"A page-turning adventure with historical detail that will make you feel as though you are really there."
Alexandra Walsh, author of *The Marquess House Trilogy*

"Recreating Pepys's voice is a heavy undertaking, but Jack Jewers has pulled it off with great aplomb and flair. The sheer pleasure of sinking back into Pepys's world so long after his last diary was an unexpected treat. Even readers who wouldn't consider themselves historical fiction fans will find something to love in this book."
C.S. Quinn, bestselling author of *The Thieftaker* series

"I have to say this is one of the best novels that I have read in the last decade. Jewers writes with a clearly well-researched style which I may even describe as 'delightfully minimalist'. However his clever, skilled use of words means that despite this, the reader's imagination is successfully triggered and the reader is soon a character within the book. One can virtually inhale the odour of Pepys' sweat as he and others tackle intense fear, surprise and anticipation during their mission. In the absence of a scientifically established time machine currently existing, worry not, Jewers' literary talents are the next best thing. Absolutely outstanding."
Julian Evan-Hart, Treasure Hunting Magazine

"The Lost Diary fits the zeitgeist and offers a likeable hero in the flawed, kind and courageous Pepys: an engaging summer read."
Country Life Magazine

"Jack Jewers has no scruples. He revels in such phrases as 'bull's pizzle' and delves into as many décolletés as are to hand… His rip-roaring yarn is also a bodice-ripper. There is something for everyone in The Lost Diary of Samuel Pepys."
The Irish Examiner

The

LOST
DIARY

of

SAMUEL
PEPYS

a novel

JACK JEWERS

MOONFLOWER

Published by Moonflower Publishing Ltd.
www.MoonflowerBooks.co.uk

1 2 3 4 5 6 7 8 9 10

ISBN: 978-1-9196187-6-0

Cover design by Jasmine Aurora
Cover image © National Portrait Gallery, London

Images from the Diary of Samuel Pepys
© The Pepys Library, Magdalene College, Cambridge

Printed and bound by Jellyfish Ltd., Curdridge, Hampshire

Moonflower Publishing Registered Office: 303 The Pillbox, 115 Coventry Road, London E2 6GG, United Kingdom

MOONFLOWER

For Christi
in omnia paratus

Cast of Characters

London

Samuel Pepys	*Clerk of the Acts to the Navy Board and (secret) diarist*
William (Will) Hewer	*Assistant and protégé of Samuel Pepys*
Elisabeth Pepys	*Wife of Samuel Pepys*
The Duke of Albemarle	*First Lord of the Treasury*
Thomas Marshall	*The Duke's long-serving secretary*
Mary Simkin	*Servant in the Pepys' household*
Mother Quick	*A bawd; owner of Samuel's favourite brothel*

Portsmouth

Lord John Maynard	*Governor of Portsmouth*
Captain James Harcourt	*Senior naval officer and associate of Lord Maynard*
Benjamin Arden	*Deputy Governor of Portsmouth; old friend of Pepys'*
Charlotte de Vere	*Wealthy widow; head of a powerful household*
Belle	*Caribbean-born servant and friend to Charlotte de Vere*
Kitty, Jane, Anne, Cecily	*Members of Mistress de Vere's household*
Alice Scovell	*A laundress*
Wolfert Jansen	*Dutch sailor; a deserter*

'Silken' Jack Gale	*Retired captain, now in more profitable lines of work*
Goody Brown	*Landlady of the Four Feathers*
Tamsin Lacey	*Serving girl at the Four Feathers*
Olly	*Potboy at the Four Feathers*
Tom Wilkin	*Regular drinker at the Four Feathers*
Doctor Grey	*Physician and town coroner*
Boatswain Stearne	*A junior officer*
Dimmock	*A Purser's Mate*
Pitt	*A gaoler*
Cobb	*Pitt's assistant*
Peter Woodfall	*Blacksmith to the village of Farlington*
Jake Hopkins	*A young boy, resident in Farlington*
Two Unnamed Mercenaries	*English soldiers of fortune, of unknown origin*

Amsterdam

Sir George Downing	*Former ambassador to Holland, and Pepys' old master*
Peck	*Sir George's young secretary*

. . . Axe-yard . . . — Ę Jane —
. . . 6 3 . . .

. . . River — Monke . . . Scott

. . . Lamb: . . .

2 Monke . . .

. . . h₃ . . .

. . . Mr Downing . . .

June 8th

It was an hour after midnight and the whorehouse was on fire.

I was woken from a slumber by shouting from somewhere down the corridor. My head was light from wine and the pleasures lately taken. I looked around, but there was no sign of the girl who had been here when I shut my eyes. The last I could remember was her going to fetch more wine.

Then I caught it on the air. The smell of burning.

I slid from the canopied bed and immediately stumbled across the floor, my legs caught up in the shirt that hung down over my bare legs. I felt for my boots.

The noises from the corridor grew louder. Panicked screams and the pounding of feet along the old wooden floorboards. I pulled on my boots as quickly as I could, my eyes straining to see in the near-darkness. Then, picking up the small clay oil lamp that provided the room's only illumination, I grabbed my little satchel and opened the door.

A cloud of acrid smoke stung my eyes and filled my lungs, causing me to choke. Figures ran past the doorway, shapes in the billowing smoke, their flickering lamps floating by like spectres.

Holding my arm to my mouth, I forced myself out into the corridor. All around I could hear screams of panic. People jostled against me, desperate to reach the staircase and the safety of outside. In the crush, the lamp was knocked out of my hand and it shattered on the floor. A lick of flame from the spilled oil ignited a pair of silk curtains.

The smoke was growing thicker by the moment. I could hardly see a thing. All I could do was run with the crowd and pray that they knew their way around the building better than I did.

We rounded a corner and all of a sudden, the air cleared a little. I could make out an open space with a tall ceiling, the glint of gilded walls, and a skylight through which the moon illuminated the hazy air.

I recalled going through an atrium as the girl led me to her chamber. That meant we were on the top floor, with three storeys between us and the safety of the street.

'This way.' Mother Quick stood at the top of a wrought-iron staircase, holding a lit candelabra. Her pink silk gown was dishevelled and torn down one side, her tall wig tilted askew.

'Move!' she repeated, as a crush of men and women ran past me and down the stairs. Only now could I see that some of them were naked.

I did not follow.

'Mr Pepys, you must go,' shouted Mother Quick.

'Have you seen Mr Hewer? The man I came in with. I must find him.'

She thought for a moment, sweat making rivulets through her thickly powdered face.

'He was at cards in the parlour. You'll find him outside. Now go.'

A great billow of black smoke made us both choke. We held on to each other, gasping for breath.

It was then that we saw them.

Standing at the entrance to the corridor, flames rising around them, they looked more like devils than men. Four of them, dressed in the clothes of fine gentlemen, but with hair styled into rigid spikes. One carried a flaming torch.

Behind them the silk drapes that lined the corridor were ablaze.

Looking around for new quarry, the men saw us and grinned. With horror I saw that their teeth were filed into points like the fangs of an animal.

Mother Quick gripped my arm. 'Mr Pepys. Run.'

I could hear their terrible cries behind us as we fled down the stairs. I knew without doubt that if they caught us we would be bludgeoned to death on the spot. And then Mother Quick tripped over her skirts, dropping the candelabra to the ground.

We were plunged into darkness.

Had the bawd let go of me at that moment then I do not think I would have survived. Fortunately, she knew the building inside and out. I held onto her for my very life, following blindly as she jerked right and left. We ran along a corridor, skirting around furniture that I could neither see nor remember from when I had last come this way, an hour or so ago, when the night had seemed so very different.

I heard an almighty crash behind us as one of our pursuers ran into a piece of furniture, or perhaps one of the fashionable *objects d'art* Mother Quick had littered about the house. Either way, it bought us precious seconds. As we half-tumbled down the last flight of stairs we heard dreadful screams from above; whether it was clients of the house, or those brutes consumed by the inferno of their own making, I could not tell.

But I had no intention of finding out.

We burst out of the open door and collapsed onto the hard ground of Bankside, coughing the acrid air from our lungs. I felt the sweat pouring off my brow turn cold in the night air and I thought for a moment I would vomit.

I turned just in time to see three of the wild men crashing through the door. I attempted to pull Mother Quick into the shadows, but they ran straight off into the night, whooping and hollering. As they passed us I saw that their cudgels were stained with blood, and they carried whatever valuables they had been able to take from the house as they went.

I staggered to my feet and turned to help Mother Quick, but she had already gone in search of her girls.

'Sam!' A voice cut through the darkness.

I turned to see Will Hewer running towards me. His white shirt was torn and smeared with dirt, his natural blond hair turned almost black with soot and ash. Like me, he had been forced to leave without his wig. He grasped my arms, scanning my face with concern.

'God be praised! I couldn't find you. Are you hurt?'

I started to reply but fell to another fit of coughing. Will slung my arm around his broad shoulders and led me across the cobbled street.

'Who were they?' I managed to sputter.

'I know not. They looked like devils. But I think they have gone.'

We reached the shelter of an empty stable. Amid the warm, sweet smell of horses, well fed and kept, Will leaned me against a wall, where I gasped in the cold air, trying to recover my strength. The nag in the stall next to us eyed me with nervous curiosity and then went back to chewing hay.

'Sam?'

I could hear the concern in his voice, and was suddenly aware of how unaffected he seemed by our narrow escape. By contrast, my hands shook, and water streamed from my stinging eyes.

There was an explosion and the sound of falling glass as the top floor windows blew out, flames engulfing the silk curtains that hung on the other side. I felt a pang of sadness as I looked over at the grand old townhouse, once known as the sapphire of the stews, the very pinnacle of the Southwark brothels. Soon it would be gone forever.

Mother Quick strode back and forth on the hard dirt road, her face tight-lipped with anger and pain. She was so close to the flames, I feared her voluminous skirts might catch an ember and be set alight, but she seemed not to notice. The nightwatchmen had started to arrive with buckets of sand and water, and she was ready to take command whether they liked it or not.

'Sam?' Will said again, placing a hand on my shoulder. 'Time to go.'

'Of course,' I replied, looking down at my filthy and torn undershirt. 'Elisabeth will murder me.'

'We shall stop at my house first. I shall lend you a suit of clothes.'

With one last look at the awful scene, we set off in search of a boatman to take us home.

In the fresh air out on the water, we coughed the last of the smoke from our lungs.

As we approached the north bank of the Thames, I noticed a long line of women standing at the river's edge, their gaudy dresses shimmering in the moonlight. There were even one or two boys, foppishly attired, their faces powdered as white as the women's.

'The ladies are working late tonight,' I said.

Will glanced back at the plumes of thick, dark smoke rising from the streets of Southwark. 'I think perhaps they have come to watch the spectacle.'

He ran his hand across his head and a cloud of soot rose up from his close-cropped hair. It occurred to me that the wig he had been wearing that night was one I had given him on his birthday last. It had been expensive, and the thought of that money going up in smoke vexed me mightily.

I felt a sudden, painful cramp in my groin. It lasted no more than a few seconds, but it was strong enough that I had to hold onto the side of the boat until it subsided. Fortunately, Will did not see. This had been happening to me for some time now. But I feared the pain was growing worse.

The ferryman tied up his boat and I stepped cautiously out onto the jetty. A sudden gust of wind blew my undershirt up, revealing my cods to the harlots.

'Got away in a hurry, did we?' one of them said, with a whoop of laughter.

'Go on, take it off,' cackled another, as I walked by, comporting myself with all the dignity I could muster.

One of the women stood in front of Will, pressing herself firmly against him. She ran her hands seductively over his muscular torso.

'Not ready to go home yet, surely, my handsome lord?' The wench reached down and cupped his balls through his soot-covered breeches.

Removing her hands from his body, he raised them to his lips and kissed them, moving her aside as gently if she were a dainty goodwife.

'Alas, madam, not tonight.'

The harlot blew him a kiss as we walked on, briefly pulling down her loose-fitting bodice to expose her nipples. Then she picked up her skirts and returned to her friends.

Although Will said nothing, he seemed much pleased. I set my lips tight, trying not to show my hurt that he had been the target of their advances, while I was a figure of fun.

An hour later, I am sitting alone in the parlour at Will's house on Seething Lane. How fortuitous that I thought to pick up my satchel at Mother Quick's, elsewise my little notebook would have been lost to the flames.

It is almost dawn. I have changed into the new set of clothes he lent me, which are much too tight around the waist and neck. In truth, they are also of a much finer cut than was strictly necessary, but I suspect the lad wanted to impress me.

A coal fire glows in the hearth and dust motes float gently in the soft candlelight. The walls are hung with fitted sheets of heavy, woven cloth stamped with patterns of *fleur-de-lis*. Dornix, I believe, which look handsome enough, but would have cost far less than the more fashionable silk. I note with satisfaction how shrewd the boy has become with money.

After freeing ourselves from the two drabs at Queenhythe dock, we made our way up the narrow slope of Stew Lane, in the direction of St Paul's. I must have passed this way half a hundred times since the Great Fire of '66, but this time I saw it with fresh eyes. The blaze at Mother Quick's had brought back unpleasant memories of the devastation that consumed this city, just three years past.

Ahead of us, atop the hill, stood the shell of the cathedral, jutting out starkly against the night sky. It is still a ghastly sight, which I fancy is made worse by the fact that from certain angles the building looks far less damaged than it truly is. Were it not for the melted lead from the old roof cleaving to its side in great hardened globs, one could almost be forgiven for believing nothing has changed.

But it is just an illusion. Soon the building will be gone forever. And with it the very heart of old London.

Much has changed in that time. How, too, has it been six years since Will left the position of manservant in my household and joined the Navy

Board as a junior clerk? My own station, through the most dedicated application, has risen to the extent that I am one of the Board's principal officers, favoured by dukes and princes. Nor do I want for money or the comforts of home.

Why then, do I feel such melancholy within me?

The answer is plain, of course. I hoped to forget about it, if only for one evening. A trip to my favourite bawdy house seemed just the remedy, but I only succeeded in making matters worse.

The moment I become aware of some happiness or joy in the moment, immediately that joy is cast away. I seem unable to permit myself to forget my troubles, and this shadow of my own making only grows longer.

Will entered the room carrying two steaming cups. The air filled with the rich, exotic scent of cloves and ginger. He handed me one, and I drank from it, with a sigh of pleasure.

'Upon my soul, Will Hewer, I miss your spiced posset.'

There was a hint of pride in his golden-brown eyes.

'Can you guess the special ingredient?'

I sipped the dark, aromatic brew, trying to identify the taste.

'Is that... nutmeg?'

'Cinnamon.'

I raised an eyebrow. Perhaps the boy is not so thrifty after all.

We drank in peace for a while, gazing out of the window as the sky slowly turned from blue to crimson. It was the kind of silence that passes easily between friends.

The kind that begs for the sharing of confidences.

'I think Elisabeth means to leave London.'

Will looked up at me with a wry smile. 'I cannot see you as a country gentleman.'

'No, Will. I mean she wishes to leave... without me.'

He grew serious. 'Are things that bad?'

'Every time we talk, it seems we must fight. She weeps for no reason. Several nights this past month she has woken late, cursing me for being unfaithful, even raining blows upon me. She sobbed for an hour yesterday, calling me liar and cheat, over and over. She says her heart is broken.'

Will seemed to choose his next words carefully. 'Have you... I mean, your new servant girl...?'

'Little Mary Simkin? No. I have sworn to Elisabeth, never again shall I make amours with another woman. And I mean it.'

'Aside from whores.'

'Aside from— Oh, damn your eyes.'

'Forgive me. Sam, I do not pretend to understand women. But I know this much. Elisabeth thinks herself gravely wounded by you. And perhaps she is right. She needs time.'

I drained my cup, swallowing the last dregs of spice that had sunk to the bottom.

'Time, yes. A precious commodity indeed.'

I fell silent again. There was more to it, of course. But I could not find the courage to tell him the full story of what had happened.

What Elisabeth had discovered.

Will jumped from his chair. 'Come. It will be a beautiful dawn. Let us walk down to watch the sunrise from the river before you go home.'

We took the short stroll down to the Thames. The ships docked at the hamlet of Rotherhithe had become all but invisible under the dazzling glare of the first rays of daylight. To the west, the new brick houses under construction on the Strand had turned pink and orange.

Will chuckled. I looked at him quizzically.

'Forgive me. I was just remembering... Was it not some comedy, watching all those fine gentlemen of the court stumbling about, bare arsed, terrified that someone may recognise them?'

I could not help but smile. 'That fellow who went to find his carriage, bollocks swinging in the wind... I think it was the Bishop of Winchester.'

'At last, a sermon of his worth going to.'

We fell about laughing. Then I thought of the poor wretches in Mother Quick's employ, who were left on the street with nothing but the clothes they stood up in – if they were fortunate enough to be wearing any. Where would they go, now the sun was up?

I stared at the ships over by Rotherhithe, bobbing gently up and down on the water. Gulls wheeled and shrieked overhead. If the wind kept up it would be a magnificent day to sail.

The ships.

The *ships*.

I gasped. 'Oh God, how could I forget? The ambassadors...'

I could hear the crowd long before I saw it.

The public jetty at the Palace Stairs was closed to allow for the royal barges, so I had the boatman take us to the Privy Steps instead. It was further, but I knew the back ways through the west wing of the palace.

Will and I had barely stepped out onto the landing stage when a guardsman came forward to question us, but luckily the fellow recognised me and waved us straight through.

We hurried into the palace grounds. It was already hot, despite the early hour, the sun blazing in a cloudless sky. Sweat stung my eyes and I tried in vain to loosen the ill-fitting collar that cut into my neck.

I cursed myself once again. Today was set to be the grandest Water Triumph since the time of the old king. Representatives of all the foreign courts were to process down the river from White Hall Palace, to be met by His Majesty at Greenwich, where a new ambassador was to be admitted into court.

My job was to greet the ambassadors at their arrival and see them safely to their barges. But to have been bestowed with such a task, and not only to be late, by Christ, but to have *forgotten* until I saw those ships at Rotherhithe dock…

How in God's name could I have been so stupid?

We passed under a wide stone arch and immediately turned down a curved passage lined with neat, timber-framed apartments. At the end of this lay the covered space of the Stone Gallery. All we had to do was cross this and we'd be in the Privy Garden. The designated meeting point was just beyond.

It was then that I heard the roar. Two or three hundred people, or so it sounded, cheering and applauding.

'Oh Lord, Sam, are they already here?'

I listened intently. 'I think not. That sounded like something else. We may yet make it.'

Entering the Privy Garden, we ran as fast as we could up the sloped ground. I barely noticed its neat box flower beds, bright with blooms, though the scent was heady in the warm air. As we passed the old sundial, I saw that the time was nearing half past seven. God be praised, they were running late.

A voice bellowed at us from up ahead. '*Pepys*. Damn and bugger you.'

I turned to Will in despair. 'Oh, Christ. We are done.'

The Duke of Albemarle stepped out from under a stone arch at the top end of the garden. An expensive black wig hung down to the shoulders of his richly tailored coat of scarlet brocade. The old man's bulky frame was raised even higher by a pair of fashionable tall-heeled boots.

'Where in Christ's name have you been?' he rasped in that rough officer's voice of his.

'I am most deeply sorry, my Lord. In truth, we were caught in a most dreadful fire this last night, and only just escaped with our lives.'

'We?' He jabbed a finger at Will. 'Who's this?'

Will bowed deeply. 'William Hewer, Your Grace.'

The duke continued without acknowledgement. 'Fire? What fire? Where?'

I hesitated. 'Southwark, my lord.'

He leaned forward and lowered his voice to a menacing purr. 'Do you mean to tell me that you were late for the ambassadors' triumph because you spent the night at some Southwark stew?'

I searched for the words but none came. My growing status, my reputation at court – all was now in jeopardy.

I felt like a fool.

The duke rose back to his full height. 'No time now. You will get out there and you will do your job, Mr Pepys, and by God's balls you will do it well. There is to be no mishap. None. Do I make myself clear?'

'Yes, my Lord,' I replied, trying hard not to stammer.

'Then go.'

I started to move, but he grabbed my arm to stop me. His fingers dug deep into my flesh. To my surprise, his tone softened, as if he were worried about something.

'Pepys, I must see you about another matter. Be at my office, tomorrow morning, at eight.' He fixed me with piercing look. 'Do not be late.'

We descended the wide stone staircase leading to the western end of the parade ground in Horse Guard's Yard. A huge crowd had gathered, spilling out into St James's Park, but there was no sign of the ambassadors.

I let out a sigh of relief. We were in time after all.

As we hurried to join the rest of the delegation at the eastern end of the yard, I could see what the cheering had been about. A troupe of acrobats had just finished an impromptu show. Two small boys were making their way through the crowd with caps held out, collecting money. Now the crowd were restless for the main event to begin.

'Good luck,' said Will, as I hurried over to take my place in the line.

There was a fit of coughing from somewhere across the yard. I turned to see the duke, now mounted on horseback, spitting out a great globule of phlegm onto the parade ground.

I strained my eyes, staring down the road towards Charing Cross. For a long time, I could see nothing. And then, slowly, figures began to take shape out of the shimmering heat.

At the head of the line was the delegation from Sweden. The prospective ambassador himself, the Baron Leijonbergh, rode out in front, mounted on an enormous steed. A small group of courtiers followed in his wake.

The Baron, a tall, handsome man of about thirty, wore a doublet of golden silk and the deep blue sash of a royal officer. He steered his horse into the yard and took the last stretch at a dashing canter, eliciting a further cheer from the crowd. Albemarle bade him welcome with a courtly bow.

Next came the Spanish, four men in short coats of rich satin, topped with neck ruffs in the old fashion. A group of young ladies waved flirtatiously and one of the men doffed his cap, eliciting whoops of delight in return.

On and on they came. Next were the Poles with their long blue robes and enormous mustachios. Then the Russians, in their brown fur habits, which must have been unbearable in the heat.

Then came the French.

Oh Lord, what a sight they were! I had heard that fashions at the court of King Louis had reached the height of extravagance, but nothing prepared me for this. All the men wore loose-fitting shirts that puffed out around the arms, tied with lengths of brightly coloured ribbon. Great tassels hung down from their embroidered silk waistcoats, and they wore stockings of pearl-white satin underneath pantalooned breeches.

They looked ridiculous.

When, at last, all the delegations were assembled in the yard, it was time for me to do my part. I looked over to the duke, who gave me a curt nod of approval.

Taking a deep breath, I walked up to Baron Leijonbergh and bowed. He looked me up and down. I hoped he was sizing up my importance rather than wondering why I was wearing a suit of clothes a good three inches too tight.

'Your Excellency, if you would care to follow me?'

He hesitated briefly, and I remembered that, until his credentials had been formally accepted by the King, the correct form of address was simply 'my Lord'. I cursed inwardly. Little tests of etiquette such as this are how men of breeding judge others.

'Please. Lead the way.'

I led the Baron and his retinue towards the Palace Gate, which opened out directly onto a wide avenue leading down to the Palace Steps. We walked in a loose procession down towards the river, where the royal barges were waiting. The short route was lined with wealthy citizens of the city and officials of the King's Council, who had come by special invitation to watch the procession from inside the Palace grounds.

When we reached the barges, I took my place among a line of aldermen. All that remained was for us to stand respectfully as the various delegations boarded.

It could not come soon enough. My feet hurt and I felt the stirrings of that pain in my groin again. Dear God. I hoped some doxy had not left me with the French pox.

There was a commotion near the jetty. I took a step forward, and to my surprise I saw the ambassadors from France and Spain jostling each other, chests puffed out, gesticulating angrily in the direction of the barges.

I looked around for the duke. He was nowhere to be seen.

Suddenly, the ambassador from France shoved the ambassador from Spain in the chest. He staggered backwards, as his aides instantly drew their swords.

My first thought was that the French courtiers were in danger, unarmed and unprotected. But then they each withdrew a wheel lock pistol from their waistcoats, training them on their Spanish counterparts.

A murmur of alarm spread through the assembled crowd. An elderly grand dame let out a yelp of fright and stepped back too hastily, treading on her own skirts and falling backwards onto the cobbles.

Where in God's name was Albemarle?

The men stood there, dangerously poised. The French ambassador grinned, knowing he held the upper hand.

I took a deep breath and stepped forward. 'My Lords. What seems to be the trouble?'

Without taking his eyes off his counterpart, the Spanish ambassador spoke in thickly accented English. 'Sir. I do not think we have been introduced.'

'I am Samuel Pepys, Clerk of the Acts to the Navy Board, and aide to His Grace the Duke of Albemarle.'

'I am the Caballero de Vatteville, Ambassador of His Majesty King Charles II of Spain to His Majesty King Charles II of England. And this French churl can kiss my arse.'

'Monsieur?'

'Je suis le Marquis de Croissy, Ambassadeur à la cour de Sa Majesté le Roi Charles depuis six ans et chaque année, cette vermine arrogante' – at this, he spat on the ground – *'me précède dans le cortège. Je ne ferai pas l'objet de cette humiliation la prochaine fois. Poussez-vous.'*

The Caballero spoke to his compatriots. 'So, this French *petimetre* complains that we have gone before him at every Water Triumph since he has been ambassador. Now he wants that we let him go first this time. What you say, boys?'

A Spanish courtier spat on the ground. One of the French men leaned right into his face.

'Putain.'

The Caballero turned to me. 'You see, *Señor* Pepys, how his Excellency the Marquis cares so little for your hospitality that neither he nor his men will even speak to you in your language. Or do you suppose he does not have much skill with the English?'

The Spaniards laughed. The marquis' jaw clenched dangerously.

'Monsieur le Marquis,' I said, as diplomatically as I could. 'If you will permit me to suggest a solution. Perhaps the Caballero and his men could travel first, at the rear.' The Frenchman's nostrils flared angrily. 'And Your Excellency would like to travel on the next barge. At its head.'

The Frenchman considered this for a moment, then the plume on his cap quivered and he spoke, curt and tight-lipped. *'Oui. C'est bon.'*

I breathed a sigh of relief. 'Excellent. Sirs?'

The Caballero slowly drew back, his eyes still fixed on his rival. Then he turned to the crowd, doffed his cap, and jumped on board the waiting barge.

The Frenchmen put away their guns. As they waited to board the next boat, I tried to make conversation with the marquis.

'My wife is French. At least, her father was. She has quite the fancy to visit. Perhaps Your Excellency might suggest some places to take her?'

Without even acknowledging me, the ambassador gestured to his men and they hopped onto the second barge.

And with that, my role in the procession was complete.

It was past two o'clock when at last I arrived home at Seething Lane.

I was exhausted. Hot and worn out from the ceremony, I was desperate for bed. But the disapproving look Mary gave me as she opened the door told me that Elisabeth was waiting for me.

'In the salon. She's not best pleased with you, sir.'

I should have dismissed the girl on the spot for such insolence, but all I wanted to do was get this over and done with, then sleep.

Elisabeth was sitting alone on an embroidered settle at the far side of the salon. She had turned to face the wall, deliberately looking away from me as I entered. A little book lay open on the table beside her.

I had come in ready for battle, but something about her appearance disarmed me completely. She looked so small, all alone in that spacious room. Her dress was rumpled and I realised that it was the same one she had been wearing last night.

Surely she could not have stayed up waiting for me, all this time?

I could not seem to find the right words through the fog of tiredness. I said nothing for so long that she turned her head to check that I was still there.

This was not a good start to my apology.

'Elisabeth, my dear. I am sorry that I did not return last night, but you will never believe—'

'Where were you?'

'Do you recall how I told you today was the arrival of the new ambassador from Sweden, and I was to play a role in the ceremony of admission to court? Well, my dearest, I fear that I quite forgot. Can you believe that?'

Silence.

'For my sins, this morning I have had to break up a diplomatic skirmish. I fear, had I not intervened, it may have become a serious incident, across three nations.'

I paused for effect but Elisabeth still did not move.

'And furthermore, my Lord Albemarle wishes to see me tomorrow. I sense he wants to talk to me about some important matter or other. I think this speaks highly of the regard in which he now holds me.'

She turned to face me at last. 'Why do you despise me, Samuel?'

'My love! How could you think that?'

'Because I am not a fool.'

'I am being straight with you, Elisabeth. I have just come from White Hall.'

'And last night?'

I paused, a little too long. 'Last night is not important.'

'Liar. Cheat.'

'My love—'

'Do not call me that. Do not even speak to me.' She stood abruptly, the book falling to the floor. Her cheeks were red with fury.

I turned to go. 'Please yourself, madam. I have no time for this.'

'How quickly you cannot stand to talk to me.'

I told myself to keep walking, that no good would come of having this argument now. I remembered what Will had said about giving her time. I should wait until I had rested, and make my case then.

I did not wait.

'Come then. Let us have it.'

'You show me nothing but contempt in the way you speak. The way you behave.'

'Contempt for what?'

'Everything. Our marriage. My every opinion. Where I am from. What I believe.'

'For goodness' sake, leave the *Pope* out of this.'

'Have you always thought yourself so superior, Samuel? Or is it just age that has made you this arrogant?'

'You are my wife, Elisabeth.'

'Come then, *husband*. Tell me you do not think yourself better than me. Truly.'

I tried to reply but I was caught so off guard by the strength of her attack that I foundered. Why, in God's name, could I not find the right words? Why was she always so composed when we fought, and I so tongue-tied?

She continued, 'Every morning you are up at dawn and to your office, where you stay all day, engaged in your great work with your important friends. Then you come home and are gone again. You return stinking of wine and sluts, if you return at all. I mean nothing to you.'

'Enough. That "great work" pays for the fine dress you are wearing, *wife*.'

'I made my vows. And I have kept to them. All of them. Have you?'

Again, I searched for the right words, but none came. Her weapons were too well aimed. She picked up the little book from the floor and opened it at a marked page. Only then did I recognise what it was.

'"And so to Mrs Martin and there did what *je voudrais avec* her, both *devante* and backward, which is also *muy bon plazer*."'

I began to speak but she held up her hand to silence me, then turned the page. '"…And there *nudo in lecto con ella*, but though I did intend *para aver demorado con ella toda la night* yet when I had done *ce que je voudrais*, I did hate both *ella* and *la cosa*.'"

Her voice dripped contempt, but still she did not stop.

'"And there naked in bed with her, though I did intend to have stayed with her all night, yet when I had done all that I wanted, I did hate both her and her body." If you would write in code, Samuel, at least make it one that a halfwit child could not decipher.'

'Damn you, woman.'

'Damn me? A fine choice of words for one whose' – she opened the book again – '"mind did *courir* upon Betty Michell, so that I do *hazer con mi cosa in la eglisa meme*." You pleasured yourself? In a church?'

'Elisabeth, I—'

'And this is just '66.' She checked the first page. 'From midsummer to Christmas. What else am I going to find, Samuel? How many have there been?'

Her lips trembled and I realised that she was fighting hard not to weep. I sank down onto the settle and buried my face in my hands.

It had been two days since Elisabeth had discovered my private diaries. I have always known that a diary, in the wrong hands, could be a compromising document. Now I was learning how compromising it truly could be.

This was the real reason I had been avoiding coming home. This was why she had threatened to leave me forever. All because the hiding place I'd chosen for my words was inadequate. And she was curious.

I breathed deeply in an effort to ward off the tears I could feel pricking the backs of my eyes. After what seemed like an age, I felt the settle move as she sat down next to me.

'What happened to us, Samuel? Was I not good enough for you?'

I took her hand in mine. She flinched, but did not pull away.

'I am sorry, Elisabeth. You deserve better than me. Truly. But know this. I love you. It pains me that you doubt it.' She drew breath to speak but I continued hastily. 'Even though I know you have good reason. I can offer no defence against the evidence of my own words. But believe this, I beg you. I am resolved to change. I shall give up my vices. The other women. I give it all up for good. For you. For us.'

I gestured at the book on the floor.

'No more doxies. No more diaries.'

She sat in silence for a long while. So long that I thought perhaps this time it really was too late. But then, she squeezed my hand lightly.

'Samuel, I do not pretend that I can see an easy way through this. And I do not know if we will ever be as we were. But I do know that I am tired of this.'

I took her other hand. 'I too. We must both be resolved to—'

'So I have decided to leave.'

It was as if all the breath had been sucked out of me. I stared back at her.

'What?'

'Just for the time being. I shall visit my family in Devonshire.'

'When?'

'Soon.'

'For how long?'

'As long as I please.'

I felt a tightness in my chest. Dear God, did she really mean to do it? I could not live without her. For all my lying and my dallying with whores, I needed her still. Every time, whatever my sins, I always came home. Could she not see that?

She patted my hand, then got up and crossed the room.

'Elisabeth,' I said, as she reached the door. 'I love you.'

She glanced back at me for just a moment, the green of her eyes sparkling in the afternoon light.

Then she turned and left the room without saying another word.

June 9th

Lord's Day. Up very betimes and straight to White Hall, where I arrived well ahead of my appointed hour. I thought it prudent not to keep the duke waiting today.

As I entered the spacious oak-panelled anteroom next to Albemarle's private office, Mr Marshall looked up from his small, neat desk.

'Ah, Mr Pepys,' he said, in his broad Yorkshire accent. 'How goes the day?'

'Fair, Mr Marshall, although I shall be fit to drop if this infernal heat does not break soon.'

'Aye. I pray for rain. My garden does too. I fear my poor roses are done for this year.' He put down his pen and ran a slightly tremulous hand through his thinning grey hair. Not for the first time, it struck me how quaint the old fellow looked, with his refusal to submit to fashion and wear a wig.

He smiled. 'How fares that lovely wife of yours?'

I almost blurted out my troubles to the old man, but I stopped myself. I have always found Thomas Marshall a comfortable fellow to talk to, though his easy manner hid a keen intellect and a resilient nature. One found oneself wanting to share secrets with the man – a valuable skill for one in his position to have. Perhaps it was why he had lasted over twenty years in the duke's service as his secretary.

'She… is well, thank you.'

Marshall studied me with those keen grey eyes that missed nothing.

'I am glad to hear it, Mr Pepys. Very glad indeed. Well, His Grace is in his office. You may go straight in.'

I hesitated. 'How is the duke today, Mr Marshall?

He put down his quill and lowered his voice, delicately. 'I fear His Grace is feeling the ravages of age somewhat this morning, sir. You may find it advantageous to tread gently.'

I thanked him and walked through to the duke's office.

Albemarle was hunched over his desk in the small but airy room, with its enviable view of the river and the meadows beyond. I stood there for an awkwardly long time, waiting for him to indicate that I might sit, but he ignored me and kept writing. I once had a schoolmaster at St Paul's who employed the same trick with naughty children.

I cleared my throat. The duke's hand shot up, peremptorily, as he put down his quill, then sanded and blotted the paper. Only then did he look up.

'Ah, Pepys. I hear you averted war between France and Spain yesterday.'

He motioned for me to sit. I knew he was being sardonic, but still I was pleased that news of the confrontation between the ambassadors had reached him. Perhaps this would help me avoid the worst of his censure.

'I merely did my best to calm the situation, Your Grace. I fear the heat has raised many tempers.'

The duke nodded absently. Picking up a stack of papers, he rifled through them until he found one in particular, which he tossed over to me. I recognised my own hand.

'The report you sent me at Candlemas,' he said. 'Concerning the *Prince Rupert*.'

I cast my mind back to February. 'The ship with the slovenly accounts.'

'Damned peculiar way of putting it. Go on.'

I leafed through the pages of my report, trying to recall what it was that had aroused my attention enough to tell the duke. 'Yes, there were some figures that did not tally. A few poorly kept records. They were badly done.'

'It is not the first time there have been problems with the administration in Portsmouth lately.'

'I fear not.'

He placed his hands gently on the desk. 'I need not tell you, Pepys, how dire the condition of England's fleet is at the present time. We are stretched to the very limit, starved of funds, and yet now it seems we are expected to prepare for another fight with the Dutch. The war of '67 took us closer to the brink than even His Majesty realises. I need not tell you how we are likely to fare if there is another.'

Gone was any sense of bluster from his words. His manner was deadly serious.

'No indeed, Your Grace,' I replied quietly.

'So you can imagine how a set of *slovenly* accounts may be cause for concern when it comes to one of His Majesty's warships.' The duke leaned back in his chair and made a steeple of his fingers. 'After I read your report, I sent a man down to investigate.'

I tried hard not to sound irritated. 'I heard nothing about this.'

'That is because you did not need to,' he snapped. 'A promising young man in my employ. His name was Elias Thorne.'

'I do not know him.'

'You wouldn't have done. Thorne's job was to work out why so much money was draining away from the navy accounts. Discreetly. Without drawing attention to himself.'

'And what did he discover?'

'His last report reached me a fortnight ago. It makes wild claims of a conspiracy to defraud the Crown, though with precious few details to back it up.'

'His last report? You mean, he is missing?'

'Not missing. Dead.'

My jaw dropped. 'Dead?'

'Murdered.'

'I am most sorry to hear it, Your Grace. Do you know what happened?'

'He was found at dawn, three days ago, in an alleyway. Stabbed to death.'

'A robbery then? Portsmouth can be a dangerous place.'

The duke opened his mouth to speak, but then hesitated, placing a bony finger to his lips. I could tell there was something else he was not saying.

'If I am not mistaken, you were made a burgess of Portsmouth, were you not?'

I shifted uncomfortably in my seat. 'I am a burgess of the town, but the appointment is not recent. Near ten years past, in fact.'

'But you must be well known there.'

I could see where this was going and I did not like it. 'I have been only once or twice since then. My work there was menial compared with my responsibilities now. I doubt there are many in the town who would even remember me.'

He smiled thinly. 'Oh come, Pepys, your name must surely carry great authority there. Beyond just the status of your office, I mean.'

In case I mistook his words for flattery, the duke gave me a condescending smile. I wanted to tell him that my rank now afforded me the pleasure of remaining in London more or less as I pleased, and I was loathe to take on a mission to a country backwater more suited to a junior clerk than a man in my position.

But it was futile. He would not have called me here if his mind were not already made up.

'It is kind of you to say so, sir,' I conceded.

His eyes flashed triumphantly. 'Good. Then you can go down there and investigate what has happened. Get to the bottom of what's been going on with the accounts of the *Prince Rupert*. Start by interviewing the Governor, Lord Maynard. I don't trust him. Find out what Thorne meant by a conspiracy. And while you're about it, I want to know who killed him and why.'

My heart sank. This assignment could well be long. And the timing could not be worse. 'Your Grace, I have much business at the Navy Office…'

'They will manage without you for a time,' he said, dismissively.

I tried appealing to his kindness. 'The truth is, sir... If you will permit me to share a confidence. My wife and I... Relations have been complicated of late. Leaving now would be... difficult.'

The old man placed his dry, dark-spotted hands on the polished oak. 'Pepys, you have a keen mind inside that puffed-up head of yours. Your actions yesterday proved that to me. But you are not indispensable. You would do well to remember how far you have climbed. And how far you could yet fall.'

The threat could not have been clearer.

'Of course not, Your Grace.'

'Then you will go?'

I nodded, miserably. It was not as if I had any choice.

He gave a satisfied smile.

'Good. You can take your man, that young pup I met yesterday. Travel light. Be discreet. You have full authority to investigate as you see fit, but I want this matter settled quickly and *quietly*. Is that clear?'

'I will do my best, Your Grace. But, tell me – why the secrecy? You said yourself that this man Thorne could offer no evidence to back up his claim of a conspiracy. And his death, while tragic, was surely just a common assault? Hardly unusual in a place like that.'

'That is what I assumed at first, too. Until the coroner's report arrived yesterday.' He tapped a paper on his desk. 'Thorne's body had been... interfered with.'

'What do you mean, interfered with?'

'Mutilated. He had been... gelded.'

My eyes widened in shock. 'Dear God. And you've no idea who did it?'

'None. And that's not all.' He paused. 'He had also been branded.'

'How do you mean, branded?'

'The letter M was carved into his skin, right in the middle of his forehead. No one can tell me why, or what it might mean.'

I did my best to pay attention to what Albemarle said for the rest of the meeting, but my mind was elsewhere. The duke wanted me to leave at once, but I persuaded him to allow me a day or two to make arrangements at home and in the office before we set out for Portsmouth.

He handed me a fresh copy of the *Prince Rupert* 's accounts ledger, together with Thorne's final report and a few other notes about his ill-fated expedition. It was as well that he did, for by that point I was in no fit state of mind to absorb anything more of what he was telling me.

As I made my way unsteadily back through the anteroom, Mr Marshall looked up with curiosity from his neat and ordered little desk. I must have looked as if I were about to be sick, so desperate was I to get away from that room.

The troubles that consumed me this morning now seem mundane by comparison. I feel as if the world has been turned upside down. Whoever killed Elias Thorne is a madman.

And I am being sent to find him.

June 12ᵗʰ

I awoke with a start at an enormous crash from outside the coach. Will and I were thrown backwards as the horses reared and the coach came to a juddering halt.

'What in God's name is the matter?' I called up at the driver, an older fellow with grey hair and a pockmarked face.

'Road's blocked,' he shouted back. 'We've nowhere to bloody go.'

We had left Seething Lane at first light, in an attempt to be clear of London Bridge before the city streets were at their busiest. But some demolition men had been taking down the last of the burned-out buildings near the north bank of the Thames. It seemed a wall had come down too hard and smashed onto the bridge, narrowly missing some passers-by.

'What can you see?' Will asked from behind me.

'A mishap at the building site. I fear we shall be here a while.'

'Fine. Wake me up when we are moving.'

'We should stay alert. Unless you wish to be robbed in broad daylight?'

'Sam, it is seven o'clock and we are surrounded by people.'

'Hawkers, pickpockets, vagabonds.'

He raised his hand. 'Alright, Sam. You take the first watch.'

He turned away from me, folding up his coat to make a pillow.

I was in an ill humour this morning. Elisabeth and I had hardly spoken since our argument on Saturday. I had expected her to be angry at the news that I was to be away in Portsmouth for a time, but in fact she seemed barely to care. 'Do as you please, Sam. It is what you always do.' That was all she had to say on the matter.

Then, the next afternoon, I returned from the office to find her gone. I asked Mary, and the girl informed me that her mistress had already left for Devon. No note, nor word to me of any kind.

I was also feeling out of sorts this morning because of a strange event that occurred last night.

I was leaving the Navy Office just before sundown, at around eight. The street was all but empty, save for a chandler's boy making a late delivery to St Olave's Church at the top of Seething Lane.

I had stopped to let a coach go by. But as soon as it had passed, I jumped – a girl was standing on the other side of the road, looking at me. I was certain there had been no one there before.

The girl, who could not have been more than fifteen, was very thin, poorly dressed, with fine blonde hair. She carried a little basket on her arm. We both started to cross the road at the same time, and as we passed each other, I caught a strong scent of flowers. I glanced at her basket. It was full of dried lavender – and just for a moment, I could swear there was something hidden underneath.

'Posy for your sweetheart, sir?'

'No thank you,' I said, brusquely, quickening the pace towards my house, a few yards up the hill. As I approached, the door opened, and Mary stepped out with a bucket of dirty water.

'Oh hello, sir. Are you home for the evening?'

'Yes, indeed,' I said, still distracted by the lavender girl.

'Her again.'

'What?'

'She's been by three times today, asking if I want to buy some of her stupid lavender. I sent her on her way but she kept coming back. One time, I had the door open for a minute while I were sweeping, and I found her standing inside the hallway. Saucy little mumps.'

I turned to look again, but the odd young woman had gone.

I took a little supper of roast capon, then retired to my solar to get a few last pieces of business in order before the morning. As I was putting my ledgers away, I noticed that the wood was broken around the lock to one of the drawers in my bureau.

I might have thought more of it, had anything important been kept in there. But this was just where I stored old family papers and a few assorted mementos. Nothing of significance.

I put it down to an accident and resolved to chide Mary about her carelessness in the morning. But something about the sequence of events unsettled me.

It was another hour until we were finally across the bridge and onto the south bank of the Thames. As we progressed slowly along the last few yards of the ancient wooden structure, a sudden noise disturbed a flock of birds who had been pecking at something mounted above the bridge. I peered up and immediately recoiled.

It was a row of severed heads. They were bloated and blackened, patches of sun-bleached bone shining behind strips of rotting flesh. Wisps of hair swayed limply in the breeze.

I thought the King had ordered an end to the barbaric custom of putting traitors' heads on pikes at the entrance to London Bridge. Evidently, word had yet to reach the people of Southwark.

'What's the matter?' asked Will.

'Nothing,' I replied.

But I was glad to be away from London Bridge at last.

After a late start, the journey south from London was easier going. We crossed into Surrey at Dulwich, where the quiet lanes heading south offered little impediment to our progress.

After a couple of hours, we stopped next to a field of buttercups near a small woodland copse. I could hear the sound of running water from nearby.

'Where are we?' I asked Will.

'Streatham. The driver needs to water the horses.'

We climbed out of the coach and stood on the dusty, sun-baked ground. We had stopped next to a spring, from which the driver was trying to persuade the stubborn animals to take a drink.

I closed my eyes. Around us, there was only the singing of birds and the rustling of the wind through the trees. I breathed deeply of the fresh country air, relishing the warm sun on my face, the smell of wildflowers on the breeze. Oh, but it was good to be out of the city.

'Why would anybody mutilate a corpse?' said Will.

'How should I know?' I snapped, the moment ruined. 'Who can explain the actions of a madman?'

'Who's to say it was a madman? Perhaps it was a message of some kind.'

'I fear you are enjoying this too much.'

'Well, it makes a change from naval accounts and supply lines to Tangier. Or would you rather we didn't talk about it at all?'

I could not deny that I had been avoiding discussion of the more disturbing aspects of our mission. There at least, my troubles with Elisabeth had been a distraction.

I sighed. 'Well, mad or not, whoever murdered Elias Thorne certainly wanted people to know about it.'

'So you do think it was a message?'

'Or a warning.'

'A warning of what?'

'That is something we must find out.'

Suddenly, I felt a spasm of pain from my groin. I leaned against the coach, clutching my stomach.

'Are you alright, Sam?'

'Yes, fine. I need to piss, that is all.'

I hastened to a nearby bush and unbuttoned my breeches. I closed my eyes for a moment, expecting to let forth a long stream of piss, but all I could manage was a trickle. Then, when I opened them again, I felt a jolt of fear.

My water had turned a pinkish colour. I was pissing blood.

Shaken, I buttoned myself up and returned to Will.

'In any case,' I said, resuming our conversation, 'that is not the main part of our business.'

'But we must still find out who killed him. Albemarle told you—'

'So long as we trace the missing funds, Will, the duke cares little for the rest.'

'This is the same duke we're talking about? I just want to make sure.'

'Listen, Will,' I snapped. 'I just want to get this over with as quickly as possible and return to London. Unlike you, I am in no mood for an adventure.'

We are lodging for the night in Guildford, at the Red Lyon, a place I have stayed before and find most agreeable. After a fine supper of mutton broth, I have sat down to write my diary.

I have, as is self-evident, already broken one of the promises I made to Elisabeth. I thought hard about whether to abandon this diary, as I had sworn, but as yet I have not had the courage. Perhaps after this journey is over I will make good on my oath. But for now, I find that I need the solace of this confessional more than ever.

I have brought along my little notebook on our journey, so that I may quickly record my thoughts in shorthand. In this I am making use of a curious new invention, a set of which has lately been procured for the office by Will. They are of German design, a kind of pencil, but with a shard of soft rock where the lead should be, bound up between two pieces of wood. They are somewhat difficult to get used to, and require frequent sharpening, but they are strong and portable.

Here I intended to close my diary for the day, but after I had finished the foregoing, I wrote a long letter to Elisabeth. I told her how much I missed her. How sorry I was, again, for the hurt I have caused her. How much I wanted to prove to her that I could change, be worthy of her trust once again. How there was nothing I craved more than her love and forgiveness.

Only when I finished the letter did I realise with great sadness that I had no idea where to send it.

June 13ᵗʰ

Up betimes and away from Guildford, with hope of reaching Portsmouth by day's end. But by this afternoon it was clear this could not be done without crossing the forest in darkness, so instead, we have taken rooms at a plain old inn called the White Hart, in the village of Petersfield.

Lord, how I hate travelling in summer. Every road is dry and pitted with potholes. My joints ache and my arse is sore after two long and tedious days inside that airless little coach. I am in dire need of a good night's rest. Not that I shall find it here, with the three of us forced to share a tiny room with a single straw mattress.

But when I said as much to Will in the taproom after supper, the boy's first reaction was to upbraid me.

'You never tire of complaining, do you?' he said, beckoning for more wine.

'That's hardly fair,' I protested.

'It is, you know. I swear, you are like an old scold sometimes. Have another one.'

'I do not want more wine.'

'It would make you feel better.'

'Enough.'

Will stared at me reproachfully, then held up his hand and leaned back in his chair, as if to indicate that he would waste no more time trying to make me feel better. I felt like a fool, though I hoped that he would apologise before I had to do so myself.

'So, what is a burgess exactly?' he said after a long pause. 'I have never quite understood how they are different from aldermen.'

I realised that, in changing the subject without comment, Will was allowing me to save face.

'It is an honorary title, nothing more. A burgess has no power, though it is a common first step to becoming a Member of Parliament.'

'And how did you end up a burgess of Portsmouth?'

I opened my hands modestly. 'The position was offered and I accepted. Though it took some years. The mayor vetoed it at first.'

'What made him change his mind?'

'As my stature grew at the Navy Board, so eventually the town saw fit to bestow the position on me. That and…' I paused.

'And?'

'There was an old alderman by the name of Arden. Benjamin Arden. A lovely man, whose star has only risen since. He put my case most vigorously and…' I looked over my shoulder before leaning in towards Will. 'I have reason to believe he bribed the mayor.'

'You sly old dog.'

'I deny everything, and don't you go repeating that either. He is an important man now. Deputy to the Governor.'

Will looked at me in surprise. 'Quite the advancement for an alderman.'

'I thought so too. There is talk the King's brother has his eye on the Governorship next, and that would be a difference in rank for the ages. An alderman deputising for a Prince.'

Will raised an eyebrow. 'He must have made quite an impression on the King.'

'I can only think so. Oh, but what fine evenings Ben and I spent together. I remember, one night, we got so drunk the nightwatchman threatened to throw us in gaol for disturbing the peace. I had to push him in the fountain to sober him up.'

I fell silent for a moment, fondly remembering the friendship I had struck up with the old man on my early visits to Portsmouth. It feels so long ago now.

We were interrupted by the sound of a man clearing his throat, and turned to see our driver standing awkwardly next to our table.

'Is there something the matter?' I asked.

'Beg pardon, sir. But I've been talking to some fellows, local men, and they tell me there's been... trouble on the road to Portsmouth.'

'Trouble?' said Will. 'What kind of trouble?'

He shifted uneasily. 'They say the woods are full of outlaws. In the forest between here and Portsmouth. Several of their customers have been set upon just this last week, sir.'

'Well, evidently they lived to tell the tale.'

The old man could see that I was taking the news more seriously than Will, and addressed the remainder of his story to me.

'And now they say a man from Buriton has gone missing. That's the next village. He was travelling home through the forest last night and hasn't come back.'

'Difficult times make for desperate men. Is there an alternative route we could take?'

'We could make a detour to the west, sir, and approach via Fareham. Tis quite a ways, but it avoids the most isolated parts of the forest.'

'Then that is what we shall do.'

He bowed, with an audible sigh of relief, and shuffled away. Will did not seem pleased.

'Sam, that will take all day. They're just trying to scare him so we'll stay longer and spend more money.'

But I was in no mood to argue. Something about his story made me uneasy. If a longer journey is the price we must pay to avoid outlaw territory, another day on the road does not seem like such an unappealing prospect at all.

June 14th

Portsmouth has changed greatly.

The detour via Fareham did indeed add several more hours to our journey, as we knew it would. But it was not just the distance that slowed us down; as we got closer to Portsmouth, the road seemed to fill up with all manner of carts, heavily laden with building materials. As soon as we crested Portsdown Hill, and caught our first glimpse of the town beneath us, I understood why.

When I was last here, in the summer of '67, the old ramparts were all but falling down. Now they have been almost entirely rebuilt. Beyond them, on the harbour, I could see the line of new defensive bulwarks, some of them manned already.

I knew all about His Majesty's great program of works, but I had no idea that so much had been completed already. I am told that as many as five thousand souls live in Portsmouth now. Judging by the huge line of tradesmen and builders I could see waiting to enter through the north gate, not to mention the hundreds of seaborne traders that must be in port at any time, the true number must be many times that. But the greatest surprise was waiting on the other side of the walls.

After waiting our turn to enter the town over the old wooden crossing to Portsea Island, then through the north gate, I pointed the driver westward in the direction of the Domus Dei, the great medieval hospice overlooking the sea. The tall spire is a useful navigational aid, and I know from experience how easy it is to get lost in Portsmouth's shambolic warren of narrow streets and alleys.

Once we were nearly there, I told him to look for Penny Street, which runs nearby. This was where we would find Admiralty House, the home of the Governor and the centre of naval command in the town. But where once it had blended in among the handsome but ordinary-looking brick townhouses that line the street, I was astonished to find the portico of a grand mansion.

This new Admiralty House was a huge, white stucco building, remodelled in the style of an Italian *palazzo*. Doric columns supported a pediment roof, which was carved intricately with the figures of Poseidon and Amphitrite. The sounds of hammering and sawing could be heard from an open window on the top floor. Clearly the extravagant work was not yet finished.

'I thought you said they didn't have any money?' said Will.

I shook my head incredulously. 'It seems I have yet more questions I should like to put to the Governor.'

The driver was anxious to start his return journey to London, so I told him to wait a few minutes while Will and I went inside and found our quarters.

We stepped through the doors and into a tall atrium, through which light poured from windows high in the domed ceiling. Opposite us was a small desk, behind which sat a young man dressed in the blue frock coat of a junior officer. From the way his head was buried in some papers, I guessed he must be painfully short-sighted.

He sat up with a jolt as the door slammed shut.

'Yes?' he demanded, peering towards us.

'Tell Governor Maynard that Mr Pepys and Mr Hewer have arrived. We are expected.'

The young officer sifted through some of the papers on his desk, scanning the text at close range. I exchanged a puzzled glance with Will.

'I do not believe so, sir.'

'I beg your pardon?'

'Your name is not on my list. When were you due to arrive?'

'Mr Pepys and I are here to see the Governor,' said Will impatiently. 'We have had a long journey and are in no mood to tarry. Check your papers again.'

The officer did so, then shook his head with a conceited smile. I stepped forward and leaned over the desk. 'Listen to me, Mr...'

'*Boatswain* Stearne.'

'Well listen to me, Mr Boatswain. I am Clerk of the Acts to His Majesty's Navy Board, here on a mission from the Duke of Albemarle. And you are trying my patience.'

'Is there a problem here, Stearne?'

I looked up to see a tall, broad-shouldered man standing in an open doorway at the rear of the atrium. His face was mostly in shadow, with the bright sunlight from above illuminating his dark hair, giving the appearance of a halo.

He could not have been much older than thirty, but he wore the uniform of a captain, his dark blue coat and pressed white breeches so impeccable that he might as well have been on parade. He carried a tricorn hat underneath his arm.

'And you are?' I said boldly, although I felt a little intimidated.

'Captain James Harcourt. And you are?'

'Samuel Pepys.' I held out my hand, and immediately regretted it, for the man did not move.

'Are you expected, sir?'

'Indeed I am, Captain. On king's business concerning your own ship, the *Prince Rupert*.' I paused, expecting a reply, but he said nothing. I cleared my throat. 'Well sir, we shall talk later. In the meantime, perhaps someone could tell me where I can find Lord Maynard?'

'He is at Mistress de Vere's hou—' Stearne began to speak, but Harcourt cut him off.

'*Governor* Maynard is currently indisposed. But I am sure he would see you on the morrow.'

I bristled at his lack of respect, but I could see that arguing would get me nowhere.

'Very well. I shall call for him in the morning.'

Harcourt shrugged in such a way as to suggest he cared not a bit whether I did or not.

Stearne cleared his throat. 'Beg your pardon, sir. Tomorrow is Saturday. The Governor likes to spend the morning inspecting the fleet on Saturdays.'

'Then I shall call for him early. Meanwhile, you can show us to our quarters.'

'I'm sorry, sir. We have no quarters available. The building work…'

I looked to Harcourt for help, but the captain merely smiled and walked away. I turned to face Will.

'Well then, it appears we have another job to do.'

While Will went off to find us alternative lodgings, I ordered Stearne to make available to me the last year's worth of accounts for the *Prince Rupert*, together with those of the other ships-of-the-line moored here in the last year. Of course, I had the ledger that Albemarle had given me, but I wanted to compare it to the records kept here.

Besides, I thought, it would do no harm to start asserting my authority.

Stearne dispatched a footman to collect what I wanted while I waited in the atrium. I had hoped he would offer me refreshment, but instead, after a few minutes of silence had passed between us, I decided I would use the time to ask him about my predecessor.

'Mr Thorne?' he said, looking up at me from the desk. 'A most unfortunate business, sir. Most unfortunate indeed.'

'Did you come to know him while he was here?'

'Only to say good-day. But he seemed a pleasant man.'

'Was he well liked among the men here?'

'Oh yes, sir. He was thought of as a most congenial fellow. One or two of the officers started many a day with a sore head after a night drinking with Mr Thorne.'

A little odd for a man sent to investigate them for corruption, I thought.

'And what about his work? Did he talk much about that?'

'Not to me, sir. I understood he was here for the same reason as you.' He paused for a moment, then lowered his voice. 'Do you know who killed him, sir?'

'No. Do you?'

'I heard a rumour that there was something… devilish about it.' He dropped his voice to a whisper. 'Is it true that they unmanned him too?'

I was about to tell him the truth, but thought there was little value to be had in spreading salacious rumours. Better to let the matter lie. Albemarle had impressed upon me the need for discretion, after all.

'You would do well not to listen to rumour, Boatswain Stearne. Now, where is that fellow with my accounts?'

The man returned carrying a box filled with accounting books, at just the same time that a young potboy appeared at the front door. His clothes were smeared with grease and he was red faced from running in the heat.

'Looking for Mr Pepys,' he said, in a thick Hampshire burr.

'I am Mr Pepys.'

'Mr Hewer sends me to take you to your lodgings, sir.'

I handed him the box, telling him he would have an extra shilling for carrying it, and followed the boy out onto the street.

Away from the modern houses of Penny Street, the town soon began to feel old again. We cut down an alleyway that led to a narrow, curved street lined with timber-framed buildings that leaned forward so far that they almost touched. Gulls screeched overhead and my nostrils were assailed with the stink of rotting fish and ordure.

After a minute or two, we turned on a sharp corner into Craven Street, and there, in front of us, was an inn called the Four Feathers. A woman was emerging from the front door, carrying a basket of dirty linen. She was red faced and sweating heavily. It took me a moment to realise that she was with child.

'Allow me, madam,' I said, hurrying forward to help with the door.

'Much obliged, sir.'

'You must let me help you with your load, too.'

'Oh now, I ain't going far. Just Bear Lane.' She smiled at the potboy. 'How now, Olly? Don't tell me you gone and grown some more, have you?'

'Hello Alice,' he replied, pushing past me and through the door. Before I could offer to help a second time, the woman had already set off down the street, huffing away with the basket under her arm.

The door opened into a large taproom, filled with wooden benches and rickety-looking tables. A stout, matronly woman of about sixty was busily scrubbing the diamond-shaped windowpanes, causing the unmistakable scent of vinegar to mix with the odours of old woodsmoke and sweat. A huge coal fire took up most of one wall. Mercifully, it was unlit.

The boy held out his hand and I fished out a shilling from my waistcoat. He put the box down on the floor and scurried off through a door to what I assumed must be the kitchen.

I looked around. A thick-set young man with thinning hair and an untidy beard lay slumped over a table near the door. He was snoring loudly, still gripping a half-empty tankard, as if somebody might take it away. Then I noticed that he had only one leg, a crutch propped up against the wall beside him.

'Sam.'

Will called to me from a table in the corner. I picked up the box of ledgers and went to join him, groaning with discomfort as I sank down into my chair and placed the heavy box on the ground.

'Sam, are you alright? You look terrible.'

'Fine. I just want a drink.'

Will flagged down a serving maid. 'Tamsin! Two more cups of ale.'

'This is a drab place,' I said, looking around.

'Oh, nonsense. The ostler at Admiralty House called it the friendliest inn for miles, and I think I agree with him.'

'So I can see. Honestly, Will Hewer, I leave you alone for half an hour and you are already on first-name terms with the prettiest girl I have seen in days.'

'You are jealous.'

'I am tired. Where is our luggage?'

'Already upstairs. I paid the coachman an extra shilling before he went on his way. We appear to be the only guests at the moment.'

The girl came over with our ale. She was around twenty years old, with cornflower-blue eyes and ringlets of light brown hair escaping from beneath her cap. Her dress was cut very low, even for a taproom wench, and I shut my eyes to stop myself from staring at her décolletage.

When I opened them again, she was looking at me with amusement.

'Who's your friend then, Will? I do believe I make him nervous.'

'This is Mr Samuel Pepys. Clerk of the Acts to His Majesty's Navy Board.'

'Not often we get such fancy gentlemen staying here. So, do you know the King then?'

I could not decide whether she was genuinely impressed, or just teasing me. 'I have met His Majesty, on occasion.'

'Saw him once, I did. Married Queen Catherine at the Domus, not ten minutes from here. Did you know that?'

'Indeed I did.'

'Fresh off the boat, she was. Oh, but she did look pretty. The king was a bit of rich sauce too, if you ask me.' She began to fan herself with her fingers. 'I hear he keeps a mistress or two. I ain't saying I got airs and graces, but I reckon he might go for a bit of rough, what do you think?'

She gave me a saucy wink and nudged my shoulder. I stared back at her.

'We shall take our supper soon, Tamsin. Before I have need to call for the Justice.'

'Best tell the mistress then.' She shrugged at Will, then withdrew.

'What was that about?' I asked.

'I told her you'd probably be in a foul temper when you arrived. She bet me a farthing she'd have you smiling in a minute.'

'You bull's pizzle. I was seeking for a fool when I found you.'

We were interrupted by the arrival at our table of the matronly woman who had been cleaning the windows when I entered. Her face was flushed and she seemed in need of sitting down.

'You must be Mr Pepys and Mr Hewer?'

'Indeed madam. And you are?'

'Goody Brown, sir. Mistress of this establishment. I trust young Tamsin has been taking good care of you?'

'A most charming host,' said Will.

I thought to make a jibe at his expense, but decided better of it.

'Will you be staying long, sirs?'

I inclined my head. 'Some weeks probably, though we hope our business will be concluded soon.'

'Oh? Business?'

'King's business. In fact, it is possible that you knew our predecessor in this matter, Mr Elias Thorne?'

I thought I saw a flicker of recognition, but she shook her head.

'Can't say I know the name, sir. But you are welcome for as long as you please. You'll find this a humble house, but an honest one.'

Though the shift in her manner was slight, suddenly she seemed a little hostile towards us. I wondered why.

'Ah, now here's Tamsin with your food.' Tamsin emerged from the kitchen with two steaming plates of roast beef and buttered carrots, which we fell upon hungrily.

I related to Will what Boatswain Stearne had told me about Elias Thorne. As we talked, I kept a close eye on the landlady, who was on the other side of the taproom clearing some cups. Once again, the mention of Mr Thorne seemed to provoke a reaction in her. I saw her back stiffen when I spoke his name.

Then, just as Tamsin was clearing away our empty plates, something strange happened. The man in the corner, whom I had seen when I entered, let out a loud cry. The room felt silent as he called out in anguish, apparently still asleep.

'Piety? Come back, Pie my love. Piety!'

Goody Brown ran over to comfort him. 'There, there,' she said, rocking him gently back and forth. 'Piety's gone, remember? Quiet now.'

She held him as he wept, quietly.

'What in God's name is going on there?' said Will.

'I don't know. But in faith, this is a strange place.'

Tamsin returned to our table. Gone were the bold spirits of an hour ago. Now she seemed subdued, almost shaken.

'Apologies, gentlemen, you mustn't pay him no heed. More ale?'

'What's the matter with him?' I asked.

'Oh, that's just poor Tom Wilkin in his cups again. He's harmless.'

I considered this for a moment, then rose from my chair and picked up the box of ledgers.

'We shall take our rooms now, Tamsin, thank you. Will?'

'I… think I'll stay and have more ale. If you don't mind – sir?'

I frowned, puzzled at the oddness of him calling me 'sir.' Tamsin called over to Goody Brown, who bade me follow her upstairs.

As we left, I saw Tamsin leaning on the table, laughing as Will shared a joke with her. Suddenly, I realised that he had probably addressed me in such a formal manner so as to draw attention to the difference in our stations – and thus to himself as the younger man. Could it be that he was growing tired of my company and wanted to be rid of me for the rest of the evening?

I began to feel very hurt and welcomed the chance to be alone.

I lie awake on a most uncomfortable truckle bed, trying to make notes by the light of a candle. My eyes are sore and tired. From downstairs, I can hear the sound of laughter. Will is no doubt making many friends. Something I seem incapable of doing.

Does it mean anything that Elias Thorne had such an easy relationship with the men he had been sent to investigate? Was he involved in some corruption himself, or was he just bad at keeping professional distance? And Goody Brown clearly recognised his name, so why lie about it?

For now, that's all one. It must be near ten and the last of the evening light has disappeared from the sky. I must sleep. Such questions can wait until tomorrow.

It is perhaps half an hour since last I wrote and something very strange has just happened.

I sorely needed to piss, so got up to use the pot. I hardly dared look at my water, but nonetheless, I took the pewter bowl over to the window and held it up. Even by the moonlight, the sight was unmistakable. Blood. More of it than last time.

I emptied the pot onto the cobbles below. With little hope of rest, I took out my tinder box and lit a new candle. The cheap tallow gave off an acrid black smoke, which did make my eyes sting.

I opened the leather satchel I had brought from London and took out the accounts of the *Prince Rupert*. Then I took the first of the ledgers I had brought from Admiralty House and, squinting in the dim light, began to scan the pages of neat, precise handwriting.

A sudden noise from outside the window caught my attention. I walked over and peered outside.

A burly young man was walking past on the street. He was dressed in a sailor's uniform, though not an English one. His long blue surcoat was faded and tattered around the edges, and he wore a wide-brimmed blue hat. I could see that the jerkin underneath his coat was smeared with dirt, and his high-topped leather boots were coming apart at the seams.

Then it struck me. He was Dutch.

Suddenly, the man jerked his head upwards and looked straight at me. His bearded face bore a menacing expression. Quickly, I ducked away out of sight.

I crouched underneath the window, breathing heavily. Maybe he did not see me? And even if he did, I reasoned, he is just a passer-by. What reason did I have to feel so unnerved? I waited there for what seemed like several minutes before daring to look again.

The man was still standing there, staring up at my window.

June 15ᵗʰ

Up betimes and to breakfast. I did not wait for Will to rise.

To my great vexation, Governor Maynard was nowhere to be found by the time I arrived at Admiralty House, though it was not yet eight. Eventually I located Mr Stearne, who told me that His Lordship had left early. Already in a bad humour, I left in search of the docks.

It took no more than a few minutes to reach the quayside. From there, I could see the masts of several large ships, about a quarter of a mile around the curve of bay.

I made my way through the crowds of people walking to and fro along the busy seafront, always keeping one hand to my purse. As I crossed the road, a pair of richly dressed Moors stepped aside to let me by, respectfully placing their hands to their hearts as I passed. I returned the gesture, familiar with their manners from my time in Tangier.

Suddenly, my stomach cramped violently and I felt a wave of nausea. The pain seemed even greater this time.

I stopped to rest on a low brick wall overlooking the quayside. Breathing hard to try and suppress the pain, I began to reflect on how angry I felt. Was it really possible that they had not received Albemarle's letter, telling them we were coming? Surely the duke could not have forgotten to send word ahead of our arrival?

After a few minutes' rest, I felt ready to press on. Wiping sweat from my brow, I walked past the huge dry dock that had been built in the days of Henry VIII, and reached the harbour. There, at anchor a little way off shore, was the enormous bulk of the *Prince Rupert*.

It was as fine a vessel as any ship-of-the-line, with a huge, impenetrable-looking hull and space for a full 92 guns when put to sea. It has been two years since those cannons have been fired in anger, in the last war with the Dutch, and, pray God, they will stay silent a while longer.

Suddenly, I became aware of a commotion nearby. A launch boat was moored at the quayside, freshly loaded with supplies. But its departure seemed to be delayed by a group of maybe a dozen goodwives, who were remonstrating angrily with the purser.

I approached a very short, bow-legged young fellow with thick wrists and a protruding breastbone. He regarded me cautiously until I presented my credentials, then identified himelf as Dimmock, the ship's mate. I asked him where I might find Lord Maynard.

'Aboard ship, sir.'

I looked at him in surprise. 'On the *Rupert?*'

'Yes, sir.'

'She's not preparing to set sail?'

'No, sir.'

'Well then what…'

'Surprise inspection, sir.'

'When do you expect him back?'

Dimmock wiped his brow. 'Don't know, sir. His Lordship often stays awhile afterward.'

I swore with irritation. This day had barely begun and yet it was already trying my patience. My head itched under my wig in the baking sun, sweat was getting in my eyes, and my groin still hurt. A few of the women started directing their insults towards me, which angered me even further. I was in no frame of mind to be made a fool.

'We could take you, sir?'

I looked up at the young mate. 'What?'

'To the *Rupert*, sir. We going across now.' The boy lowered his voice. 'That is, if Mr Purser can get away.'

Ten minutes later, I was sitting uncomfortably between a coil of ship's rope and a barrel, heading out to the *Rupert*. The faint smell of dead fish and vinegar suggested to me that the barrel may have a leak, and the contents within were long past their best.

My eyes were drawn to another ship at port, some distance behind us and to the left. Her sails were ragged and the starboard side was in dire need of cleaning.

I tapped Dimmock on the shoulder. 'You, boy. What is the name of that cutter over there?'

He squinted. '*Nonsuch*, sir. My uncle served on her.'

'A fine-looking vessel,' I said, though my tone was far from convincing.

We reached the *Prince Rupert* and they threw down a sturdy rope ladder for me to climb. I thanked the purser and young Dimmock, then was given over to the charge of a surly midshipman, who escorted me below decks, towards the prow of the ship. We stopped outside a heavy wooden door.

'Captain's Cabin, sir.'

I expected him to announce me, but instead he turned and left me there alone. I knocked. There was no reply. I knocked again, harder this time. A voice from within called sharply for me to enter. I pushed the door open and stepped inside.

A beam of dazzling sunlight shone through the cabin's single leaded window, casting jewel-like patterns across the neat but cramped little space. Tidy shelves were lined with logbooks and sealed wooden boxes, held in place by iron rails. A portrait of King Charles was fixed to the wall. Beneath it sat a well-dressed man, leafing through some papers. He was short and muscular, with dark eyes, and a severe countenance. Were it not for his neat grey beard, he could easily have passed for forty, although I suspected he was ten years older. He wore a high brown wig and a red velvet coat. Around his neck was a small gold medallion tied with ribbon.

'Governor Maynard, I presume?'

'Yes, what of it?' he said, barely looking up from his papers.

'I am Samuel Pepys, Clerk of the Acts—'

'I know who you are.'

I tried to control my anger. 'Then tell me, sir, is this how you treat all your guests? Why was nobody informed of our arrival?'

'Knew you were coming, just didn't care,' he said, rising from his chair and removing a bottle from a sideboard. 'Drink?'

'I have been sent by the Duke of Albemarle to investigate irregularities in the accounts of His Majesty's Navy in Portsmouth. You will have met my unfortunate predecessor?'

'Elias Thorne. Yes. Terrible business. Terrible.' He handed me a glass of port.

'Did you spend much time with him?'

'Hardly saw the fellow. Kept himself to himself. Couldn't hold his drink, though.'

'I find it hard to believe you had no dealings with him directly.'

'Oh, he came and talked to me a couple of times. He spent most of his days here auditing the accounts. I can't say any of the officers got to know him that well.'

This is not what young Stearne told me, I thought, making a note to come back to this point later.

'Sir, you must be aware that the duke takes the inconsistencies in your accounts very seriously. I have his personal charge to investigate the matter, with his full authority. Not to say…' I puffed out my chest for the fullest effect. 'That of my own position as Clerk of the Acts to the Navy Board.'

Maynard held my gaze steadily for a moment, his glass half raised to his mouth, then let out a sudden burst of laughter.

'Well then, sir, I am glad that you are here. We have much to discuss.'

He sat back down at his desk, motioning for me to sit opposite. He opened a drawer and thumped a thick wad of papers down, then picked one up and tossed it to me.

'This is a list of my men who are owed wages. The most indebted on that list goes back to November 1668.'

I was about to respond when another paper landed in front of me.

'An inventory of my stores. On a war footing, barely a third of my guns would be operational under sustained attack. I have provisions enough to feed a full crew for no more than a fortnight at sea, even on combat rations.'

'Lord Maynard—'

'That is to say nothing of the conditions in which my men must be billeted, the rancid vittles, and the repairs needed to barracks, which are still outstanding despite my repeated applications to your office for extra funds.'

'But the great works, the new defences—'

'Barely a fraction of what is needed.'

'As Your Lordship knows, the rebuilding of London has placed great strain on the Exchequer—'

'Which somehow finds the money to pay the King's gambling debts, to say nothing of his expensive taste in whores. How is Lady Castlemaine, by the way?'

I stiffened. I was used to hearing innuendo against the King and his extravagances, but this was dangerously close to sedition. 'Those are bold words indeed, sir, given what I have seen up at Admiralty House. Dear God, what money is being spent on that place, that could be better used elsewhere!'

'I quite agree with you. Stupid waste. But it is the King's wish that the military command in Portsmouth carries with it the trappings of his authority. And that means more money we do not have.'

I was beginning to wonder if I had misjudged this man. Perhaps he was not quite the buffoon for which I had first taken him.

'I sympathise, Governor. But the King, while he has his foibles, understands the gravity of what is facing us. You must see what a fine job his commissioners have done with Portsmouth's defences, but this is not the only port in dire need of refortification. What of the East Coast, for example? I am sorry for the conditions in which your men must live, but these are straitened times and we must all tighten our belts.'

'A fair point, Mr Pepys. Perhaps you would care to convey it to the crowd of goodwives you may have seen on your way over, whose husbands do not have the money to feed, clothe or house their families? I think perhaps you would have a lively reception.'

I took a sip of port. It was good.

'We stray from the point, My Lord. I am here primarily to investigate irregularities in the accounts of the *Prince Rupert*. I am aware that you have your own problems to deal with, and believe me, I want to deal with them too. But this matter will not go away and it must be addressed – urgently. I must and will have your cooperation. Do I make myself clear?'

Maynard looked at me, as if carefully weighing up my ability to match him in this battle of wits. Then, without warning, he leaped up from his chair.

'Very well. Then you shall have it.'

'Thank you, sir.'

He went over to a cupboard and removed a thick sheaf of paper. He handed it to me.

'Copies of the accounts held on the ship. You will find the rest at Admiralty House. Take what you want.'

'Thank you, sir. I already have done.'

'Marvellous.'

'I will need to interview you too.'

'I have business to attend to this afternoon, but tomorrow I am yours.'

'I suppose there will be enough to keep me occupied for the day,' I conceded, aware that by delaying he was once again making it plain who had the real power here. But for the sake of peace, I bit my tongue.

'Tell me, Mr Pepys. Have you brought your best clothes with you?'

'I beg your pardon, sir?'

'There is to be a banquet at Admiralty House tonight. Local worthies. A few friends. You will join us as my guest?'

Though I suspected this was just another tactic, I will not deny that I was flattered.

'I… Thank you, sir. I would be glad to.'

'Excellent,' he said, pouring another glass of port.

'You will not object if I bring my assistant?'

'You can bring who you want. Bring your dog, for all I care.' He leaned back against the desk in a way that seemed casual, but also rather threatening.

I bowed slightly and turned to leave.

'Pepys?' A hint of ice crept back into his tone. I turned again. He seemed harder, all traces of levity vanished.

'You won't find anything, you know. There is no corruption in this town.'

'I hope not, Your Lordship,' I said, and left the room. Then, as a parting shot, I added, 'And so, no doubt, does the King.'

I had hoped to call on my old friend Ben Arden before returning to the Four Feathers, but to my great frustration I was unable to find his house. I could clearly picture the place, an old-fashioned timber building no more than two or three hundred yards from where the launch boat brought me to shore. But the very layout of the streets appeared different from when I had last been here.

Then, after half an hour of searching, I realised that not only was his old house not there anymore, but nor was half the street on which it had once stood. A whole row of handsome dwellings from the time of the last King Richard, razed to make way for Lord knows what! Portsmouth, like London, would be unrecognisable soon.

I recalled how much Ben had loved that rambling old house, with its little rose garden at the back, where one night we drank so much that we passed out under the stars and did not wake until morning. I felt a sudden melancholy at the recollection of a happier time, though I suppose it stands to reason that if my old friend has gone up in the world, he will have moved to grander quarters too.

I was about to return to the inn when it occurred to me that there was another call I could make while I was in this part of town. I found the office of Doctor Richard Grey, coroner, on Peacock Street, not far from the harbour. It did not take me long to locate which among the row of smart new red brick townhouses was his. I knocked and waited.

The door was opened by a tall, wiry man of about fifty, with angular features and a prominent Adam's apple. I waited for him to address me, but he merely stood there, regarding me with insolent silence.

'Good day. I am Mr Samuel Pepys of His Majesty's Navy Board.'

'Indeed?' the man replied, in a slight Scotch accent. 'And do you have an appointment?'

'It is the King's business.'

'Ah. No appointment. Come back Monday.'

He started to close the door but I jammed it with my foot.

'You listen to me, churl. I do not know who you believe yourself to be, but I can assure you, this is no jest. Go and tell your master that I am here to see him.'

'Oh, my master, is it? And who might that be?'

'Doctor Grey,' I said, with clenched jaw.

'In that case, you've found him, sir. I am Doctor Grey.'

My first thought was to ask him why everyone in this town was so damned impertinent, but I forced myself to remain calm.

'I am here to see you about an official matter, Doctor. May I come in?'

Doctor Grey led me into his neat and ordered study. I caught the appetising smell of meat on the air, and noticed that there was a half-eaten plate of hot bacon on his desk. Evidently, I had interrupted his morning meal.

'Do you have no servants, sir?' I said, as he closed the door behind him.

'Of course I have servants. I'm just not too proud to open my own front door. What can I do for you, then?'

'I am here to ask you about a case of yours. The murder of Elias Thorne.'

He sucked air through his teeth. 'Aye, a nasty business, that one. Very nasty indeed. What do you wish to know about it?'

'To begin, where was the body found?'

'In an alleyway off Bear Lane, not far from Admiralty House.'

'And the injuries he sustained, did they give you any clues as to who might have killed him?'

'Well, I can tell you that he was killed by a single blade thrust to the abdomen. And that the killer was shorter than him. Otherwise, no.'

'How can you tell a thing like that?'

Grey looked around for a prop with which to demonstrate. He picked up the knife from his plate.

'Elias Thorne was a man of five feet, ten inches tall. I am six foot two. So if I were to stick this knife into his gut' – he made a downward stabbing motion – 'you can see the wound would be of a certain angle, like so. But if I were much shorter than him, it would be different. Do you see?'

'I do. And judging by the angle of the wounds found on this body, how tall was his assailant?'

'I would say between five feet and five feet four. That is, whoever killed him. I cannot speak for the other wounds.'

I frowned. 'What do mean?'

'The mutilations. Those were made post-mortem.'

'Are you sure?'

'Aye. By at least an hour.'

'How can you possibly tell?'

'The body was lying in a large pool of blood, as you would expect. Wounds to the stomach bleed grievously. I fear the poor soul who found Mr Thorne's body was alerted by the fact that his blood had gushed downhill and pooled in the gutter.'

I began to feel a little sick. 'He had several wounds, as you said. How can you tell if they were made at different times?'

He thought for a moment, then placed his unfinished plate of food between us. 'Now, if you were to cut yourself, sir, what would happen to the wound?'

'It would bleed, of course.'

'Yes, but after that. Later.'

'Eventually, it would close up.'

'A scab forms, yes? Now watch.'

Using the knife, he began to score the slab of bacon. 'Now, what do you see?'

'Just… meat,' I said, puzzled at the question.

'No scab, correct?'

'Of course not. It is dead.'

'Precisely. No scab, because this is dead flesh. It was the same with Elias Thorne. The wound to his abdomen had started to congeal normally by the time he took his last breath. The wounds to his face and genitals, on the other hand, showed no congealing of the blood. Ergo, whoever mutilated his body must have done so some time after he was killed.'

I considered this information carefully. Then, suddenly, I felt the cramp in my groin again, stronger than ever. I doubled over in pain, clutching at the desk.

'Are you ill, sir?' said Grey.

'It is nothing. Just… Something I ate.'

He regarded me sceptically. 'You should be careful, sir. Perhaps you should make an appointment to see me?'

I looked at him with irritation, assuming this to be a joke in poor taste, but he brought me a chair and had me sit. 'I am not just a coroner, sir, I am also a practising physician. Not all of my patients are beyond help.'

'It… Just a little… It will pass in a moment.' I could hardly get the words out, so strongly did I have to grit my teeth.

'How long has this been happening?'

'Some months, but never this bad until recently.'

'And your waters? How are they?'

'Fine.' Suddenly I was in dire need of fresh air. I rose to my feet. 'Doctor Grey, I thank you for your concern, but I must go now.'

'Very well. Though you should never just ignore pain like that, Mr Pepys. Do not let pride endanger your life.'

'I thank you for your advice. I shall see myself out.' I started to take my leave, but then one last thought occurred to me. 'Doctor Grey, do you know who found the body?'

He thought for a moment, then produced a notebook from his desk and flicked back through the pages. 'Ah yes, here it is. A man by the name of Wilkin. Thomas Wilkin.'

I walked slowly back to the Four Feathers. The pain had subsided, but it had left me shaken. It was not just the intensity, which was worse than ever, but the suddenness with which it had overtaken me. One moment I was fine; the next, all but unable to move.

Meanwhile, I had made no progress on the missing funds, although at least I had got a flavour of the Governor's opinions on how the Crown's money was being spent. But would that give him motive enough to steal?

I arrived back at the inn and made straight for my chamber, meaning to take a nap. But as I opened the door and stepped inside, I was surprised to see Will sitting at my desk.

'There you are,' he said. 'What happened to you?'

'I have been with Governor Maynard. What are you doing here?'

'I came looking for you, but you'd vanished. Thought I'd look through these account books until you reappeared.'

I sat on the bed and said nothing.

'What did you find out?' he asked.

I told him about my conversation with Maynard, and the Governor's litany of complaints against the King. Then I related what Doctor Grey had told me about the wounds on Elias Thorne's body having been made at different times.

'Interesting,' said Will. 'So, are we looking for more than one assailant?'

'Perhaps. Or a madman who went back later to finish his work.'

My stomach began to cramp. I held onto the bedclothes, expecting a repeat of the agonies of before, but mercifully it dissipated swiftly.

'Sam? Did it happen again?'

'It is nothing, I—'

'It is not nothing; you should see a doctor.'

'How good of you to be concerned, Will Hewer. Seeing as how you could not wait to be rid of me last night.'

'What are you talking about?'

'In the taproom. You made it clear you wanted to be left in the company of your new friends.'

He looked at me blankly. 'Sam, I just wanted to stay for another drink.'

'You called me sir.'

'I— No, I didn't.'

'Yes, you did.'

'Well, maybe I did, what of it?'

'So we are not friends, is that it? You still see us as master and servant?'

'Alright Sam, stow your beans. What in heaven's name is the matter with you?'

I wanted to argue the point further, but already I felt like a child for being so hurt by something so small. I pulled off my wig and rubbed my sweaty pate.

'I am sorry, Will. This place does not agree with me.'

Will leaned forward in his chair. 'Sam… If I offended you, in faith I am sorry. Of course we are friends.'

I waved away his apology, though in truth I was glad to hear him say those words.

He continued, 'But I will admit, it did occur to me that I might get more out of them on my own.'

'And did you?'

He smiled. 'Indeed, I did. For a start, I think you're right about Elias Thorne. They do know who he is, but for some reason they're lying about it. Almost…'

'Almost?'

'Like they're scared of something.'

'Interesting. What else?'

'You remember that cupshot fellow in the taproom last night, Tom Wilkin? The one who woke up wailing about a girl called Piety?'

'I do. And I have news of him as well. But tell me yours first.'

'Tamsin told me that he was madly in love with this girl, Piety Blake, who used to work here as a serving wench. They grew up together. He was besotted with her.'

'Were they lovers?'

'Not according to Tamsin, though they dallied a little. He asked her to marry him; she refused.'

'And where is this girl now?'

'Dead.'

My heart skipped a beat.

'Dead? How?'

'Choked to death.'

'When?'

'Three weeks ago.'

Only days before Elias, I thought.

'Good heavens. Did they find whoever did such a terrible thing?'

'No. She was discovered on the road between here and Farlington, a little village a couple of miles away.'

I contemplated this for a moment. Of course, that was no reason to suppose that the two murders had anything to do with each other. Portsmouth is a violent place. Thieves and cutpurses abound in these streets, and the country roads are unsafe for travellers – particularly lone women.

And yet, there was something about the connection to this man Tom Wilkin, and the behaviour of the innkeeper, Goody Brown, that gave me pause.

I told Will what I had learned about Tom Wilkin having discovered Thorne's body. Will rubbed the stubble on his cheeks thoughtfully.

'An interesting coincidence, I would say.'

'You know, Will, I am beginning to think we should have a word with the unfortunate Mr Wilkin.'

'Shouldn't be too difficult. By the sound of things, he comes here all the time, pining for Piety Blake like a lost dog. He'll probably be in tonight.'

I suddenly remembered Lord Maynard's invitation.

'Oh Lord, I almost forgot. You and I are to dine with the Governor tonight. He is hosting a revel at Admiralty House.'

'Do you think that's wise? Should we not maintain our distance?'

'That is what I thought at first. But tonight is an opportunity to get the measure of the man and the company he keeps, at close quarters. And besides, if he truly believes me weak enough to be swayed by a pat on the back and a glass of good wine, why disavow him of the notion? The less he thinks of me, the more likely he is to make a mistake.'

This evening, Will and I presented ourselves at Admiralty House. A footman led us through to a small salon, then promptly left without bothering to announce us.

There were perhaps twenty men and half as many women inside the long, elegant room, conversing cheerfully with each other as they sipped wine from crystal glasses. None so much as looked at us.

'Who do you suppose I have to fight for a glass of wine?' muttered Will.

'No doubt Maynard wants to put us in our place,' I replied. 'Take my advice, do not rise to the bait.'

Will scanned the room. 'Do you recognise any of these people?'

I peered into the candlelight, trying to distinguish the faces of the guests. 'A few, perhaps. There's Captain Harcourt. I don't think I can place any others by name. Country squires, a few aldermen and their wives.'

'I feel under-dressed.'

He was right. It was notable how many of the guests seemed to be garbed for an occasion far grander than the one they were attending.

I smirked. 'One almost expects to see the Empress Messalina swanning around, flaunting a bill of sale to prove how much she paid for her dress.'

The doors at the opposite end of the room opened and we were summoned to the dining room. We had just started to move when a voice called from the other side of the room.

'Samuel Pepys? Is that really you?'

I looked around to see an old man walking towards me, his arm outstretched in greeting. He walked with a slight stoop and had a thin white beard. It took me a moment or two to recognise him.

'As I live and breathe – Benjamin,' I said, shaking his hand vigorously. 'My dear man, it is good to see you.'

'And you, Samuel. It has been… How many years?'

'Five at least, if not more. You look well.'

'I look old and tired, Samuel, but you are kind to say so. And who is this?'

Will shook his hand. 'William Hewer, sir.'

'Will is my assistant at the Navy Board,' I said.

The footman standing by the open door cleared his throat and I realised we were the only ones left in the salon. Ben took my arm and the three of us walked towards the dining room. Through the open door I could see that most of the other guests were already seated.

'I congratulate you on your new position, Ben.'

'Thank you. In truth, I dislike this world of politics, but one does one's duty. What brings you to Portsmouth?'

'A bad business, I am afraid, but perhaps one that is best discussed elsewhere.'

'An intrigue? Why, you have gone up in the world too. Well then, let us talk of it another time. Would you come and dine at my house tomorrow?'

I smiled. 'It would give me great pleasure. Although I am sad to find that old place of yours gone to ruin.'

Ben looked at me quizzically and I explained how earlier in the day I had gone looking for his old house, only to find a pile of rubble. He shook his head sadly.

'Ah yes, a great sorrow upon my heart. But I am an old man now. I have no wife. It is just me and my small household. So when the King's commissioners offered to buy it at a fair price to knock down as part of their great works, who was I to refuse?'

We stepped into the dining room and my heart sank a little as I saw that, of the three places left unfilled, only two were next to each other, the other being beside Lord Maynard himself. I was about to ask Will to let me sit with Ben, when Maynard saw me and beckoned me over.

'Better not keep his Lordship waiting,' said Ben, patting me on the arm. 'We shall take this up again later.'

As he sat down next to Will, several places away from where I would have to spend most of the evening, I suppressed a sudden pang of jealousy.

There would be time enough for reunions later. For now, I had work to do.

Oh, but how we ate.

Whatever Lord Maynard's complaints about not being able to feed his men, they clearly did not extend to his own table. Dishes worthy of the finest houses in London were laid before us: plates of roasted capon and duck, covered in rich sauces; stewed carp, pike and lamprey; enough roast chicken for a whole one apiece and more; and an abundance of breads and French cheeses.

No expense was spared. A plate of smoked salmon was flavoured with a sharp, woody spice I learned was called pimento, imported from the West Indies. Even the beef pies were encased in a kind of pastry I'd never seen before, all flaky and puffed with air.

But even that came nowhere close to matching the quality of the cellar. Burgundy and Oléron, hot Scotch toddies and strong port flowed as freely as water.

Maynard proved to be surprisingly good company, and the two of us passed a pleasant hour sparring wits and exchanging tales of naval life – his in far more exotic climes than mine.

At one point, he held the whole table in rapt attention with enthralling tales of his encounters with pirates in the Caribbean Sea. No matter what mischief the Governor may have been up to, I cannot deny his fine wit.

None of the other guests spoke to me much at all, until a chance mention of my old employer, Sir George Downing, piqued the interest of Captain Harcourt, who was seated a few places to my right.

'You know him?' asked the dour young officer.

'Yes indeed. I first met him as a boy at St Paul's School. Then he became my patron. He secured me my first position as a young man, working at the Exchequer.'

'In the service of Lord Cromwell, was it not?' said Maynard, slurring his words. There was a definite edge to his voice.

'Indeed, Your Lordship,' I said. 'This was before the restoration of His Majesty.'

'Ah,' said Maynard, pouring himself more wine.

Harcourt leaned forward. 'Tell us, Pepys: what is he like, Sir George? I have heard he is a difficult man.'

I wanted to reply that Downing was a hateful boor, who had worked me to the bone while taking all credit as his own. But I chose to be diplomatic.

'I… did not always get on with Sir George, if you would have it true, Captain. But he was a fine administrator, I will give him that.'

'And a turncoat,' added Maynard.

'He… was instrumental in negotiating His Majesty's return, Your Lordship. We had our differences, but I cannot deny he proved himself loyal to the Crown.'

'Just as he was loyal to the Commonwealth and Lord Cromwell,' Maynard growled, topping up his glass once more.

'His Majesty saw fit to forgive him. Just as he did with many men of rank.'

The Governor puffed out his cheeks scornfully.

Captain Harcourt spoke up again. 'You say he was a difficult man. And yet you seem to have done very well out of him, is that not so?'

'Indeed, he provided me with many opportunities as a young man, and for that I must be grateful.'

'George Downing is a festering sore on Satan's arsehole' bellowed Maynard with sudden passion. He struck his open hand on the table for emphasis, causing wine to splash from his glass onto his uniform.

All conversation came to an abrupt halt. Ben caught my eye from the other end of the table and raised an eyebrow. I stifled a laugh.

Captain Harcourt cleared his throat. 'That… was a most excellent meal, Your Lordship.'

'Not over yet, my friends,' said Maynard, leaping to his feet. He strode over to a connecting door and threw it open, indicating for us to follow.

As we filed out of the room, I leaned over to Will and whispered, 'I fear Maynard cannot hold his drink as well as he thinks he can. He should be more careful. I wonder whether we should leave?'

'Or we stay and see what more trouble he gets himself into. And besides, this is the best night out I've had in ages.'

We crossed into the withdrawing room, a large, richly furnished chamber with blue silk wallpaper. Servants were already at work ferrying dishes of sweetmeats in from the kitchens to the sideboard, where we were encouraged to help ourselves from the selection.

Generous bowls of fruit and nuts were laid out, alongside sugar cakes, and even a bowl of rose-flavoured cream ice, which seemed to me the most extravagant luxury in the middle of summer.

I had just sat down on the far side of the room with a plate of orange pudding when Ben came and sat on the settle next to me.

'Quite a show, I think,' he said.

'Does Maynard often sail so close to the wind when it comes to affairs of state?'

'He can be a trifle passionate sometimes, perhaps.'

'Passionate? I cannot decide if the man's a hothead or something more sinister.'

'Oh, John is a good governor, I can assure you. And a good man besides. I should know.'

I cursed myself inwardly for letting my guard down. No matter how friendly we once were, Ben's position here is such that I cannot discount the possibility that he may warrant investigation too, unpleasant though the thought may be. But before I could ask anything else, he changed the subject.

'Let me ask you something about Downing. Do you think the King has made a wise choice, appointing him as envoy?'

It took me a second to remember that my troublesome old mentor had recently been sent to Holland as head of a special diplomatic mission. He had once held the post of Ambassador to the Dutch Republic, and the King felt his presence there might help to ease the rising tensions.

That must be why they are all so interested in him, I thought.

'He… is certainly a shrewd man. Apt to get his own way.'

'Many of us here fear that an invasion by the Dutch might be closer than His Majesty believes. Downing's role will be vital if we are to avoid war. Is he equal to the task?'

I considered my words carefully. All this talk of Downing was making me uncomfortable. He was a cruel master to me as a young man, bullying and belittling me constantly while I worked tirelessly in his service. This was not a man whose memory I liked to dwell upon, but I did not want my enmity towards him to be widely known – even to one I trusted as much as Ben.

'My years with Sir George were not happy ones, I confess. But I do believe him to be a shrewd negotiator.'

At that moment, Will perched himself on the arm of the settle next to me, his plate stacked high with sweets. Ben smiled at him then rose to his feet.

'If you will excuse me, I heard tell of some marchpane.'

As he shuffled away in the direction of the sideboard, I turned to Will.

'I would do well to remember his position before speaking my mind in future.'

'I thought the same at supper. Amiable fellow but he asks a lot of questions.'

'What did he want to know?'

'Oh, how you were doing. London. Elisabeth… He was also very keen to know more about your connection to Sir George Downing, for some reason.'

'Ah. He's just been appointed diplomatic envoy to the Dutch.'

'Oh Christ. We'll be at war in a week.'

It was just after midnight when the mysterious guest arrived.

Hours had passed for us in a happy daze of drink and dancing. A band of musicians arrived, and while their playing began with the sedate rhythms of ballettis and pavanes, a quick word from the Governor had them shift to a series of fast and bawdy jigs.

Maynard had the furniture pushed to one side and we all danced in circles, faster and faster, until I felt quite dizzy and had to steady myself against the wall.

Ben, red-faced with exertion, put his arm around my shoulder. 'I am too old for this sort of thing, Samuel.'

'I too,' I replied, catching my breath.

'Then take solace in the fact that, should you ever decide to leave the Navy Board, you are sure to find work as a dancing master.'

'You will be my first pupil, Ben.'

I had thought Maynard was so drunk that he might pass out at any minute, but when, a little later, his valet arrived with a message that there was a lady there to see him, he seemed to regain his composure immediately. I watched as the Governor excused himself to his companions and slipped out to the hallway.

My interest was piqued. With a quick glance to check that nobody was watching, I went and peered through the open door to the hallway.

Maynard was standing at the far end of the room, talking to a tall woman in a crimson velvet riding cloak. Her back was turned to me but I could tell by the cut of her clothes that she was a lady of means. Her long hair was pulled back with a silver band and styled into ringlets, which pooled in the open space of her hood.

They were talking too quietly for me to hear, so instead I watched them curiously. Were they lovers? Or was their relationship of a different kind?

Suddenly, from somewhere behind me, there was a clatter of metal and breaking glass. I spun around to see that one of the officers had collided with a servant carrying a tray of glasses. When I turned again, Lord Maynard and the woman in red were staring directly at me.

Maynard nodded politely. I bowed my head in return and hastily withdrew.

I found Will picking at a plate of sweetmeats. 'Come. It is time you and I took our leave.'

I looked over my shoulder. The woman in the red cloak was still watching me. Then she strode over to the connecting door and firmly pushed it shut.

'Stop making a fuss, Sam.'

Will tried to resist as I lifted his legs up onto the bed and pulled his boots off. The walk back to the Four Feathers had gone some way towards sobering me up, but it seemed not to have had the same effect on my companion.

'Keep still. Time for bed.'

'I have an idea, why don't we go out and—'

'Sleep it off, Will. You will feel better in the morning.'

He let out a sigh, which turned into a yawn. 'Perhaps I will close my eyes. Just for a moment, you know.'

'A fine idea. I shall see you in the morning.'

I rose unsteadily to my feet and made my way back to my own room.

I started to undress, but my eyes were drawn to the window. Somewhere in the distance, a church clock struck two. This must have been about the same time that I had seen that man outside the window, in the early hours of the morning. Tentatively, I crept over and peered outside.

The street was empty. There was no sound except the distant murmur of the sea. I laughed at my own foolishness, but all the same, I dragged the chest in which I keep my belongings over to the door to wedge it shut. Then I climbed into bed to complete my diary for the day.

I shall have another reckoning with Maynard tomorrow.

June 16th

I was awoken by a pounding at the door. I opened my eyes. Somebody was calling my name. I sat up and immediately gripped my aching head.

'What is it?' I snapped.

'Boatswain Stearne, sir. You must come quickly.'

I pulled on some clothes and my boots, then dragged the chest out of the way and cracked the door open.

The boatswain was standing alone in the corridor, holding a candle. His face was white as ash.

'What is the matter?'

'Please, sir. You must come now.'

I hesitated for a moment, then pushed the door open. Stearne headed straight for the stairs, but I hurried over to Will's room first, banging on the door to rouse him.

'What is it?' he called from within, groggy and irritated.

'Will! Something's happened.'

A few moments later, Will appeared at the door, still dressed in last night's clothes, his eyes only half open.

'Hurry, sirs, please,' Stearne called from the stairs. There was something about the urgency in his voice that sobered us up like ice-cold water.

We followed him down the narrow staircase and into the taproom, where Goody Brown stood in her nightgown, holding a candle.

'What is the meaning of this, Mr Pepys?'

'I cannot say, madam,' I replied, as we hurried out into the street.

Will and I almost had to run to keep pace with Stearne as we hurried up Craven Street. I guessed from the sky that it must be nearly dawn.

'What is the matter?' I asked again, but Stearne would not look back. As we emerged from the alleyway leading to Penny Street, I saw Admiralty House ahead of us, and immediately knew something was wrong.

The front door was open and a group of officers were standing there, looking at something on the ground. The officers looked up as we approached. One of them was Captain Harcourt. His mouth was covered with a trembling hand.

Sprawled out in the gutter lay another man. A huge gash had split the man's throat wide open, blood pooling on the cobblestones. His mouth was frozen in a rictus of pain, his lifeless eyes staring up at the early morning sky.

It was Lord Maynard.

Harcourt sent some men to conduct a search of the surrounding area. Within an hour, the whole place was spurred into action as if we were going to war.

The captain told us to wait inside while his men removed the body. The hallway was cold and draughty, and a group of servants huddled together. A few of them were crying.

So Maynard was well liked, I noted. But could he have had enemies here too?

I went over to ask if any of them knew what had happened. They told me that Maynard's body had been discovered by a guardsman on patrol, who had immediately raised the alarm. Given how regular the patrols were, this meant that Maynard could not have been dead more than half an hour by the time we were awoken.

Still more than enough time for the killer to disappear.

A short time later, Harcourt entered and strode over to us, his heavy footsteps echoing off the marble walls. I offered our condolences, which he dismissed with a wave of his hand, getting straight to the point.

'Did you two return directly to your lodgings after you left here last night?'

'Yes,' I replied. 'Sometime between midnight and one o'clock.'

'And you saw and heard nothing suspicious?'

'It is only a short walk and we were drunk. But no, not that I recall.'

He turned to Will. 'And you?'

'I... was in no state to observe much last night, sir.'

'There was one thing,' I said, the fog clearing in my head. 'Shortly before we left, the Governor was talking privately with a visitor in the hall. It seemed odd that they had called so late.'

'You do not know who it was?'

'A woman. Maybe in her early to middle thirties. Richly dressed. She wore a red velvet riding cloak.'

Harcourt's mouth twisted into a disdainful smile. 'Charlotte de Vere.'

'Who?'

'It is no concern of yours.'

He turned on his heel and was gone.

'What woman?' said Will.

'Perhaps you wouldn't remember. Maynard had a late caller.' I lowered my voice. 'I need you to find me a fast rider. I must get word to Albemarle.'

'Of course. And then?'

'Then I need to speak to Ben. Harcourt may have taken charge here, but as Maynard's deputy, Ben is acting governor now. So where is he?'

The sun was beginning to rise as the messenger took my hastily written report and spurred his horse towards the north road. A faint mist hung over the ground outside Admiralty House. There was a sickening trail of fresh blood in the gutter where Maynard's body had been.

London is seventy miles from here. Riding hard, a skilled messenger could reach White Hall by the evening. Today being the Lord's Day, at least the roads would be clear.

I wanted to make sure my report reached the duke before anybody else's. I prayed that the rider Will had managed to press into service, with the reluctant help of Mr Stearne, was just such a man.

Will nudged my arm and I became aware of another horse approaching at speed. At first, I thought it was the messenger coming back again, but then I saw a familiar figure riding towards us down Penny Street.

Before the horse had even come to a complete halt, he eased himself out of the saddle, handing the reins to a servant who had just arrived to scrub the ground clean of blood.

'Ben,' I said, stepping forward.

'Where have they taken his body?' His eyes were red and I wondered if he had been crying.

'I do not know. Captain Harcourt—'

'*Harcourt,*' spat Ben, striding across the hall in search of his colleague. I started to follow, but he spun around and held up a shaking hand.

'You should keep out of the way, Samuel, for the time being. Return to your lodgings. I shall send for you in due time.'

He disappeared into the building. I turned to Will, who seemed as surprised by his reaction as I was. Was the old man just taking the news badly? Or did he have other reasons to be so angry?

We were too shocked to say anything for most of the way back to the Four Feathers. I was glad that the sun was now up and we did not have to walk those narrow streets and passages in darkness.

It was when we made the final turn into Craven Street that we saw the body in the gutter. I froze with shock as Will gripped my arm.

We approached the figure without saying a word, both of us fearing the worst. I looked around, but there was no sign of another soul.

Then the body let out a grunt and we sighed with relief.

'Thank Heaven,' I said.

Will knelt down and rolled the man over. He was a plump, ruddy-cheeked young fellow, with thinning hair and a reddened nose. Mucus trailed from his cracked lips and I realised that he was lying next to a puddle of his own vomit. His right leg only went down as far as his knee and a broken crutch lay on the ground next to him.

He opened his eyes and stared at us, uncomprehendingly.

'Why, Mr Wilkin,' I said. 'Perhaps you would come inside so we can talk?'

'Drink this.' Will pushed a tankard of pale liquid across the table. Wilkin sniffed it and grimaced.

'It is weak beer, sir,' I said. 'Best, in your current condition.'

We were sitting in a corner of the taproom in the Four Feathers, waiting for the three plates of breakfast I had ordered from Goody Brown. A small fire burned in the grate next to us.

Tom Wilkin made for a pathetic sight. He could be no older than twenty-five, and had probably been quite handsome once, though the skin under his beard was marked by the red lines of a habitual drunkard. His hands were shaking so strongly as he lifted the cup to his parched lips that some of the beer splashed onto his filthy shirt.

Will opened a pouch of tobacco and offered him some. Wilkin filled his pipe and lit it from the fireplace.

'Tell us about yourself, Mr Wilkin,' Will said, gently.

For a while he merely sat there, smoking his pipe, his bloodshot eyes staring at a fixed point upon the table. It was as if conversation itself were a burden, to be borne reluctantly as the price of living.

'Nothing to tell,' he replied, eventually. 'I ain't nobody.'

'Now that's not true.' Tamsin walked up to the table and set down three plates of bread and cheese in front of us. 'Tom here were a seaman. Served on the *Monmouth* and the *Prince Rupert*, he did.'

She spoke to him encouragingly, as one might to a shy child. But I could see pity in those cornflower-blue eyes.

'Two very fine vessels,' I concurred.

'And then when he got hurt in the war, he took up work as a shipwright. Ain't that right, Tom?'

He said nothing.

'In which war did you serve, Mr Wilkin?' asked Will.

'Dutch. '67.'

'And do you still have work at the shipyard?'

'No, sir, I do not.'

At that, the conversation stopped short. We might have sat in silence for longer, had Goody Brown not come rushing over to our table.

'Mr Pepys. Is it true? About the Governor?'

Word travels fast in this town, I thought, bowing my head solemnly. 'I fear it is, madam.'

'What about him?' asked Tamsin.

'He's been done for.'

Tamsin put a hand to her mouth in shock. Wilkin raised his head, suddenly more animated than we had ever seen him.

'Captain Maynard dead? How?'

'*Governor* Maynard had his throat cut open,' I said, emphasising his proper title. 'A tragic business. And I fear the assailant is still at large.'

Wilkin slumped back in his chair, a look of genuine shock on his face. Will regarded him curiously.

'Did you know him, Tom?'

'Aye, sir. I did. He were skipper of the *Rupert* when I were an ordinary seaman. Most of the officers wouldn't so much as look at the likes of us, except when giving orders. But he were different. He'd come talk with us, check we had all the pay and provisions we were due. Even ask our opinion sometimes on how the ship could be better run.'

Wilkin emptied his tankard and wiped his damp beard. It was evident that this was one subject at least about which he was happy to talk.

'Now mark me, we knew our place, mind, and he knew his, and he could be as harsh as the next man, let me tell you. He expected you to work and do your part, or you'd feel his wrath. But he were fair with it too. Never did we think he looked down on us just on account of who we was, right down to the lowest cabin boy.'

Tamsin patted him on the shoulder and took his cup.

'I'll get you another one, Tom.'

'I best be getting back to work too. Terrible business. Terrible.' Goody Brown set to polishing tables with a rag, though I could tell that she was still listening to every word of our conversation.

'Did you ever see him again?' Will asked.

Wilkin let out a short laugh, which turned into a deep, guttural cough.

'What'd you think, he'd invite me for dinner? No, sir, I've not seen him since then. But Maynard were a fair man and as good a Captain as any I knew. God rest his soul.'

A look of melancholy returned to his eyes and he resumed sucking on his pipe.

Tamsin returned with another tankard of ale, then went to work replacing an empty barrel. My attention turned back to Goody Brown. I wanted to keep my eye on the landlady as I asked my next question.

'Tell us about Piety Blake, Mr Wilkin.'

Goody Brown's head jerked up, her eyes briefly making contact with mine. She looked away almost immediately, but it was enough time to confirm one thing in my mind. There were secrets here and she did not welcome us prying into them.

'Oh, Pie! My sweet angel.'

'She was your sweetheart, wasn't she?'

'I loved her, sir. But her heart was promised to another.'

Hearing him say this, Goody Brown could hold her tongue no longer.

'Now, now, Tom,' she said. 'These good fellows don't want to hear your tales of woe. Perhaps it's time you were on your way.'

'We will decide what we want to hear, madam,' I snapped.

Her nostrils flared angrily, though she tried to keep her tone civil. 'My apologies. Just don't want no one causing a scene. Do we now, Tom?'

She stared at him pointedly, then went back to her work. All but the slimmest pretence that she was not hanging on our every word had disappeared.

'Can you read, Mr Wilkin?' I asked.

'Aye, sir.'

'Mistress,' I called after the landlady. 'Might I trouble you for a pen and some ink?'

She did not say yes straight away, no doubt trying to decide whether there was any way for her to refuse without being openly rude. I hoped she cared enough about keeping our custom to give me what I wanted.

'Tamsin,' she said reluctantly, and the girl fetched me a quill and a small pot of ink. I removed a small piece of paper from my pocket and spread it out on the table. 'I am going to write something down,' I said to Wilkin, lowering my voice almost to a whisper.

I scratched out the words *Elias Thorne*, then turned the paper towards him. He looked at it, then up at me.

'Do you recognise the name?'

He nodded, slowly.

'Goodwife Brown,' I said, folding up the paper, 'Mr Wilkin is tired and he needs a new crutch. We shall take our breakfasts upstairs so that Mr Wilkin may rest more comfortably until such time as one can be made for him.'

The woman glared at me. 'Very well, sir. Maybe I'll set one of the potboys to it now so that young Tom here can be on his way nice and quick.'

'Why are they lying, Tom?'

It was Will who asked the question. Wilkin was sitting on the bed in my room, a half-eaten plate of bread and cheese beside him.

'I do not know, sir. 'Tis a mystery to me too. A fortnight ago, Elias Thorne was sitting downstairs in that taproom, laughing, buying drinks, and making everyone his friend. Then after he... after he was murdered, suddenly it was like he'd never existed. Goody Brown, Tamsin... even the boys in the kitchen. If you said his name, they'd tell you to be quiet.'

'What kind of man would you say Elias Thorne was?' I asked.

'People loved him. Everyone wanted to be his friend.'

'Did you?'

'No, sir. I hated him.'

'Why?'

'Because he took Piety, that's why.'

'They were lovers?' asked Will.

Wilkin nodded. 'I know she weren't as sweet on me as I was on her. I ain't daft. But I hoped, in time…'

'How did you know each other?'

'Grew up together, didn't we?'

'And Tamsin? Goody Brown? They knew her too?'

'Piety were a serving girl here, like Tamsin. That's how she—' The words caught in his throat. 'That's how she met Mr Thorne. He were always in here of a night.'

We let him compose himself for a moment. Then I asked, gently, 'How did Piety die?'

He did not look up, as if not meeting our eyes was the only way to hold back tears.

'Piety lived on the outskirts of town, near Farlington. I worried about her, walking back and forth between there and Portsmouth, on her own, even late at night. But she wouldn't listen to me.'

He trailed off, lost in some memory. Will prompted him. 'Tom? Tell us what happened to her.'

'She was found one morning, three weeks past. On the road. I… don't want to say the rest, sir.'

I chose my next words carefully. 'Tom, I am sorry for your loss, truly. But we know that it was you who found Mr Thorne's body. So I must ask you this – did you kill him?'

He stared up at me. I had been prepared for my question to be met with anger, perhaps even violence, but to my surprise his bloodshot eyes were filled with tears.

'No, sir. I swear it. I do not deny I wanted him dead, God forgive me, but I could never have done a thing like that to a man. I seen dead bodies before, but that…' He closed his eyes as if to force away the memory. 'No man deserves to die like that.'

Will crouched down in front of him. 'Tom, I am not saying I disbelieve you. But you tell us that you hated Thorne and wanted him dead. Many men would, in your shoes. And to have been the first to discover his body and raise the alarm… You must understand how that looks to us?'

'I do, sir. But I swear on Piety's soul, I did not kill him. And I can prove it.'

'How?'

'I'd just been released from gaol when I found Mr Thorne's body. I was making my way home and… That's when I found him.'

'What were you doing in gaol, Tom?' I asked.

'I got in a brawl outside the Four Feathers. Some lads were teasing me about my leg. Nightwatchman came by and had me locked up for the night; said I was lucky not to end up in the stocks. I ain't proud, but that's the truth of it.'

I regarded Tom closely. If he was lying, then he was a fine actor.

'Very well, Tom, we believe you,' I said, as reassuringly as I could. 'But tell us more about Piety's relationship to Thorne. You say they were sweethearts. Would you say she was privy to any of his private business?'

'What d'you mean?'

'Might he have told her something of his mission, the reason why he was here in Portsmouth?'

Wilkin puffed out his cheeks. 'No, I don't think so… Wait. 'Tis probably nothing, but…'

'Trust us, Mr Wilkin. Any detail may help.'

'Well, Mr Thorne… He were always giving her gifts. Jewellery, silks, perfume. One day, I overheard them outside. He handed her something; at first I thought it was just another trinket, but then she promised to look after it for him. Keep it safe.'

'Safe from whom?'

'I don't know.'

'A dangerous game for a serving girl to play, perhaps.'

He shook his head. 'That's just it, though. She'd changed. She weren't the same no more. It weren't just Elias. It all started before he came.'

'What do you mean, changed?'

'She'd become bold. Foolish. Her head filled with ungodly ideas. I think it were ever since she met that woman.'

'What woman?' asked Will.

He looked up at us suddenly, an expression of hatred on his face. 'Charlotte de Vere. That bitch. She-devil.'

Before he could say anything else, there was a knock at the door and Tamsin entered.

'Mr Pepys, sir, there's a messenger downstairs; says you're to return to Admiralty House straightway.'

'Very well. Mr Wilkin, I thank you for your time. Your stick should be repaired by now. Will you be alright to make your way home?'

'Don't you worry about me, sir.' He smiled sadly. I wondered if he had been grateful of the opportunity to unburden his troubles to sympathetic ears.

I turned to speak to Will, lowering my voice so Wilkin could not hear. 'While I am gone, why don't you see what else you can discover about this Charlotte de Vere? Hers is a name I seem to keep on hearing.'

'Yes. I'll see if I can get more out of him, then ask around here. Maybe visit some of the other taverns in town.'

'Good. And Will, be discreet. Do not draw attention to yourself.'

I stepped out into the corridor, and was surprised to find Tamsin still waiting for me by the door.

'Stay away from her, sir,' she whispered.

'Tamsin? Stay away from whom?'

'That woman you were talking about. Charlotte de Vere. She's dangerous. Stay away. If you value your life.'

Before I could ask anything else, she hurried down the stairs and returned to the taproom.

Ben had wasted no time in assuming control of the investigation. He had spent the last hour interviewing everyone who had been on the scene, summoning them to his office to give their account of what had happened.

Now it was my turn.

I began by extending my condolences for the loss of his friend in so brutal a fashion. He smiled, deep sadness etched upon his face.

'I have not felt a loss this keenly since my own dear wife went to God, ten years ago. Cherish those you love, Samuel, for you never know which day will be their last. Lord Maynard was a good friend. I shall miss him.'

Once again, I chastised myself for having shared my doubts about the late Governor so hastily, the night before.

'Where is he now?

'His body is in the navy chapel. He will be laid to rest tomorrow.'

'Did he have any family?'

'His wife died a year since. He had a child, a daughter, but she passed a long time ago.'

'Have there been further developments since this morning?'

'No. This is why I want to talk to everybody who was here and make sure nothing has been missed. Tell me what you saw last night.'

I recounted my role in the events of last night and this morning. All the while, Ben took notes. I watched his reaction as I mentioned the woman Harcourt had identified as Charlotte de Vere. There was a flinch, and a slight hesitation, but he did not ask anything more about her.

When I had finished, he laid his pen down and let out a deep sigh.

'Who could have done this, Samuel?'

'Did the Governor have any enemies?'

'None. He was well loved by all his men.'

'A crime of opportunity, then?'

'And yet, I am told no money was taken from his purse.'

I shifted uncomfortably in my chair. My groin suddenly felt tight, the pain beginning to rise again.

'I should tell you, Ben, that when I met with him yesterday, Lord Maynard agreed to give me free rein in my own investigations.'

'Investigations?'

I realised that I had not yet had a chance to tell Ben the reason for my visit here. Nor, I noted, had Lord Maynard seen fit to do so either. I recounted the story as succinctly as I could.

'A bad business,' said Ben, when I had finished.

'I trust that you will honour Maynard's promise and grant me full cooperation?'

'Of course, my friend. I shall be only too glad. Though I fear we shall have to postpone our dinner tonight. Now, if you will excuse me?'

I nodded sympathetically and began to rise, but a wave of pain shot through my abdomen. I held onto the chair to steady myself, breathing heavily.

'Samuel?'

'Just a touch of indigestion,' I said through gritted teeth. 'I—I will be fine in a minute.'

'It does not look like indigestion to me. I will summon a doctor.'

I was determined that Ben should not think of me as weak, particularly in the midst of all of this. But dear God, how it hurt.

'No, please; it will pass. But perhaps a short rest will do me good.'

I made my excuses and left. Keeping as steady as I could, I walked across the atrium and out onto Penny Street. I fought to control a rising panic at having to walk the five minutes back to the Four Feathers.

Just five minutes, I thought. Five minutes.

Every step I made caused an agony of pain to spasm through my groin, so intense I could barely place one foot in front of the other. I began to doubt whether I could even make it halfway there without passing out.

It will end, I told myself. I just have to get back to the inn.

Then, as I emerged through the little alleyway onto Craven Street, I suddenly realised with horror that there was a dampness forming in my underclothes.

Dear God, I thought. Please say I haven't pissed myself too.

I entered the inn and staggered straight up the stairs. I fumbled with the door to my room, almost falling over a wooden stool on my way in, and collapsed onto the bed, gasping with pain.

I reached underneath and pulled out my chamber pot, then rose enough to loosen my breeches. But again, though the pressure in my bladder was immense, I could only manage the smallest trickle. Passing water felt more like passing nails, and when I looked down I could see that once again my water was tainted with blood.

I lowered myself back down onto the bed, exhaling with relief as the pain began to subside. I closed my eyes and thought longingly of home.

Of London.

Elisabeth.

It must have been near midday when I was woken by a knock at the door.

'Sam? Are you in there?'

It was Will. I sat up, shaking myself awake.

'Come in,' I called, only just remembering to kick the blood-spattered chamber pot out of sight before he opened the door. 'Will, I—'

I stopped short at the sight of him. An angry bruise was forming on his cheek and there was dried blood around his nose. His knuckles were grazed and red.

He swiftly held up a hand. 'Don't.'

'Will, what happened to you?'

'I was accosted.'

'My God, man, by whom? Are you alright?'

'I'm fine. Nothing to worry about.'

'Will, if you were attacked you should tell me about it.'

'I said it was nothing,' he snapped.

Why didn't he want to tell me? What was he hiding? I decided to let it go for the time being.

'Very well. Did you find out anything?'

He picked up the overturned stool and sat down.

'Charlotte de Vere was Maynard's lover. Their affair was a badly kept secret. The officers around here hate her.'

'Did Tom Wilkin tell you this?'

'No, I got nothing more from him. This came from some of the servants at Admiralty House.'

I was about to admonish him for disobeying my instructions about being discreet, but he raised his hand defensively. 'Do not fret, I was careful. They seemed to respect her, but the officers see her as a woman of loose morals.'

'Is she married?'

'A widow. Sole heir to her late husband's fortune.'

'Who was he?'

'Captain Edmund de Vere. Do you recognise the name?'

I thought for a moment, then it came to me. 'Yes. I met him once, in '61. A fierce fellow, I recall. Not one to suffer fools. Fought for Cromwell, then defected to the cause of His Majesty shortly before the Restoration.'

'Well, he certainly left her well provided for. She's rich. Very rich. Lives not far from here, in an estate the size of Kew Palace, by the sound of things.'

'A widow with means. Interesting. What else did you discover?'

'I didn't want to press his servants too hard, so I went into the town and spoke with some people in a few taverns.'

Will shifted uncomfortably in his seat. Was this where he had got into a fight, I wondered? He continued, 'Again, people spoke of the animus between her and the officers. A few men held her in high esteem, while others seemed…'

'Seemed what?'

'Frightened of her.'

'Interesting. They are not the only ones.'

I recounted the warning Tamsin had given me earlier. *Stay away from her, if you value your life*. Between that and what Will had discovered, we were beginning to build up quite a picture of the mysterious Charlotte de Vere.

Here was a powerful woman, liked and feared in almost equal measure. We knew of her intimate connection to Lord Maynard, whom we also suspect of embezzlement – a charge that his death cannot undo. We knew, too, of her connection to Piety Blake, and through her, to Elias Thorne.

It would appear that an awful lot of people connected to this woman had ended up dead.

'Well then,' I said, getting to my feet. 'I think it's about time we paid a visit to the mysterious Charlotte de Vere, don't you?'

We walked to Charlotte de Vere's house on the edge of town, about half a mile east of the inn. I had been apprehensive about walking all the way there unaided, but for now at least the pain was under control. I prayed that it would stay that way for at least as long as our audience lasted.

Dione House, as the polished brass plaque proclaimed it to be, lay at the end of a quiet avenue lined with plane trees. The wrought iron gates at the front were not locked, and we approached the front door down a paved pathway.

A row of well-kept hedges on the front lawn helped disguise how large the house was from the street. There must be at least twenty bedrooms, I thought, counting the tall, rectangular windows on the upper floors of the large brick building.

'That's a lot of space for one widow,' said Will, quietly.

'Do you know if she has any family, or is it just her and her servants?' I asked.

'As far as I know, it is just her.'

I knocked and waited. There was no answer. I knocked again and we heard the sound of footsteps approaching from the other side.

The door was opened by a short, muscular young woman in a simple blue dress. Her skin was dark brown, darker than a Moor's, and she had keen eyes, the colour of amber. Her long black hair was tied up in a white headscarf.

The peculiar thing was that Will seemed shocked to see her. Almost as if he recognised her.

'Good day, madam. My name is Samuel Pepys, Clerk of the Acts to His Majesty's Navy Board, and this is my assistant, Mr Hewer. I wish to see—'

'She ain't at home,' interrupted the woman. She spoke in a loud and powerful voice, completely without deference. Her accent had the strong lilt of the West Indies.

'May I ask where she is?'

'I mean, she ain't at home to you. Nor any caller.'

I bristled, but kept my tone even. 'Madam, I am here on official business. If you would just tell her—'

'Sir, I don't think you heard. My mistress is not receiving guests today. You could be the King of England or the Sultan of Turkey for all I care, you ain't coming in.'

I could feel my face reddening with anger, but before I could respond, Will put a cautioning hand on my arm.

The girl continued, 'My mistress has had a terrible shock. I'm sure as gentlemen' – somehow she made the word seem like an insult – 'you will understand.'

'Very well,' I said, before adding with as much authority as I could, 'But tell your mistress that I shall call again tomorrow. Early.'

'You do that, sir. I got work to do.'

She made a little sound almost like a kiss, but with an obviously contemptuous meaning. I didn't even have time to respond before she slammed the door in our faces.

'Pert little wench. Who does she think she is?'

We were retracing our steps back up the secluded little street. A breeze was blowing in from the sea, bringing with it the distant sounds of construction work from the dry docks.

I continued. 'Whoever Charlotte de Vere is, she keeps a slack rein on her staff. How dare she speak to me like that?'

Will said nothing. I couldn't decide if the sight of that girl had downright unsettled him.

'Well then, what now?' I continued, exasperated at both his silence and our lack of progress. 'We shall get no useful answers out of the officers for a while. I have no desire to spend the rest of this day cooped up at the Four Feathers, staring at the same books, hoping they give us answers that do not seem to be there.'

Will was suddenly possessed of an idea that seemed to lighten his mood.

'You are right. So let's leave.'

'What are you talking about?'

My irritation was clearly showing, for he frowned reproachfully. 'I do not mean give up. The avenues of our investigation in Portsmouth seem closed to us for the time being. So let us follow the other lead that has opened up this day.'

'What do you mean? What lead?'

'Piety Blake. Tom said she lived a place called Farlington, did he not?'

The village of Farlington lies on a bleak stretch of road to the northeast of Portsmouth.

We had procured horses from Admiralty House and set out on the four-mile ride, which took us back out through the old north gate, before branching off down a lonely track through desolate ground that quickly turned to marshland.

The landscape was flat and featureless, save for the reeds that swayed in the breeze on either side. It was an eerie, isolated road, even in bright sunshine. I would not have cared to make this journey in the dark. No wonder Tom Wilkin was uneasy about Piety coming this way alone and on foot. I shivered, wondering if we had already passed the spot where the girl had met her end.

We were at least a mile away from the edge of Farlington when we first glimpsed the squat stone tower of the village church, standing like a beacon against the near-cloudless sky. When the sea wind blew in our direction, we caught the echoes of a hammer clanging against metal. A blacksmith was at work somewhere nearby.

As we rode into the village, I noticed the blackened trunk of an enormous dead oak tree in the churchyard. A line of crows sat on what was left of its gnarled branches, watching as we rode past. Beyond the church, there were maybe two dozen timber-framed dwellings, their whitewashed fronts dazzling in the bright sun.

'A pretty little place,' said Will.

'You are too generous,' I replied, raising a kerchief to my nose. The wind had changed direction again, bringing with it the stink of rotten fish and marsh gas.

Suddenly, my horse reared. I leaned forward, reining her in to make it stop. The beast hobbled forward with a limp.

'She's thrown a shoe,' said Will, leaping down from his own horse and patting the agitated creature on the nose. 'Easy there, girl. Easy.'

I slid painfully down from the saddle. The shoe on her left leg had indeed come loose, and a nail was scratching at the flesh on her fetlock.

I leaned down and cautiously pulled the nail out. The horse whinnied, then calmed.

'There now,' said Will, gently stroking her mane. 'All over now.'

'Damnation. I could have been thrown. This is the last thing we need.'

Will looked towards the sound of hammering metal.

'Well, at least we know where to find help.'

Peter Woodfall, blacksmith to the village of Farlington, was sitting on a stool, firmly gripping the horse's leg. Next to him was the thrown shoe and a pile of sharp nails. We watched as he began hammering them into place one by one, with steady, powerful strikes.

He was a burly man of around forty, with arms the size of coiled rope. Will and I stood next to the open door as he worked. I was glad of the sea breeze, however much it stank, as a bulwark against the heat of his workshop.

'I was lucky to find your shop open on the Lord's Day, sir,' I said.

He grunted. 'Got to make a living in times like these. So, where you gentlemen headed then?'

'In truth, we have already arrived. We have come from Portsmouth, on a matter connected with a woman late of this parish. Piety Blake?'

Woodfall paused in his work and looked up at us suspiciously. 'What about Piety Blake?'

'We are king's men. I am Mr Pepys of the Navy Board, and this is Mr Hewer. We think whoever killed her may have some connection to another matter we are investigating.'

This seemed to satisfy him.

'So, they ain't caught the bastard what did for her then?'

'Sadly not, Mr Woodfall.'

'Do you have any idea who it might have been?' asked Will.

'How the hell should I know? Some outlaw, as like as not. This road's full of them.'

'We should very much like to talk to her family. Do you know where we may find them?'

Woodfall hammered in the final nail and rose from the stool. The horse stamped her hoof, unused to the feeling of the newly fixed shoe.

'Well now, if it's the family you're after, you gentlemen have had a wasted journey. She was the last Blake in this parish.'

I cursed inwardly. More dead ends. 'Surely the girl did not live by herself?'

'Piety's pa went to God about a year ago. Her ma died in childbirth. She had no brothers or sisters.'

'So she continued to live here alone after her father's passing?'

'Aye.'

'Is that not rather unusual?' said Will.

Woodfall grunted disapprovingly. 'Aye, that was our Piety, right enough. We thought she'd marry once her pa died, but she'd hear none of it. Said she didn't need no man to keep her.'

An uncommon girl indeed, I thought. Perhaps even more so than we already knew.

He crossed his arms. 'If you ask me, that girl got what was coming to her, the way she carried on. Now I'm not saying she deserved it, mind. But she were a different person these last few months, staying out all hours of the night. God only knows where she was and what she were doing. Wouldn't be talked to. Said how she lived her life were her own choice and she could take care of herself.' He let out a mirthless chuckle. 'Well... Look how that worked out for her.'

I exchanged a glance with Will. This tallied with what Tom Wilkin had told us about the change in her behaviour. A change that had happened after she began consorting with Charlotte de Vere.

'Thank you, Mr Woodfall. You have been most helpful.' I handed him his fee and led my horse outside.

Just as we had mounted up, Will called back to the blacksmith. 'Mr Woodfall! Piety's cottage. Is it still empty?'

'Aye.'

'Do you think anybody would object if we had a look around?'

'Can't stop you. Carry on through the village; it's the last house you come to, just after the crossroads. But you won't find nothing there.'

We thanked him and spurred our horses on. Once we had gone a little way, I turned to look back over my shoulder.

Woodfall was standing in the middle of the road, watching us go.

Even without his directions, finding Piety Blake's cottage would have been easy.

The little two-storey building was in poor shape, as if nature had begun to claim it back. Patches of straw from the thatched roof had gone, the spaces filled with nesting birds. Tom Wilkin had told us how Elias had wooed Piety with expensive trinkets, but she must have lived close to poverty.

We dismounted from our horses and tied them to a nearby tree. I could feel the pain rising again within me, still a low ache rather than the agonising spasms of earlier this day, but enough to make me anxious that we should not stay here too long.

We approached the cottage through a vegetable garden that was already overgrown with grass and weeds. Rows of beans and summer cabbage lay ripe for picking, and would rot in the ground soon if not harvested.

I peered in through the small windows. The cheap shutters were cracked and broken. Cobwebs draped across gaps in the wood like curtains, layered with grass seed and dead insects.

Peter Woodfall had been telling the truth, right enough. This place was deserted.

'This is a waste of time, Will. We should head back.'

'Just a minute,' he said, circling the abandoned building.

'What do you expect to find?'

'Nothing, probably. But since we have come all this way…'

'Will, this was a fool's errand. There is nothing here and we have serious business to attend to in Portsmouth.

Will tried the latch on the front door. It creaked open. With a smile, he ducked inside.

'Will… Oh, damn you.'

Reluctantly, I followed.

The room we stepped into smelled of damp and bird shit. A broken chair sat at one end, next to a ladder propped up against the open hatch that led to the top floor. Pools of sunlight shimmered on the dusty floor, broken by the shadows of undulating trees. The only sound was the cooing of some pigeons that had taken up residence in the chimney.

'Everybody talks about how much Piety changed because of this woman, Charlotte de Vere,' said Will, looking around. 'What do you suppose they mean?'

'I do not know. Evidently her father was a country yeoman at best. There could hardly have been a greater difference in their stations.'

'Who was this girl, Sam? Was she some sort of free-spirited libertine?'

'You are getting obsessed. This business strays too far from our path.'

'It is all relevant.'

'It is a distraction. The tragedy of Piety Blake would make a fine subject for a Drury Lane playhouse, but that is not why we are here.'

Will looked like he was going to argue some more, then he sighed with resignation. 'Oh, I suppose you are right.'

'I fear I am.' I closed my eyes against a sudden wave of pain, mercifully short, but enough to make me steady myself on the wall.

'Sam?'

'I am fine.'

'You keep saying that. But we both know it is a lie.'

I nodded, taking deep breaths of the damp air while the pain faded. 'You are right. I should seek treatment.'

'What is it?'

'Blood and burning when I piss. And such pain in my gut, that comes without warning.'

'That does not sound good. We must take you to a doctor.'

'Yes, yes.'

'Tomorrow.' His voice was firm.

'Very well. In truth, I have been putting it off for some time. But I fear I already know the truth of what it is, and—'

Will raised his hand. 'Wait. There's someone upstairs.'

'Are you sure?' I whispered.

'Yes. I heard movement.'

'An animal.'

'No. I am telling you. *There is someone upstairs.*'

We stared at each other. My arms prickled with gooseflesh. Surely it was his imagination?

Carefully, I stepped forward and peered up the ladder. But I could see nothing in the empty space beyond except the slowly decaying rafters.

Then I heard it too. The unmistakable creaking of floorboards. He was right. We were not alone.

My first instinct was to leave. To run, fetch our horses, and ride straight back to Portsmouth. No matter how I may have denied it, our enquiries thus far had in part been spurred on by a sense of adventure. But now all that fell away like a shade. This was no game.

There is someone upstairs.

'Hello?' I could hear the uncertainty in my own voice. 'We know you are there. Show yourself.'

Will stepped onto the ladder.

'This is your last chance,' I shouted. 'We are on the King's business.'

Still nothing. Will took another step up and peered through the open hatch. He looked around, then climbed inside.

'I cannot see anybody. Perhaps I was—'

Suddenly, I heard the pounding of feet from above, together with a terrifying shriek. Will cried out in shock, spinning around to face his attacker, as a shape ran at him from the shadows.

'Will!' I shouted, clambering up the ladder just in time to see him swinging his fist into the path of the advancing figure, causing them to sprawl on the ground with a crack. But as we braced ourselves for a counter-attack, we saw that the danger was not as great as we had feared.

Our assailant was a child.

'You could've done for me, you old madge cull. Why'd you have to hit me so hard?'

The lad was sitting up against the wall, rubbing his jaw. Thankfully, the bone had not been broken, only bruised. The only real injuries were to the boy's pride.

We had learned that his name was Jake Hopkins, and that he was the ten-year-old son of a local farmhand. What we did not yet know was what he was doing there.

'Well, you shouldn't have accosted us, young man,' I said, sternly. 'Why did you not answer when we called?'

'Thought I were in trouble, didn't I? Besides, what's your excuse? You're here too, ain't you?'

I was about to admonish the lad for his insolence, but Will seemed to find it amusing. At least he had spirit.

'You have to admit that young Master Hopkins has a point, Sam. Perhaps you should consider a career in the law, Jake?'

The boy frowned. 'You talk funny. Where you from?'

'London.'

'My pa went to London once. Is it true they have cats big as horses?'

'At the Tower of London, yes. They are called lions. There are also beasts called elephants, ten feet tall with horns on their face and noses like this.'

Will used his arm to mimic the trunk of an elephant, swinging it about in a silly pantomime. The boy laughed appreciatively.

'Young man, do you know who this cottage belonged to?'

He looked at me as if I were a fool. 'Course. It be Piety Blake's.'

'You knew her?'

'Don't be daft, course I knew her. Everyone knew her.'

Will sat down on the floor next to him. 'Did you like her, Jake?'

'Aye, I suppose.'

'What about her friends? Did you know any of them?'

'I met her swain once or twice.'

'Can you remember his name?'

Jake shook his head.

'Might it have been Mr Thorne, Jake?'

'Aye, perhaps.'

'And did you like him?'

Jake seemed hesitant to answer at first, then shook his head again.

'Most of the time, people tell us that Elias was a nice man,' Will continued, gently. 'What was it that you did not like about him?'

'I heard them fighting once. She said he was hurting her and had to stop.'

'And did he stop, Jake?'

Jake shook his head. His eyes began to moisten. 'Piety kept saying no, and he should stop it. But he didn't. I told my ma and she said it was just a game grown-ups play.'

'How did you hear all this?' I asked.

'Listened in at the window.'

'Answer me one more question' said Will. 'After Piety was—after she passed away, did you see anybody else coming to her house?'

'Aye, folk came and took all her things. Even her clothes. My pa said it weren't really stealing as she didn't need them no more and other folks did.'

'I see. Anybody you did not recognise?'

'No. Just folk from the village.' His face broke out into a smile. 'They didn't get everything, though.'

'Oh?' I said. 'What do you mean?'

'She had a hiding place, didn't she? I found things in there.'

'What sort of things?'

'Treasure. Twelve shillings. A mirror. A pretty jewel. I gave that to my ma.'

'I see. Anything else?'

'Only some stupid book. But I didn't take that on account I can't read.' Will shot me a look. 'Is it still here?'

'Aye. Up there.' He pointed at the rafters.

Will squatted back down so that his face was level with the boy's. 'Jake, if I gave you half a crown, would you do something for me?'

Half an hour later, Will and I stood staring in astonishment at what we held in front of us. Jake had gone on his way, coin in hand, after retrieving the object from its hiding place in the thatch between the rafters.

It was a thin, leather-bound accounts ledger. I recognised it immediately as naval issue, of a similar kind to those we had taken from Admiralty House. The margins of each page were covered in notes, diagrams, and calculations, obviously made by a different hand to the neat columns of figures.

'The property of Mr Elias Thorne, I presume?' I said, flicking through the dusty pages.

'Why hide a thing like this?'

'I do not know. But I think we may assume that it was the book he entrusted to Piety Blake for safekeeping.'

Will looked anxiously out of the window. 'Sam. This can wait. The boy was harmless enough, but…'

'We have drawn enough attention to ourselves already. Yes, I agree. Come, it is time we were on our way.'

We were halfway along the lonely road through Farlington Marsh when we realised something was wrong.

'Sam.' Will's voice cut through my thoughts, low and urgent. 'Look.'

I narrowed my eyes, squinting at the road ahead.

'Is that a horseman? Why isn't he moving?'

'There are two of them. Just standing there, watching us.'

I began to see more clearly now. Will was right. Two mounted figures, about a hundred yards ahead, facing us in the road.

'Who might they be?' I said.

'What do you want to do?'

'Keep going. It may be nothing.'

We were both determined to stay calm, but I could sense that Will was as unnerved as I was. There was something unusual about the way these riders looked, bolt upright in the saddle, waiting for us to draw near. They were dressed all in black, with long leather coats and tricorn hats.

At first I could not quite make out their faces, then I realised with a horrible sense of dread that it was because they were wearing masks.

The words of Peter Woodfall echoed in my mind, when asked who he thought had killed Piety Blake. *Some outlaw, as like as not. This road's full of them.*

I looked over my shoulder, trying to decide if we should make a bolt for the village, but my hopes were immediately dashed. There were more of them behind us. Masked riders, dressed in black.

We were trapped.

There was something about them that was utterly chilling to me. It was not just that they appeared to be outlaws; there was a slowness and poise in the way they moved that seemed to exude menace, like animals stalking their prey.

These were no ordinary highwaymen.

'Courage, my friend,' I whispered to Will.

Closer and closer we came. My heart began to pound. My throat was dry as dust.

We drew so close that I could see the sun glinting in their eyes. Our lives depended utterly on what would happen in the next few seconds. Live or die. Escape or be captured. Our fate was in their hands.

And just like that, the two riders ahead of us separated to let us pass. There was no attack. Nobody stopped us. Nobody made a move.

Cautiously, we rode on past, then as soon as we were clear, we spurred our horses, galloping away as quickly as we could.

I turned in my saddle, watching the sinister group as they in turn watched us. And then suddenly it hit me like a bolt of lightning. I knew what was unusual about them.

'My God, Will. They are all women.'

We arrived back at the Four Feathers at dusk, still shaken by what had happened on the road through the marshes.

We had stopped at Admiralty House for long enough to return the horses and get word on the investigation. Ben was not there, but we were able to find Captain Harcourt, who informed us that there had been little progress. Without witnesses to the murder of Governor Maynard, or suspects with a motive of any kind, there was little that could be done.

By the time we returned to the inn, I was sorely tired. The pain that had come and gone all day was sapping my strength, making it hard for me to think. I desperately needed to rest.

But we had hardly stepped through the door when we were waylaid by Goody Brown. 'Mr Pepys, there's a man here to see you. Royal livery,' she added, with interest.

She indicated the uniformed messenger seated in the corner. As soon as he saw me coming over, he leaped to his feet and produced a sealed letter from inside a small leather satchel. He handed it to me and I swiftly broke the seal.

Immediately, I recognised the neat, fastidious hand of Thomas Marshall, the Duke of Albemarle's secretary.

Pepys,

I received your message with the gravest concern. What in God's name is going on down there? I have just come from the King, and I must tell you that he is in a very ill humour about the whole affair. His Majesty admired Governor Maynard, and greets the news of his murder with outrage.

Do not tell him that you know this, but Mr Arden is to be formally appointed to the governorship by His Majesty. I confess to you that this does not sit easy with me, given the gravity of what he must face, and I do not just mean the investigation into Maynard's death. This is no time for a man so untested as he to be in charge, no matter how highly Lord Maynard held him in regard.

Pepys, what I will tell you next must go no further. Tensions with Holland are near breaking point. As you are aware, we have been braced for a resumption of hostilities these last two years. But the situation is worse than you know.

We have received intelligence that the Dutch are preparing fresh attacks on our shipping, perhaps even an invasion fleet. War may be coming, Pepys, and soon.

The navy will devote much effort into apprehending the killer. Assist them in any way you can. Report any developments back to me. And do not lose sight of the other matters on which you were sent there.

I want answers, Pepys. And I want them soon.

The letter was signed in Albemarle's own hand.

A sudden image flashed through my mind. A man, wearing the tattered uniform of a Dutch sailor. Staring up at my window.

I shivered. This was bad.

I thanked the messenger and ordered some supper to be sent upstairs. Will followed me to my room, looking on with concern as I lowered myself painfully onto the bed.

'Sam, you really must see a doctor.'

'I shall. First thing on the morrow. As I agreed.'

'Good. And if you do not, I shall make you.'

He sat on the edge of the bed, rubbing his neck. The evening shadows accentuated the bruises on his face.

'What happened this morning, Will? Who attacked you?'

'It is not worth talking about. Shall we go over this?'

He took out the leather volume we had found at Piety Blake's cottage. Again, I noted how quickly he tried to change the subject.

'We must. But I am tired. Leave it here. We will examine it properly tomorrow.'

'Very well. Is there anything you need?'

'Just food and sleep. Thank you.'

Tired though I am, sleep has not come to me tonight.

The pain continues to come and go in waves, but it is other matters that keep me awake. I find myself unable to stop ruminating on our investigation.

For every answer, there seems to be another question.

First, there are the discrepancies in the accounts of the *Prince Rupert*. The last man to investigate this, Elias Thorne, died with a knife to his guts and his balls in the gutter.

Surely that points to more than just petty corruption? On the other hand, could we just be inventing connections where there are none, simply because we want it to be so?

Yesterday, I might have been more doubtful. But the discovery of the accounts book, hidden away at the house of his dead lover, must surely narrow our thinking? Tomorrow we shall make a proper examination of its contents. Maybe that is where we shall start to find real answers.

And what of Piety Blake? Was she silenced because of something she knew? Elias entrusted that book to her for safekeeping. But in doing so, was he condemning her to death? Was it the cause of whatever ill-feeling existed between them, according to the boy Jake? On the other hand, this was the observation of a child. Who is to say what he really overheard? It is not as if lovers do not quarrel. In faith, I know that all too well.

And had we not been given cause to question the prevailing view of the late Mr Thorne as a gregarious and popular fellow, liked by all who knew him? The conspiracy of silence among the women at the inn must at least give us pause for thought. Why would they not even acknowledge the existence of a dead man? What did they have to fear?

Or is her death, tragic though it is, not related to our investigation at all? The blacksmith echoed what we had heard at the inn, on our journey down to Portsmouth. *The woods are full of outlaws.* Given our encounter on the ride back, it can come as no surprise that a girl walking alone at night should have met such a fate.

Then there is the murder of Lord Maynard. How I wish I had taken more time to question him before it was too late. Now I will have to take my enquiries to Ben, and Maynard's other associates, such as Captain Harcourt. What more do they know?

Ben loved Maynard, that much is clear. I cannot believe he had anything to do with the Governor's death. But even if the man is no murderer, I must not allow our friendship to place him above suspicion in the matter of the missing funds.

And finally, there is the enigmatic figure of Charlotte de Vere. Sooner or later, all roads seem to end up at her door. We must call on her again. And this time, I will not take no for an answer.

Now I must try again to sleep. I have a feeling that I will need all my reserves of strength for whatever is to come tomorrow.

June 17ᵗʰ

Doctor Grey sat behind his desk, making notes as I buttoned up my breeches. It was still early in the day, but the room felt unpleasantly hot.

Grey had started his examination by squeezing my cods and examining my prick. Thus far, he offered little but tuts and grumbles as clues to his findings. I wished that he would just tell me the truth and be done with it.

The dour old man followed this by asking me a long list of intrusive questions: what I ate, how much I drank, whom I bedded. As with many in his profession, his manner was like that of a wagging finger, constantly judging the moral failures of his patient.

This morning, that patient was me. And, just a few minutes earlier, that finger had been stuck up my arse.

I cleared my throat, impatiently. 'Doctor Grey, I fear that I already know the answer, so you may as well tell it me now. It is the clap, is it not?'

Grey put down his quill and looked at me with raised eyebrows. 'Well, despite evidently poor taste in the company you keep, sir, I can assure you this is no venereal disease. You have bladder stones.'

I exhaled deeply, with more obvious emotion than I had intended to share. 'That is a great relief. What is the cure?'

'The stones may yet pass of their own accord if you are lucky, though I fear they have grown too big. It would be painful, but not as bad as the alternative.'

'What alternative?'

'In the worst case, a severe fever, or even death.'

'How likely is that?'

'If it remains untreated? I would say, almost certain.'

I felt as if my blood ran cold. Suddenly this diagnosis did not seem so much of a relief after all. 'What is the treatment?'

'The only other cure is to operate. My examination of you revealed that the stones are at least accessible. This makes you very fortunate in one regard. But the only way to get them out is to cut open your perineum and retrieve the stones manually. I must tell you, it is a very dangerous operation.'

I blanched, and thought for a moment that I might be sick.

'Mr Pepys?'

'I am fine. It is a shock, that is all. Thank you, Doctor Grey. You have given me much to think about.'

I hurried out of the room, feeling a good deal colder than when I had arrived.

We walked in silence along the pathway to Dione House. I told Will the bare minimum about my prognosis. I could not afford to be distracted, and I knew that if I let myself dwell on the enormity of what Doctor Grey had told me, I had no hope of being equal to the task of what we must do next. There would be time enough for contemplation later.

The door was opened by the same maid who had greeted us so rudely yesterday. But while her manner was still sorely lacking in grace, at least this time she invited us in without argument.

We were led through a spacious hallway into the parlour, a tall-ceilinged room papered in rich blue silk. A large window at one end looked out over acres of well-kept gardens.

The girl indicated for us to sit while she went to fetch her mistress. To my surprise, as she left the room, I saw her exchange a brief glance with Will, and her face broke out into a smirk.

'You *do* know her,' I whispered, as the girl's footsteps receded across the hallway.

'I'm telling you, I do not.'

'Why are you being so evasive? She's not some trug you once tupped in the stews, is she?'

From somewhere down the corridor came the sound of a door closing, followed by the echo of boot heels along the marble floor. They moved slowly, with the confident gait of one who never has any need to hurry.

We stood waiting anxiously. And then, finally, Charlotte de Vere entered the room.

She was dressed in a black silk gown of mourning and she wore her dark hair up in a tall chignon, laced with pearls, in the French style. Up until now I had only seen Lord Maynard's mistress in semi-darkness, but by the full light of day I could see how striking she looked. She is perhaps in her middle thirties, nearly six feet tall, with high cheekbones and a surprisingly clear complexion for her age. Her eyes an unusual shade of deep brown., almost obsidian.

'Gentlemen.'

We bowed.

'Mistress de Vere. Thank you for allowing us into your home,' I said.

She inclined her head. The way she looked us up and down, curious and appraising, reminded me of a cat deciding what to do with a pair of trapped birds.

'Please, be seated.'

De Vere lowered herself onto a chair and we took our place on the settle opposite. As she brushed her skirts to one side, I saw that they were in fact made of dark green silk, not black, and embroidered with gold thread that glowed like the embers of a fire when caught by the sunlight.

Perhaps you are not quite so deep in mourning after all, I thought.

'My condolences, madam, at what must be a very difficult time.'

'Thank you. I understand that you knew my late husband? Captain Edmund de Vere?'

'I met him only once, I am sorry to say. He was a most accomplished man.'

She smiled tightly. 'Many would say so. Did you know he marched on Parliament with General Monck in '59? And helped negotiate the Declaration of Breda?'

How convenient for a turncoat, I thought, to have helped write the document that forgave him for fighting on the other side.

'I did not, madam. Your husband obviously had a most exceptional career.'

'He was a good soldier. But Mr Pepys, you had your own part to play in the Restoration of His Majesty, did you not?'

'I… do not follow you, madam.'

'Were you not with our Sovereign aboard the *Royal Charles*?'

I was astounded. How in God's name did she know that?

'You are remarkably well informed, madam. Indeed, I attended His Majesty on the vessel that returned him to England from exile. But forgive me, how did you—'

We were interrupted by the maid who had let us in, who entered carrying a tray piled with small dishes and a steaming earthenware pot.

'Ah, Belle. Gentlemen, would you care for coffee?'

We accepted gratefully, not having tasted coffee since we left London. Belle poured out three dishes and set them before us on dainty little side tables.

'Is that all, mistress?' she asked.

De Vere nodded and Belle left the room.

'Now, to what do I owe this pleasure, gentlemen?'

Somehow, she made the question sound like an insult. I hesitated, sipping the coffee. It was strong and bitter.

'Mistress de Vere,' I said, cautiously, 'I know that you were… close to Lord Maynard.'

'Indeed. He was a dear friend.'

'How long had you known him?'

'Since he took up the post of governor here. He has been—' The word caught in her throat. She swallowed, burying the emotion. '*Was* a loyal companion to a poor widow.'

'Madam, while I do not wish to suggest anything improper, might it be fair to say that your relationship with him was—'

'I was his mistress, yes. This is what you wanted to ask me, is it not?'

'For how long?'

'Two years.'

'So, since before his wife died?'

'Do you judge me, sir?'

'Not at all. I am merely interested in the facts.'

'In that case, the facts are that John and his wife were locked in a loveless marriage and each pursued their own affairs of the heart for many years until her death. Of natural causes, in case you were wondering.'

Her tone remained level, but I could sense anger growing beneath the surface. 'When did you last see Governor Maynard?'

'About three hours after you left his party. Drunk, as I recall.'

'Forgive me, but when I saw you together you did not appear to be discussing affairs of the heart.'

'We had business.'

'What kind of business?'

'None of yours.'

'Were you the last guest to leave the party?'

'I was.'

'Why did you stay so late?'

She tilted her head defiantly. 'We were fucking, Mr Pepys.'

Will spat out his coffee. De Vere turned to him and frowned, noticing the bruise on his face for the first time.

'Mr Hewer, have you hurt yourself?'

'Madam,' I continued, 'if, as you say, you left Lord Maynard in his bed in the early hours of the morning, why then would he have bothered to dress and leave Admiralty House again, after you had gone?'

'Some other business.'

'Business that could not wait?'

'Evidently.' Her lips remained fixed into a taut smile, but her eyes, never straying from my own, were far from innocent.

Suddenly, I realised that my hand was shaking. I gripped the arm of the settle, hoping she had not noticed.

'Madam, you have been most generous with your time. But there is one other matter I would trouble you with before we leave.'

'Oh, I would not say you have been any trouble, Mr Pepys.'

'Are you by any chance acquainted with a serving girl by the name of Piety Blake?'

This time her smile faded, and those deep brown eyes flashed dangerously.

'How did you know Piety?'

'*Did*, madam?'

'Indeed, sir. You will know that Piety was most vilely murdered. Have you come to ask me if I did that too?'

'Madam...' It was Will who spoke now, in that manner of his that was like pouring sand on fire. 'We meant no disrespect. Piety Blake worked at the Four Feathers, where Mr Pepys and I have lodgings. We have come to suspect that her death may have some connection to another matter we are investigating.'

De Vere arched an eyebrow. 'Indeed? Yes, I knew Piety Blake. She was in my service for a time. She was very dear to me and her death affected me greatly.'

'So she was employed in your household?' I asked.

'Not exactly.'

'Then in what capacity did she work for you?'

'Why do I feel as if this is an interrogation, Mr Pepys?'

'What about a man named Elias Thorne? Do you have any knowledge of him?'

The look she gave me was as cold as ice. 'I find myself growing tired. Perhaps it is time for you to leave.'

'Very well. Thank you for your time, Mistress de Vere.'

We rose from the settle, but she stayed seated.

'I trust you got what you came for. Tell me, how long are you staying in Portsmouth?'

'As long as it takes to find the answers I seek, madam. There is no need to call your maid. We can see ourselves out.'

'What in God's name is going on in that house?' said Will.

We were standing on the quayside, where I had stopped to take a rest.

'God rot her, did she utter a single true word the whole time?' I replied. 'She knows more about the death of Governor Maynard than she is letting on, of that I am certain. And I thought her more upset at the mention of Piety Blake's death than his. Is he not supposed to have been her lover?'

'Perhaps she was too?'

I was about to tell Will that he had the mind of a French bookseller, but then I began to wonder if there might be any truth to it. Would I really put it past this unconventional woman to have had a Sapphic bond with one of her servants?

If, indeed, that is what Piety had really been to her.

Will continued, 'I mean she's obviously lying about something. And as for the way she talked to you...'

He trailed off, as I bent double, my stomach cramping violently. He placed a hand gently on my shoulder.

'Sam, are you sure you're up to this? If you are sick, we should return to London. Albemarle will not blame you.'

'No. I am out of favour enough as it is. We must see this through.'

'The duke will understand, surely, for something like this. And even if he didn't...' Will hesitated. 'You should write to Elisabeth. If she has sent word of where she is, then a letter could be forwarded.'

'I shall,' I agreed with a sigh. But in truth, I knew that even in our state of estrangement, if Elisabeth were to find out about my condition, she would only make me return home. Or come and fetch me herself.

But on the other hand, if the worst were to happen... Was it possible that the last words ever to pass between us had already been spoken?

I shook my head, pushing the morbid thought from my mind. 'Perhaps I could go and rest for a while. Besides, I am anxious to start examining that accounts book we found at Piety's cottage.'

'I could come with you?'

'No, I shall be fine on my own. Why don't you stay around here for a while longer? Talk to some of the men around the docks. Put your talent for making friends to use once more; see if you can find out anything useful. But be careful. I want no repeat of whatever happened to you yesterday. Is that clear?'

'I promise. Now, go and rest.'

We parted ways and I started to walk in the direction of the Four Feathers. The curved roof of the Domus Dei, opposite Admiralty House, once again made for an easy landmark for navigating my way through the narrow, crowded streets. I calculated that it should take me no more than half an hour.

I had just stopped to rest when I realised I was being followed.

I was leaning against the wall next to a baker's shop, catching my breath. The smell of fresh bread should have made me hungry, but instead I started to feel nauseous.

A young boy came out of the shop, carrying a basket laden with fresh loaves. He looked me up and down.

'You alright, master?'

'Fine, thank you,' I replied, shortly.

'Looks like you're about to sling a cat.' He screwed up his nose in distaste, taking off in the direction I had just come from.

My eyes followed him through the crowd, envious of his swift and easy movement, which at that moment seemed the most carefree thing in all the world.

It was then that I saw the figure darting into the shadows, maybe ten yards or so behind me. I frowned, instinctively checking my purse was where it should be. I am practised enough in dealing with cutpurses, and did not suppose that the petty thieves of Portsmouth would be any more skilled than those I was used to in London.

I walked on, occasionally glancing back to let the fellow know that I had the measure of him. For a time, I could see nothing and supposed that he had gone. In my experience, footpads usually give up when they are discovered, particularly the sort who work in daylight.

But then I saw the figure again. He was dressed in a green cloak with the hood down. A flash of colour, moving swiftly between the overhanging eaves.

I jumped at a sudden shout, halting abruptly as a horse and cart went by, just inches in front of my face. I had been so engrossed in keeping track of the hooded man that I had not realised I had come to an intersection.

A small crowd was standing there, waiting for a long line of carts to go by, laden with fresh goods. The pace was agonisingly slow and I had no choice but to wait. Anxiously, I glanced over my shoulder, and my heart skipped a beat.

He was walking straight towards me. I was trapped.

I jumped out into the busy road, bypassing the small crowd. One of the carters swore and yanked his reins to avoid me, causing his horse to rear, but I dared not stop as I hurried away down a lane that curved around to the right.

I checked back over my shoulder. The hooded figure was pushing his way through the crowd to keep pace with me. Then, to my horror, I saw a flash of metal underneath the green cloak.

It was a knife.

The lane curved so sharply that I was unable to see more than a few yards ahead. More carts went by, which at least helped put some obstacles between us, but I desperately needed to find a cross-street or an alleyway if I was to stand a chance of losing my pursuer. There was nothing.

All the time, I could hear footsteps behind me, drawing ever nearer. Then, suddenly, I realised that the lane had grown quiet. We were alone.

I broke into a run. It felt as if the walls were closing in, waiting to engulf me, to trap me like an animal to be finished off by my pursuer.

Sunlight flickered through gaps in the overhanging eaves, casting intermittent shadows on the rough cobblestones in front of me. At first it was just my shadow that I saw, but then there was another, gaining speed, closing the gap between us, until it had almost reached mine...

All of a sudden, the lane ended abruptly, and I found myself standing on the edge of a busy market square. Dozens of stalls were packed into the open space, which was lined on all sides by poor-looking tenement buildings.

It was market day. God be praised.

Hardly daring to break step, I plunged myself into the crowd. The sudden mass of people was disorienting, but I forced my way through, sweat stinging my eyes.

I hazarded a glance behind me. The green robed figure was still following, the knife hastily concealed beneath the cloak. But his progress was also being slowed by the mass of people. This bought me precious time, but I had to think fast.

I came level with a weaver's stall, where sheets of newly spun cloth were hanging from an awning. Seizing the opportunity, I dived off to one side, entangling myself in the cloth as I pushed my way through. The weaver shouted at me angrily, but I was already on the other side, running headlong down the next row of stalls.

My heart pounded in my chest, and my muscles cramped in agony. Then, from behind, I heard the weaver cursing and swearing again. The hooded figure was still on my tail.

The crowd ahead parted enough for me to see the end of the row. There was a man loading up a cart with some barrels he had just bought from a wine merchant. And behind him was a short passage that led directly onto a busy street.

My chance at escape.

I pushed as hard as I could against the flow of people. Ahead of me, the man with the cart was beginning to climb on board. If I could just reach him in time…

I looked over my shoulder and gasped in fright. The hooded figure was nearly upon me. I looked down and saw him draw his knife again, holding it down at his side. I was transfixed by the razor-sharp blade, glinting in the midday sun.

The man with the cart cracked the reins and his horses started to turn. The hope I had felt began to drain away. I was so nearly there, but I would never make it in time. I heard a commotion behind me. People being pushed. Heavy footsteps, coming up behind me fast, getting closer and closer…

So this is how it ends, I thought. Knifed to death in a marketplace, alone, a long way from home.

Then a face flashed into my mind.

Elisabeth.

With one final burst of effort, I spurred myself forward. I was only a few feet away from the turning cart. Next to me was a stall selling fruit and vegetables. The fellow had almost run out of produce, his table nearly bare.

Seizing the opportunity, I hauled myself up onto the rickety trestle and leaped at the moving cart. I landed painfully on my side.

The driver shouted indignantly.

'I beg your pardon,' I said, gasping for breath. 'Take me to Admiralty House and I'll give you a guinea.'

The man looked at me incredulously for a moment, then shrugged and cracked his whip over the horses. As we clattered off down the little lane, I looked back to see the hooded figure standing where I had been just moments before, still holding the knife by his side.

I leaned forward and thumbed my nose at him. Then we turned the corner and he disappeared from view.

'What in Hades' name were you doing questioning Charlotte de Vere without asking me first?' Ben snapped at me from the other side of his desk.

Much to my annoyance, he had not taken my ordeal very seriously. Portsmouth was a dangerous place, he had told me reprovingly, as if I were not an old friend but just another of the people around here whom he suddenly and unexpectedly outranked.

'Ben, you told me I had carte blanche to investigate however I chose. I was under the impression your permission had already been granted.'

He was about to argue, but instead he sighed deeply and sank into his chair. 'Forgive me, Samuel. I have hardly slept these last two days. This awful business…'

'There has been no progress?'

'None. Did you find out anything from Mistress de Vere?'

'Perhaps. It seems she stayed for some time after the other guests left on the night Governor Maynard was killed.'

'Yes, I can imagine,' he replied, sardonically. 'And now I have even more to worry about. Albemarle has written, informing me that I am now formally appointed Governor of Portsmouth.'

I feigned surprise. 'Congratulations.'

Ben looked at me sharply. 'I do not want this. I do not want any of it. They want me to move into John's quarters now, assume the trappings of office, but how can I take his place? I do this out of duty to His Majesty and nothing more. How am I expected to be worthy of such a thing?'

'I would suggest that doubting your ability to lead is a mark in your favour.'

'You are kind, Samuel, but there is much you do not know. Are you aware of the Dutch situation, for example?'

'I have been briefed by Albemarle. Which reminds me, I should like your opinion on something. A strange thing happened to me, three nights past.'

I told him about the Dutch sailor I had seen from my window on our first night at the Four Feathers.

'About what time was this?'

'Two, maybe three o'clock.'

'I am not aware of any Dutch ships in port this week. But the next time you see anything suspicious, raise the alarm. Day or night. Until the killer is caught, we must take no chances. And take better care when wandering around.' He raised a finger and smiled. 'That is an order, old friend.'

I inclined my head. 'I will do my best. There is just one more thing before I go. Have you met de Vere's housemaid, a girl called Belle?'

He thought for a moment. 'The Jamaican girl? What of her?'

'Do you know anything about her?'

'Only that she has been in Mistress de Vere's service for… Hard to say. Two, three years perhaps. Why?'

'Oh, it is nothing. Just a small mystery wrapped up inside a bigger one.'

'It is an outrage, Mr Pepys. An outrage, I tell you.'

Goody Brown fussed around me, pulling up a chair and making me sit.

'It was nothing, madam. An altercation in the street, that is all.'

'What is the world coming to when gentlemen are accosted in broad daylight?' She clapped her hands. 'Tamsin, fetch Mr Pepys some ale.'

'Just a little brandy will suffice, thank you. And perhaps some bread and cheese.'

In truth, I was anxious to go upstairs and get to work on the secret accounts book, but after everything that had happened in the last few hours, I was suddenly aware of how ravenously hungry I was.

'It is a disgrace, is what it is,' Goody Brown continued. 'This town wouldn't have stood for it in my day. Villain like that. Hanging be too good for him.'

Tamsin came over, carrying a pewter cup.

'Thank you,' I said, taking a long sip of the brandy.

'I am sorry to hear of your trouble, sir.'

The sunlight though the window made the girl's blue eyes sparkle. I smiled.

'Thank you, Tamsin. And you, Goody Brown. I am grateful for your concern, but I assure you I am quite unhurt. But while I have you both, I would ask you a question. Are either of you aware of any Dutch sailors currently in these parts?'

Brown drew her tongue slowly across her rotten teeth. 'Aye. Time to time, Dutchies come in here when they got shore leave.'

'And you welcome them as you would any other guest?'

'So long as they can pay and they keep their heads down, I'll take their coin good as anyone else's.'

'But there have been none in this past week?'

'Not that I've seen. Mind, they'd need some balls to show themselves at the minute, things the way they are.' She must have read the surprise on my face, for she crossed her arms defensively. 'This is a seafaring town, Mr Pepys; we ain't daft and we keep our eyes and ears open. We know war's coming. Mind you, good war might knock sense into a few people if you ask me.'

'Forgive me, Mistress Brown. Only, it is a Dutchman I seek. A large man, perhaps thirty years old, with a thick brown beard. I know he was in these parts as recently as three nights ago.'

'What for?' Tamsin asked, I thought perhaps a little too hastily.

'Nothing of any great importance. Why, might you know the man I seek?'

She shook her head, but I was not sure I believed her. Goody Brown smacked the girl's arm lightly.

'What you still here for? Fetch Mr Pepys his bread and cheese, then leave him in peace.' Tamsin hurried away. 'I tell you, if that girl spent as much time serving as she does yacking, I'd never work again. She's lucky my late husband ain't still in charge. I'm too soft.'

Her voice trailed away as she shuffled off to greet some new customers at the door.

I sat there, alone. I was still shaken by my ordeal in the town, but the brandy was helping to calm my nerves.

Had my assailant really been a common thief? No, about that much I was certain. He was an assassin, sent to kill me. But by whom?

I had entered Charlotte de Vere's house already thinking the woman was capable of murder. A quarter of an hour in her company had done nothing to disabuse me of the notion. And besides, had Tamsin not warned me to stay away from her, or risk my own life?

Tamsin. The girl seems to know too much not to be involved in this business in some way, I thought. I waited patiently until she emerged from the kitchen, carrying a dish piled high with cold meat and cheese. She placed it on the table in front of me.

'Thank you, Tamsin. And more brandy, if you will?' I held out the cup, but when she tried to take it I did not let go. 'I know you are lying.'

'In faith I do not know what you mean, sir.'

'I have been to Farlington.' I stared into her eyes. This clearly unnerved her.

'Farlington?'

'Yes. I spoke with some of the people there. They told me some interesting things about Piety Blake. And Elias Thorne.'

She looked hesitant, as if there were something she wanted to say, but did not dare.

'Tamsin, I know you are lying to me. You do know who he was, don't you?'

She nodded.

'If you are frightened of somebody, we can protect you. I swear it. But you have to trust me.'

She leaned in close. 'Not here. Meet me at the stables in an hour.'

Then she pulled the cup out of my hand and was gone.

Twenty minutes later, I am sitting on the bed in my quarters.

The ledger we recovered from Piety Blake's cottage is open in front of me. At first glance, its contents looked just like those of all the others. Pages upon pages of neat columns, tallying up the costs of everything from rope and tar to ship's biscuits.

But as we saw before, every page of this one is covered in notes. In some places, figures have been crossed out; in others, totals corrected. Meticulous care has been taken to cross-reference each calculation, with the results collated into tables every few pages.

Elias Thorne certainly did his work in unpicking the discrepancies. A little here, a little there, I could see the irregularities begin to add up. A picture was emerging of a clever fraud to divert funds from the coffers of the *Prince Rupert*. But to where? And why?

To that last question, there is only one tantalising clue. Beside several of the tabulations had been scrawled a peculiar acronym:

O.R.O.

Over and over I have I tried to remember if I have seen it before, but my mind comes up blank. What can it mean? Is it a person, a place, or some other thing?

I was so absorbed by trying to work out this piece of the puzzle, I almost missed the sound of some church bells striking three o'clock. Nearly an hour has passed since Tamsin said she would meet me.

I must return the book to its hiding place in my luggage and hurry outside.

It did not take me long to find the stables. I pushed open the gate to the cramped little yard, which stank of dirty straw.

'Hello?' I called. There was no reply.

I looked around. There was no sign of an ostler, nor even a stable boy. The place was deserted, save for an old nag in a stall, blinking away a cloud of flies.

'Hello?' I said again, my voice echoing around the empty space. I began to feel uneasy, and wished that I had waited for Will to return.

Suddenly, I heard the gate close behind me and spun around. With a sigh of relief, I saw that it was just Tamsin.

'Didn't mean to startle you.'

'I take it Mistress Brown does not know you are here?'

'No. And I must be quick before she realises I am gone.'

'Then tell me straight, Tamsin. Who is it that you are scared of?'

She let out a long, quivering breath. 'The night after Elias was killed, two men came into the taproom. Right pair of radgie bastards, they were. They told the customers to leave, then them's that wouldn't, they set about with cudgels and knives. One or two tried to fight back, but they beat them to a pulp. They were like a pair of devils.'

She swallowed hard. Her cheeks had grown red and I saw that she was shaking. 'They... they made everyone leave, except me and Mistress Brown. They helped themselves to some ale, then made us sit down and drink with them. I thought they planned to do for us.'

'Go on,' I said, gently.

'They took out a purse filled with coin and told us it was in payment to keep our mouths shut. Said as long as we didn't say nothing to nobody about Elias Thorne, we'd get to keep it. But if we did...'

'They would come back.'

'We was to act like he never existed. If we did that, they said, no harm would come to us.'

'And if you did not?'

The fear in her eyes said it all. 'We swore to it, but then one of them started... His hand was up my skirts. I was so scared. I thought he was going to do more, but the other one stopped him; said they had to go.' She flicked away a tear. 'Then they finished their ale and left.'

'Have they been back?'

'No, thank the Lord.'

'Do you have any idea who they were?'

'No. But they weren't local, I can tell you that. The mistress thought they sounded like Essex men.'

'Can you describe them to me? Were they big men? How old were they?'

'More your age than Mr Hewer's. They were strong as devils, but only one of them was tall.' She shivered. 'The short one frightened me most.'

Could they have been sailors, I wondered?

'Tamsin. I know this is difficult for you. But I want you to tell me about Elias Thorne.'

Her jaw became tight. 'Damn his black heart. I wish to God that man had never come here.'

'Almost everybody we have spoken to has had nothing but good to say about the man. We have been told he was a most congenial fellow, everybody's friend, loved by all…'

She let out a short, bitter laugh. 'Let me guess, Mr Pepys. All men what told you that, was it? Elias was alright when he was sober. You'd know he'd had a few when he couldn't keep his hands to himself, but that ain't nothing new around here. It was when he got proper drunk that his temper came out.'

'Was he ever violent with Piety?'

She closed her eyes. 'God have mercy, Pie was a fool. The girl was besotted. I told her and told her, but she refused to see the bad in him, even after he starting laying hands on her.'

'He beat her?'

'She would come into work sometimes, bruises on her face. Denied it at first. Then switched her story, said it was just rough swiving. That she gave back as good as what he give her and we shouldn't worry.'

'So he was violent with her… even though they were lovers?'

'Even though they were lovers? Christ, you really don't know much about the ways men treat women, do you, duck?'

'What I meant was, she chose not to leave him, despite all this?'

Tamsin shrugged. 'What can I say? I tried to warn her. But he was her charming swain, and she was a free woman who could handle his rages. Until…'

She turned away. I took a deep breath.

'Tamsin, did Elias Thorne kill Piety Blake?'

She stared at me for a moment, then nodded her head slowly.

'And Elias Thorne? Do you know who killed him?'

'I… I cannot say.'

'Cannot? Or will not?'

She took a step back. 'I must go.'

'Tamsin, please.'

'In faith, sir. I cannot.'

I was so close to learning the truth about what had happened to Elias. But she had risked enough already. I would not push her further, this day.

'Very well, Tamsin. Thank you for everything you have done.'

Her eyes welled up with tears. 'He was not a good man. He was not.'

'I understand that now. Be assured, your secret shall be safe with me.'

She opened the gate. Then, just as she was about to leave, she turned back to me. 'Mr Pepys? If it is a Dutchman you seek, try the laundry on Bear Lane.'

I opened my mouth to speak but she was already gone.

As I turned into Bear Lane, I heard a loud rumble in the distance. My first thought was that it was cannon fire, and that we were under attack. Then I realised the truth and sighed with relief.

It was thunder. At last, a storm was coming.

I had no trouble finding the laundry. An acrid, sulphurous smell drifted out onto the street, the cause of which was plain to see as soon as I turned down a little side alley and entered a wide courtyard.

Great vats of piss stood ripening in the hot sunshine, ready to be mixed with wood ash to form soap. A handful of washerwomen were pouring fresh lye into barrels full of dirty linen. Clouds of flies and gnats buzzed around, and I wondered how the women could stand to work in such a vile place.

Another distant rumble sounded, causing the laundresses to look up from their work. One of them saw me and smiled. She was young, ruddy-cheeked, with wispy, ginger-coloured hair tied up in a white headscarf. Her skirts were knotted beneath her protruding belly, exposing short, swollen legs.

Suddenly I realised that I had seen her before, on the day I arrived at the inn with Olly, the potboy. It was the pregnant girl, Alice.

'Can I help you, sir?' she said, wiping away the sweat from her face.

'I am Samuel Pepys. I am with the navy.'

'Not often we get gentlemen come for their own laundry. Maid off sick, is she?'

Her lack of deference should have aggravated me, but there was something disarming about this girl's manner. To my surprise, I found myself smiling back. 'No, madam. I am here on other business. Perhaps you would sit down and talk with me a moment?'

She called over to one of the other washerwomen. 'Maggie, take over for a while, will you?'

An older woman walked over and took the paddle she had been using to stir a barrel of linens. Alice rubbed her back and let out a long sigh, then led me to the rear of the courtyard and down a short walkway. It took us towards a second, smaller courtyard, where laundry was hung out to dry.

Just off to our right was a little storage area, open to the elements, where baskets and other supplies were piled up, ready for use. We stepped in here and she sat down on a wooden stool, groaning loudly with relief.

'That's better. Pour us some beer, will you?'

I looked around and saw a pewter jug set on a small table, and covered with cloth to keep away the flies. Next to it was a stack of beakers. I filled two and sat down opposite her.

She gulped down the beer thirstily and let out a little belch. 'Beg pardon, sir.'

'This awful heat must be unbearable for you, Mistress…?'

'Alice Scovell. Say now, I seen you before, ain't I?'

'I have lodgings at the Four Feathers.'

'That's right. The other day. I were fetching Goody Brown's laundry.'

'You have a good memory, madam. But perhaps you should be more careful in your present condition.'

'Now, I'm not sick, sir. And as for the heat, I'd take this over a winter frost any day.' She drained her cup and handed it to me. I got up and refilled it for her, waving away the persistent flies.

'Portsmouth man, are you?' she said, curiously.

'London. A place even less becoming in midsummer than your own, I fear.'

'London, eh? My pa was a London man.'

'Oh? From where?'

'Don't know who he was, chick, do I?'

I smiled again. In spite of the heat, the wretched flies, and my continuing pain, I was enjoying this woman's company. I took a long gulp of beer. My throat was so parched that even this cheap, bitter brew tasted good.

Another rumble of thunder sounded and the air above us crackled slightly. I began to feel tiny droplets of rain on my skin.

Alice put down her cup. 'Now, sir. Don't think I mind a good yack and all, but you didn't come to talk about the weather now, did you?'

'I seek information about a certain person who I believe has been seen around these parts.'

'What kind of man will that be then, sir?' Her tone shifted, the easy banter now gone. Had I offended her, or did she have other reasons to be nervous?

I described the Dutchman as best I could, watching her face closely for signs of recognition. But she claimed to have no knowledge of such a man, and if she was lying, her expression gave nothing away.

I wished I had pressed Tamsin for more information. Had she meant that the Dutchman was staying here? If so, was somebody concealing him? Or could these women be ignorant of the fact?

Suddenly there was a bright flash, followed a few seconds later by an ominous rumble of thunder. The rumbling shook the buildings around us and the hair on my arms stood on end.

It was coming.

Alice looked up at the darkening sky. 'Hello, here we go. Been needing this a while, ain't we?'

'I should take my leave. Thank you for your time, Mrs Scovell.'

''Tis no bother, sir. You know the way out?'

'Indeed. Good day to you.'

I left the little storage area, but instead of returning the way we had come, I turned to the right and entered the second courtyard.

A breeze was rising. The sheets that had been hung out to dry were billowing softly to and fro. On the opposite side of the courtyard was a locked iron gate, beyond which lay a narrow street lined with humble wooden buildings. From somewhere nearby I could hear the sound of small children playing a boisterous game of war. Otherwise, there was nobody to be seen.

I walked past a derelict shed, briefly pausing to look inside, but there was nothing there except a long-dead fox being picked at by rats. Then I crossed to another outbuilding. This one was larger, with a rickety-looking staircase leading up to a small door. I took a few cautious steps up, trying to peer through the small windows.

Then came the deluge. Fat droplets of rain bursting on the bone-dry ground, filling the air with the smell of hot earth. I looked around for shelter, then suddenly I heard voices approaching. It was the women, come to fetch the laundry.

Swiftly, I ran the rest of the way up the stairs to the upper room, pushing gently at the door. It opened. Inside I could make out a small truckle bed and a wooden chest, but otherwise it appeared to be deserted.

I looked over my shoulder just in time to see Alice Scovell and the woman she'd called Maggie hurrying into the yard. I ducked inside, pulling the door to behind me.

Taking care to stay low, I made a brief search of the room, but it was indeed empty save for the simple pieces of furniture I had seen from the window. I tried the lid of the chest. It was unlocked. Inside were some plain clothes, men's and women's, neatly laundered and folded. I lifted them up. Underneath were a pair of pewter plates and two eating knives.

I closed the chest, then returned to the window. The women were still gathering in the laundry. I had no alternative but to stay where I was for the time being.

Suddenly, I felt another cramp in my stomach and needed to sit down. It kept growing and growing, until I was doubled over in pain. I clenched my teeth, trying desperately not to cry out.

Another crack of thunder shook the walls around me. Rain was streaking down the windows and I could no longer see enough outside to know whether the women were still there.

I sat for a couple of minutes, shaking, until the pain subsided enough for me to move again. I went over to the door and opened it a crack. The women had gone.

I was about to leave when, glancing around the room one last time, I saw a small dark shape protruding from underneath the straw mattress. I bent over and pulled it out.

It was a small leather book. I opened it. On the plain, cheap-looking frontispiece were printed the words:

BIJBEL DAT IS DE GANSCHE HEILIGE SCHRIFT

It was a Bible. A Dutch Bible.

Suddenly, there was a noise at the doorway. I spun around. A man was standing there, his eyes wide open in shock. He was tall and muscular, with dark hair and a thick beard.

I recognised him instantly. It was the man I had seen from my window. Perhaps also the man who had tried to kill me in the marketplace. But instead of attacking me, he turned and ran down the steps. Ignoring the lingering pain in my stomach, I scrambled to my feet and ran after him.

Outside, the sky had turned dark and the ground was saturated with rain. The Dutchman splashed through puddles, slipping and almost falling as he raced towards the locked gate. He pulled frantically at the metalwork, but it would not open, so he vaulted straight over the top.

Seconds later, I reached the gate and tried to pull myself up as hard as I could. My legs kicked in search of a firm foothold, but water had made the metal slick. My arms ached with the effort as I jumped down onto the other side with a splash.

The Dutchman was younger and fitter than me, but the torrential rain had slowed him down. I took off as fast as I could down the narrow street, straining to close the gap between us. My guts roared with pain, as if imploring me to stop, but I kept going.

Then, without warning, the Dutchman swerved left, skidding on the slick ground and disappearing down an alleyway. I followed, only just managing to keep him in sight as he turned again into a small yard behind a row of shops.

I raced around the corner after him – and stopped. It was a dead end. The Dutchman stood facing me. I didn't know if he had miscalculated or led me here deliberately, but now I stood between him and the only way out.

The rain poured down between us. I raised my hands with the palms facing outward.

'Please… I just want to talk.'

He stared at me coldly, then reached into his pocket and pulled out a knife. I started to back away, but he leaped towards me, forcing me to move away from the entrance and into the yard.

We circled each other slowly. I could just make out Bear Lane through the dirty glass of an empty shop. The street was tantalisingly close and yet completely unreachable. I was trapped.

He slashed at me with the knife. I only just managed to pull back in time.

'I just want to talk. I mean you no harm.'

He stabbed at me again, aiming for the chest this time. I swerved to one side, and as I did so, I caught a glimpse of two shapes passing by on the street, one tall, one short. My heart leapt.

'Will, help!'

As the Dutchman slashed at me again, I saw Will looking around, unable to tell where my shouts were coming from.

'Behind the shop. Will, hurry!'

Will pressed his face against the glass, trying to see through to the yard. Then he saw me and began frantically pushing at the door. It was locked. My eyes darted back and forth between Will and the Dutchman.

'We're coming,' shouted Will.

He disappeared from view, just as the Dutchman ran at me hard. I raised my arms in a futile attempt to shield myself from the attack, but he lost his footing at the last moment and slipped in the mud. As he fell, he grabbed onto me, and we hit the ground together.

'You will not take them away from me!' His voice was filled with rage.

I kicked out frantically, crying for help, as he dragged me backwards and turned me over to face him. He slammed his fist down into my face and my head cracked against the muddy ground. The metallic taste of blood spread through my mouth.

He raised the knife to strike the killing blow, but I grabbed his arm, pushing back as hard as I could to try and keep the blade away. But my strength was no match for his. I watched in terror as the knife edged closer and closer to my neck.

In a last, desperate attempt, I leaned forward and bit his knuckles as hard as I could. He screamed, raising his knee up sharply into my cods. I gasped as pain shot through me like fire, forcing me to let go of his arm – just as Will ran into the yard and kicked the man in the side of the head.

I rolled away as the Dutchman stood up, dazed but on his feet. Rain mixed with the blood that was now coursing from his forehead, streaking his face with red.

Will took off his coat and raised his fists. 'Come on then. Let's see what you're made of.'

I tried to stand, but the pain was too great. All I could do was lie helplessly, clutching my stomach, as Will and the Dutchman circled each other like animals, each waiting for the other to strike the first blow.

The Dutchman lashed out with his knife and Will jumped back, but it was a feint, and the knife came slashing back from the other direction, only just missing its target. Will threw a well-aimed punch to the man's jaw, hitting it with a loud crack.

I thought he was going to topple backwards, but instead he parried, swiping the knife at Will's arm once again. This time it made contact and blood started to spread from the wound, turning the torn sleeve red. The

Dutchman took advantage of Will's momentary confusion and launched himself forward, knife outstretched.

'Look out!' I cried. Will quickly sidestepped, then he grabbed the man's arm and twisted it back sharply, forcing him to drop the knife into the mud.

Immediately he pressed his advantage with a hail of punches. The Dutchman put up a strong resistance, but Will stood firm, hammering the man's face and body with blow after blow.

For a moment, I thought Will had him beaten – but then the man rammed into him with the full weight of his body and they crashed to the ground together, rolling over and over in the mud, each desperately trying to gain the upper hand.

Will fought as hard as he could but I could see that he was getting tired. His opponent was too strong. The Dutchman rolled him onto his back and began choking him. Will pushed and kicked, gasping for air, but it was no good. The man was going to choke the life out of him.

With all my remaining strength I hauled myself to my feet and fell onto the Dutchman, throwing my arms around his neck to pull him away from Will. He loosened his grip just enough to elbow me hard in the stomach and I staggered backwards, my vision starting to blur.

I was losing consciousness. There was a loud ringing in my ears and I was unable to keep my balance. Then I became aware of other sounds all around me. The pounding of feet. Shouting. The sounds of another struggle.

Then somebody grabbed my shoulders and shook me hard.

'Pepys? Pepys, are you alright?'

I shook my head and my vision swam back into focus. Captain Harcourt was staring into my eyes. Suddenly, I was awake again.

'Will?' I cried, looking around urgently.

A group of Harcourt's men were hauling the Dutchman out of the yard, as he protested violently. Behind them, Will was on his feet, rubbing his throat. I felt a surge of relief. His rain-soaked shirt was torn to rags and there were deep cuts on his chest. But at least he was alive.

'Will,' I said again, staggering over to him. He reached out an arm to hold me steady.

'It is over, Sam,' he said, his voice cracked and strained. 'We've got him.'

That is the last thing I remember hearing before my legs gave way and the world turned to black.

I awoke in an unfamiliar room. It was dark, save for the flicker of candlelight. Somewhere in the far distance, the storm was still raging. My nostrils twitched at the smell of woodsmoke.

'He is awake.' Will threw a log onto the fire and brushed dirt off his hands. His voice was still hoarse and there were livid red marks on his neck. 'How are you feeling, Sam?'

'The pain is bearable, if I do not move,' I croaked.

'Then you should keep still, sir.'

The stern voice came from the other end of the room. I looked over to see Doctor Grey standing over a table with his back to me. I could not quite discern what he was doing, but it seemed to involve taking items out of a bag and carefully laying them on a cloth, one by one.

'Where am I, Will?'

'Admiralty House.'

I started to ask why, but was overtaken by a fit of coughing.

'Easy, Sam,' said Will. 'You need to save your strength.'

'How did you find me?'

'I returned to the Four Feathers but you weren't there. Tamsin told me where you had gone. I took the little potboy, Olly, to show me where it was. When I saw you were being attacked, I had him run to Admiralty House for help.'

'I should put that boy on a salary. You saved my life.'

I touched Will's arm. He took my hand.

'And you mine. Bastard fought like a tiger.'

'Where is he now?'

'Town gaol. They say he killed Maynard.'

I began to cough again. 'Could I have something to drink?'

Will shifted uneasily. 'I am… afraid not, Sam.'

'Why not?'

Doctor Grey turned to face me, his hands clasped behind his back. 'Mr Pepys, I fear that your condition has grown worse. The stones are larger than I first thought, and it appears they have caused some corruption to your bladder. Time may now be short.'

'What does that mean?'

'It means that if Doctor Grey does not operate, you will die, Sam,' said Will.

I looked at Grey in disbelief, but his face was impassive.

'When?'

'Now.'

My eye caught a momentary glimmer of candlelight on metal and I looked over to where Grey had been standing. A row of scalpels, grips, and other implements had already been laid out in a neat row.

I felt the blood drain from my face. 'No. There must be another way.'

'I'm afraid there is not, Sam,' said Will. He was trying to appear calm, but I could tell he was frightened. 'Is there anything I can get you?'

My heart was pounding. I could hardly think. 'P-paper and some ink, please.'

Will handed me a sheet of parchment and a quill, resting them on top of a wooden tray on my lap. I dipped the quill in the ink pot and tried to write, but my hands were shaking too much to form words. Tears welled up in my eyes.

'What is the use?'

'Let me write for you.'

Will took the tray and waited. Still no words came. Fear had made my thoughts weak and hard to grasp.

'Just tell Elisabeth that… that I love her above all, and that I beg her forgiveness for the wrongs I have done her.'

Will nodded his understanding and set the tray down.

There was a knock at the door and two muscular young men I had never seen before entered, carrying a large wooden table. The kind a butcher might use, I thought.

Doctor Grey directed them to place it in the middle of the room. Then one of them picked up some heavy coils of rope.

Will turned to me. 'Are you ready, Sam?'

I began to weep. 'Can—can I at least have some brandy? Or some wine, to drink myself to a stupor?'

'I am afraid not,' said Grey. 'It is necessary that your bladder remains empty for such an operation as this. I am sorry, sir.'

He signalled to Will. Together, the two of them lifted me from my bed. I fought to be free of their grip, but Will looked at me and I saw the sadness on his face.

'Sam. I am truly sorry.'

I closed my eyes. 'Very well. Do it now.'

It is, I must now confess, several days later that I write these words. I have recorded it as best I could, but hope never to read back of my ordeal. Besides, I shall remember every terrible second of what happened next until the day I die.

First, they stood me up and undressed me, until I stood naked in front of the fire. Then Grey took out a razor. I recoiled, but Will spoke reassuringly.

'It is just to shave you, Sam.'

When the doctor had finished, they laid me down on the table. The two men who had come in earlier, who I realised must be Grey's assistants, released a catch, and part of the table pivoted upwards. When I had reached a sitting position, they locked it in place and bound my chest and arms tightly with rope. As they were doing this, Will placed a large piece of wood in my mouth and bound it shut.

Then they lifted my legs so that my knees touched my chest, and spread them as wide as they would go, before gripping onto them with all their strength so that I was pinioned, totally unable to move.

Grey told Will to hold my prick upright. Then he took out a long thin wooden staff. Before I had even registered what was happening, the doctor forced it down the shaft of my piece. I bit down as hard as I could, screaming, as Grey drove the rod deeper and deeper until I could feel it enter my bowels. I looked down and saw blood oozing out through the narrow opening and pooling onto the table.

But, oh God, there was worse to come. Much worse. As I struggled to bear the pain of having the rod stuck inside me, Grey started feeling around in my arse with his fingers, looking for where the stones were lodged. It was then that I realised that the rod was only a guide for what was to come next.

Grey nodded at Will, who went over to the fire. Taking a thick cloth in his hand, he lifted a metal object out of the flames. The doctor pulled on a glove and took it from him. Flames danced across the polished blade of a hot scalpel as he turned it in his hand.

I felt his cold fingers lift my cods out of the way, then an agony of red hot metal piercing my skin. I screamed, but still that was not the worst of it, as he plunged the blade into my cod sack and dragged it sharply downwards towards my arse, ripping through the soft skin and muscle so that I thought my balls would fall out.

I could feel the hot blood gush out of my loins and around my body, pouring onto the floor like water. I retched violently against the piece of wood that held my mouth open, but there was nothing within me to throw up. Desperately, I prayed for the mercy of oblivion, but all I could do was scream.

Doctor Grey held up his gloved hand, which was dripping with my blood. Will pulled off the glove and swiftly handed him a pair of pincers. Grey took the implement and plunged it straight into the open wound.

I screamed over and over as the pincers moved around inside me. I was dimly aware that they made contact with the stones, then Doctor Grey stuck two fingers inside the wound, pulling it open as wide as it would go. Then I heard something small and hard drop onto the table. They went in again, and a few seconds later, out came another.

I was nearly insensible by now. I felt my arms and legs being untied, and a cold wet cloth being placed against my injured skin. There was a dreadful stinging sensation and the wound felt hot. Then my legs were closed and I could feel bandages being wound tightly around my nether parts.

The last thing I remember before passing out completely was Will leaning in close and telling me that it was over.

June 19*th*

I remember little of the day after my ordeal – only images, as I drifted in and out of a fitful sleep. I believe Doctor Grey must have given me a draught to make me rest, else I might have been driven mad by the pain – and the memory of what I had just endured.

Once again, I piece together the events of this day from some time later. Today is, in fact, the twentieth of June, and I remain in my sickbed at Admiralty House.

I believe that it was around noon on the nineteenth that I did finally wake. The pain flooded back as I came to my senses and I tried to move, only to find that my legs were still bound tightly together.

'Sam.'

Will hurried over from a chair by the fire. He lifted a cup from the bedside and gently raised it to my mouth. My throat felt raw and parched as I gulped the liquid down. It was a cold syrup that tasted strongly of lemons and sugar.

When I had finished the cup, Will laid me gently back down.

'How are you feeling?'

'Alive.' My voice was hoarse and feeble. 'How went it?'

'It went well. Doctor Grey is very pleased. You have been asleep for nearly two days.'

I tried to speak but my throat was too sore.

'Sam, you must rest.'

'No. There are things I must tell you. I know who killed Piety Blake.'

'Who?'

I began to say the words, but started coughing again. Will lifted the cup once more to my lips.

'Elias Thorne,' I said, finally. 'We were right about him.'

Will seemed about to say something, but hesitated. He leaned over and tucked my sheets around me. 'Sleep now, Sam. We will talk of such things later.'

'Wait, there is more—'

'Later,' he said, firmly. 'Now you must sleep.'

June 20ᵗʰ

I was awoken by a knock on the door. Will had evidently fallen asleep in the chair next to my bed, for it was he who got up to answer it.

I felt disoriented, still lost in the nightmare that had gripped my sleeping mind. Whenever I closed my eyes, it seemed that I must relive those terrible moments.

Ben stepped into the room. He paused in the doorway, shocked by my appearance, then came over and held my hand.

'How do you fare, Samuel?'

'If you are here for your dancing lesson, Ben, I fear I must disappoint you.'

He laughed. 'It can wait. I bring news. The Dutchman has been arraigned, and is in Portsmouth gaol awaiting trial.'

'Good,' said Will.

'There is more. He has confessed to the murder of Lord Maynard. And that of your predecessor, Elias Thorne.'

I was aghast. 'What?'

'It is true. He admitted as much after questioning.'

'I do not understand. Why?'

'It is not yet clear, but Captain Harcourt suspects his mission was to help provoke a war with England. It would suit the Dutch to take us on now, while our defences are still weak.'

I felt confused. Events were catching up with me too fast. I was about to ask more, when Ben produced a small, folded piece of paper with an unbroken seal.

'I informed the Duke of Albemarle of all that has happened, leaving out no detail of your bravery. His reply arrived by messenger last night.

His Grace ordered me to give you this.' He placed the letter in my hand. 'You are a hero, Samuel.'

With a brief nod to Will, Ben left the room.

I opened the letter.

Mr Pepys,

I have just come from the King, who commends you on your achievement. To have apprehended the man who killed Governor Maynard would be cause enough for celebration, but Arden tells me that the brute has also admitted to having murdered Elias Thorne. This is indeed fine work, Pepys.

The Dutch traitor will now be tried and executed, God be praised. What is more, the machinations of this wicked man have left His Majesty more convinced than ever of the threat that faces us.

I am sorry to hear of your recent troubles, and trust that you are recovering well. Once you are fit to travel, consider yourself under orders to return to London. I know not the state of your enquiries into the other matter, but hope that you have made some progress.

That's all one. You have done enough. Conclude the remainder of your investigations at home.

I wish you a safe return.
Albemarle

I handed the letter to Will. He read it quickly.

'So we are to return to London?'

'Yes,' I said. 'Though I cannot help but feel that our work is unfinished.'

'You have found the man who killed both Maynard and Thorne.'

'Have we?'

'You doubt it?'

'You do not?'

'Well, guilty or not, it is no longer our business. You read what the duke said. What else is there to keep us here?'

'Who sent the assassin after me, for a start.'

Will frowned. 'What assassin?'

Suddenly, I realised that we had not yet had a chance to talk about what happened after we had parted company at Charlotte de Vere's house. I told him all I could remember about the attempt on my life, and my narrow escape in the marketplace. He listened with interest as I recounted the discoveries I had made in the secret accounts ledger.

Counter to my expectations, however, he seemed unsurprised when I told him that according to Tamsin, Elias Thorne had killed Piety Blake.

'I had reached the same conclusion. And besides, I think this explains the way Tamsin's been acting these last three days.'

'What do you mean?'

'The girl's been avoiding me. Won't even meet my eye.'

'She is scared. It was also she who suggested I look for the Dutchman at the laundry on Bear Lane. No doubt she fears reprisals.'

'Perhaps.'

'You think there is more to it?'

Will shrugged. 'How did she know he was there in the first place?'

'That is one of many questions I still wish to ask her.'

I considered all this for a moment. He was right about Tamsin. The girl was still holding something back. I knew that as soon as she refused to say more about Elias Thorne's murder. But what could she be so afraid of? Especially given all that she had told me, possibly risking her life in the process?

'Who do you suppose those men were who came to silence Tamsin and Goody Brown?' I said. 'And who sent them? I assume they were not acting alone. All she could tell me was that they were closer in age to me than you, that one was tall and one was short, and both had the accents of Essex men.'

'And that they left money, as well as making threats?'

'Yes. A most handsome sum, by the sounds of things. So their employer must be a man of means.'

Will arched an eyebrow. 'A man? Or a woman?'

He did not need to say whom he had in mind. I was about to reply when he stood up and made me take another gulp of Doctor Grey's draught. 'But it is all as one. This is out of our hands now; we have our orders, and you are a hero.'

'Perhaps you are right. It would be good to go home. To see…'

Suddenly, I felt as if I might weep. Will placed his hand on my arm.

'I know. And you shall. But now you must rest.'

I closed my eyes and hoped the nightmares would not come again.

June 21st

Too weak to write. Too much pain. Will try tomorrow.

June 23rd

Lord's Day. I slept for most of yesterday and today. Will has been with me all this time. His waking hours are divided between tending to me, and carrying on my work in auditing the accounts ledgers against the work of Elias Thorne.

Doctor Grey visited this morning on his way back from church, and seems pleased with my progress. He warned that I may need to stay in bed for several weeks, but so long as his instructions are followed to the letter, he is confident I will make a full recovery.

Ben has been the most gracious host that I could wish for. The kitchens prepare me special dishes, following the advice of Doctor Grey. For the most part I am given a soothing preparation of hot water infused with cinnamon, though once a day I am allowed a light, bland broth.

There is even a permanent guard on my door, which I think excessive, but given the events of the past week, I confess I am glad of it.

The pain has settled into a constant soreness and my legs remain bound together, which causes me unbearable cramps. The greatest indignity is having to beg help for my most intimate needs. Fortunately, the servants here are at hand for the tasks I would not wish Will to perform, though it makes me feel as impotent as a babe.

Impotent. A poor choice of word, perhaps. I pray at least that the ministrations of Doctor Grey's knife have spared me that fate.

Unfortunately, Will knows that I am attempting to maintain my diary during this period of convalescence, and implores me to stop until I am well again. The boy is like an old shrew, but I concede the wisdom. I need as much rest as possible if I am to be strong enough to make the journey to London soon.

So, until such time, I shall stay my pen. I only pray that day shall not be long in coming.

July 1st, 1669
Bideford

My dearest Sam,

I was shocked to receive Will's letter informing me of your current condition, which Mary has forwarded to me in Devonshire by post rider from London. I pray God that you are recovering well.

But Samuel, why did you not write to me yourself and tell me that you were in such terrible straits? Are you too weak, or do you seek to avoid me?

Mary says that there has been no word from you since you left, nor any indication of when you will return. I do not know what I expected. Perhaps I hoped that during my absence from Seething Lane, you would at least write to me there so that I might read your letters at a later date.

And yet it fell to Will, not you, to tell me that you are gravely ill, and recuperating in bed after what I am told was a most agonising surgery. Surgery!

Do you really think so little of me, Sam? Am I unworthy of such simple courtesies as a note to say you are well? Once again, you wound me. In the days before you left for Portsmouth you gave me a little hope, but your actions since have caused those hopes to fade. You do not have to miss me, but do not presume that your silence goes unnoticed or uncared for.

Forgive me, my love. Will says you are safe, thanks be to God, and that is all that truly matters. But will you not write and tell me this yourself? I know Will did not give me the full truth of what has happened. (The boy has become a true friend, but he was ever a terrible liar.)

I am leaving Devonshire for London so that I may be there when you return. In truth, I tire of this place. It is too hot or too wet and I am plagued by mosquitoes. One of the devils bit me on the arse last night. At least it will be autumn soon. Do you remember how we used to ride our little coach around St James's Park, watching the leaves fall? What happy times they were.

I miss you, dearest one. And, in spite of all the pain you have caused me, know this above all else: I love you. Three tiny little words, and yet never have I spoken them to a soul in all the world, except you.

Come home, Sam Pepys.

Elisabeth

August 9th

I knew something was wrong as soon as I emerged from my quarters.

I could hear a commotion from somewhere below, shouts and the barking of orders. Admiralty House is usually a calm place, where voices are seldom raised. This was unusual.

It has been more than six weeks since my ordeal, and at last, we are shortly to go home. Doctor Grey has declared me well enough to travel – God be praised, as I think I would go quite mad if I were forced to spend much longer cooped up in that tiny, airless room.

Will, who has been quartered in a room adjacent to mine so that he could finally move out of the Four Feathers, was to spend the day making preparations for our journey. Captain Harcourt has generously offered to send a detachment of men to escort us back to London and we will leave on the morrow.

But, as we discovered when we descended the stairs into the white marble hallway, there is a new danger looming here.

'What's going on?' Will demanded, as Boatswain Stearne hurried past us in the direction of the atrium.

'Sir, it is grave news. One of our cutters, the *Nonsuch*, has been stolen.'

I was aghast. 'Stolen? How?'

'She was grounded for careening. The nightwatchman had his throat cut. The ship was boarded and they were away before anyone could raise the alarm.'

'My God,' exclaimed Will.

'Do we know how many attackers there were?' I asked.

'I can say nothing else. Forgive me, sir, I must go.'

'At least tell me where I will find the Governor.'

'At the docks, inspecting the damage,' he said, hurrying deeper into the building.

The half hour it took us to reach the docks on foot was the longest I had gone since the start of my recuperation. I no longer need the aid of a cane to walk, but I cannot move fast, and the market-day crowds slowed us down further.

I was glad of Will's presence. Memories of the last time I was here on market day were uncomfortably fresh in my mind. But, despite the myriad of people, an eerie quiet seemed to have descended on the town this day. Conversations were conducted in nervous, subdued tones. Everywhere we heard the same word, spoken clearly above all others.

War.

Then, as we approached the docks, I saw a woman shout angrily at a guardsman on duty. I recognised her immediately. It was Alice Scovell. I noticed that she was holding a small babe in her arms, wrapped up in swaddling.

So, I thought, she has had her child at last.

Hoping to intervene I made my way over, but before I could get close enough to call out, Mistress Scovell had turned and hurried away.

'What do you suppose that was about?' Will said.

'That is Alice Scovell. The girl from the laundry.' I watched the red-headed woman disappear into the crowd on the other side of the street, then added, 'I wonder how much she really knew?'

The guard on duty at the shipyard looked anxious. He recognised me, but not Will, so I continued alone towards where the missing ship had been moored. Despite the gravity of the situation, I allowed myself a moment to pause and inhale the sea air.

Oh, but it felt good to be out. The creaking of masts, the murmur of the waves, the crying of gulls – sights and sounds that at any other time would be unremarkable, now felt like symbols of my liberation.

Suddenly, I caught the sound of familiar voices on the wind. It was Ben talking to Captain Harcourt. They appeared to be having some sort of argument, in hushed but angry tones. I looked around, unable to see them at first, then spotted the two men standing a little way off, on the other side of some empty wooden barrels. I edged over to them, carefully, trying to make out what was being said.

'Keep your voice down,' snapped Ben. 'Remember where you are.'

'The Dutch fleet grows stronger by the day, and yet we are starved of men and money.'

'What do you expect me to do? This was an act of war.'

'Behave like a Governor. Or, if you cannot lead, get out of the way so somebody else can.'

'The king will not listen.'

'Then you must make him listen.'

'We are sworn to the order.'

'Damn the order.'

There was a sudden clatter of metal on stone and I realised that I had accidentally kicked a nail. It rolled across the ground, coming to rest just a few feet away from the two men. They looked up and immediately saw me.

Ben's face broke out into a broad smile and he walked over to me, arms outstretched.

'Good heavens, Samuel, it is good to see you out at last. You are feeling well?' He clasped my hands warmly.

'A little uneasy on my feet, but I am myself again.'

'This fills me with joy. And good news is hard to come by these days, it seems.'

He indicated an empty mooring, a little further down from where we stood. I could just make out a patch of something that might have been blood splashed across the ground.

'Is there any news at all?'

'Nothing,' said Harcourt, grimly. 'We were taken completely by surprise.'

'What I do not understand is how so many men could do this without being detected. A cutter is a forty-man vessel.'

'Fully crewed, yes,' he replied, a little defensively. 'But with a skeleton crew, ten, maybe fewer. They knew what they were doing.'

I turned back to Ben. 'Has Albemarle been informed?'

'Of course, by dispatch rider this morning.'

'I fear we should not discount the possibility that this could be in some way connected to the other affair, do you not agree?'

'*We* shall not discount anything in our investigations,' Harcourt interjected.

'I could delay my departure, if I can be of assistance?'

Ben patted my arm. 'You have done enough, Samuel. Without you, we would never have caught the killer, nor recovered the money he stole. Return to London. This is a tragedy, but we can cope – whatever comes next.'

For a moment, I was lost for words. I had told no one about the secret accounts ledger and the discoveries made by Elias Thorne.

'The money, Ben?'

He looked at me in surprise. 'Did nobody not tell you? The missing funds you were here to investigate, they were found in the possession of the Dutchman.'

'They were?'

'Eight hundred and fifty guineas, secreted in the man's hideaway.'

'But I searched his room myself.'

'The money was hidden under a loose floorboard,' said Harcourt. 'I led the search party myself.'

I was about to respond, when the bells of a nearby church began to strike the hour. Ben waved his hand.

'Nine o'clock already. I should have been on the road an hour ago. Samuel, do you have everything you need for tomorrow?'

'Yes, Captain Harcourt has been most helpful to us. But Ben, are you going somewhere?'

'London, to attend His Majesty. I have been summoned. No doubt these latest developments shall give us much to talk about.'

'I shall walk with you as far as the quay.'

'I would enjoy that very much, Samuel.'

As Harcourt strode off towards the *Nonsuch's* mooring, Ben took my arm and we walked slowly in the direction of the street.

'The man is a churl and you should not let him talk to you like that,' I said, when I was sure the Captain was out of earshot.

Ben laughed mirthlessly, and patted my arm. 'Would that you were governor instead of I. Perhaps you would demand more respect.'

'Nonsense, Ben. You are doing a fine job, under the worst of circumstances. What was he talking about, making the King listen?'

'He... believes that His Majesty is not doing enough to prepare for the possibility of war with the Dutch.' The old man lowered his voice to a whisper. 'In fact, Samuel, he thinks the King has little understanding in matters of war at all.'

'Oh?'

'To Harcourt, the King is a good man led by sheep. He thinks His Majesty relies too greatly on diplomacy. What the French would call a *libertin*: a soft man obsessed with the pleasures of the flesh, with no awareness when it comes to matters of war.' He lowered his voice. 'Is he not, after all, the man who lost the Battle of Worcester and condemned us to a decade of Puritan rule? In Harcourt's eyes, the path the King has chosen will lead inexorably to war, and conquest by the Dutch.'

'What is your opinion?'

Ben inclined his head. 'I have faith in the King. Though I will admit the recent news from Holland gives me a certain sympathy with Harcourt's frustrations.'

I frowned. 'What news?'

'You have not heard? The mission has been called off.'

'Sir George Downing's mission?'

'Yes. He is to be recalled to London. Evidently, he did not prove quite the skilled diplomat you hoped he would.'

'This is troubling news.'

'Indeed. No doubt I shall hear more from His Majesty in person.' By now we had reached the entrance to the shipyard. Ben let go of my arm and put his hands on my shoulders.

'I wish you a safe journey, Samuel.'

'And you. How long do you intend to stay in London?'

'A week, perhaps more.'

'Then when I am returned there myself, you must come to my house for that dinner we were denied.'

He smiled. 'Oh, I would enjoy that. You know I have never met your wife?'

'She will like you.'

'And I her, no doubt.'

'Then it is settled?'

'Nothing in the world would give me greater pleasure.'

Earlier this evening, Will and I were sitting by the fire in my quarters. We had just finished a light supper of boiled ox's cheek and peas. I had sent a message to Elisabeth via post rider to London, informing her that we would be home in a matter of days.

The thought that our time here was nearly at an end should have made for a joyous evening. And yet our minds were preoccupied with other matters.

'I still don't understand how it could happen,' said Will, staring into the glowing coals. 'Stolen right from under their noses.'

'When I first met Lord Maynard, he told me that on a war footing barely a third of his guns could be put to use, so depleted were their resources.'

'But a whole ship? The king will be furious.'

'I expect even Albemarle has been given cause to shrink from his wrath by now. Whether this was piracy or an act of war, at least it makes Maynard's point clearly enough. If a powerful enemy chooses now to invade, England is like to fall.'

We fell silent for a moment. I thought of Ben, and what a momentous task lay ahead of him. 'I wish to God the King had not picked him.'

Will looked at me with a sympathetic smile. 'You are concerned about Ben?'

'He looked so tired when I saw him today. I fear for his health.'

'He has done better than anybody expected.'

'You and I both know he is no leader of men, no matter how acute his sense of duty. And how long has he been acting Governor now? Two months? From what I saw today, I could not say that he commands the respect of officers.'

I gazed into the fire, recalling my conversation with Ben. 'These are dangerous times, Will. Downing's mission was a failure. And whether it be criminals or spies, if our own ships are apt to be stolen with such ease, I must confess I agree with Captain Harcourt. We are gravely ill-prepared for another war.'

'You should say as much to Albemarle when we are back home.'

'Home. Yes. And I think perhaps not a moment too soon.'

August 10th

Our departure was scheduled for noon. With the developing crisis in our midst, I had not expected more than a perfunctory goodbye. But as we stepped out through the polished brass doors of Admiralty House for the last time, we were hit by a great wave of applause.

Servants and footmen were arrayed down the steps, in rows two deep, cheering as we passed. I recognised Boatswain Stearne, and a few others who had been at Lord Maynard's supper on the night he was killed. We shook hands with the officers in turn, each of them congratulating us warmly on our achievements.

At the bottom of the steps, Harcourt waited next to a grand-looking coach. Any anxieties I may have had about our safety on the journey home fell away when I saw our escort, two uniformed men armed with pistols and swords, mounted atop a pair of stallions.

Through the open door, I could see that they had even provided me with a specially upholstered seat, so that I might ride in greater comfort.

'God speed, Mr Pepys,' said the Captain, clasping my hands firmly. He hesitated for a moment, then, without quite being able to meet my eyes, he added: 'England owes you a debt, sir. As do we.'

I inclined my head, surprised to hear him compliment me so directly. Then, with a final wave to the assembled crowd, I climbed on board.

'Look at this!' exclaimed Will, opening a hamper that had been placed on the floor. Inside was an assortment of roast meats, bread, cheese, and weak ale. Plates, cutlery, and even crystal glasses had been strapped into place, ready for us to break out the feast.

'No wine, though,' I said, gloomily. 'Doctor's orders, I suppose.'

With a crafty smile, Will opened up the little leather travelling bag he had brought with him, and took out a small cask and two pewter cups.

'Medoc. Compliments of Goody Brown.'

I rubbed my hands together with glee as he poured us each a glass. 'You old dog.'

'Don't tell the quack.'

'Here's to old Sawbones Grey. May his knife stay far away from my cock.'

I took a long sip of the ruby-coloured liquid. It was a little sour, but I do not think I have ever enjoyed a drink so much in my life.

'You settled our bill at the Four Feathers?' I asked.

'Yes. Though Tamsin still refused to say more than two words to me, more's the pity.'

With our escort to lead the way, the journey out of Portsmouth was much faster than it had been coming in. In no time at all, we had reached the north gate and the driver cracked his whip over the horses. We sped along the London road, Portsmouth receding fast behind us.

Hours passed, and the wide expanses of farmland and hills gave way to forest. The trees were thick and dark, but I was not afraid. Any outlaw would shy away from the sight of two fully armed guards in the livery of His Majesty's Navy.

As we sat there, drinking the wine and picking at the food, I became possessed of a contentment I had not felt in weeks. More than once had I come close to death during our stay here, but now we were finally going home.

And yet there was much about what had transpired yesterday that sat uneasily in my mind. The Dutchman had confessed to the murders of Elias Thorne and Governor Maynard. Now, according to Ben, the missing funds were accounted for too – regardless of the clues we had found in Elias Thorne's hidden accounts book.

Are we to assume he was simply wrong about everything? The man might have been a murderer, but that does not make him a bad investigator. Indeed, his work seems nothing short of meticulous.

Suddenly, a thought struck me. The letter M carved into Elias Thorne's forehead. *Murderer*. I have no trouble believing the Dutchman capable of such a desecration. Does it therefore mean he knew Piety Blake? Was he another of her lovers?

What I cannot accept is that he stole the navy funds all by himself. The fellow is a brute, to be sure, but a theft such as that would require keenness of intellect. No. If he is involved at all, it must be as part of a wider conspiracy.

I worry that Ben has been too distracted to see for himself that all this does not add up. Harcourt was the one who found the money. Could he have placed it in the Dutchman's room himself? If so, might it also be possible that I was correct about Maynard to begin with, and the two of them were in league?

It would not be the first partnership of criminals to end in murder. It would also make the Dutchman a convenient scapegoat, given that he will already hang for his other crime. And there is one other thing that has been bothering me, over the many hours I have had to consider the events of six weeks ago in my mind.

'Will, when I was fighting with the Dutchman, just before you got there, he said something. "You will not take them away from me." What do you suppose he meant by that?'

'I have no idea. Who can say what other business the brute was mixed up in?' He went back to staring out of the window, and I realised that he was a little cupshotten. 'I shall miss Tamsin. Eyes of a princess. Breasts of a goddess. Mouth of a sailor.'

Suddenly, without warning, there was a loud *whoa* from the driver, and the coach slowed rapidly to a halt. I heard the driver calm the horses and one of the outriders dismount. Otherwise there were no sounds, save for the chirping of birds and a light wind rustling the leaves.

I leaned out of the window. For as far as I could see, a dense canopy of trees stretched in every direction on either side of the little track. We were deeper into the forest than I had thought.

'What's going on?'

'Tree down ahead of us, sir,' replied the driver, with a reassuring lack of concern. 'Won't be long. Five minutes.'

'I may take the opportunity…' said Will, pointing towards the trees. I said I'd join him, suddenly aware of how uncomfortably full my bladder had become.

We were in a small clearing, through which the track passed before widening out to a patch of more exposed ground up ahead. I relieved myself, delighted by the healthy yellow colour of my piss, then walked over to see how the guards were getting on with moving the fallen tree.

It was a young silver birch, big enough to be an obstacle, but not so much that two strong men could not shift it by hand. The two of them heaved at the thing with groans of exertion. They were already close to getting it cleared from our path.

Then one of the men looked up at me and grinned. There was something in his face that made me uneasy. An insolence beneath the deferential veneer.

'Don't you worry yourself now, sir. You sit tight and we'll be away in a—'

He froze mid-sentence. Suddenly his body arched and stiffened, then he fell forward onto the ground. I looked down with horror.

There was a knife sticking out of his back.

The second guardsman immediately drew his pistol, just as two figures stepped out from behind a nearby tree. They were dressed in simple leather jerkins with cloth masks pulled up over most of their faces. Both wore swords at their waists.

Both were women.

It was them. The outlaws from the marshes. The ones who had let us go.

The guardsman fired and one of the women flew backwards, blood spurting from her arm. Behind me, the horses whinnied in panic. The driver jumped down to stop them from bolting.

'*Take cover,*' shouted Will, and we ran behind a tree as the guardsman fired his other pistol. But the uninjured woman had already anticipated his move, pushing her wounded compatriot out of the way, just as the bullet exploded into the tree trunk and showered them with fragments of bark.

With expert speed, the guardsman started to reload his pistol, but before he could even raise the weapon again, the woman leaped to her feet and kicked it clear out of his hand.

Immediately he drew his sword. She drew hers in response, and they circled each other, neither wanting to make the first move.

'Look,' said Will, pointing into the woods. Two more masked women were approaching from the shadows, each with swords drawn.

'Behind you!' I called. The guardsman turned just for a moment, but it gave his opponent an opening and she lunged forward. He parried, and the clang of steel filled the air as their blades clashed.

The two others burst out from the wood, startling the guardsman, who narrowly avoided a swipe to his face. One ran straight over to the injured woman and started binding up her wound, while the second went for the coachman, sword pointed at his neck.

The coachman raised his hands as if to surrender, but instead threw himself down, rolled over, and pulled a pistol out of his boot. But before he could fire, there was a flash of metal, and a stream of blood arced from his forearm.

He dropped the gun with a cry of pain, right as the woman turned her sword around and brought the hilt down sharply on the back of his head.

Meanwhile, the surviving guardsman was gaining the upper hand. His opponent was skilled with the blade, but she was smaller, and her strength could not match his for sheer force. His sword cut left and right with mighty swings, dislodging her weapon from her hand. She was defenceless.

Just as he was about to go in for the kill, the woman launched herself into the air, swinging her leg around to make contact with his hand. There was a loud crack, he cried out, and his sword went flying.

She pressed her advantage, pulling a stiletto from her boot, but the guardsman was too quick for her. He grabbed her arm and twisted it sharply, forcing her to drop the knife, then he pushed her face first to the ground.

Immediately he fell on her, flipping her onto her back. She struck at his chin with her outstretched palm and his head snapped backwards, but it was not enough to dislodge him. He wrapped his hands around her neck.

The woman's bright red hair fell loose as she struggled frantically to get free. She gripped his wrists and pushed back with all her strength, eyes bulging behind her mask as she fought for breath. But it was no good. The guardsman's face twisted with rage as he pressed tighter and tighter, choking her, knowing that any moment her neck would be crushed beneath his hands.

Then a look of shock crossed his face and he began to loosen his grip. He convulsed, blood pouring from his mouth. A second later, a leather boot pushed the man forward into the dirt. Behind him stood the same woman who had just felled the coach driver, blood dripping from her sword.

We watched from our hiding place as she helped her friend to her feet. Then they turned and fixed their gaze on us. The one with the sword started walking slowly in our direction. I wanted to move, but I was frozen to the spot.

As she got closer, I realised that this woman had darker skin than the others. Her dangerous, amber-coloured eyes met mine with a look of pure defiance, as if challenging us to run just to see what would happen.

She pulled the mask down from her face and I recognised her immediately.

It was Belle.

I already knew we were underground when the hoods were pulled from our heads. After a ride of more than an hour, during which we were bound up inside a sealed coach, we had come to a halt in a stable yard.

I could hear the murmur of people and the clatter of hooves in the distance, but otherwise it was quiet. We were somewhere near a town, but that was all I knew. There was a flurry of activity as the injured women were taken away to be treated, then I heard the creak of heavy trapdoors being opened.

'Take them below.' It was Belle's voice, clear and direct.

Hands gripped our arms roughly and we were guided down a steep flight of stairs. Only when we were tied up did I hear another familiar voice.

'Take them off.'

The hoods were pulled away from our heads. It took my eyes a few seconds to adjust to the dim candlelight but I could tell that we were in some sort of cellar.

Standing directly in front of us was Charlotte de Vere. She wore a dress of dark red velvet, embroidered with a black floral pattern, and a string of white pearls around her neck. She was flanked by Belle and two other women, both of whom wore the simple clothes of servants, although they carried mean-looking cudgels.

'Did they give you any trouble?' de Vere said to Belle.

'Gentle as babes.' She raised an eyebrow at Will. 'Think this one learned his lesson last time.'

'Anne and Kitty?'

'Anne took a bullet in her arm. She won't be no good for fighting for a while but she'll live. Kitty just got a sore throat.'

De Vere rounded on her angrily. 'How did this happen? You promised me they were ready.'

Belle raised her hands in a placating gesture. 'They did well. Those men were good fighters. And we all came home.'

'And the men?'

Belle responded with that same contemptuous kissing sound she had made the first time we met. De Vere smiled.

'Good. Now go and check on the injured.'

Belle climbed the steps and went out through the trapdoor. De Vere turned to us. I raised my chin defiantly.

'Charlotte de Vere, queen of the outlaws.'

'Outlaws,' she scoffed. 'Please, Mr Pepys. We are the law.'

'Two men dead? Or was it three, with the driver?'

'Those weren't navy men. They were hired thugs. Their orders were to take you deep into the forest and kill you.'

'Nonsense. We are heroes in Portsmouth. Who would have done such a thing?'

'Harcourt, you want-witted simpleton. He has been behind this whole thing. The Governor's murder. The framing of Wolfert Jansen. Did you truly have no idea?'

She must have read the confusion on our faces, for she looked at us with a mixture of disappointment and contempt. 'You don't even know the man's name, do you?'

I opened my mouth to answer, but no words came. She was right. I had never even thought to ask. To us, he had just been the Dutchman.

'If he was so innocent, why did he try to kill us?' said Will.

'He was scared.'

'No,' I insisted. 'We caught a dangerous criminal.'

'You caught a desperate man who thought you were going to take him away from his wife and unborn child. Which you did.'

I remembered again what he had said during the fight. *You will not take them away from me.*

'Oh Lord,' I said, quietly.

Her voice became softer. 'It is the easier path, is it not? The glory of action. The splendour of achievement. It feels good to be a hero. But is it really that easy for you to let an innocent man die?'

I had nothing to say. Will filled the silence for me.

'Why would Harcourt want us dead? It makes no sense.'

'He knows that once you got back to London, and time passed, you would start to see things more clearly. Despite all appearances, you are not fools and he knows it. Albemarle knows it too. Much easier to have you out of the way, while handily shoring up some blatherskite tale about Dutch spies.'

'The Governor would never allow it,' I insisted.

'The Governor would not have to know. I hardly think he would be a difficult man to deceive, do you?'

I was about to protest the insult to Ben's character, but something made me hold my tongue. There was some truth to what she said. Ben is a decent man, but no politician. And were her accusations towards Harcourt not just giving voice to the doubts I already had?

Despite this, I continued to argue. 'I simply do not believe it. What would Harcourt have to gain?'

'That is what I want to know. But I tell you this, Mr Pepys. Wolfert Jansen did not kill John Maynard.' She pulled up a chair and sat across from me. 'On the night he died, John told me that he had discovered certain truths about his naval colleagues, and that he believed the Captain might be corrupt. We were due to meet the next day to discuss it further.'

Talking about Maynard clearly made her emotional. If nothing else, I thought, she truly believes he was innocent in all of this.

'And what do you want us to do about it, madam?'

'I want you to help me prove Wolfert's innocence. And expose Captain Harcourt while we're about it.'

'You cannot make me do anything.'

'Oh, but Mr Pepys,' she said, with something that almost sounded like regret. 'I am afraid I can.'

She held her hand out towards one of the guards, who reached into her bodice and passed her a folded piece of paper. Slowly, de Vere opened it and held it up before my face.

It was a letter, yellow and faded. It took me a moment to recognise the neat, boyish handwriting, but as I read to the end, I felt as if my blood had run cold.

I looked up at her in disbelief. She spoke softly, but with the confidence of a woman who knew exactly what power she held in her soft, white hands.

'Now will you help us, Mr Pepys?'

'What's going on, Sam?'

We were alone in a small, cramped room, sitting across from each other on truckle beds. The only light was provided by a cheap tallow candle that stank of animal fat.

I had hardly talked since de Vere had shown me the letter. My mind was still reeling with the implications. How in God's name had she obtained it?

After de Vere put away the dangerous piece of paper, she told us that we were to be given time to think things over. Then, at a signal from their mistress, the two armed guardswomen led us to the far end of the wine cellar, where they unbolted a heavy wooden door and indicated that we should go through. With only the dull, flickering candle to light our way, we could barely see for more than a few feet, but we appeared to be in some sort of tunnel. The smell of damp was overpowering. I nearly slipped on a patch of wet slime on the floor, above which grew little stalactites, glistening with water.

After a short while, we reached a row of small doors. One of them was opened and we were pushed inside, our hands still bound. At first, I thought that we were to be left in darkness, but the woman carrying the candle used it to light another that had already been placed on the ground. It cast just enough light to reveal a low, sloping roof and the two small beds.

Then the door was locked and we heard their footsteps receding. We were trapped.

'Sam? What was it?' Will said again. 'What did she show you?'

I took a long, deep breath. 'When I was a young man, I wrote some… intemperate things about the old king.'

'What do you mean, intemperate?'

'You know I was at his execution?'

'You told me. You shirked off school to see it.'`

'Shortly afterwards, I wrote a letter to my cousin Montagu, describing what I had seen. I was just a hot-headed boy then, weeks from turning sixteen. I thought I understood the world and I believed things then that… Well, what man does not regret things he said as a youth?'

'What was in the letter, Sam? You can trust me; I will not tell a soul.'

I took a moment to gather my thoughts, then I continued with my confession. 'I was a great believer in the Republican cause back then. I truly thought Cromwell had come to deliver us from the evils of wealth and privilege. And I wrote these thoughts down in a letter.'

'Sam, a lot of people felt that way back then. The king issued pardons on his return to those who took the oath of loyalty, you know that.'

'It is the strength of the letter that is the problem. I wrote of how glad I was that the hated tyrant was dead. I praised the Lord Protector for slaying the kingly despot. I pledged my soul to the Republican cause and beseeched God that one day soon…'

'Go on?'

'One day soon, Charles, his fugitive son, would be caught and be put to the sword like the filthy dog he was.'

Will blanched. 'Oh God. Does anybody else know about this?'

'Sir George Downing knew of my Republican beliefs when he took me into his employ. We both worked under Lord Cromwell then of course, so that hardly counted against me. But Downing was ever the skilled politician, always seeing which way the wind was blowing. And he liked to know people's secrets. He used to say that knowledge was the greatest weapon of all.'

'Did Downing see the letter?'

'No. In truth, I had forgotten about it myself. I assumed it lost or burned by Montagu, so much time has passed. No, Downing played a more subtle game than that. He teased my sympathies out of me, bit by bit, in conversation, as if we were friends. Except the real confidences always came from me, never him. Sometimes he would get me drunk, have me confess the worst of it. All of this he stored up as if it were ammunition, to be used at a later date should the tide turn. And turn it did. When the King returned, and pardons were issued, I took the oath just like everyone else. And with joy in my heart, too. Any allegiance I had had to the Republic had long since died. But Downing made sure there was just enough doubt hanging over me. I was questioned about my loyalties, and believed, as Downing knew I would be. But he also knew how badly it would go for me if proof were ever to emerge that my old beliefs had been more… emphatic than I was prepared to admit.'

'So he blackmailed you.'

I shrugged, wearily. 'He would make me turn a blind eye to his petty corruption. A lost accounting book here, a purse full of gold there. All to line his pockets. He knew I could never talk.'

'But wait – if Downing never had the letter, how did Charlotte de Vere get it?'

'I wish I knew. When Montagu died, his wife sent me a box of our correspondence. Keepsakes, mostly. I never really found the time to go through them. It may have been in there. But as to how it then came into her possession?' I sighed wearily. 'Dear God, if only I had known…'

'I still think Downing could be mixed up in this.'

'Perhaps. But one way or another, de Vere knows how damaging it would be if that letter ever came to light. I have risen in the world since then, with much to lose should I fall. By God's mercy, it is a long time since my path has crossed with Downing, but I have long thought there were others at court who still look at me askance. I wonder how often Sir George once whispered in their ears that I should not be trusted? I have no doubt he would give up my secrets in an instant, should the worst happen.'

'But you have many friends at court. They would help you.'

'Perhaps. On the other hand, if the letter came to the attention of the King, what do you suppose he would call it then?'

Will spoke the word in barely more than a whisper.

'Treason.'

After another hour or so, the candle had burned down almost to nothing.

We had both lain back on our beds, but with our hands tied, it was impossible to get comfortable.

Will eventually broke the silence. 'Tell you what, though. That housemaid fights like a tiger.'

I turned to him. He grinned at me sheepishly.

'It was her, wasn't it?' I said. 'The reason you came back with so many bruises that day?'

'I could have beaten her,' he protested. 'She took me by surprise.'

'What happened?'

'Before I even knew she was there, she had me pinned up against a wall, demanding to know why I was going around asking people about Charlotte de Vere. Told me to mind my own business or it would go badly for me.'

I smiled. 'Will Hewer, did you really keep that from me just because you did not want to admit that you had been beaten by a girl?'

He opened his mouth to object, when suddenly we heard footsteps. A few seconds later, they stopped outside our door. Anxiously we waited as the key turned in the lock and the door creaked open.

One of the women who had escorted us here stood in the entrance, regarding us with the cold detachment of a gaoler. She held a lamp in one hand and her cudgel in the other.

'Mistress de Vere requests your company at dinner,' she said. I recognised her accent as that of a Londoner.

We started to manoeuvre ourselves off the beds, but she pointed her cudgel straight at me.

'Just you. We'll fetch a bowl of soup for the boy.'

I started to object, but Will shuffled back onto the bed with a sigh.

'It is alright, Sam. I am not hungry anyway.'

'At least untie him,' I protested.

The girl hesitated for a moment, then rested the lamp on the bedpost and pulled out a knife. Still gripping the cudgel in her other hand, she swiftly cut away his bonds and stepped back, pushing me out into the corridor and closing the door.

'Have a pleasant evening,' Will called after us.

The girl took me back along the tunnel and through the wine cellar. We climbed the stairs through the open trapdoor and into the yard. It was dusk by now and the sunset had turned the sky a vivid shade of pink. In the evening light, I suddenly had the strangest feeling that I had seen this pale young woman somewhere before.

'This way,' she said brusquely, and led me through an archway onto a large, well-maintained lawn. Ahead of us was the rear of a familiar grand brick building.

Dione House. So we were back in Portsmouth.

We found Charlotte de Vere standing on the rear terrace looking out across the grounds. She had changed into an elegant dress made of grey silk, cut low, with a string of pearls around her neck. The skirt was slashed with gold, which shimmered brightly in the evening sun.

As we approached, I thought once again how powerful this woman looked. Beautiful, yes, but there was more to it than that. She had a presence that is simply impossible to ignore. This was her world and she commanded it absolutely.

She looked up as we approached. 'Ah, Mr Pepys. It is a beautiful sunset, is it not?'

'Why must Mr Hewer be left alone in that pit?' I shot back, in no mood to play games.

To my surprise, she seemed genuinely regretful.

'I am sorry that I did not invite your friend. But I thought it was time you and I had the chance to talk – alone. Oh, but you are still bound. Jane?'

The girl sliced through my bonds, then curtseyed and went inside, leaving me alone with her mistress. I watched her go, again filled with the oddest notion that it was not the first time we had met.

De Vere must have read my confusion, for she smiled wryly. 'Is something the matter, Mr Pepys?'

'It is nothing. What is this place, madam?'

'A refuge. A haven.'

'A den of criminals, more like.'

'There speaks one who has never been an outsider.' Her attention was drawn by something across the lawn and she started to applaud. 'Excellent, Kitty. Well done.'

I followed where she was looking and saw there was a girl standing about a hundred yards away from us. I could just make out a knife protruding from a target that had been affixed to a tree, some distance away from her. From her bright red hair, I recognised her as the girl who had almost been strangled in the woods.

'Fifty yards, mistress,' she called back, as proud as if she had been showing off a dance step.

'Good, good,' shouted de Vere, then turned back to me. 'I am proud of Kitty. She is such a clever girl, and has overcome much.'

'Her skills as a marksman are impressive. Though I cannot think what good such a thing would do a lady of breeding.'

'Other than saving your life, you mean? Shall we go inside?'

She led me through an open door. A motto had been carved into the lintel stone: *Feminae Pares Omnibus*. I translated the phrase in my mind. *Women are equal to everything.*

We walked along a darkening corridor and entered the dining room. Jane was lighting candelabra that had been placed on a large, polished oak table. Thin fingers of blue smoke rose from the freshly lit fire, dancing beneath the intricately plastered ceiling.

Just two places had been set for dinner, one at the head of the table, and one to its side. I could guess which I was expected to take. As we sat down, I noticed the large portrait above the fireplace, its gilt frame shining against the dark green walls. I recognised the face. It was Edmund de Vere, although his hair was a good deal greyer than when I had met him, a decade ago.

'Tell me, madam. Did you live such a wicked existence while your husband was still alive?'

She let out a sudden peal of laughter, stifling it with a hand to her mouth. 'Forgive me, Mr Pepys. I was not expecting to find your attitude to be quite so… antediluvian. To answer your question, I do not keep his picture out of fondness and I care not what he would have thought. You will take some wine?'

Jane came forward to fill our glasses from a crystal jug. The wine was an unusual pink colour. I took a sip and spluttered, finding it much stronger than expected.

'I trust Rhenish is to your taste?'

'Fine,' I replied curtly.

'Now, Mr Pepys, I would like to ask—'

'Madam, I will say nothing until you tell me how you came to be in possession of that letter.'

She considered for a moment. Then she turned to Jane and nodded. The girl put down the jug on a side table and looked at me with an impertinent smile on her thin, pale face.

'Posy for your sweetheart, sir?'

For a moment, I had no idea what she was talking about. Then a series of images flashed through my mind. Seething Lane. A painfully thin girl. Something hidden in her basket.

'The lavender seller?' I gasped.

Jane raised an eyebrow triumphantly, then curtsied to her mistress and left us alone. De Vere took another sip of wine.

'Jane lost both her parents in the Great Fire. At twelve, she became the sole provider for two young brothers. Unable to find work in service, she was left with two options, prostitution or larceny. So she became a thief. Clever girl.'

'How did you find her?'

'Sometimes we are fortunate in that the good ones find us. Sadly, God saw fit to take Jane's brothers. She would likely have followed, were it not for certain associates of mine who sent her to me. She had skills we could use.'

'But how in God's name did she know about the letter? It was under lock and key in my study, known to nobody but me.'

'That was a happy accident. When John told me that you were being sent here, I had some enquiries made. Discreetly, of course. We felt that you could be a useful ally, so I sent Jane to obtain a little… collateral, shall we say? I had no idea that her work would prove quite so fruitful.'

I struggled to contain my anger. 'You spied on me, broke into my house, and now you threaten my very livelihood – perhaps even my life? And you presume to take offence when I call you an outlaw? Madam, I fear I have much harsher words than that for what you really are.'

I expected this to antagonise her, but instead she placed her hands calmly on the table.

'I do not expect you to understand this, Mr Pepys, but the law is an instrument of men. As women alone, we are all but powerless. Even more so, without means such as those I am fortunate to possess. But together—'

She was interrupted as two young women entered, carrying dishes of bread, cheese and steaming hot fish. As they were set before us, I caught the sweet scents of marjoram and juniper, and my stomach began to growl.

'I was not sure if you had eaten dinner before we rescued you. So I took the precaution of ordering a large supper.'

The women were in their early twenties. One of them was Kitty. Up close, I could see that there were angry red marks around her neck, but otherwise she looked as delicate and beautiful as a courtesan, with green eyes and pale skin. It was hard to imagine she was capable of such ferocity as I witnessed during the fight in the woods.

'Stay a moment, girls, will you?' De Vere turned back to me. 'Kitty was married to a gentleman at the age of nineteen. He was a cruel man who would beat her savagely if she displeased him. She went to the law, but it was her word against his, and I do not need to tell you how that went for her. So she turned to me and I… took care of the situation. Meanwhile, Cecily here escaped from a brothel on Cheapside, where she was all but a prisoner to debt, used by as many as thirty men in a day. Never again will she have to sell her body just to survive.' She paused to let this sink in. 'Do you frequent whores, Mr Pepys? Why, perhaps you have already met her too?'

I found myself unable to look either of the women in the eye. Aside from their unusually toned physiques, both looked exactly as other women to me. I would never have guessed the torments they had endured.

'I am… sorry for both of you.'

De Vere dismissed them and started serving herself from the dishes in front of us. She indicated that I should do the same.

'All of my girls are like Kitty, or Cecily, or Jane. The abused and outcast. But together we are strong. And we have a common purpose, to take justice from a world that gives us none. That is the power of a sisterhood.'

I began to eat my fish, but was troubled by an ache in my stomach.

'Is there something wrong with the sturgeon?' asked de Vere.

'Just a cramp. After enduring such horrors as I did only weeks ago, the ordeal of today has taken its toll.'

'The washerwoman who bore Wolfert Jansen's child was forced to return to her backbreaking work the day after giving birth. Does that not bother you?'

I put down a morsel of fish. Suddenly I did not feel like eating.

'Alice Scovell,' I said, quietly.

'And now her husband will hang and she will have to raise her son alone.'

'Madam, I grow weary of your judgements. I am not a bad man.'

She raised an eyebrow. 'I did not realise we were talking about you.'

'Kidnap. Blackmail. Murder. I call you a hypocrite.'

'And yet here you are, a loyal servant of the crown that in your youth you so despised.'

'I lived through those years, madam. I saw the disorder, the chaos, that resulted from that unhappy time. Are you even old enough to remember the war?'

'I lived through the siege of Chester. I too saw many terrible things. Fighting. Starvation. I joined a band of smugglers who would go on raids to bring food in from outside the city. I was ten.' She inclined her head. 'Were your masters angry when you took the day off school to watch the King die?'

I banged the table. 'For pity's sake, silence, woman.'

De Vere said nothing. A few moments later, I heard footsteps, then Kitty's head appeared around the door.

'Mistress?'

'It is alright, Kitty. Mr Pepys is just explaining war to me.'

Kitty shot me a warning look. 'We shall be outside if you need us.'

I forced myself to be calm. 'The return of His Majesty brought order. And how can there be justice without order?'

She fixed me with her deep brown eyes. 'It is like I said, sir. That depends on whose justice you mean.'

I said nothing for a long time. She continued to watch me, resting her chin on her hand. When she next spoke, her voice was quiet and gentle. 'I do not think you are a bad man, Mr Pepys.'

'And what of Maynard? Was he mixed up in all this?'

She smiled with sadness and longing. 'John was an enlightened man who saw the possibility of a better future and was willing to risk his life to work for it.'

And then it hit me. The realisation that had been in front of my eyes since the first time I met the Governor on board the *Prince Rupert*. 'He was a Republican, wasn't he? And whatever strange ideas about justice you cleave to, you were useful to each other's causes. Is that not how it was?'

She took another sip of wine, but did not look away. 'John had no wish to see war return to England. Whatever he believed in his heart, he was no traitor to the King. I do not know the nature of this plot he claimed to have uncovered, but I do know he was murdered for that knowledge. Of that I am certain.'

I felt a sense of great conflict at that moment. I no longer thought the woman sitting before me was mad, although I believed her to be gripped by a longing for power in ways that went against the very natural order of the world. Whether or not she would kill us if I refused to cooperate, I could not say. But I knew she was capable of doing so.

On the other hand, I could no longer deny the truth about the Dutchman. The evidence against him was clearly fabricated. And if we did nothing, we were condemning the man to certain death.

'My wife... She will expect me back.'

'I can get word to her that you are delayed, but safe.'

'I would like to send a message to Governor Arden too, to tell him what has happened.'

'That I cannot agree to.'

'Why not? You don't think he is involved too?'

'Perhaps. Perhaps not. But for now, the risk is too great. Secrecy is a powerful weapon.'

'And once this is done, after we have somehow proved this man's innocence, you will let us go back to London?'

'I give you my word.'

I looked again into her eyes, watching the fire reflected in them. 'Then I will help you. On one more condition. We are not treated as prisoners. I will give you my oath that we shall not leave, and so will Mr Hewer. But if we do this, we do it as free men.'

She considered for a moment, then raised her glass.

'Welcome to the Hidden League.'

August 11th

'Gaoler Pitt?'

I handed the scroll to the wiry young man with thin, greasy hair, who regarded it suspiciously. Evidently, he was not expecting visitors on the Lord's Day.

After allowing me to hold out the scroll for an awkwardly long time, the boy placed the pipe he was carrying in his mouth and took the document from me. I did my best to maintain an imperious air as he unrolled it and scanned the writing, but in truth I was far from convinced this was going to work.

I was standing next to Will at the entrance to Portsmouth gaol. After discussing many potential plans of action to gain entry, legally or otherwise, we opted for a simple deception. For the time being, I was Sir Thomas Grant, His Majesty's Inspector of Prisons – a title that did not exist, although I was hoping that the boy would not know that.

I was also gambling that he could not read.

'Mr Pitt's in his office,' he mumbled. 'This way, gentlemen.'

Will leaned in close as we followed him inside. 'What was that?'

'Bill of sale. Ten casks of claret and a Parmesan cheese.'

We were led into an office containing a wooden desk and a small fireplace. Behind the desk sat a hunched, thick-necked man, chewing on a greasy hunk of meat. In front of him was a stack of pewter plates, caked with the dried remains of several meals, and a half-drunk tankard of ale. A small window cast sunbeams through the cheap sot-weed smoke that hung heavily in the air.

The gaoler looked up as we entered, evidently startled to see us.

'King's men,' said the boy, sliding down onto a wooden stool next to the unlit fire.

'Mr Pitt, I presume?' I said, haughtily.

'Gentlemen. To what do I owe this pleasure?' He made the words sound like an insult.

'We wish to see Wolfert Jansen. Take us to him.'

He snorted a great lump of phlegm and spat it out on the ground. 'Ah, the Dutchie. Cobb, take them to him.'

Cobb sighed, rising again from his stool as if it were the greatest imposition. But before he could lead us away, I held up my hand.

'Just a moment, Cobb. First, Mr Pitt, I would see your admissions book.'

The gaoler shrugged insolently. 'Why?'

'Never mind why, man, I wish to see it and I will do so now.'

Glowering, he opened a drawer in his desk and took out a thick sheaf of cheap paper, bound with black leather. He held it up, but kept it far enough from my reach that I was forced to lean forward and snatch it from him. His breath stank of meat and ale.

I flicked backwards through the pages of untidy scrawl until I reached the date of June 17th. There was just one entry, which read:

Jansen, Wolfert. Sailor (Dutch). Suspected of murdering His Lordship Govn'r Maynard & others.

I turned back a page further and ran my finger down the entries, pausing at June 5th. There were eleven prisoners admitted on that date, mostly for petty crimes such as theft and larceny. I alighted on the final entry of the day, which read simply:

Wilkin, Thomas. Brawling.

'This man, Thomas Wilkin,' I said, pointing at the entry. 'Do you remember him?'

Pitt took the book from me, staring at it as if trying to conjure an image from the page. 'Aye, I remember him. The cripple. We've seen a lot of him around here lately.'

'Do you recall what time of day he was released?'

'Aye, I do. First light. Nightwatchman only brung him in so he could cool his heels and we was full enough as it was, so I chucked him out at dawn.'

'So you are certain he was here all night?'

'Unless he can walk through walls, yes I am. What's all this about anyways?'

'Another matter. We will see the prisoner now.'

Cobb reluctantly led us out to a heavy wooden door and unlocked it from a set of keys tied to his belt. Beyond was a narrow spiral staircase. I could smell the cells immediately; the wave of ordure from below was almost enough to make me gag.

As we descended to the lower level, I reflected on what we had just learned. Despite our natural sympathies towards the man, I had until now believed Tom Wilkin to be the most likely suspect in the murder of Elias Thorne. But it appeared he had the perfect alibi.

On the other hand, we had already established that the man who killed Thorne and whoever mutilated the corpse were not necessarily one and the same person. Could Tom have found the body, then committed such an horrific act in a moment of passion? I believe that he could. In either case, it meant that whoever killed Thorne was still out there.

We emerged from the stairs into an underground chamber with a vaulted stone ceiling. It was obviously much older than the upper level, and I wondered if this had once been the cellar to some long-forgotten building. Along one side of the room, a series of iron bars had been set into stone archways to form cells.

The only illumination came from tiny skylights, set high up into the walls. They were far too small to climb through, but wide enough to make the cells effectively open to the elements. I dreaded to think how the poor wretches down here must have fared on the night of the great storm, six weeks ago.

The night we caught Wolfert Jansen.

'Dutchie's over there,' Cobb said in a disinterested tone, pointing with his chin towards the far end of the room. He stretched himself out on a rickety chair and continued to suck on his pipe.

We made our way in the direction Cobb had indicated. Suddenly, a rat darted across my boots. I kicked out and yelped with surprise, causing several of the prisoners to laugh. I could not see well in the gloomy light, but I judged that there were as many as five or six people to each cell.

As we passed one of the cells, I noticed a huddled shape leaning motionless against the bars. I looked closer and saw that it was a woman. She was panting and sweating profusely, her face covered in oozing sores. The wretched creature looked up at me with pleading eyes and her mouth began to move, but she was too weak to form words.

Wolfert Jansen lay asleep on the hard stone floor of the furthest cell. The sun was shining directly through the little window above, encircling him with a halo of light. Behind him, two other inmates were engrossed in a game of dice.

Jansen was much thinner than when we saw him last. His filthy clothes were the same ones he was wearing on the day he was arrested. His hair was matted with dried blood and dirt, and his skin looked pallid and waxy, save for the livid bruises on his cheek and jaw.

I had been nervous about meeting Jansen again, but seeing him like this caused me to feel nothing but shame.

Will cleared his throat and Jansen's cellmates looked up from their game of dice. 'Wake him, would you?'

One of them leaned over and shoved Jansen in the back. The Dutchman opened his eyes and frowned.

'Wolfert?' I said. 'Do you know who we are?'

Jansen got to his feet and hobbled unsteadily to the bars. Leaning forward, he stared with a dazed expression, then his eyes widened in recognition and he spat in my face.

I took out a handkerchief and wiped myself clean. 'We are here to help you, sir.'

'I have nothing to say to you.'

He turned and sat back down on the ground, turning his back to us.

'We are telling you the truth. We mean you no harm. We know what happened between us was a misunderstanding. And we also know you did not kill Maynard, or Elias Thorne.'

'I have no need of your help.'

'We are here for Alice,' said Will.

Suddenly he was animated. 'You have seen Alice? How does she fare?'

'I believe she is well, yes, although anxious for your safe return,' I said.

'And the child? Has she had our child?'

He does not know, I thought. Dear God, they hadn't even allowed him that.

'Yes. It is a boy. You are a father.'

'God be praised.' Tears welled from his eyes and he began to pray.

Seeing this sudden outpouring of emotion from the man I had once thought of as a vicious killer caused a rush of guilt within me. I thought of Alice Scovell, arguing with the guardsman on the quayside, then running away with their infant child in her arms. Had she been pleading for an audience with the Governor?

'She has not been to see you?' asked Will.

'I have been allowed no visitors, except you. And the navy men.'

My eyes were drawn to the bruises on his face. 'We are going to help get you out of here any way we can. And we are truly sorry for our part in your trouble.'

'My son, he is strong? He feeds?'

'I am sorry, I have no more information for you. But I will find out what I can. And I will try and ensure Alice and the boy are allowed in to see you for herself.'

Jansen put his head in his hands and took a deep breath. 'Thank you, sir,' he said at last. 'In God's name, I just want to be there with them.'

'I understand. But I must be straight with you. It will not be easy to prove your innocence. In the eyes of the law, the case against you is settled. You confessed, did you not?'

'Under irons a man will say anything. That does not make it true.'

'You were tortured?' asked Will.

Wolfert stayed silent. I wondered if he was ashamed.

Will continued, 'Torture is illegal in England, Wolfert. If they did that to you, it may help your case.'

I placed my hand gently on Will's arm to silence him. I knew he was only trying to lift the man's spirits, but I thought it unwise to give him false hope.

'Mr Hewer is right. But I fear it will do us little good in the circumstances. As you know, the situation between our two countries means that it is politically convenient that you should be found guilty. Your chances are poor.'

Jansen's shoulders sagged. It was dreadful to see a man with so much reason to live so devoid of hope.

'How did you come to be in Portsmouth?' asked Will.

'I… needed to get away.'

Something in his tone warned us not to pry any further.

Deciding it was best not to press the matter, for the time being at least, I asked him how he came to meet Alice. He told us that he had been employed as a carpenter aboard the *Gelderland,* a Dutch ship that had stopped briefly in Portsmouth a year ago, to effect repairs.

Whilst here, he had met and fallen in love with a young laundress – Alice Scovell. He soon got her with child and the two of them married hastily. He deserted his ship and had been living in hiding with her ever since. To aid in the deception, she had continued to use her maiden name to strangers.

In order to supplement Alice's meagre income from the laundry, Jansen had taken whatever work he could. He had spent a few weeks as a stable hand, then managed to get himself taken on as a labourer for the new fortification works. Recently, however, the upturn in anti-Dutch sentiment had made it impossible for him to keep steady employment. Besides, he had to keep his head down, in case his old ship should ever return to port and enquiries be made as to his whereabouts.

He told us he was worried about how Alice was making ends meet and I chose not to tell him that she had returned to work just a day after giving birth. When I brought up the subject of the money hidden in his room, Jansen laughed bitterly.

'Do they think I am a fool? If I had money like that hidden away, would we be living in such a way as we do?'

I raised my hand and placed it gently on the bars between us, as if somehow that could lessen the blow of what I was about to say.

'Wolfert… We will continue to fight for you. But if the worst should happen, what are your wishes when it comes to Alice and your child? Do you have family to whom we should send word?'

'No family,' he said uneasily.

'No cousins? Nobody who may be able to—'

Suddenly, he reached his hand through the bars and gripped my arm. Even in a weakened state, he was surprisingly strong. 'I beg you, sir. For Alice's sake. Nobody who knew me in Holland can know of her. Promise me.'

'Of course; you have my word. But why? You think Alice is in danger?'

He let go of me and ran his hand through his filthy hair. 'Not now. But if certain people in my homeland learned I had married and she was my wife, I fear she could be.'

'I know it is hard for you to trust us, and with good reason. But if Alice needs protection, it will help us if we know more. So tell us. What made you leave Holland? The truth now.'

His eyes met mine, steady and appraising. I leaned in closer, lowering my voice so that there was no chance we could be overheard.

'I swear to you, upon my life, all we want to do is help.'

For a long while, I thought he was going to say nothing. Then at last he seemed to make a decision to trust us.

'I had to leave because they said I was a traitor.'

'What do you mean? Who did?' said Will.

'You had your civil war, did you not, sir? It is not just Englishmen who would fight for liberty.'

'Be careful what you say in here,' I whispered.

'Or what? English justice has already done its work on me.'

'But your country is already a Republic,' said Will. 'Are you saying you were a rebel for the Royalist cause?'

He scoffed. 'It is a Republic only in name. What man has ever been *stadtholder* unless he is a prince of the House of Orange first? No, sir, I fight for the cause of a true Republic, one in which the common man may have a say in how he is governed.'

'But you were in the navy, were you not?' I said.

'I was. The company of rebels I was part of, they were discovered. Many were arrested. But one of my comrades managed to get word to me that the militia was coming. So I fled.'

'A naval vessel hardly seems a good hiding place for a man wanted for treason.'

'It was good fortune that saved me. And God's mercy. I was wasting away the day in a tavern, like the sinner I am. There I heard that the carpenter aboard the *Gelderland* had been taken sick, and the ship was due to leave port that afternoon. So when the message reached me, I went directly to the ship and volunteered myself.'

'Clever,' said Will.

'I take no pride in my deception, sir. If I had not escaped, I would have hanged.' He let out a bitter laugh. 'It seems fate has caught up with me one way or the other.'

'It is not for me to judge a man for his beliefs,' I said, softly. 'That is of no consequence. All I care about is that you are innocent of these crimes and we shall do what we can to save you.'

He looked up at me. I wondered if I could see resentment in those sad eyes, or whether it was merely my own guilt reflected back at me. After all, if it were not for me, he would still be free.

'We will do what we can for you, Wolfert. There is hope.'

'If they find me guilty, I hang. If they send me home, I hang. It is not hope I need, sir. It is a miracle.'

We said our goodbyes with a pledge to return. Then, as we left, I saw the sick woman once again, and felt a rush of anger. Will clearly felt the same. We marched over to Cobb, who was taking a nap in his chair. Will kicked him in the shin and he woke with an affronted cry.

'Hey, what—'

Before Cobb could even get the words out, Will dragged him to his feet and pinned him up against the wall by the throat. His pipe fell and shattered to pieces on the floor as he struggled to break free, but Will was too strong. Behind us, some of the prisoners began cheering. 'Do him! Go on, kill the bastard.'

'Will, no,' I said, firmly. 'He is not the one we want.'

Will stared at him, teeth clenched with rage. Then he dropped the boy to the ground and we hurried up the stairs, leaving the hellish place behind us.

We emerged from the gaol and made our way back up the lane. Waiting on the corner was an elegant black coach trimmed with gold. Keeping watch for anybody who might recognise us, I opened the door and we ducked inside.

'Well?'

Charlotte de Vere was seated beside the window next to Belle. Kitty sat opposite. She shuffled up on the bench, allowing us to squeeze in next to her.

'We saw Jansen,' I replied. 'He has been roughly treated but fares well enough under the circumstances.'

'Did he give you anything to go on?'

'The story of how he came to be in England was of some interest, but in truth I cannot see how it helps us. He is concerned for the safety of Alice. Did you manage to see her?'

'No. The laundry was closed and the gates locked. But it is Sunday. We shall try tomorrow.'

'By God, they are cruel men,' I said, anger once again swelling within me. 'Did you know they had not even told Wolfert he—'

'Get down,' de Vere hissed, suddenly catching sight of something outside.

Will and I hastily ducked onto the floor, but it was impossible in the cramped space to get completely out of sight of the window. De Vere leaned forward as far as she could to block us from view, but we were still not hidden enough.

Kitty gave Belle a look of silent entreaty, to which she responded with a wry shrug that suggested she had no intention of helping. The younger girl stretched her legs out awkwardly, lending us as much cover as she could with her voluminous skirts, just as we heard the sound of approaching footsteps.

'Captain Harcourt,' said de Vere, brightly. 'What a pleasure to see you.'

'Mistress de Vere. Ladies. I trust you are well?'

I peered from beneath the fabric of Kitty's skirts to see the tip of Harcourt's head. He was obviously trying to see what was going on.

'Quite well, Captain. What news of the Dutch affair?'

'None to speak of, mistress, and all the better for it. But I fear I have sad news to impart on another matter.'

'Oh?'

'Two of my men and a coach driver were attacked and killed in the forest, en route to London. Ambushed by outlaws.'

'My God! Captain, this is most distressing news.'

'Alas, that is not all. You will remember our visitors, Mr Pepys and Mr Hewer?'

'How could I forget them?'

'I am most sorry to say that they were in the coach at the time.'

She gasped. 'Heaven preserve us. Are they safe?'

'I… do not know, madam. For now, I fear they are missing, presumed dead.'

'Those poor men! What times are these, that the innocent are preyed upon while the wicked walk freely among us?'

'Indeed. But rest assured, we shall see these outlaws hang.'

'I have no doubt of it, Captain.'

Harcourt cleared his throat. A hint of suggestiveness entered his tone. 'I wonder, madam… Perhaps you would do me the honour of having dinner with me soon?'

'I… would like that very much, Captain.'

'Good. We shall arrange it.'

'I look forward to it.'

There was an awkward pause. I guessed Harcourt was once again trying to see into the coach. Then at last he took his leave.

De Vere pulled the curtain shut and slumped backwards with a sigh. Belle knocked hard on the roof to indicate that it was time to go. As the coach pulled away, Kitty shuffled awkwardly back to her seat and Will and I picked ourselves up off the ground.

'I would choose death before I had dinner with Captain Harcourt,' said de Vere.

Belle grinned. 'Did you see how he wanted to know what you were up to in here? Probably thought you were entertaining some gentleman in line with your scandalous reputation.'

De Vere placed a hand on her arm. 'Death before dinner.'

The coach made its way through the busy streets towards Dione House. After a little while, Will turned to me and spoke in a low voice.

'Did Harcourt not seem a little too keen to tell that story? To spread word that we were probably dead?'

'Yes. I believe he did.'

'Why do you suppose that is?'

I thought about it for a moment. 'What if he is looking for a way to turn our disappearance to his advantage? He is bound to have people out looking for us. He must hope he can find and dispatch us before we can make it back to London – and tell Ben what happened. But in the meantime…'

'A pair of dead heroes would be most convenient for him.'

'Exactly. How I wish we could get word to Ben. You and I need to keep our heads down if we are to stay undetected. I fear Portsmouth may be even more dangerous for us than we thought.'

De Vere paced anxiously up and down the drawing room. 'I am not happy with this. I am not happy at all.'

'Today was a waste of time,' said Belle. She was sitting on a chair, smoking a long clay pipe. 'All that talk and what have we gained? Nothing.'

'She is right,' I said. 'We have managed little other than to confirm what we already knew.'

'Why don't you just write to Albemarle?' asked Will. 'Tell him the truth about what's happening. Have Harcourt arrested.'

'On what evidence? I may have the ear of the duke, but it would be our word against his. No doubt backed up to a man by his fellow officers.'

De Vere took a seat next to the fire and stared into the flames, her expression grim and determined. 'Pepys is right. Your escape will have made him nervous. Play your hand too soon and he will stop at nothing to finish what he started. Secrecy is our weapon. We find proof first.'

'We have little time. If they intend to make Wolfert a scapegoat, it will not be long before he is put on trial.'

Belle blew out a mouthful of smoke. 'So we have nothing. Like I said, waste of time.'

De Vere slapped her leg with frustration. 'Damn it. There must be something we are missing. If only time were not so short.'

There was silence. She was right; any hopes we had had that questioning Wolfert could lead to an easy solution had quickly been dashed. Alice Scovell might yet provide us with new information, but it would be foolish to expect much from her. If the girl would even talk to us after what we had done...

It was Belle who broke the silence. 'Reckon we're going about this the wrong way.'

'What do you mean?' replied de Vere. 'What other way is there?'

'Rich folk talk around their staff, as if the likes of us don't have ears. But ask in the right places and maybe you'd learn a thing or two.'

'I asked around in the taverns but gleaned little of use,' said Will.

'Aye, most folk got enough sense to see a rum cully like you coming.'

'Well then, where do you suggest, madam?'

Belle exhaled a cloud of smoke. 'Most Sunday nights there's a cock fight at the Old Ring o' Bells, over by Guy's Bulwark. Reckon we might have better luck there.'

'Is that not dangerous?' I asked.

She smiled. 'Aye.'

'A fine idea, Belle,' said de Vere. 'There could be value in listening to gossip.'

Will turned to me. 'What do you think?'

'You ain't coming, boy,' Belle scoffed.

'I can handle myself in a fight.'

'Aye, I can tell by all them scars on your pretty face.'

I could not help but smile as Will instinctively raised a hand to his smooth and unmarked cheeks.

'Stop torturing the puppy, Belle,' said de Vere. 'Mr Pepys and Mr Hewer know more about the whys and wherefores of the navy than you or I. They will be useful.'

'Suit your own selves. But if you're coming, keep your heads down. And you'll need plainer clothes. Not many fine gentlemen to be found where we're going.'

I drew my arms around my chest as we picked our way through the warren of dark and stinking back alleys. It was late and we were heading to the far end of the docks.

Will and I were dressed in the poorest clothes that could be found for us. Torn shirts and old jerkins did little to keep out the chill winds blowing in off the sea.

But it was not only with cold that I shivered.

Ghostly faces followed our progress from the shadows, rough men stinking of gin and grog with danger in their eyes. Emaciated figures lay sprawled out on the ground in puddles of their own piss and vomit. We kept close to Belle, who strode ahead, undaunted. I was reassured by the knife and wheel-lock pistol I knew she had concealed underneath her long black leather coat.

I breathed a sigh of relief as finally we emerged onto the quayside, directly opposite the imposing edifice of Guy's Bulwark. The century-old fortification jutted out to sea, waves crashing against its solid stone walls. I could just make out the figure of a lone watchman patrolling the battlements.

A short distance away stood an inn. Its uneven timbers and crumbling plaster gave it the appearance of being very old, although the sea no doubt took quite a toll on the dirty little building. The glow of firelight bled weakly through its filthy windows, while a crudely-painted sign creaked back and forth in the breeze.

This was it. The Old Ring o' Bells.

As we got closer to the entrance, I could hear the sounds of rough laughter and carousing from within. Belle pounded on the door. The top half swung open to reveal a bald, thick-set man of about sixty, fumbling with a pipe. He had the wide neck and leathery skin of an old mariner. Half of one ear was missing and a heavy gold ring hung from the distended lobe of the other.

He carried on lighting his pipe, not bothering to look up. 'Password?'

'The password is: how's about you pay me the money you owe, you cheating dog?'

I tensed, but the old sailor looked up at her and laughed.

'Belle, you black devil. How do you fare?'

'All the worse for seeing your ugly face,' she said, with what I took to be affection. 'How goes trade?'

'Very fine. There is profit in this game, I tell you.'

'Never thought I'd see the day old Silken Jack got himself an honest living.'

He laughed again, a throaty hack that swiftly became a cough. 'Never said nothing about honesty, now did I? You here for the fight, then?'

'No, but I'd have a few minutes of your time.'

'Oh?'

'I want information. Reckon you're the man to ask.'

'Like that is it, eh? Aye, well, stand me an ounce of sot-weed and I'll sit with you awhile.'

He opened the door, allowing us to pass into the dark taproom. The place stank of ale and sweat. Three long benches ran the length of the room, packed with rough-looking men, drinking and gambling.

'There,' said Will, pointing to some spare places at the far end of the nearest bench. We were about halfway there when the trouble started.

'Here, lads. Want to split some cunny?'

There was a roar of laughter as a man rose from the bench and stepped into our path. He was well over six feet tall, with a broken nose and a scar down one side of his face.

'How much then?' he leered, towering over Belle. He placed an enormous hand on her arse, pulling her body close to his.

What happened next was so fast that I barely had time to react. Belle grabbed his wrist, twisting it around sharply. He lost his balance, raising the other arm to break his fall as he slammed into the bench. Before he could turn around, there was a blur of metal and his hand was impaled to the wood.

The man looked down at the quivering blade sticking out of his hand, then let out an agonised scream. Two of his drinking companions got to their feet but Belle already had her pistol trained on them.

'Come on then, which one of you's man enough to go first?'

The men slowly raised their hands and sat back down on the bench. Belle retrieved her knife, leaving the injured man clutching his bleeding hand.

Will and I stared at each other, incredulous.

As we approached the spare seats, Belle hailed a passing potboy.

'Ale, lad. And quick.'

He scurried away. Belle took out her pipe and tobacco.

The rhythmic pounding of a drum started nearby. I looked around and saw that some men had picked up a bodhran and fiddle. Others from across the taproom answered with whoops and cheers as they struck up a popular sailor's tune.

'In Amsterdam there lived a maid
Mark well what I do say
In Amsterdam there lived a maid
And she was mistress of her trade…'

'How did he get that name, Silken Jack?' asked Will.

'Old Jack used to trade in fine silks and… other things,' replied Belle.

'He was a merchant?'

She stared at him pointedly through a cloud of blue smoke. 'Aye, my boy. That's right. A merchant.'

The potboy returned with three tankards of ale. Belle tossed him a coin and he hurried away, colliding with the broad torso of Silken Jack. The old man swatted him away and sat down with us.

'Who are you?' he said, immediately turning to me and Will. Gone was the cheerful rake who had greeted us; now he seemed altogether more hostile.

Words stuck in my throat. I became aware that I was shaking. Meanwhile, the sound of singing had grown louder and more raucous.

'Then a great big Dutchman rammed my bow
Mark well what I do say
For a great big Dutchman rammed my bow
And said, "Young man, dees ees mein frau!"'

The crowd broke into uproarious laughter, but Silken Jack did not smile.

Belle broke the tension at last. 'Friends of my mistress, Jack. You can trust them.'

This seemed to satisfy him and he turned back to her. 'So, what's this business of yours?'

'You heard about this Dutchie they say did for Governor Maynard?'

'Aye.'

'What do folks say about him?'

'Knifed him on the street, I heard. Right by Admiralty House.'

'And you ain't heard no gossip about it?'

'What sort of gossip?'

'We think—' I began to interject, then cleared my throat, forcing myself to sound less timid. 'We think that there may be some question over his guilt.'

'That right? First I've heard of it.'

'Your customers, none of them have expressed doubts?'

'Can't say I've heard none. Whole town's baying for Dutch blood.'

A new round of cheering went up, drowning out the players. We craned our necks to see two men walking out into a makeshift ring that had been set up on the far side of the room. They appeared to be carrying large cages.

Will leaned in close. 'If it's blood they want, it looks as if they're about to get it.'

Belle continued her questioning. 'What about anything to do with the navy? Any gossip there?'

'No, can't say I heard much.' He sucked on his pipe, watching as the two men lined up the fighting cocks opposite each other. One of them shouted for bets to be placed, and there was a rush of eager bodies crowding around the ring.

'Wait, I tell you a lie,' Jack continued. 'I did hear of something strange. Dock workers been complaining about a pair of new men been seen around.'

'New men?' I asked. 'What new men?'

'That's just it, no one knows. They ain't navy, but they seem to answer to the big man. What's his name?'

My heart skipped a beat.

'Governor Arden?' asked Will.

'No. An officer.'

'You mean Captain Harcourt?' I said, feeling a surge of relief.

'Aye, that's him. I heard he's paying them for whatever it is they do, and a fair packet and all, which don't go down too well around here, let me tell you. Not with how long it's been since ordinary folk got no wages.'

'Interesting,' I said. 'And you've no idea what it is they do?'

'No. Work around the docks is all I know. Mean pair too, by all accounts. Don't take kindly to questions.'

Suddenly, a great cheer went up from the ringside. I could no longer see through the crush of people, but the sounds of shrieking birds and the beating of wings told us that the fight had begun.

Silken Jack got to his feet and looked over excitedly. 'Go on, my son! Belle, you coming to watch the fight?'

'You go on. I'll be seeing you.'

The old man shrugged, then pushed his way into the crowd and was gone.

'Two men,' I said loudly, trying to be heard above the commotion. 'Strangers in town, and violent at that. Remind you of anything?'

'The men Tamsin said came to the Four Feathers,' said Will.

'You ask me, the man's a smuggler,' said Belle. 'Wouldn't be the first corrupt captain this town ever had.'

I considered this for a moment. 'It is possible. But either way, something is going on, and we should investigate. The sooner we can prove Harcourt has a role in all this, the sooner we can win Wolfert his freedom.'

'How do we find them?' asked Will.

'We could set a watch,' said Belle. 'See who comes and goes for a day or two. Get a feel for anything unusual going on.'

'Not a bad idea,' agreed Will. 'But how? Sooner or later, we'd be seen.'

The corner of Belle's mouth curled into a smile. 'Don't you worry, my boy. We got our ways.'

She downed the remainder of her ale and indicated that it was time to go.

As we made our way back to the door, one of the fighting birds let out a terrible screech, then fell silent. Half the men roared in approval, while the other half started to make their way sullenly back to their chairs.

The thinning of the crowd opened up a line of sight to the ring once again, revealing a scene of carnage. One of the birds lay on the ground, blood pouring from an open wound on its neck, while its legs twitched pathetically. The other was being held aloft in a declaration of victory.

'Poor creature,' I said.

Belle spat on the floor. 'Better dead than in a cage. Let's go.'

August 12th

Will and I set out a little after nine this morning. Mindful of how close this would bring us to Admiralty House, we kept away from the main thoroughfares as best we could, traversing the warren of quieter lanes and alleyways until we reached the laundry on Bear Lane.

We found Alice beating some linens that were hanging from a line. Her baby was strapped to her back, sleeping soundly. As she looked up at our approach, her face became a mask of hostility.

'No,' she said, pointing angrily at me. 'Leave.'

'Alice, I—'

'Go. You're not welcome.'

The baby opened its eyes and began to cry.

'Alice?' the other laundress called from the other side of the yard.

'It's alright, Maggie. These men ain't staying.'

'Alice, please,' I said. 'We have been to the prison. We have seen Wolfert.'

Her eyes lit up with fury. 'What did you do to him?'

'You misunderstand. We know he is innocent.'

'We are on your side, madam,' added Will. 'I promise.'

Alice moved the cloth sling around to her front and started to cradle the wailing infant. 'There, there. Alright.'

'Just give us five minutes,' I said. 'Please.'

She considered for a moment, then let out a weary sigh. 'Alright. Baby needs feeding anyhow.'

She put down the beater and walked over to Maggie. The two women exchanged some words, while Maggie regarded us with hard, watchful eyes.

Alice indicated that we should follow her and we went through to the same little storage area where we had sat together before. She picked up an old piece of cloth that was lying on top of a stool, then sat down and untied the sling. The baby grizzled, waving its tiny hands in the air.

'You have a fine son, madam,' said Will.

Alice shot him a look that indicated she was not yet ready to indulge us with small talk. Covering herself and the baby with the cloth first, she attached the boy to her breast. His legs wriggled as he began to suckle hungrily.

'Well? How does my husband fare?'

We recounted the story of yesterday's meeting with Wolfert at the gaol. I did not spare her any of the distressing details, reasoning that if she could see I was holding nothing back from her, she might be more open to believing the other things I was there to say.

When I told her how Wolfert had reacted to the news of their son's birth, Alice began to cry, just as he had done. Her voice was dull with despair.

'They will not let me see him. I have begged and pleaded to be allowed in, just for five minutes, but they deny me even that.'

Will's jaw tightened. 'They want a bribe.'

'Those men are cruel. And it is because of you that he lies there, alone, rotting in that hole. And now he will hang.'

Her voice choked with tears. I wanted desperately to move forward and touch her, to put my hand on her shoulder and promise that everything would be alright, but I stayed still.

'Alice, I am sorry that—'

'I do not want your apology.'

'Alice,' Will said, gently. 'What happened was a mistake. We believe your husband to be innocent. But equally, you must understand that he attacked Mr Pepys. He nearly killed both of us.'

Her jaw clenched tightly. I expected a new tirade of anger, but instead her tone became softer. 'Well. No use me wailing like an old mulligrubs. What's done is done. What do we do now?'

I was relieved that we seemed to be making progress. 'Tell us what happened after Wolfert's arrest. Anything you can remember may prove useful.'

'Navy came and turned the place upside down. Said they found money in our room. All my eye and bollocks to that.'

'And you're certain there was nothing there?'

'I cleaned that room every day. Scrubbed them floors till they was smooth as stone. If there were money in there, I'd have found it.'

'Those men, did they harm you?'

'No. Just asked a load of questions.'

'What kind of questions?'

'Mostly about Wolfert. How long he'd been here. If we was married. Funny thing was, they didn't seem interested in me at all. Like they was questions that had to be asked, but none of them led to more questions.'

'In other words, they were just making a show of it?' said Will.

'Aye. I think they knew the answers they wanted and nothing else mattered. Left the place all smashed up too. Me and the babe been shacked up with old Maggie since then, God love her.'

'These men. Can you describe them?'

'There was maybe four or five... One who did the talking were an officer, thirty-odd. Miserable bastard with dark hair.'

Will looked over at me. 'Captain Harcourt.'

'And they took nothing else?' I asked.

'No. Like I said, got what they came for, didn't they? Or, what they came to say they got, at least.'

'An astute way of putting it, Mrs Scovell. I think we have what we came for. If you need anything, you can send word to us through Mistress de Vere at Dione House.'

We stood, but Alice motioned for us to wait. 'My husband, sir. You think they'll let me in to see him now?'

'Tell him you are there with the permission of Sir Thomas Grant and I think he will listen. The gaoler is a cruel man, but he is also a fool. I made him think the King himself would hear of it if he did not comply with my orders and he damn near wet his breeches.'

Alice smiled, then swiftly detached the baby from her bosom, pulled her dress up, and wrapped the boy back in his sling. 'Well then. If we're done clacking, I best be getting on, hadn't I?'

Although it was obvious that she still harboured resentment towards us, I was glad to find myself back on the same side as Alice Scovell. I enjoyed the company of this simple but spirited woman.

'Alice, take this,' I said, handing her a purse of coins.

She hesitated, then took it from my outstretched hand. 'Thank you, sir. I'll pay it back, mind, once my husband is free. If there's one thing I can't abide, it's being in debt.'

We stood across from a row of ancient timber-framed dwellings. Gulls wheeled overhead and I could see the tops of ships' masts as they swayed back and forth in the breeze.

Many of the buildings on the poor-looking street were in such bad repair that they looked ready to collapse – all except for one. At the corner, abutting the harbour, stood a fine-looking new warehouse, made of solid red brick. It stood out incongruously, a strong modern structure next to what amounted to little more than crumbling hovels. No doubt they would be demolished before long, razed for the valuable land on which they sat, their residents moved on to who knows where.

'Stay here,' said Anne, crossing the road.

The girl had been waiting for us on Bear Lane as we emerged from the laundry. I recognised her as the one who had taken a bullet to her arm during the fight in the woods. Her arm was bound in a kerchief tied around her neck, and she looked pale, but otherwise I was relieved to see that she was well.

We had followed her down a warren of backstreets and narrow cut-throughs – a route so circuitous that we could not possibly have found our way without her – until we had arrived in this gloomy little backstreet.

Now we watched as she went up to the last building before the warehouse and knocked on the door. A moment later it opened and she swiftly beckoned us over.

Jane, the pickpocket, was standing inside as we entered. She wore a pistol strapped to her waist. Only a little light penetrated the small, permanently shuttered windows of the empty room, and it took a moment for my eyes to adjust to the dark. The place smelled powerfully of damp.

'Follow me,' said Jane, leading us towards a wooden ladder propped up against an open trapdoor.

The girl went up first, followed by Will. As he stepped off the ladder, the ceiling above my head creaked precariously, and I hoped that the ancient boards could take the weight of all three of us standing together. Cautiously, I climbed up after them.

A hole had been knocked through one wall of the little attic room. One by one we stepped through the opening and into the starkly different space of the building next door. The beamed ceiling of the warehouse was tall, the walls new and sturdy. It was late morning and the sun was high in the sky, illuminating the dust that floated in the clear air. Everything smelled pleasantly of new wood.

A row of small windows was set into the wall opposite, overlooking the docks and the sea beyond. A figure sat in the far corner, looking out through a spyglass. Unable to see clearly, I started to walk closer, my footsteps echoing loudly on the thick floorboards.

Then the figure stood. My heart skipped a beat as I realised they were wearing a green cloak. An image flashed through my mind, of the assassin in the marketplace running at me, brandishing a knife.

'Mr Pepys?'

I sighed with relief. 'Mistress de Vere.'

'I did not mean to startle you.'

'It is nothing.' I waved my hand, a little embarrassed at my nervousness. 'You reminded me of somebody else for a moment, that is all.'

'Jane, send Anne to fetch the girl.'

'Mistress.' She curtseyed, then disappeared back through the hole.

'You seem anxious, Mr Pepys. I take it your visit went badly?'

'On the contrary. It went well. Alice forgives me.'

'Good. That is after all what matters.'

I looked out of the window. We had an excellent view of the docks from where we were. The *Prince Rupert* was visible at a diagonal to our left, while a little further away, I could see the empty space that had, until three days ago, been occupied by the stolen cutter, the *Nonsuch*.

'Anything?' I asked.

'Look for yourself,' she said, handing me the spyglass.

I scanned the docks through the lens, looking for any faces that I recognised. Small groups of men were unloading cargo, while others were engaged in cleaning, minor repairs, and the other menial tasks that make up the everyday work of a place like this.

In other words, nothing whatever out of the ordinary.

Then my eye was caught by a beggar woman sitting on the quayside. She was wearing a filthy, ragged dress, and a cap that obscured most of her face.

'Is that Belle?' I said in surprise, lowering the spyglass.

De Vere grinned enigmatically, as if she had merely been waiting for me to discover her secret. 'She makes a fine *espion*, does she not? We have pre-arranged signals should she identify anyone or anything suspicious. Did you find out anything new from Alice?'

'A little,' said Will. 'She confirmed what we suspected about the money having been a plant. And we're pretty sure she identified Captain Harcourt as the man responsible.'

'Hearsay, Mr Hewer. Speculation. The word of a foreign deserter's wife. Worthless in the eyes of the law. We need proof.'

'Speculation is all this whole enterprise is built on, madam,' I protested. Her relentless cynicism towards our efforts was beginning to try my patience. 'It is not as if you can offer us real proof that there is a conspiracy at all, other than the opinion of your late paramour. A man you freely admit was a Republican sympathiser.'

'Oh, come now. Harcourt tried to have you killed.'

'Did he? We have no real proof of that either.'

'He is in this whole sordid affair up to his neck and you cannot seriously believe otherwise.'

'We agree with you, madam,' said Will, calmly. 'Don't we, Sam? But no matter what our differences of opinion, we can surely concur that none of this is enough to act upon yet. Our priority must be to gather real evidence, and it will do no good squabbling among ourselves.'

De Vere snatched the spyglass back from me. The room fell to an ill-tempered silence as we resumed our watch.

I looked out of the window and once again my eyes were drawn to Belle. Nobody seemed to pay her much heed. Many of those who walked by seemed not to see her at all. I found myself gripped with curiosity to find out more about this extraordinary young woman from the other side of the world.

'Where did Belle come from?'

De Vere looked up at me. 'I beg your pardon?'

'Belle. How did she come to be in your service?'

She considered this for a while, as if deciding how much to tell me. 'She has said nothing to you?'

'No. Though I think she has spent time at sea.'

'One could say that,' she said, and lifted her spyglass again.

No more was said for a few minutes, and I assumed that to be an end to the matter. But then, to my surprise, she continued.

'Belle was born in Jamaica. As a girl of fifteen, she was kidnapped and sold as a slave in Kingston. The transport she was on was set upon by outlaws off the coast of Charleston, and she was captured again. Most on board were either murdered or sold, but the crew seemed to take a liking to Belle and kept her on as a cook. Soon enough they found out that she had other skills, too, and she was accepted as one of them. Had quite the successful career, by all accounts.'

'Wait,' said Will. 'Do you mean to say that Belle was a *pirate*?'

'That is your word, Mr Hewer,' said de Vere with a wry smile. 'I, of course, could not possibly comment.'

'How in God's name did she end up here?' I asked.

'Their ship was captured by the navy in the Straits of Florida, five years ago. Those who had not been slain were taken back to Portsmouth, where they were sentenced to hang. When word reached me that a woman was among their number, I resolved to engineer her escape. And with John's help, I did. I offered her a place in my household, and there she has remained ever since.'

'And now she is your servant?'

'Belle is more than that to me. She trains the women under my care to defend themselves. To be fighters – strong, fierce, without the need to depend upon men for protection. Belle is my loyal friend and most trusted companion.'

It occurred to me that she had once talked about Piety Blake in similar terms. How peculiar that there should be so much affinity between a gentlewoman of great means and two lowborn girls!

'The ties that bind you are indeed strong, madam,' was all I said in reply.

I heard a noise and turned to see Jane stepping through the hole in the wall. Behind her was another woman, who appeared to be waiting on the other side.

'Come on, moppet, we ain't going to bite,' said Jane.

The other woman stepped through into the warehouse. She looked around, nervous as a trapped animal. Recognising her immediately, I strode up and took her hands.

'Tamsin! It is good to see you.'

'Mr Pepys! I can hardly believe it. You are alive.'

'As you can see. Thank you for coming.'

'When Mr Hewer sent word that you were both well and needed my help…' She lowered her voice to a whisper. 'I did not want to come, but he said it was important. Didn't I warn you about that woman?'

'You did. But I believe you can trust her.'

She looked away. 'No. I will not.'

'Then at least trust me. You have my word that no harm will come to you. Can you do that?'

She hesitated. 'Alright.'

I led her by the hand over to where the others were standing. She greeted Will with a smile, then turned to face de Vere. I could feel her hand shivering with nerves.

'And you are?' de Vere asked, impatiently.

'Tamsin Lacey, mistress.'

'Tamsin was a close friend of Piety Blake,' I added.

The older woman's face immediately softened. 'Well then, any friend of Piety's is a friend of mine. You are welcome, Tamsin Lacey. How long can you spare us?'

Tamsin worked the sleeve of her dress nervously. 'I told Mistress Brown I were sick and she said she could spare me. I didn't like to lie, mind, but you say it might help catch… them?'

'You are doing a brave thing. Now, come. Sit with me by the window. Perhaps we might send one of the girls to the cook shop to fetch us some luncheon.'

We spent many hours on lookout, patiently watching for any sign of the two men. De Vere soon put Tamsin at her ease with genuine warmth and kindness. Before long the two of them were exchanging memories of Piety Blake, both as a friend and a protégé. I said little, preferring instead to listen, though I learned nothing of consequence I did not already know. Soon enough their conversation was less about the pain of their loss, than the happy memories they both had of the girl.

Several times, Tamsin was asked to take a look through the spyglass at some fellows or other among the workers coming and going from the docks, but none sparked any sense of recognition.

In time, the warmth of the day, combined with the exertions of the night before, conspired to make me drowsy, and I closed my eyes. When I opened them again, the sun was going down and someone was calling my name.

'Sam? Sam?' Will was standing next to the window.

I stood up. De Vere was gently shaking Tamsin, who appeared to have fallen asleep on her shoulder.

'What is it?' I asked.

'Something's happening.'

I reached the window at the same time as de Vere, who took the spyglass from him.

'Yes. Belle is signalling.' She paused for a moment, trying to work out what Belle was telling her, then held her hand out towards me.

'Look. There, at the steps.'

I took the instrument from her. Belle, her face turned away so as not to draw attention to us, was making gestures with her outstretched hand. I followed where she was pointing, towards the set of steps that led down from the quayside to a steep little beach. There stood two men talking to a watchman. They were mean-looking fellows, one taller than the other, though both were powerfully built. They wore the clothes of ordinary labourers.

I handed the spyglass to Tamsin. 'Take a look at those men down there. Think carefully. Are they the fellows who threatened you and Mistress Brown that day at the Four Feathers?'

Tamsin studied them intently for a moment. 'That's them. Oh God!'

She handed back the spyglass and began to weep. Will dragged over an upturned crate and had her sit down. He put his arm around her shoulder as she sat there, gently rocking back and forth. I was about to say something, when de Vere knelt and took her by the hand.

'Tamsin? Tamsin, listen to me. Whatever those men did to you, I promise you are safe. They do not know you are here. And they never will. But if they threaten you, even once, I will protect you. And if they harm you, I swear to God, I will find them, and I will make sure they can never do it again. To anyone.'

Her words were intended as a comfort, but I found myself unsettled by the steel in her voice. I have little doubt that this woman would go to great lengths in defence of those she saw as under her protection.

Even if it meant murder.

The docks were wreathed in shadow. The quayside lay below us, still and silent, save for the whispering of the sea. The light of the full moon was our only illumination, though it did not penetrate far into the gloom of the warehouse.

Her job done, Tamsin was thanked and sent home. The girl was so distressed that de Vere had no wish to keep her here for longer than we had to. Then Belle came to join us and we told her what we had just learned. She, in turn, had news for us.

She had moved as close as possible to the men without being discovered. A bag of coins was slipped to the nightwatchman and there had been a brief exchange in hushed tones. Belle had been able to make out little, but the meaning had been clear enough – they would return later tonight and would expect not to be disturbed.

It was quickly decided that we would return to Dione House to eat and rest for a couple of hours. When we returned, it was near nine. Jane and Anne, who had been left on watch, confirmed that the men were yet to come back. There was nothing to do but wait.

I stood by the window, next to Will and de Vere. Behind us, Jane sat next to Kitty, who had come back with us from Dione House. Both women were dressed in simple black breeches and heavy cloaks. Both were armed with pistols at their waists, and once, when Kitty moved, I could see the hilts of twin stiletto blades protruding from the tops of her boots.

Will and I were also dressed plainly, in the clothes we had worn on our mission to the Old Ring o' Bells. De Vere, by contrast, wore a rich dress of slashed blue silk, with an ermine-trimmed cape slung around her shoulders. She shivered in the cold, but when I offered her my coat, she refused.

Down on the quayside, in the shadows of an overhanging building, stood Belle. In her long thick leather coat and tricorn hat, she would have been all but invisible had we not known she was there.

The trap was set. All we needed was our prey.

'I think I see something. Blow that candle out.' De Vere held the spyglass to the window as a heavily laden wagon approached on the road below. We watched as it came to a halt and two men jumped down from the front.

'Is it them?' I asked.

'Yes. And they seem to have come prepared.'

The men walked to the rear of the wagon and pulled aside a tarpaulin that had been secured over the cargo. Underneath was a collection of barrels. Working swiftly, they unloaded them one by one. Then, once they had them stacked on the quayside, they each picked up two at a time and hurried down into the docks, where they loaded them onto a small rowboat.

'What have they got there?' asked Will.

'Whatever it is, they're in a hurry to get it unloaded.'

'Let me see,' I said. She handed the spyglass to me and I watched as the men ran back to fetch more barrels. As they did so, I managed to get a clear look at their faces.

'It is them, right enough.'

Outside, the men were unloading the last of the barrels. Then they hurried back down to the boat, swifly pushing off and rowing out in the direction of the *Rupert*.

Patiently we waited. Then, not half an hour later, we saw them once more, rowing as hard as they could back across the dark water. The boat had been emptied of its cargo.

De Vere turned to Kitty and Jane. 'Prepare to move.'

The men swiftly moored the little vessel and hurried back to their wagon. I watched as they started to secure the tarpaulin.

'Pepys,' said de Vere, impatiently.

I looked up to see her and Will already standing at the hole in the wall. I hurried over and we ducked through into the abandoned cottage. A small candle still burned over by the hatchway, allowing us just enough light to see Kitty and Jane making their way down the ladder.

De Vere's coach was waiting for us outside, with Anne standing on watch, a cudgel gripped tightly in her good hand. I could hear the empty wagon trundling away along the seafront.

Kitty and Jane wasted no time in climbing on top of the perch, Kitty taking up the reins. Will and I climbed on board, just as Belle rode around the corner on the back of a grey stallion.

'We need to leave,' she said, with the composed urgency of one prepared to do battle.

'Go,' de Vere replied, climbing into the coach. 'And be careful.'

Belle spurred her horse and galloped away. I heard the cracking of a whip and we pulled out into the street.

The hunt was on.

It had been Kitty's idea to invent a relay.

We knew that Belle would have the advantage of stealth, allowing her to move fast and remain unseen. Our conveyance, by comparison, was slow and noisy. There was no way we could hope to keep pace with her.

So before we left the house, Kitty suggested we prepare small bundles of kindling for Belle to drop at regular intervals. They were tied with coloured ribbon. White meant we should continue to follow. Red meant to wait for her.

It was two or three miles before the ribbons turned red. We had reached a lonely crossroads where the north road was intersected by a dirt path that wound its way up a short hill towards thick forest. It was clear from the tracks in the mud that this was where they had turned. The route looked difficult enough for a cart, let alone a coach and pair. So there was nothing to do but wait.

In truth, I was glad to have stopped. The journey along the rough and pitted road had been painful for me, so this came as a welcome opportunity to rest.

An hour or more had passed when we heard the sound of galloping hooves from the woods. A few moments later, Belle rode out of the trees atop her grey horse, her black hat outlined with a thin halo of silver moonlight.

De Vere jumped down from the coach. 'What did you discover?'

'They're hiding out in an old windmill at Brakspur Point.'

'Where's that?' I asked.

'About two miles from here,' said de Vere, before turning back to Belle.

'No trouble?' she said.

'I thought they were getting suspicious for a while, so I dropped behind. Sure enough, they doubled back on themselves to check. After that, I took more care.'

'Did you get close enough to see what they are doing?'

'Inside, eating supper. Should have full bellies by now.'

'Then our timing is fortuitous.' De Vere turned to Kitty. The girl was still on the perch, holding the horses' reins. 'Do you know how to reach Brakspur Point from here?

'Yes, mistress. It is further by the main road, but I can get us close enough.'

'Close enough is all we need. Let's go.'

We rode further along the north road, Belle bringing up the rear this time. Then we turned sharply right down a dirt track that led to an old hollow way. The sounds of the night were all around us. Vixens barked and birds of prey flew from the trees as we approached, scared by the clatter of our wheels. Kitty drove the horses as fast as possible down the rough path. Dappled moonlight through the overhanging trees lit our path as brightly as the sun.

I closed my eyes. The pain was growing unbearable as the carriage jolted violently over the rutted ground. I prayed that my freshly healed wound was in no danger of reopening. Mercifully, we turned again onto a winding road through open fields, slowing our pace. Then, at last, we slowed to a halt.

We had stopped next to the ruins of an old shepherd's hut. I leaned out of the window just as Belle reined in her horse and came alongside the carriage.

'Brakspur Point is over that ridge,' said Kitty. 'It should come into view around the next bend.'

'Excellent,' said de Vere. 'Then you, me and Jane will keep going as far up the track as we need to in order to be seen from the door, but no further.'

'And slowly,' added Belle. 'Remember, girl, surprise is a weapon.'

'What about us?' asked Will.

De Vere indicated that we should get out. 'You stay with Belle. Do exactly as she says.'

'Look like a nursemaid to you, do I?' said Belle.

'I am serious. Take no chances. That goes for all of you. We do not know who these men are, and we would be fools to underestimate them.'

Will and I climbed down. The coach moved off and within seconds they were out of sight.

Belle dismounted and tied her horse through a hole in the ruined wall. 'You'll stay close to me.' Will opened his mouth to speak, but she cut him off. 'Say nothing. This ain't a game. Do you hear me now?'

She led us down the track at a swift pace. As the road curved around, we saw the windmill atop a short, steep slope, about a hundred yards away. It was a stark and ominous sight, outlined against the dark sky, its cracked and broken sails swaying in the wind. From behind one of the small windows, I could just see the faint flicker of candlelight.

Suddenly, Belle swerved into the woods and broke into a run. We followed, trying hard to keep up as she ducked between the trees, dodging roots and other obstacles that lay on the ground, barely visible in the cold light of the moon.

My heart was racing. The hairs on my arms stood on end, though I no longer felt the cold. Belle was right. This was no game.

We emerged from the woods onto an open patch of ground at the base of the hill. There were no windows on this side of the building, so at least I felt safe that we were not being watched as we ran up the slope and pressed ourselves flat against the dirty white stone.

We crept slowly around the base of the windmill, until we had a clear line of sight to the entrance. At first nothing happened, then de Vere appeared out of the darkness, walking calmly up the pathway to the door. She was alone.

She knocked. I held my breath. There was no answer. She knocked again. Then I heard the sound of footsteps and the door swung open. One of the men stepped out. He was tall, looming over her by at least a foot or more.

Suddenly, for the first time, she looked vulnerable.

'I beg your pardon, sir, for troubling you at this hour. My horse has thrown a shoe and I have nowhere else to go for help.'

'Who is it?' called a voice from within. He spoke with a rough, hard-bitten manner, in what I recognised as the accent of an Essex man.

'A woman,' the man at the door called back.

He looked de Vere up and down and crossed his arms. I saw Belle's shoulders stiffen.

'Where is it, then?'

'My driver is but an old man, sir, and the climb to your door is steep.' She gestured to where the coach stood, near the bottom of the hill. 'I fear we took a wrong turn, and became grievously lost. Will you help a poor woman?'

The man reached forward and started to finger the ermine trim of her cape. Belle silently drew her pistol from her belt.

The second man stepped into the doorway next to him. He was much shorter than his cohort, but even more powerfully built, with huge forearms and a thick, muscular neck.

'Who's this, then?'

'Says she's lost.'

'Yes,' said de Vere, a touch of anxiety creeping into her voice. 'We became lost on the country roads, returning late from Petersfield. Please, sirs, it is not safe for a woman and an old man to be out so late, with such little protection. Will you help me?'

The men looked at each other. Will, Belle and I pressed ourselves tightly to the wall, trying to keep them in sight without being spotted.

'Don't you worry, my love, we'll help you,' the shorter man said, with a leer.

'I am grateful to you, sirs. My coach is just up—'

She started to move, but the tall man grabbed her arm and held onto it tightly. 'No need to be in such a hurry. Won't you stop a while and share some ale with us?'

'Yes, you must be thirsty,' said the shorter man. 'We keep a poor house, but there is a warm fire and… other things.'

Belle started to raise her pistol and take aim, but I placed a restraining hand on her arm. 'No. It is too risky.'

'You are most kind,' said de Vere, 'but if you could just help me be on my way, that would be—'

'Oh, but I'm not asking, my pretty one.'

Suddenly, the shorter man screamed with pain as a small knife buried itself in his shoulder. He pulled it out, as the tall man looked around, confused. De Vere pulled away, leaving them exposed. Belle ran forward, pistol raised, but de Vere misjudged her direction and stepped into her line of fire.

'Move!' shouted Belle, but by now the tall man was alert to the threat and lunged towards her.

'Get down!' Will cried, anticipating what was about to happen.

I hit the ground, and at the same moment, the tall man threw a punch at Belle, which clipped the side of her head. She reeled just as the gun went off, and the shot exploded into the stonework, showering us with fragments of stone.

I looked over to see the tall man gripping Belle in a choke hold. She struggled, her legs kicking wildly backwards, but he was too strong even for her.

Will ran forward, picking up Belle's pistol from where she had dropped it, and hit the tall man over the head with the butt as hard as he could. He yelled angrily, pushing Belle away with a sharp kick to her spine, which sent her sprawling onto the ground.

Will raised his fists as the man turned to face him. 'Come on then. Let's see what you're made of.'

The tall man threw a punch, but Will dodged to one side, and returned it with a powerful strike to his jaw. As the two of them traded blows, I hauled myself up and helped Belle to her feet. She drew a knife from her belt and calmly stepped behind the tall man, holding the blade to his neck.

'Easy now. Or someone might get hurt.'

The man's face twisted with rage, but he had no choice but to submit. I got to my feet, wincing in pain where my shin had hit a rock, and limped to where the shorter man stood with his hands raised. Jane and Kitty had their guns levelled at him.

De Vere strode over to us. 'Belle, are you alright?'

'I thought you said there were some men we had to fight?'

'Pepys, you're hurt.'

'It is nothing. I hit a stone when I fell, that is all.'

'Good. Take them inside and tie them up. Jane, give Belle your gun.'

Jane broke off and started to walk towards Belle, leaving Kitty to guard the shorter man alone.

'Hey, you might want to go easy on the fellow, Belle,' Kitty called over to her, cheerfully. 'His friend over here looks about ready to wet his breeches.'

Kitty only took her eyes off him for a moment, but it was enough. With the speed of a practised fighter, the man lunged forward and grabbed the barrel of her gun, twisting it free of her hand. Before she even had time to react, he had her by the waist and spun her around, pressing the barrel to her temple.

'Alright, you filthy bitches. Let him go.'

Nobody moved or spoke. I hardly dared to breathe.

'Mistress?' said Belle.

My eyes darted between Kitty, frozen in terror, and the tall man, who was standing just feet away from me. His hands were still raised in submission to Belle's knife, but the grin on his face said everything we needed to know about who now held the power.

De Vere spoke through tightly gritted teeth. 'Let him go.'

Belle's arm shook with anger, but she threw her knife down. The tall man walked calmly over to Jane, who stood helplessly with her gun half-raised by her side. He held out his hand to take it, but she did not move.

'Jane,' said de Vere steadily, 'Give it to him.'

With a look of burning hatred in her eyes, Jane slowly turned the pistol around in her hand. The tall man snatched it, then gestured for her to join the rest of us. He backed away towards his friend.

I felt Will step in close behind me. 'Sam… I think this is it.'

'Quiet,' hissed de Vere.

'Well, then,' shouted the tall man, triumphantly. 'Here's what's going to happen. If you want your little whore to live, you'll all take yourselves in there.'

His gun flicked towards the open door.

Belle shook her head. 'Don't do it. They'll pick us off like rats.'

'What choice do we have?' replied de Vere. 'They will kill her.'

This was not the first time I had faced mortal danger in these last few weeks. But I was tired of shrinking in the face of death. If this really were to be the end, I resolved not to die a coward.

'On the contrary, sir,' I said, stepping forward. 'We shall stay right where we are.'

The tall man pointed his gun directly at me. I raised my hands.

'Sam—' Will began to move, but Belle held him back.

The tall man sneered at me. 'You soft in the head? Or do you just want to die first?'

'As you can see, sir, I mean you no harm. I merely wish to negotiate.'

'Did you hear that? He wants to *negotiate*.'

'Maybe he's blind as well as stupid,' ventured the shorter man, with a burst of mocking laughter. Then he pressed the gun harder into Kitty's cheek. The girl moaned with fear.

De Vere and Belle started to speak at the same time, but the tall man held up his hand for silence.

'Pretty thing, your friend. Be a shame to waste a face like that.'

'Not her face I'm interested in,' added the shorter man, fondling Kitty's breasts. She squeezed her eyes shut.

'Please, gentlemen,' I said. 'You are not thinking this through. You have the upper hand for now; this is clear. But you only have two shots.'

The shorter man started slobbering over Kitty's neck. Then he reached down and began lifting her skirts.

The tall man held out his free hand in my direction, counting theatrically with outstretched fingers. He pointed first at Kitty, then at me, then shrugged with exaggerated innocence. 'Two shots. After that I suppose it's us against whoever lives.'

'And you may well triumph. Or you may not. It would be unwise to underestimate these women. Believe me, I have seen them fight.'

'So have we,' said the shorter man. Kitty whimpered as his hand moved beneath her petticoats. 'And look at where we are now.'

'I am Samuel Pepys, Clerk of the Acts to the Navy Board. If I die here, there will be an investigation. The king himself will want to know.'

The tall man leaned forward, peering at me with what seemed like genuine interest for a moment. Then he smiled, a leering, sinister grin. 'Thought I recognised him. Been to the market lately, have you?'

'What does he mean?' said Will.

'I think, perhaps, we have found our assassin.' I swallowed hard. 'Who sent you? Was it Captain Harcourt?'

'Don't think you're in no position to ask us questions, Mr Clerk of the Acts.'

There was a groan of distress behind him, and Kitty went limp in the shorter man's arms.

'What's wrong with the redhead?' asked the tall man.

'I think she's fainting. Never mind, eh? Makes for an easier job.' He laughed again, a disgusting, feral sound, as Kitty slumped almost to the ground.

'*Let her go*,' I demanded. The tall man looked at me in surprise, then seemed to lose interest in me altogether.

'I've had enough of you,' he said, and pulled the trigger.

I closed my eyes, expecting to feel the searing pain of a bullet tearing through me, ending my life. But nothing happened. I opened my eyes again to see him pulling the trigger, over and over.

Before any of us had time to react, Kitty suddenly leaped into action, slicing upwards with the second knife that she had hidden in her other boot. It slashed across the shorter man's hand, causing him to cry out in pain and drop the pistol, which she scooped up off the ground and levelled at him. Her face was a mask of rage.

Belle ran towards the tall man with a terrifying cry, her own knife raised above her head like a sword. He held up his arms, hoping to fend off her attack, but she was too quick for him. She leaped forward, her heavy boots thudding into his chest, knocking him hard onto the ground. A second later, she was on him, her blade ready to slice his throat.

'No,' shouted de Vere. 'We need him.'

'At least let me cut him,' she growled.

'Patience. Will, you go inside and see if you can find some rope.'

Will ran inside the windmill, while de Vere went over to Kitty and took the gun from her. I wondered for a second if she was going to kill the shorter man, but instead she ordered him to kneel on the ground with his hands on his head.

Kitty leaned against the wall, breathing heavily. Jane went over to comfort her, but the girl waved her away. Belle saw that I was watching.

'Don't worry about her. She's stronger than you think.'

Will returned with two large coils of rope and immediately set to binding the hands and feet of the two men. As he worked to render them immobile, I went over to Jane.

'Your gun – why didn't it fire?'

'Removed the breech plug before handing it over, didn't I? Bit cunning with the old fingers, me.'

'Jane, I always knew you were a good investment,' said de Vere, approvingly.

'What now?' asked Belle.

'Now we get them inside and secure them well.'

'And then?'

De Vere smiled.

'Then, finally, we get can get some answers.'

'For the last time, what are they planning?'

'For the last time, I don't know.'

De Vere stood over the tightly bound men. The taller of the two stared back up at her defiantly, while his comrade looked down at the floor, blinking blood out of his eye. Belle leaned forward and punched the tall man in the jaw, sending a shower of blood spraying outwards. He spat some out on the ground.

'Try again,' she growled.

Neither man had spoken much at all since we had brought them inside and tied them to the old grain chute. They had admitted to being employed on private business, but would say no more than that. They claimed to know nothing of any plot.

They had refused to tell us their own names, so we had decided to call the tall man Red and the shorter man White.

Will and I were sitting on the floor, watching the two women make rough work of the prisoners. Kitty and Jane were outside on watch. It was late and every muscle in my body ached. Somewhere in the darkness, beyond the flickering light from the semi-circle of candles we had gathered together, I could hear the scurrying of rats.

Knowing that it was Red who had tried to kill me that day in Portsmouth made the situation all the more unnerving, even if we were now gaoler and prisoner. I had already seen how quickly the power could be reversed.

'This is going nowhere,' whispered Will.

'I fear you are right. These men will be hard to break by force.'

Red fixed me with a cold stare, drawing his tongue across blood-stained teeth. De Vere's voice cut across the silence.

'Why did you try to murder Mr Pepys?'

'Just following orders. Ain't personal. Wouldn't mind finishing the job though.'

'Orders from whom?'

He shrugged insolently. De Vere came over to us and spoke in a low voice.

'Your presence seems to aggravate him. Perhaps you should make yourselves scarce.'

'You may be right. Will, let us take a look around. Then we shall take the next watch.'

We picked up two candles from the semi-circle on the ground. For a moment, I thought I saw a flicker of concern on the faces of the men as we walked away into the shadowy depths of the building.

Once we were away from the small area that had been used as the men's living quarters, the ground became filthy with dried mud and animal droppings. A pile of empty sacks lay decaying on the ground, small remnants of the building's days as a working mill, but otherwise it seemed empty.

'Sam, look.' I followed where Will was pointing and saw a small door set into the space underneath a collapsed wooden staircase. We went over and I tried the handle. It was unlocked.

'What are you doing?' Red called over to us. The unease in his tone had become plain now.

'Why?' I heard de Vere ask. 'What will they find in there?'

'Just tell them to stay out. There's nothing to see.'

'Ain't a problem them going in, then, is it?' said Belle.

Will and I looked at each other with apprehension. He pushed the door gently and it creaked open on rusty hinges. Inside was a small storeroom, no more than about twelve feet square. Our candles cast flickering shadows across the plain white walls. In one corner stood several wooden barrels. I moved closer, holding up my candle to inspect them. They were of the same sort that we had watched the men unload at the docks.

Will started looking around for an implement of some kind. He picked up a small iron bar that was leaning against the wall.

'Hold this,' he said, giving me his candle. Then he started to pry open one of the barrels. It was nailed down tight, and he had to strain to get any leverage, but eventually the wooden lid started to crack and strain.

'*Stop!*' shouted Red.

Suddenly there was a loud snap and the lid splintered in two. I pulled aside the loose wood and held up one of the candles, peering in close to see what was inside.

I recognised the smell immediately.

'Gunpowder,' I gasped, jerking away the candle. We backed out of the room hastily.

Will stared at me, aghast. 'What the devil are they planning?'

White looked up us me with a sneer. 'How about you pay us, and we might tell you what you want to know.'

'How about you do it anyway and I might let you live?' replied Belle, turning the blade over in her hand.

The men were still refusing to talk. Only now, one important factor had changed in our favour. They were scared.

De Vere was pacing slowly back and forth, carrying an oil lamp. We had found two of them among the men's possessions, which was fortunate given how risky it had now become to work by candlelight.

Will and Jane approached from the storeroom carrying the last of the barrels, their way lit by Kitty. We had found ten of the barrels in the storeroom, filled not only with gunpowder, but muskets and shot too. I wondered how many had already been moved to the docks. Now they were arrayed in a horseshoe shape around the prisoners.

'Stupid bitch will blow us all to Hades,' said Red, sweat glistening on his face.

'Quiet, dog.' Belle pressed her knife against his throat, piercing the skin enough that a thin trickle of blood ran down his neck.

'That's all of them,' said Will.

'Good. Carry on.'

At de Vere's signal, Will picked up the crowbar and prized the lid away from the nearest barrel. Then he and Jane picked it up and started pouring the gunpowder out in a thick trail leading to the door and beyond.

'You wouldn't dare,' said White.

Belle drew the knife slowly across his face, gently enough not to draw blood. 'I hope you say nothing. Devil take me, I hope you keep your mouths shut and see what happens.'

The men looked between the three of us, fear spreading across their faces. And yet, they kept silent. My heart was pounding. Even though I knew it was just a bluff, I wanted it all to be over.

Will came back inside. 'It is done.'

'How far?' said Belle.

'All the way to the bottom of the hill, just like you said.'

'Good. We'll make a man of you yet, my boy.'

De Vere crouched down in front of the prisoners. 'This is your last chance.'

He looked up at her, then spat in her face. She wiped it away with a sigh.

'Very well then. Belle, proceed.'

Belle went over to the door and signalled to Kitty, who was standing at the bottom of the hill. A moment later I heard the shattering of glass as she threw her lamp to the ground, followed by a whoosh of flame as the gunpowder ignited. I caught a whiff of sulphurous smoke as the trail slowly burned towards the mill with an ominous fizz.

'You are bluffing,' said Red, though he sounded far from certain.

'Tell us what they are planning.'

'You would die too.'

'I estimate the distance between here and the door to be, what would you say, Pepys, twenty feet? That would give my friends and me plenty of time to get clear, before you were torn to tiny pieces of flesh and bone.'

'You fucking mad bitch.'

I glanced nervously outside. I could see the trail of fire burning its way slowly towards the door. With a sigh, De Vere got to her feet, motioning for us to leave.

'Gentlemen, there was no need for you to die this day. I wish you good fortune in the next life.'

'Give my regards to Old Nick,' added Belle.

I moved swiftly away from the gunpowder as we stepped out of the building to join the others.

'Sam,' Will said, nervously.

'This isn't going to work. You have to stop it now,' I said, but de Vere held up her palm to silence me. I looked down at the powder then back to her. Sweat poured off my forehead as the flames finally crossed the threshold.

'Alright! We'll talk. God have mercy.'

De Vere flicked her hand and Kitty hurried forward into the doorway, carrying a bucket of earth. She poured it over the flames, dousing them in an instant. We went back inside. The men looked up at de Vere, terror written on their ashen faces.

'Now. Talk.'

Once they started talking, the information came fast. The men told us that they were soldiers of fortune, hired by a senior officer of the navy. At first, they were still reticent to confirm his name, but when Belle elaborately took out her tinderbox and started lighting her pipe close to the unburned powder, they swiftly gave in.

Captain Harcourt. We had already suspected the truth, but it was still a shock to hear it from someone else. De Vere had been certain of his guilt; now I was too.

When they described how they had been given the task of loading barrels filled with gunpowder aboard the *Prince Rupert*, I stepped in with questions of my own.

'How are you allowed on board? Even at night, a ship-of-the-line like that would never be left unmanned and unguarded.'

'Harcourt bribes the watchmen,' said White. 'And we move the stuff in small consignments only, so as not to arouse much suspicion. Dozy whoresons probably think it's just a bit of ordinary smuggling.'

'Perhaps if they were paid on time, they'd be more vigilant,' muttered Will.

'Why the attempt on my life?' I asked.

Red shrugged. 'I was offered five pounds to stick a knife in your gut. Ain't paid to ask questions.'

'Try harder,' said de Vere.

'He said you was sniffing around in things that ain't your business. That's all I know.'

'And what of Lord Maynard? Did you kill him too?' I could tell she was struggling not to show emotion.

Both men looked back at her with genuine puzzlement. 'No. Never heard of him.'

They really do not know, I thought. So his killer is still out there. I steeled myself before asking my next question.

'Is a man called Benjamin Arden involved in this plot?'

'That ain't a name I've heard. But I know that Harcourt gets his orders from a man called William Jackson.'

'William Jackson? Who's he?'

'I don't know.'

De Vere leaned forward. 'Stop lying.'

'I'm not. The Captain don't even know we've ever heard the name. But we ain't daft. We hear things.'

'Do you know anything about this Jackson?' said de Vere.

'Just that he's the big man.'

'Is he here in Portsmouth?'

'I don't know.'

'Were there any other names you might have heard?' I asked.

'No. Wait, yes. We heard him talking once, about a man… What was the name?'

'Downing,' said White.

'Wait – Sir George Downing?' I said. 'Are you quite sure?'

'That's him.'

'Heard how?'

'It was behind a closed door. Heard the big man talking. Somewhere we shouldn't have been.'

'Talking to whom?'

'Don't know.'

Belle started fingering her knife. 'Anything else?'

The men related what little other scraps of information they had, but I was too distracted to listen. What business did Harcourt have with Sir George Downing? And then there was this new name – William Jackson, the leader of the conspiracy. Who was he? Somewhere, deep in the recesses of my mind, I could not help but think I had heard the name before. But where?

I was so absorbed by this thought that I did not notice the interrogation had come to an end until Will spoke to me in a low voice. 'What do you think is going on here?'

'I wish I knew. Downing... And now this man, William Jackson.'

'More questions in place of answers. And I'll tell you what else. Something is not right with them.' With a subtle movement of his head, he motioned to where de Vere was engaged in a hushed conversation with Belle and the other women.

'What do you mean?'

'I don't know. They've been like that ever since the answers dried up. We should be leaving but... What more is keeping us here?'

We did not have to wait long for an answer.

De Vere detached herself from the group and stood in front of the men. 'You swear that is all you know?'

'Aye.'

'There is nothing else you wish to say?'

'No.'

'You swear it?'

'We swear, lady.'

'Good.'

For a long time, she said nothing else. I allowed myself to breathe a quiet sigh of relief. There was still the problem of how we could safely let the men go, but I suspected that by now they were too scared to try and make trouble again. And we had learned much from them. At long last, this night was nearly over.

'Kill them.'

I looked up at her. 'What?'

Belle unsheathed her knife. The men started to struggle.

'You promised,' cried White.

I stepped forward. 'Wait! We had an agreement.'

'We agreed to make them think we were in earnest. And so we are,' said de Vere.

'We could use them as witnesses.'

'They would knife us as soon as our backs were turned.'

'I will not allow it.'

De Vere looked at me. There was defiance in her eyes, but also the hint of an apology. 'Oh Pepys! Don't you see? It was always too much of a risk. They must be silenced.'

'Listen to me.' I raised my hands in a final attempt to placate her. 'Mistress de Vere. Charlotte. Doing this will not bring back Lord Maynard.'

'It is not your decision.'

She motioned to Jane and Kitty, who took our arms and led us outside.

'You cannot do this,' I protested.

Kitty spoke to us gently. 'Come on. There is no need for you to see this.'

I looked at Will, in the desperate hope that he would somehow have a way to stop them. But I could see in his eyes that he thought it was futile.

We walked back towards where the coach had been left, on the little track at the bottom of the hill. It was quiet, save for the wind and the cries of a fox somewhere in the woods. I looked back at the mill, wondering what was happening inside. The faint glow of lamplight was still visible through the little window.

Then it went out and the building was left in darkness.

When it was finally time to depart, the first ribbons of light were starting to spread across the horizon. I sat in the coach opposite de Vere. Kitty was asleep, resting her head on her mentor's lap. Will took the seat next to Jane on the perch outside, while Belle rode ahead of us.

We did not speak to each other for most of the ride back to Portsmouth. I did not ask her if she had made good on her threat and executed those two men. Perhaps it is best that I do not know.

'I do not want you to think that your bravery went unnoticed, Mr Pepys,' she said at last.

'I beg your pardon?'

'You showed great courage back there, putting your life in danger to save Kitty. To save us all. You have done more than enough this night to earn my respect. Thank you, Mr Pepys.'

'If that is the case, I believe I have the right to demand something of you in return.'

'Oh?'

'One question, madam. And I would have the truth of it, no dissembling. No matter what the answer.'

'You intrigue me, sir.'

'Do you swear to it?'

'Very well, I swear.'

I took a deep breath. 'Did you kill Elias Thorne?'

Her expression hardly changed, but it felt as if her brown eyes were boring deep into my very soul.

'And why would you think that?'

'You loved Piety Blake, as evidently you love all your girls. I suspect you know that she and Elias were intimate with each other. And that he murdered her. His death was your revenge, was it not?'

She closed her eyes. 'Piety was a wild soul. A free spirit, who swore to live her life beholden to no man. But she had faults. A yearning for excitement that blinded her to the darkness in men's souls. Her love for Thorne – no, not love, lust – was passionate. Raw. She told me that their lovemaking was often so violent, they caused each other injury, did you know that?'

'I am led to believe it so.'

'I warned her it was a dangerous line that she must never let him cross. But she thought she could tame the beast within him. There was always an excuse for the things he did to her. She provoked him. That they were as bad as each other. Eventually it all became too much. She went to break with him and she ended up dead. A story as old as time.'

'I am sorry for it. But I repeat, did you kill him?'

She stared into my eyes again. 'The answer to your question, Mr Pepys, is no. But are you sure it was the right question to ask?'

For a moment, I did not understand. What other question could there be? Then, suddenly, I realised what she meant.

'Did you *intend* to kill Elias Thorne?'

'The men of the law had no interest in pursuing a man like Thorne. To them, Piety was just another dead peasant girl. A slut, killed by vagabonds on a road that she was a fool to have been travelling alone at night. To them, she got what she deserved. So I sent some of my girls to get the truth out of him, and if necessary, to mete out our own justice. Only somebody had beaten us to it.'

I remembered what Doctor Grey had said. Whoever had killed Thorne and whoever had mutilated his body were not necessarily one and the same.

'And so instead, they desecrated the body. Unmanned him. Carved an M into his forehead. M for murderer, I presume?'

'I concede they went a little far. But it served as a pretty warning, did it not?'

'But if it was not you who killed him, then who did?'

'I do not know. Truly. But I do know that I was not the only one with reason to wish the man dead.'

Sleep has eluded me. I am alone in my room at Dione House, trying to make sense of what occurred this night.

We said little else for the rest of the journey back to Portsmouth. In spite – perhaps because – of all that had just happened, I began to feel myself awed by Charlotte de Vere's presence. She is an enigma: capable of such brutality, yet also such love, with an intensity I have seldom encountered.

I fancy she interpreted my silence as unease, but in fact, I was coming to terms with the implications of what she had just told me. I no longer believed that she was Elias Thorne's killer. But without her, this leaves another suspect uppermost in my mind.

If I am right, the truth saddens me greatly. But I shall not dwell on that for now.

Nor shall I speculate on what might have come to pass inside that mill. They were evil men, of that I am satisfied, and the world is better without them. And yet, I feel a shadow on my conscience. Should I have done more to save them?

On the other hand, perhaps what should really concern me is how little thought of their deaths affects me, not how much. Though there is much else to think about. The conspiracy is real. What can Harcourt be planning that is worth so much risk?

Then there is still the matter of the mysterious order on which they were supposedly acting. What order? At least now we have the name of the man behind it all – William Jackson. But who is he?.

Maynard got close to the truth. That must be why he was murdered. Could Harcourt have been using the missing funds to pay mercenaries? Were those two men the only ones, or are there more? And to what end? What in heaven's name were they doing filling the *Prince Rupert* full of gunpowder?

If the answer is treason, just what could they expect to achieve with a single ship?

For every answer, another question. Meanwhile, with every hour that goes by, Harcourt's plan draws nearer to fruition. And Wolfert Jansen a step closer to the noose.

For all the strength of the Hidden League, I believe we have reached an impasse. There is only so much it is possible to discover from the outside. We need access to that ship, to investigate what is going on.

I can feel the realisation grow like a hollowness in the pit of my stomach. There is only one way forward now.

It is time for Will and me to come back from the dead.

August 13th

I was woken by a pounding on my door.

'Sam, are you awake?'

It took me a moment to remember where I was. 'Will?'

The door opened and he stepped inside. I looked at him, groggily.

'What is it? What is the time?'

'Just after seven. Sam, word from the town. Wolfert Jansen was tried yesterday and found guilty of murder.'

'What? Please tell me he lives.'

'For now. He is to hang in a few days.'

'Was he given any warning? Any chance at a defence?'

'I do not know.' Will slammed his hand against the wall in frustration. 'Damn them. Alice is so distraught she can hardly speak.'

'Alice? She is here?'

'Yes. Downstairs. De Vere and Belle are with her in the parlour.'

I threw the covers off and rose to my feet. 'Very well. I will dress and come down.'

'I shall meet you there.'

'Just a moment, Will. There is something I must tell you first.'

'No. It's much too risky. We have seen first-hand what these men are capable of.'

'We have seen what they are capable of making others do for them,' I countered. 'They would not act against us in the open. We might be knifed in the back by an assassin, but not set upon in full view of the world.'

'That is less reassuring than you might think. Surely the point is not so much that we may not get out of the *Prince Rupert* alive, but more that as soon as we reveal ourselves, we are vulnerable.'

'Well then, let us hear your idea. I am sure it is an infallible piece of strategy.'

'Calm down. I am not your enemy. I am disagreeing because it is a bad plan, not because it is your plan.'

I sank onto the bed. Will sat down next to me.

'Forgive me,' I said.

'I do not blame you. We have both been through an ordeal, you especially. We will see this through together. But I still think your plan is suicide.'

He thought for a moment, then seemed to have an idea.

'Although…'

Alice was sitting on the settle, cradling her baby. Her eyes were red and sore from crying. Belle sat next to her, while de Vere stood next to the fireplace. They looked up as Will and I entered.

'Alice,' I said. 'I have heard the news. I am so very sorry.'

'Don't talk about him like he's dead, sir. He ain't dead.' She wiped a fresh tear away from her eye.

I turned to de Vere. 'What do we know?'

'He was dragged from his cell just after sunrise. No opportunity to present a defence. The judge condemned him without a fair trial.'

'That is outrageous. Objections must be made.'

'There ain't time for that,' said Belle.

'She's right,' said Will. 'And even if we made representations in London, what reason would they have to listen to us?'

De Vere let out a short, humourless laugh. 'They have their man. A foreigner, too. Such fine red meat for the *patrie*.'

His hanging will be quite a spectacle, I thought, though I did not say so aloud.

'The question is, what is our next move? If we cannot rely on help from London, then we certainly cannot expect any here.'

The babe began to gurgle. Alice bounced him up and down gently as he squirmed in her arms.

'What is he called, your boy?' I asked.

'He has no name, sir. And he shall go without one until his father is a free man again, God willing.'

'Your faith does you credit, madam,' I said, as reassuringly as I could.

We saw Alice off with more confidence than any of us felt, then de Vere began pacing the room, anxiously.

'If he has been condemned, there is little we can do. It is not like we can raid the prison.'

Belle smiled. 'We could try.'

'Our best chance – our only chance – is to remain undistracted from our course of action. We have to expose whatever it is Harcourt is up to. We are so close, and yet...' She broke off, noticing the look that passed between me and Will. 'What? Well, come on – out with it.'

'Sam had the idea that it was time to confront Harcourt in the open.'

'Just when I had decided he wasn't a complete imbecile.'

'I said much the same thing at first. But I think there is merit in this. Sam?'

I leaned forward in my chair. 'The *Prince Rupert* is obviously key to their plan. We know from what we saw last night that the cargo of explosives is near enough fully loaded. We must find out where it is going.'

'And how do you suggest we do that?' said de Vere. 'Walk up and ask them?'

'Immediately prior to most sea voyages, the captain will usually have two charts, marked up with the expected route. One is usually kept upon his person, but the other will be secured in his quarters.'

De Vere turned to Belle for confirmation.

'He's right. But getting on board ain't easy.'

'It would be for me,' I said. 'I could order one of the men to ferry me across. Then all I would need to do is avoid being seen by any of the officers on board.'

'No, Sam.'

I stared at Will. This was not what we discussed upstairs.

He continued, 'The men may be under orders to look out for you, but they're much less likely to notice me. And I can fight my way out better than you can, if that's what it comes to.'

'If there's any fighting to be done, I'm coming too,' said Belle.

'I mean no offence, Belle, but the odds of you going unremarked aboard an English naval vessel are next to none.'

'Neither of you are going on that ship,' I protested.

'Will is right,' said de Vere. 'He would stand a better chance than either of you.'

'It is too dangerous.'

'It wasn't when you wanted to put yourself in harm's way,' said Will.

'I forbid it.'

'What choice do we have, Sam? You said it yourself, we have no other plan. I am doing this.'

I was angry with him for letting me believe that I might board the ship myself. But then, if he had told me the truth upstairs, I would never even have suggested the plan to the others. Reluctantly, I conceded.

'Very well, I agree. But under protest. So how do we get you on board? Without my involvement, that part of the problem remains the same.'

We thought for a moment, then de Vere snapped her fingers.

'I have an idea. Belle, how would you feel about another trip to see your friend Jack Gale?'

We hurried down the narrow alleyway, trying to reach Grape Lane before it was too late. De Vere led the way, along with Cecily, the girl I had met at dinner on our first night at Dione House.

Will and I struggled to keep up as they sped through the stinking backstreets, cutting through empty yards, stables, and anywhere else that could save us valuable seconds of time.

While discussing the plan in greater detail, we quickly realised that Will would need to wear the uniform of an officer in order to stand the best chance of passing through the dockyard unchallenged and securing passage to the *Prince Rupert*. Unable to come up with a way to break into Admiralty House, where most of the officers are billeted, we needed another solution.

It was de Vere who suggested a brothel. She knew Cecily was in contact with some of the whores in Grape Lane, where the greatest number of the town's stews can be found. Cecily got word to them and, within a couple of hours, a message came back that an officer had arrived to take his pleasures.

All we had to do was get there before he left.

We had travelled as close as we could by coach, but there was still some way to go. I tried desperately to keep pace with the others, but I feared too much exertion would risk inflaming my wound. Will tried to stay back with me without losing sight of the women, who ignored all of my entreaties to slow down.

At last, we rounded the corner into Grape Lane. The quiet street of old timber-framed houses stank of ordure, made all the worse by the heat of the midday sun. I leaned on Will's shoulder, gasping for breath, as de Vere looked around impatiently.

'Which one is it?'

'There,' said Cecily, hurrying over to a small unglazed window, hung with a red curtain. She whispered something and the curtain parted to reveal a lank, pox-scarred young woman in a threadbare robe.

With a swift glance over her shoulder to check she was not being observed, the girl slipped a large bundle to Cecily, then took a small pouch of money in return and pulled the curtain shut.

'Got it,' whispered Cecily, running back over to us.

'Excellent,' said de Vere. 'Time to go. Pepys, keep up.'

Before I could respond, the women had taken off towards the end of the lane. Will lifted my arm around his shoulder to take some of my weight.

'Come on, Sam. It's not far.'

We emerged into a small patch of wasteland, past which was a busy thoroughfare. A cart stood near the road, laden with barrels. In front stood a large, bald-headed man, feeding his horse. Immediately I recognised him as Silken Jack, landlord of the Old Ring o' Bells. Belle was standing next to him, dressed in plain black breeches and a leather jerkin, her long hair tied up in braids. She strode over to us.

'What took you so long? You got it then?'

'We should hurry,' said de Vere. 'Will?'

Cecily handed him the bundle, but he hesitated. Belle raised an eyebrow.

'Ain't shy are you, my boy?'

With an irritable shrug, Will started to pull off his clothes. De Vere turned away. Belle did not.

'Cecily, you'd better keep watch,' said de Vere. 'If the poor man comes out looking for his clothes, try to keep him there.'

The girl smirked. 'Almost worth hanging around to see, ain't it?'

I went over to Jack Gale. 'Do you really suppose this plan will work, Mr Gale?'

On hearing me use his real name, he glared at me warily for a moment, as if still unsure whether to trust me. 'Can't say. But if Belle wants to try, we try.'

'They're loading the supply boat, now' added Belle. 'Got about twenty minutes, I reckon.'

'It… almost fits,' said Will.

I turned to look at him. The blue coat and white waistcoat were far too tight around his broad chest. 'Well… so long as nobody looks too closely.'

De Vere clapped her gloved hands together. 'Come. We must hurry.'

Belle lifted a barrel from the back of the cart, tipping it forward to show that it was empty. Will looked down at the narrow opening.

'You expect me to fit in there?'

'It was your idea.' She replaced the barrel and leaned back against the cart with a roguish grin.

Will hopped up and stepped into the open barrel. At first I thought he would never fit, but after some careful manoeuvring, he narrowly managed to lower his head below the top. Belle picked up the lid, hammered it loosely into place, then tapped the side.

'Alright in there, my boy?'

'Stinks of rum in here.'

'Have all the luck, you do.'

'Ready?' said Gale.

'Aye,' replied Belle, pulling on her tricorn hat.

The two of them jumped on board and Gale whipped the horse into action. Seconds later, they disappeared out onto the thoroughfare.

I stood with de Vere in a narrow passageway facing the entrance to the shipyard. From our vantage point we had a clear view of the quayside and the supply boat, which was near fully loaded, yet still no sign of Gale. If he did not hurry, we would lose our chance.

Fortunately, we did not have to wait long. I held my breath as the cart rolled into view. Gale dismounted and walked over to a squat young man, whom I recognised as Dimmock, the purser's mate I had met several weeks ago on our first morning in Portsmouth. Gale's manner was forceful but disinterested, as if he had a job to do but did not much care to be there.

Just like any other tradesman, I thought.

Dimmock scratched his head doubtfully as Gale spoke to him. I could hear only snatches of their conversation.

'Ain't expecting no more… I'll have to check…That your lad? Queer looking, ain't he?'

I held my breath as Dimmock walked up to the cart in his disinctive, loping gait, and started inspecting the barrels. For a moment I thought he would order some to be opened, but then with another scratch of his head, he gestured for them to pass.

'Go on. At least purser's not here to tell me I done the list wrong.'

I sighed with relief and looked over to de Vere. She had been holding her breath too.

We retreated to the rendezvous point at the patch of wasteland near Grape Lane. Cecily was there waiting for us.

'Any trouble?' said de Vere.

'I heard shouting from inside, then the cull came out and off he went in nothing but a blanket and a pair of old breeches.'

The three of us settled down to wait, perching on what remained of a low brick wall. It was uncomfortable, but I was relieved to be at rest. The strain of the day was starting to take its toll.

We sat there in silence for what seemed like an age. In the distance, the bells of the Domus struck midday.

'How long has it been?' I said.

'Forty minutes, perhaps?' said de Vere. I noticed that she had been working the hem of her dress with her fingers.

Forty minutes. Too soon for them to have returned here. But surely enough time for Will to be off the ship, at least?

I must have been restless, for de Vere turned to look at me. 'Are you anxious?'

'How could I not be? This was a bad idea.'

'They know what they are doing.'

'Belle and Gale, maybe, but Will is headstrong. For all his bravado, the boy is out of his depth with this.' I struck my leg with frustration. 'Madness. I should never have let him go.'

'Panicking serves no one.'

'How can you be so damned calm? Anything could have happened to him.'

To my surprise, she reached forward and placed her hand gently on mine. 'Listen. I am anxious too. But this is not about you or me. If they have succeeded, they will be here soon. If they have failed, they will need us to stay calm. As I said, panicking serves no one.' I began to speak but she cut me off. 'Strategy. It does not mean that we do not care.'

I rubbed the sides of my forehead. 'Very well. How long has it been now?'

'About two minutes after the last time you asked.'

We fell to silence once again. I could hear the people and horses from the streets nearby, but nothing that sounded like Gale's cart approaching.

'How long have you known him?'

I turned to de Vere. 'I beg your pardon?'

'Will. How long have you been friends?'

'Friends? I would say two or three years. He left my employ in '63.'

'Your employ?'

'He was my manservant.'

'Interesting. I never would have guessed. He is a fine lad, you know. You should be proud of him.'

I smiled, grateful for the compliment. A slight breeze ruffled her hair, and I caught a wave of her scent. An expensive perfume made of bergamot and cloves. The faint undertone of sweat.

It gave me gooseflesh.

Suddenly there was the sound of approaching wheels and we sprang to our feet. A few seconds later, Gale's cart hurtled around the corner. My heart raced. I rushed towards them, sitting on the perch, only to stop dead in my tracks when I saw the look on Belle's face.

'What happened?'

'He's gone.'

I felt sick. 'What do you mean he's gone?'

'The ship. He got on board right enough, but then the anchor went up and…'

'Nowt we could do,' interrupted Gale. 'But it ain't a full crew, I tell you that.'

'Speak plainly,' said de Vere. 'Do you mean to say they've put to sea?'

He looked at her gravely. 'Aye.'

I could hardly breathe. Blood pounded in my ears and I felt my legs beginning to sway. The women steadied me before I fell. I attempted to speak, but the words came out as little more than a whisper.

'My God. Will…'

I watched through de Vere's spyglass as the *Prince Rupert* sailed westwards out of the bay. The wind had dropped, perhaps buying us a little time, but soon the ship would disappear from view altogether.

And with it our hopes.

'If that girl ain't here soon, we'll lose them,' said Gale, blowing out a cloud of tobacco smoke.

'She will be,' snapped de Vere. 'Just concentrate on making sure we're ready to leave when she does.'

We were standing on the shore at a secluded inlet about half a mile up the coast from the town. A little way off, accessible via a ledge that could only be reached by wading through knee-deep water, was a tall and narrow sea cave.

The perfect place for a smuggler to hide a boat.

After the initial shock wore off, our minds had quickly turned to forming a plan. I had believed the situation to be all but hopeless, but Belle suggested we hire Gale's ship to give chase. If we could at least make it to wherever they were going, we might yet be able to rescue Will – assuming he had not been caught already.

It was only a sliver of hope, but one I had gladly taken.

'I don't like it,' the old man said. 'Who knows where they're headed? The *Rupert's* a ship-of-the-line. You could sail her to the New World and back. Fastest boat I've got is a small ketch hidden out at Monkton Cove. Fast, but she'll not go much further than France or the Low Countries. And if the weather turns – forget it.'

'I will pay you,' said de Vere.

'Aye, you will. But that ain't the point. Even if it worked, you ain't got a hope of saving him.'

'How much?'

'Face it, the boy's probably dead already.'

'How *much*?'

'Jack.' Belle stepped between them. 'I know this ain't your fight, but you're the best chance we got. What say you just get us there and let us worry about the rest?'

Gale scratched his bald head. 'What's the boy to you anyway, Belle?'

'He ain't nothing to me. But he's one of us now.'

'I ain't doing no fighting for him.'

'We just need your boat.'

'And me as skipper, is that it?'

'Aye, that's it.'

She looked at him steadily. Narrowing his eyes, Gale turned back to de Vere.

'So how much you offering?'

The sound of boots on shingle brought me back to the present. It was Cecily, running towards us with Kitty by her side. Cecily was carrying two baskets, while Kitty held a small wooden box.

'At last,' said de Vere. 'You brought the money?'

Kitty opened the box to reveal a large pile of gold coins. Gale leaned forward to inspect them, then with a grunt, he turned and started wading out to the cave.

'The victuals too?' said de Vere.

'Everything you asked for, mistress. But…'

'I know, Cecily. But this has to be done.' She placed her hand on the girl's shoulder. 'I promise we will be back.'

I raised the spyglass and looked out at the *Rupert* again. The outline of her sails against the sky was rapidly diminishing. If we were to do this, it had to be now.

Just as I was about to ask what was keeping them, Gale's boat began to emerge from the cave. It was a ketch, sturdy, and large enough for a crew of five or six. The sails had been set and the oars were down, with Gale rowing on one side and Belle on the other.

Steadying himself against the motion of the waves, Gale threw a guide rope around a mooring post and heaved in tight, taking care to keep the vessel at oar's length from the rock face. He cupped his hands around his mouth and called over to us.

'Come on then, what you waiting for? Scared to get your feet wet?'

As I write this, we have been at sea for several hours. I told the others I was going below to get some rest, but the truth is that I need to be alone for a time. I dare not let myself think too hard about Will and the danger he is in. But I feel an unquenchable guilt in the very pit of my stomach. I could have stopped him and I didn't.

After setting sail, we struggled to catch enough wind to keep the *Rupert* in sight. We lost her altogether as she disappeared past Selsey Bill, but after an anxious wait, we rounded the headland ourselves and I had her in my sights once again.

Our vessel has a single, discernible advantage – size. The *Rupert* is a formidable warship, but slow. Her top speed would only be around ten knots. Meanwhile, we are flying twin sails, rigged fore-and-aft, making us swift and nimble by comparison.

On the other hand, we are sailing blind. As soon as we left, I knew that unless we could get a clear indication of where the *Rupert* was heading, it would not be long until Gale insisted on turning around.

All the time there was a shadow hanging over us that was even darker still. If Harcourt found Will on board, he could have him killed there and then.

The chances are that he already has.

But I have tarried too long down here. Time enough to write later. I am serving no one being shut away from the action. Least of all Will.

As the sun began to set, Gale knelt down on the deck and spread out a chart in front of him. He made a few calculations using a compass and an astrolabe, marking lines on the chart with a stick of charcoal. Then he beckoned us over.

'We're here.' He pointed at the Strait of Dover on the map. 'The *Rupert* set sail just before noon. If she was bound for Calais, she'd have turned east by now. But she ain't, she's heading nor'east.'

'What does that mean?' asked de Vere.

'Now, she's still got time to change course and head up the coast of England, but she ain't shown no sign of that so far. So...' He jabbed a finger at the map. 'I'll wager she's making for the Low Countries.'

'Or Dunkirk?' said Belle.

'Aye, right enough. Could be. Too soon to tell.'

I took my writing stick from my pocket and used the blunt end to trace the outline of the coast northwards from Calais.

'If that is so, and if we assume Dunkirk is not their destination, then the next major ports would be Flanders: Ostend and Knokke. If not there, then Holland – Rotterdam, Scheveningen, Amsterdam, or...' I trailed off.

'What is it?' said de Vere.

'Amsterdam is where the mission is based.'

'The what?' asked Gale.

'Two or three months past, the King sent a special diplomatic mission to Holland, in an attempt to ease tensions with the Dutch. At its head is a man named Sir George Downing.'

'The one those churls spoke of last night?' said Belle.

'But why?' asked de Vere. 'To what end?'

'I don't know. But if I am right, Harcourt is at this moment sailing towards Amsterdam with a ship full of stolen explosives. And two known associates of his told us that the plan has something to do with Sir George Downing. Surely this cannot be a coincidence?'

It was dark when we sailed past Dunkirk. The course of the *Rupert* remained fixed in a nor'easterly direction – which in another day or so would take her to Amsterdam.

I am right; I know I am. But why? How does Downing fit into the plan? If any harm were to come to him before he left Holland, it would seriously impact our relations with the Dutch, perhaps even lead to war. Harcourt must know that as well as anyone. Unless that is the object of this whole conspiracy, in which case, the man is a traitor as well as a criminal.

A traitor. Just as Lord Maynard suspected.

The moon was clear and bright, and we were taking it in turns to keep watch on deck. Had there been rain this night, we might have lost sight of the *Rupert*, but we were able to track her almost as easily by night as we could by day.

It was agreed that de Vere and I would go below for some sleep while Gale and Belle took it in turns to steer. It was cramped below decks, with barely enough room for both of us. I tried to settle as best I could on an old straw mattress, my coat folded into a makeshift pillow, under which I placed my wig for a little extra padding. The only light came from slivers of moonlight through cracks in the deck above.

I could scarcely imagine two more exhausting days than those I had just experienced. But sleep would not come. By the light of day, spurred on by the camaraderie of the group, I found that I was able to push morbid thoughts from my mind. As de Vere said, panicking serves no one. And yet, in the darkness of the hold, a new melancholy overtook me. What were our chances of saving Will, truly? I feared they were next to nothing. Even at best, he would be clapped in leg irons now, awaiting prosecution on their return to England. But in my heart I knew that the alternative was more likely.

How will I ever go back to life as it was, if Will is dead? What will it be like to pass by his empty house on Seething Lane, knowing he will never return? How could I possibly get used to seeing some other fellow at his neat little desk at the Navy Board, without each time being compelled to relive this awful day?

I sat up, rubbing my eyes to try to force such tormenting thoughts from my mind. Then, to my surprise, I saw that de Vere was also awake, her knees drawn to her chest, staring at the ground in contemplation. I watched her for a while, alone in the dark, unaware she was being observed. Could I ever truly know this woman? What manner of thoughts came to her in times of solitude? Suddenly, I felt compelled to be near to her.

Crouching low to avoid hitting my head on the low ceiling, I made my way across to her side. She looked up as I approached, surprised at first, but then she shifted so that I could sit down next to her.

'Pepys, I did not know you were awake too.'

'I thought perhaps those of us with less hardy sea legs may provide each other with a little company.'

'Indeed. I take it that thoughts of Will are what keep you awake?'

I sighed deeply. 'I should never have let him go.'

'I am not sure you could have stopped him.'

'What about you, madam? What troubles you?'

'Me? There is a whole world out there to trouble me. But you have burdens enough of your own without taking on any of mine.'

I had never been quite so close to her as I was in this moment, sitting there with my arm pressed against hers. I found my eyes wandering about her person, noticing tiny little imperfections for the very first time. The subtle lines at the corners of her eyes. A grey hair or two, almost invisible among the dark ringlets that hung down to her shoulders. Her ears – how had I never noticed that her ears were quite so small?

'Pepys?'

I looked up. The darkness made her expression hard to read. Cautiously, I moved my hand on top of hers, waiting to see if she would pull away. But instead, she smiled. My heart raced. Did she truly want me to kiss her? I began to lean in closer, but then I stopped.

What was I doing? A part of me wanted this so badly. There was a time when I would not have hesitated. And yet, I had sworn to be a better man. If I am ever to have a chance of winning back Elisabeth's trust, it is time for those days to end.

'Forgive me,' I muttered, rising abruptly and returning to my bed. I closed my eyes and lay still. There was a long pause before I heard Charlotte lie down too. Then there was no sound at all, apart from the gentle creaking of the ship on the waves.

I lay awake for a long time, thinking of home.

August 14th

The sun had almost set when at last we saw the port of Amsterdam.

Belle had been right about Gale. The man was as capable a skipper as any I have seen. We got all the way here without ever losing sight of the *Prince Rupert*, until at the last we reached the Zuyderzee, a large and busy inlet that leads from the sea into the port itself. It was completely dark by the time we made landfall, by which time we had little hope of picking out the *Rupert* among the myriad of vessels.

No matter. We would find her again soon enough.

This was my first visit to the Dutch lands, and never before had I seen a port that wears its wealth quite so openly as this one. Vast brick warehouses spread out from the harbour, and behind them were a dozen church spires that the evening light had turned the colour of burned orange as we approached.

Nor have I ever seen as many vessels in one place as were arrayed in its hundreds of moorings. Schooners, carracks and brigantines; Dutch fluets and pinnaces; barques of all kinds; vast Spanish galleons; even junks all the way from China, with their curious square sails.

I knew the coffers of the Dutch Republic swelled more bountifully than those of almost any kingdom in Europe. But I had not quite grasped by how much until today. All the more reason that war must be avoided at any cost. With England's finances in the perilous state they are, could we hope to stand against an enemy such as this?

'I reckon the *Rupert* put to harbour on the other side of them warehouses.' Gale stood on the deck, pointing to a row of tall brick buildings near the far end of the quayside. 'Port's busy enough for you to approach unseen, but you won't have much time.'

'Very well,' I said. 'Then we shall just have to rush the gangway.'

'You want to commit suicide, that's your business,' he grunted.

Belle lowered the spyglass. 'Aye, he's right. We'd not even make it across the deck.'

'Well, what then? Are you suggesting I just announce myself instead?'

'More than one way onto a ship,' said Gale, sucking on his pipe. 'Ain't that so, Belle?'

She grinned broadly. 'Aye, Captain. That there are.'

'What the devil are you talking about?' asked de Vere.

Gale took his pipe from his mouth and used it to draw shapes in the air. 'We approach by sea. Climb to the quarter galley, right under the stern. Then from there we can get below.'

'Madness,' she replied. 'But I can see it may be your best hope. You would go, Belle?'

'Aye.'

'What about you, Gale?'

'I ain't shying from a fight, but you'll need me manning the boat. Unless either of you think you can handle a pair of oars well enough?'

'I fear not. Very well, I shall go with Belle.'

'No,' I said emphatically. 'I will go.'

'A noble gesture, Pepys, but trust me, you are no fighter.'

'Will is my friend and I will see this through.'

De Vere turned to Belle. 'What do you say?'

'You're right, he ain't no fighter. But that's an English navy ship. He knows his way around it better than either of us do.'

I looked around at the assembled faces. 'Good. Then it is settled?'

Gale shrugged. 'If Belle's happy, I won't argue.'

'Then we should go.'

De Vere held up her hand. 'And what are we do to for a boat? This one is much too big.'

Gale nodded. 'Aye, we'll need to steal one. Small fishing boat would do – a buss, maybe a wherry. How about it, Belle?'

She smiled. 'Just like old times, eh, Jack?'

I pressed my body against the side of the fishing shed, hoping I could remain unseen. A little way off, two rough-looking men were warming their hands over a brazier. Behind them sat a little rowboat, tied to a mooring. My legs were trembling with anxiety.

Just as I began to wonder if something had happened to them, Gale came into view, approaching the men as nonchalantly as if he were out for an evening stroll. He held his unlit pipe in one hand. When he got close to the men, he stopped to pat the pockets of his breeches.

'*Tondeldoos?*' he asked, in halting Dutch. The men looked at him suspiciously, then one of them reached into his pocket and handed him a tinderbox.

Gale lit his pipe. '*Dank je.*'

He held out the little brass box, but just before the man could take it, there was a quick flash from behind him and a metal bar swung into his back. He collapsed with a gasp. The other man barely had time to react before the metal came swinging his way and he, too, fell to the ground.

Belle stepped from the shadows, pulling a mask down from her face. She had a large satchel slung over her shoulder. Gale examined the tinderbox admiringly for a moment, then dropped it in front of the two prone bodies.

'You'll have need of that when you wake up,' he said, then turned towards the fish sheds. 'You can come out now, Pepys.'

I hurried over to them, anxiously looking over my shoulder. 'Well, that is enough to hang us if we are caught. We must hurry.'

No more than a minute or two later, we were rowing towards the warehouses at the end of the quay, Gale and Belle each taking an oar of the stolen vessel. A thick mist was rolling in from the sea, impeding our visibility. I looked back in the direction of Gale's ship, but all I could see through the opaque haze were the shapes of swaying masts and the spectral lights of the city beyond. We had left de Vere alone on guard with a pistol. I prayed she would have no need of it.

Gale navigated as best he could by the light of the moon and the shape of the bay ahead of us, picked out by the glow of tavern windows and the flickering lanterns of vessels arrayed across the harbour. I shivered, but not from cold. It was eerily quiet.

Then at last I saw it – the *Prince Rupert,* at anchor, maybe a hundred yards ahead of us. Her sails were furled and she didn't appear to be flying any flag. She had put to harbour in a quiet section of the port; even the warehouses around here looked to be deserted.

I nudged Belle. She indicated that she had seen it too.

We rowed closer and closer until we drifted under the enormous bulk of the *Rupert*'s hull. I began to hear English voices from the quayside and craned my neck to try and see.

'What's going on there?' whispered Gale.

I knew that time was short. But this could be our only chance to find out what they were up to. 'Can we get any nearer, Jack?'

We rowed a little closer to the dock. Suddenly I was glad of the mist, with its power to cloak us from view. Belle took something out of her satchel and handed it to me. It was de Vere's spyglass.

From where we were, I had a clear line of sight to the front of the ship. A cargo of wooden barrels was being unloaded onto rowboats. There were maybe a dozen men, mostly English sailors, but the others were dressed in the simple clothes of artisans and were speaking Dutch. It was these men who seemed to be in receipt of the goods.

'Those the same barrels as the ones we found in the mill?' whispered Belle.

I nodded. One of the men seemed to hear something from behind them and turned. I froze. Could they see us?

'*Een hond,*' he said, returning to work.

So, I thought, Harcourt is supplying Dutchmen with English gunpowder and weapons. But to what end? And who are they?

I scanned the faces of the English sailors, but did not see anybody I recognised.

'Can you see Harcourt?' asked Belle.

'No. He must be inside. We need to hurry, before they are finished.'

Gale took over both oars and rowed the boat into position, straining to keep us from being carried too close to the hull by the motion of the waves. Belle reached behind her and picked up a long, coiled rope, one end of which was attached to a piece of metal with four sharp prongs.

A grappling hook.

Motioning for us to stay low, she stood up and swung the rope around her head, letting it grow longer with the force of each rotation. The metal had become little more than a blur when at last she let go. The rope uncoiled rapidly as the hook flew upward and embedded itself with a sharp crack in the outer ledge of the quarter galley.

I held my breath, certain the impact had been loud enough that someone must have heard. We waited for what seemed like minutes, but must only have been a few seconds.

Nobody came. I guessed they must all be busy unloading their cargo.

Gesturing for Gale to row even closer, Belle picked up her satchel and placed one foot on the side of the rowboat, gripping the rope tightly. Then she crouched down and leaped forward, legs outstretched, coming to rest a moment later with a painful thud as her boots slammed onto the hull.

She teetered precariously, struggling to hold on, but quickly regained her balance and started to climb. I watched, my heart pounding, as she crept up the outer surface of the ship, which looked as tall as a cathedral spire. I hardly dared breathe as she reached the quarter galley, then with a final lunge, disappeared over the edge of the balcony.

The wait was agonising, but after a few seconds, she leaned over the edge and waved twice – the signal to get ready. Then she reached into her satchel and threw down a rope ladder, which I managed to catch and hold before it clattered onto the hull.

As gently as he could, Gale let the boat drift so close to the *Rupert* that it was almost touching the sides, then gave me the signal. I swallowed hard. Then, gripping the ladder with white knuckles, I began to climb.

I kept my eyes raised upwards as I lifted one foot above the other, trying not to give in to the temptation to look down. Every muscle in my arms strained with the effort of holding on as the enormous vessel rose and fell slowly in the water.

Barely halfway up, I started to doubt if I could make it. My limbs screamed with the effort and I began to feel sick with fear. In one dreadful moment, I lost my footing and had to scrabble so fast to regain it that I caught my fingers in between a rung and the hull. I stifled a yell of pain. Truly, I thought I could go no further. But then I thought of Will and went on climbing.

At last, I caught sight of Belle's hand, stretching out towards me from the balcony. Just a few steps more. My legs were trembling and I had chafed the skin on my hands badly, but with enormous effort I pulled myself up over the edge.

I was almost insensible from fear as I took that final step forward into the darkness, but then I felt Belle's strong hands guiding me softly to rest on the deck, and I knew at last that it was over. I had made it.

I lay there for a moment, panting with exertion. Belle gestured impatiently for me to get up. There was no time to lose. Leaving the hook and ladder in place, we hurried over to the hatch and paused there for a moment, listening for sounds of movement from within. Then, as softly as she could, Belle pulled it open.

Proceeding almost on tiptoe, we climbed down the stairs and moved through the empty room below. From the long table and rows of shelves that lined the wall, I guessed it must be the great cabin. We were fortunate that any officers on board must be engaged elsewhere.

We reached a door. Belle cracked it open and looked out, then motioned to me that the coast was clear. We stepped out into a corridor, which stretched off in both directions. There was no movement; no sign of life. Aside from the gentle murmuring of the waves against the hull, everything was quiet.

'Which way?' she whispered.

I looked left and right, trying to recall everything I knew about the layout of a second rate ship-of-the-line. If Will was alive, it was likely he would be held in the brig. That meant we had to continue for about half the length of the ship, then go down as far as we could.

'That way. Through the officers' stores and then the cuddy. That will take us to the first gun deck.'

'Ain't no way that won't be guarded.'

'Not necessarily. Most of the men appear to be engaged in moving the cargo. If we are lucky, we may have a chance of reaching the main hatch way and getting down to the hold undetected.'

We crept down the long corridor. The oil lamps fixed to the wall cast long, flickering tendrils of light that barely penetrated the thick shadows. Whether we were truly alone or not, it was impossible to tell. Perhaps we were already being watched, I thought, as my heart pounded so hard that I could hear the blood rushing through my ears.

Suddenly, there were voices from up ahead. We froze, listening as they drew closer. Two men, maybe more. I looked at Belle. Her hand hovered near the pistol in her belt, but I knew that she would use it only as a last resort. The noise would bring the whole ship down on us, and at best she could only take one man before having to reload.

I grabbed her arm and pointed back the way we came. We began to retreat as quickly as we could, but then I heard other voices, approaching from behind us this time.

There was nowhere to go. We were trapped.

Suddenly I noticed a door set into the wall, a short distance ahead of us. I grabbed Belle and pulled her towards it. There was no way to know what was on the other side, but it was our only hope.

I pushed it open to reveal a staircase, leading downwards. We slipped inside and I closed the door silently behind us. It was almost pitch dark, but just enough light seeped in to enable us to make our way down the stairs. The steps creaked underfoot at what seemed like a deafening volume. Meanwhile, the voices outside kept getting closer.

We reached the bottom of the stairs and looked up. We could hear talking. Shadows began to move back and forth on the other side of the doorway. Evidently the two parties had met.

Belle and I gripped onto each other, hardly daring to move or make a sound. Sweat trickled down my brow and stung my eyes. Then at last, with agonising slowness, the voices receded and faded to nothing. They had gone, for now. We exhaled with relief.

By now my eyes had adjusted enough to the gloom that I could see we were in a storage hold. Next to us was a row of casks. This must be where the victuals are stored, I thought.

I was about to say that it was probably safe for us to leave when I felt the coldness of metal press into my neck. Belle's eyes widened in shock and I braced myself for the bite of the killing blade that I knew was about to come...

'Sam?'

My eyes shot open. I spun around. 'Will! God be praised, you're alive!'

He sheathed his pocket knife and we embraced warmly. He turned to Belle and she punched him in the arm.

'What you want to go and get yourself trapped for, you lack-witted whoreson?'

Will put his arms around her. She tried to seem affronted, but instead her hands rose slowly to rest on his back.

He pulled away and looked us up and down. His pallid, stubbly face shone with dirt and sweat, but otherwise he seemed unharmed.

'How did you get on board? And where are we?'

'Amsterdam,' I said.

'Amsterdam? I knew we had been at sea awhile, but... Are the others here?'

'De Vere is guarding the ship. Jack Gale is waiting for us outside in a fishing boat.'

'What, old Silken Jack?'

'The same.'

'You have been busy.'

'Aye,' said Belle. 'Saving your sorry arse. We'd best be going.'

She led us up the stairs, gesturing for us to be as quiet as we could on the creaking steps. Gently she pushed the door open and looked from left to right.

'All clear,' she whispered.

We hurried along the corridor and through the empty great cabin, out onto the quarter deck. The rope ladder and grappling hook were still in place over the edge of the balcony.

'Go. I'll follow,' said Belle, as she removed the hook and began winding it up around her forearm.

Will went first, unsteadily to begin with, but soon getting used to the precarious motion of the ladder against the hull. Steeling myself, I held on to the rope and put one leg over the edge.

I breathed heavily, telling myself that I had done this once and I could do it again. Then I caught a glimpse of the roiling sea below and thought I would be sick.

'Go on,' hissed Belle. 'What are you waiting for?'

Closing my eyes, I swung my other leg over the edge, gripping the ladder so tightly that my fingernails dug into the palms of my hands. I do not know how I managed it, but somehow I was able to take another step. Then another. And another.

With agonising slowness, we descended towards the water. I could only trust that Gale was still there in his boat, waiting for us, for even when I did open my eyes again, I could not bear to look down.

Belle finished winding the rope and began the descent herself. I envied the speed and fearlessness with which she moved, and before long she was directly above me.

'Can't you go any faster?' she whispered.

'I am doing my best, madam.'

From below, I heard the sounds of oars in the water and dared to hazard a glance downwards. I felt a surge of relief. Gale was rowing into position. We were almost there.

Will reached the bottom of the ladder and jumped. Gale caught him, then started gesturing at us to go faster.

It was then that I heard the shouting.

'You! Stop!'

Belle cursed. 'They've seen us. Hurry!'

I scrambled down the ladder as fast as I could, all hesitation gone. But the shouting was getting louder. I glanced upwards to see several men looking over the edge. I just had time to wonder if Captain Harcourt was among them when there was a loud bang and a bullet whizzed past my head, splashing into the sea.

'Sam, jump!' shouted Will, stretching his arms up towards me.

I was not quite to the bottom of the ladder, but I knew I had no alternative. As another gunshot fired from above, I said a brief prayer and let go. With a cry of effort, Will caught me. A moment later I heard Belle landing too.

'Go. Now!' she yelled, picking up one oar as Gale took the other.

They began to row with frantic intensity, but we had covered barely any distance at all when the third bullet came, slamming into the boat with an almighty crack. I shielded my face as splinters of wood flew upwards.

We were hit.

'Harder!' shouted Gale. 'Row harder!'

Will grabbed onto the end of Belle's oar and I took Gale's, adding our strength to theirs as we rowed as hard as we could. More shots landed in the sea around us, but the moon had disappeared behind a cloud, making us a difficult target in the darkness.

Then I felt it – wetness, seeping in through holes in my shoes.

'We're taking on water!' I yelled.

'Starboard turn!' Gale shouted back. Belle and Will eased off their oar as Gale and I doubled our pace, heaving over and over as the little boat veered sharply towards the shore.

Will pulled off his blue officer's coat and jammed it against the hole in the deck, but it was enough to slow the leak only a little. Cold water was still pouring in, up to my ankles now.

Harder and harder we rowed, as the quayside crept nearer with agonising slowness. I could hear more shouts from the *Rupert*, no doubt ordering men to meet us on the shore and cut off our escape. We would never make it.

'*Land!*' shouted Gale, and a moment later there was a sharp jolt as we slammed into a sandbank. We dropped the oars and leaped over the side, wading as fast as we could through the waist-deep water and onto the shore, then up the muddy slope that led onto the quayside.

'Which way now?' asked Will.

I looked around. We had come ashore just south of the warehouses. The quickest way back to the ship would be to turn right and go along the main thoroughfare that ran next to the port. But that would leave us dangerously exposed.

'There,' I said, pointing instead to a small cobbled lane that ran between two of the warehouses. But before we had got there, a group of English sailors rounded the corner to our left. They were armed with muskets and swords. Among them was a man in civilian clothes, whose face I could not quite see, but who seemed to be in charge.

'That must be Harcourt,' I said.

Our only hope was to reach the alleyway before they spotted us. We were almost there when a loud, commanding voice cut through the night air.

'Pepys?'

I felt my blood run cold. I knew that voice. Slowing my pace, I turned just in time to see the line of men parting and the man in civilian clothes step forward. It was not Harcourt at all.

It was Ben.

He stared at me, his face a mask of pure shock. For a moment, I actually thought we were saved, that this had somehow all been a terrible misunderstanding. That everything would be alright.

Ben turned to his men. '*After them.*'

I leaped into action, running as fast as I could to catch up with the others. Will was standing halfway up the lane, waiting for me.

'Sam, what in God's name—'

'Run, Will. *Run!*'

The lane opened out into an empty street lined with poor-looking houses. Belle and Gale were already there, waiting for us, impatiently.

'It's Ben,' I said, barely able to get the words out.

Will turned to me in shock. 'What? It can't be.'

'Who's Ben?' asked Gale.

'You mean the Governor?' said Belle.

From behind us I could hear the sound of heavy boots on cobblestones. Belle spurred herself into action. 'No time. This way.'

We followed her down a narrow alleyway that ran behind the warehouse to our right. The dark passageway stank of damp and rotten meat, and I could barely see where we were going, but this was no time to be squeamish.

We were running all but blind through the dark space, praying that it would soon open out and provide us with another escape route. I prayed that the men had not seen where we had gone.

'They went in here.'

The voice came from behind, quickly followed by the sound of men running. My breath was growing short, and ahead of me I could see that Gale was slowing too. Even Will seemed to be flagging. Only Belle kept up the pace, leading us further and further into the darkness.

'Stop!' she yelled suddenly, and we came to a juddering halt. It was only after I slammed into Will that I saw we were facing a brick wall.

It was a dead end.

We looked around, desperately searching for a way out as the sound of running boots drew ever closer. But we were trapped like rats.

'Up there.' Will pointed above our heads. About twelve feet up there was a little window set into the wall of the warehouse.

'We can't—' I began, but he had already made a stirrup of his hands for Belle to step into.

'Come on, help!' she said, gesturing to me and Gale.

She balanced one leg on my shoulder, then in a single motion she vaulted upwards, gripping onto the windowsill with both hands and swinging herself up as hard as she could. Her shoulder rammed into the window pane and she fell through, in a hail of shattering glass.

'Now you,' said Will.

Using his hand as a foothold, I climbed onto his shoulders and he pushed me up with all his strength. Belle reached down and grabbed me with both hands, hauling me in through the window. Broken glass slashed my clothes and scratched at my skin as I dropped down onto the hard wooden floor on the other side.

'Now you, lad,' said Gale, and gave Will a foothold.

A few moments later, Will hauled himself up through the opening and landed on the ground next to me. We helped each other to our feet and looked around. Moonlight shone through the windows on the far side of the spacious room, which appeared to be empty.

'Come on, Jack!' Belle shouted out of the window.

I looked back down the alleyway. Two men in English naval uniform had almost reached Gale. Belle pulled out her pistol, priming it with shot and gunpowder with the speed of an expert fighter. She began to take aim, but hesitated, then shoved her pistol into my hand.

'Leave me,' Gale called up to us.

'Not while you owe me money.' Belle swung round to face Will. 'Hold me. And don't let go.'

Will put his arm around her waist and she leaned out of the window, stretching down as far as she could, but it wasn't enough to reach Gale.

'Lower,' Belle called back to Will, and carefully he adjusted his grip so that he had his arms wrapped around her thighs instead. It was just enough for Gale to grab hold of her outstretched hands.

'Now *pull*.'

Will heaved backwards with all his strength. I could see Gale scrabbling against the wall for a foothold as they dragged him towards the window. Then, just when I thought he would make it, the old man let out a sudden cry and they stopped with a violent jolt. The men had got hold of his legs.

Belle looked at me. 'Now.'

I stared at the pistol in my hand.

'Sam, do it!' cried Will, his face twisted with exertion.

'What are you waiting for, damn you?' shouted Belle.

'I… have never fired one before.'

She looked at me with exasperation. 'You point the end at the other fellow and squeeze.'

I leaned out of the window, aiming the gun. My arm was shaking wildly. Thoughts raced through my mind. How could I aim properly in the dark? How could I be sure not to hit Gale? And was I really prepared to take a man's life, even if it was to try and save us?

'*Do it, damn you!*' cried Belle, straining as hard as she could to keep hold of Gale.

I pointed the gun over their heads, closed my eyes, and fired.

There was a loud bang and I was thrown backwards, nearly losing my balance. Black smoke filled the air and my ears were ringing so hard that I could barely hear a thing as Gale tumbled through the window, crashing onto the ground.

Choking on the acrid smoke, I stood and peered out of the window. I was relieved to see the men standing there, unharmed, covering their heads for protection. After a moment, they dropped their arms and looked up at me with rage.

'Sam, we have to go.'

Will and the others were already hurrying across the empty warehouse. With a quick bow to the men on the ground, I ran after them.

Half an hour later, we were sitting on the deck of Gale's ship. Will was recounting his story, while filling his belly with some of the rations we had brought with us.

After he had found himself trapped on board the *Rupert*, he had managed to find his way to the storeroom without being challenged. Despite a narrow escape when some men had come in to fetch some goods, he had managed to remain there undetected until Belle and I had found him.

But I was hardly listening to his words. I was too busy thinking about Ben. A man whom I had once trusted with my life; one I have loved as a true and dear friend. All of it had been a lie. I had just been too blind to see.

Did this mean that it was really he who tried to have me killed in the forest? And at the marketplace in Portsmouth? No, it could not be. The men we had interrogated in the mill had been adamant – Harcourt was the one who gave them their orders.

In that case, Ben and Harcourt must be working together. Again, I recalled what I had overheard that day in the shipyard. *We are sworn to the order.* But what order?

'What do you think, Sam?'

I looked at Will blankly. 'What did you say?'

'Who were they?'

'I am sorry, Will, I missed what you said.'

'I was asking about the men on the quayside. You said they were Dutch?'

'Yes. Criminals, by the looks of it. They were certainly ready to give fight if they were disturbed.'

'And now they have got a lot of gunpowder too,' added Belle grimly, from her position on watch.

I pinched the bridge of my nose. 'There is something we are missing, I know it. And what of Sir George Downing? Is he in danger?'

'You think they plan to assassinate him?' asked de Vere.

'Perhaps. But then again, why go to all the trouble? If they want him dead, there are a hundred easier ways to achieve it.'

Gale blew out a cloud of sweet blue pipe smoke. 'Well – can't sail till this fog clears. It'll be dawn, I reckon. We best take it in turns on watch.'

'And until then we are expected to wait here like sitting targets?' said de Vere, testily.

'Perhaps, perhaps not. But I ain't sailing in this, and that's that. We get some rest, then we leave at dawn.'

Somewhere nearby a clock struck eleven, followed by another, and another, bells ringing out, almost but not quite in unison, from all around the sprawling city.

Again, I pictured those men on the quayside. Who were they? I knew there was a connection I was missing. But what was it?

'Dawn. Yes. There is still enough time.'

Will frowned. 'Sam?'

In truth, I did not realise I had spoken the words out loud. An idea had been forming in the back of my mind – one that I had been all too glad to push from my thoughts at first. Now, knowing that we were to be stuck here for at least a few more hours, I could ignore it no longer. This might be our only chance to find out what was really going on here. And perhaps avert disaster.

'Sam?' he repeated. 'Still enough time to do what?'

I looked up at him.

'To find Sir George Downing.'

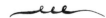

I shivered and pulled my surcoat in tighter. Where we stood could not have been more than a hundred yards from the harbour, but the cool night air was almost free of mist.

Even though Will and Belle were only on the other side of the tavern door, I felt dangerously exposed. The street looked empty enough, but this was night-time in a strange city. I had no wish to linger a moment longer than we had to.

De Vere stood opposite me, her face illuminated by the glow of the candle in the window. The fact that her heavy shawl concealed a primed flintlock was of small comfort.

After I had declared my intention to seek out Sir George Downing, Will was the only one who had agreed to go with me straight away. I would have left with him alone by my side, had Belle not spoken up.

'What's your plan then? Knock on doors till the sun comes up in the hope you find him?'

'We shall make enquiries in the taverns,' said Will.

'How's your Dutch, then, my boy?'

'I speak a few words,' I interjected. 'But it matters little; this is the richest port in the continent. It should not be difficult to find a man conversant in English or French.'

'Aye, you might at that. Or someone might stick a knife in your guts first.'

'Well then, what do you suggest?'

'I know some Dutch. Enough to get by. And I reckon I got a better nose for when a place is trouble than either of you.'

Her insolence was beginning to annoy me, but before I could respond, Will leaped to his feet.

'Belle, if you will come with us, I would be glad of it.'

'Aye, well, try not to do nothing stupid for once.' She turned to de Vere for confirmation. 'Mistress?'

'I will not stop you. But I don't like it either. So if you are going, I am going too.'

I shook my head. 'No. There is no reason for all of us to go. You have risked enough as it is.'

'It is enough of a risk just staying here. And there is safety in numbers, is there not?'

I began to object, but she was already readying her flintlock with gunpowder and shot.

I looked up at the painted sign of a sheep's head, swinging gently in the breeze outside the timber-framed building. De Vere and I had been standing outside the tavern for several minutes now, neither of us saying a word.

I wondered if she bore any ill-will towards me for what had passed between us last night, fleeting though the moment had been. Then I shook away the thought. It was only a touch of the hand. Nothing more.

'It has been a challenging few days, has it not?'

It took me a moment to register what she had said. 'Indeed it has. Perhaps more so for me than you.'

She arched an eyebrow. 'Oh?'

'I am not used to such adventure, madam. The pace at which you live your life is too fast for me.'

'You may have a point.' She paused, then her tone softened. 'You know, we are all apt to behave in ways that we later come to regret, when faced with questions of our own mortality.'

'I do not follow.'

'I heard you weeping last night. When you thought I was asleep.'

I looked at the ground, not wanting to meet her eyes. 'I… It was thoughts of my wife. That is all.'

'Ah, yes. Your wife. What is her name?'

'Elisabeth.'

'You must miss her.'

'With all my heart.'

'Truly?'

'Truly.'

She smiled. 'Then upon my oath, Samuel Pepys, I think it possible you have learned something after all.'

Suddenly I felt compelled to apologise. 'Madam, if I gave you cause to think I was—'

'There is no need,' she said, holding up her hand to silence me. 'As I said, we are all apt to make poor decisions, once in a while.'

'So… we remain friends?'

She extended her hand and I took it gladly.

'Friends.'

At that moment, the tavern door opened and Will stepped outside, Belle following right behind him.

'At last,' I said. 'Did you find out anything?'

Belle nodded. 'Aye. We'll find him on *Paternostersteeg*, which is near the *Oude Kerk*.'

'And where is that?' asked Charlotte.

She grinned and pointed behind us. I turned to look. A giant spire loomed against the dark, cloudy sky, no more than a few streets away.

I felt a rush of hope. The night might yet be ours.

'Come. There is no time to lose.'

I looked up at the tall brick building. It was narrow but handsomely built, with an unusual crenelated roof, rising in stacks to a narrow peak with a single window on the top floor. Behind this I could see the glow of candlelight.

Will hammered on the elegant black door, but there was no answer.

'There is somebody home,' I said. 'Try again.'

He pounded his fist against the wood once more, and did not stop until we heard the sound of a heavy bolt being drawn from the other side. The door opened a fraction and a young, thin-faced man wearing a nightgown and a long black overcoat looked out at us cautiously. I doubted he was yet twenty.

'What do you want?' he said, in a high, English-accented voice.

'Is this the residence of Sir George Downing?' I asked.

His manner began to shift from apprehensive to indignant. 'sir, it is the middle of the night.'

'I apologise for calling at this late hour, but my business is of paramount urgency. I have to talk to Sir George Downing now.'

'Come back in the morning.'

I jammed my foot in the door to prevent him from closing it. 'No, Mr…'

'Peck. Sir George's private secretary.'

'Well, Mr Peck, this cannot wait. You will tell Sir George that Samuel Pepys is here. He will know me; I was once his teller at the Exchequer and I am now Clerk of the Acts to the Navy Board.' Peck looked over my shoulder. 'These are my associates. Mr Hewer is my secretary, and Mistress de Vere is the widow of Captain Edmund de Vere, who once attended His Majesty in exile. I repeat, we must see Sir George now.'

Peck hesitated, but he did not move back from the doorway. De Vere stepped forward.

'Sir, we would not have come here at this hour if our business were not in deadly earnest. At the very least, will you afford us safe harbour while you inform your master and let him make the decision for himself?'

Peck pursed his lips, and with a final, priggish shake of his head, he opened the door and invited us inside.

We stood in the neat little parlour, the only light coming from a freshly lit candle and the glowing embers of a coal fire.

'God, how I wish we were back in London,' I said to Will.

'And we shall be. Soon. What will you say if he does agree to see you?'

'I will tell him the facts and hope he believes me. What else can I do?'

Will glanced over his shoulder at Charlotte and Belle, who were standing by the window. He lowered his voice.

'How do you fare, otherwise? I am so sorry about Ben. I know what he meant to you.'

'Thank you. I admit, the sight of his face was like a knife to my gut. But at least now I know the truth. What is done is done.'

'Sir George will listen, you know. I am sure of it. He must.'

'You have never met the man. Oh Will, if only I had not come up with this absurd plan and we had gone straight to Albemarle instead. No, I fear we are on a fool's errand.'

'Perhaps. But listen, even if Sir George has you thrown from the building, you can at least ask him about William Jackson first. He might know him.'

'True. It is not as if we have much else to go on. Oh, why is that damn boy taking so long? I have a mind to march up there and demand to see the old goat myself.'

'*Demand*, eh? As I live and breathe, little Samuel Pepys has finally grown up.'

We turned to see Sir George Downing standing in the doorway. It was a shock at first, seeing how much older the man looked than when I saw him last. Aside from a fleeting glimpse at a distance, two years past, when he was made Secretary to the Treasury, my life had been blessedly free of this odious man for near a decade. When I had known him, he had been filled with the strength and boorishness of an inveterate bully.

Now, he looked like an old man. His face had grown jowly and covered in dark spots. His eyes, though still as narrow and cruel as I remembered them, were milky. And while the expensive dark wig he wore gave the slight impression of a younger man, his thinning eyebrows betrayed the fact that he was now completely grey.

I had wondered how I would feel, coming face to face after all this time with the man who had once made my life such a misery. And indeed, my first instinct was to feel like I was that bullied young man all over again.

But that is not who I am anymore.

'Sir George. It is good to see you, after all this time. You are well, I hope?'

Ignoring the question, he turned towards Charlotte. 'Who is this?'

'Charlotte de Vere, Sir George,' she replied, with a curtsey.

'I knew a de Vere in the war. A Captain.'

'My husband.'

'How does he fare?'

'He is dead.'

'I am sorry.'

'I am not.'

Sir George turned back to me. 'Pepys, what in buggery's name is this about?'

'Sir, we have come to warn you. We have reason to believe that you are in danger.'

'Danger? From whom?'

'A man called Ben Arden, who is the acting Governor of Portsmouth. He is at this moment on his way here to take you back to England.'

'The escort from the King?'

'Yes, sir.'

'Pepys, are you out of your damn mind?'

'No, sir. I am quite serious.'

He frowned, not taking his narrow eyes off me. For a while I thought that he was going to have us ejected, then he sighed with irritation.

'Very well, come to my solar. But just you. Mistress de Vere and the boy will stay here. That can wait in the hall.'

Downing waved his hand at Belle and left the room too quickly to see the dangerous look she gave him in return. Out in the hallway, he paused and whispered something to Peck. The boy indicated his understanding, then eyed me suspiciously as we began to climb the stairs.

Sir George stood at the window of his solar, looking out over the city. Cold moonlight shone through gaps in the clouds, illuminating row upon row of misty rooftops.

The room was filled with boxes and trunks, stacked and ready to be moved out. The furniture had been covered with sheets of cloth, giving the place an air of impermanence that underscored how soon Sir George must be due to leave for London. Only a small writing bureau remained in use, on which rested several papers, and the candle that I had seen burning from the street.

I began to recount the story as clearly as I could. I told him how Lord Maynard had spoken of a conspiracy just before he was murdered, and of the two attempts on my own life that followed.

I described the events leading to our discovery that Captain Harcourt was employing mercenaries, who had secretly been loading explosives aboard the *Prince Rupert*. This at least got Downing's attention, and he listened quietly as I described how we had watched those same explosives unloaded at the port, earlier this night. It was only at the mention of Ben's involvement that he turned to face me.

'Governor Arden. You are quite sure?'

'I am, sir.'

'It is a misty night. Could you not have been mistaken?'

'I saw him as clearly as I see you now, sir.'

I was about to continue with my story when there was a knock at the door and Sir George's secretary entered, carrying a bottle and two glasses on a tray.

'Ah, Peck. Set it down on the desk.'

Peck began to pour, but Sir George waved him away. He bowed and left the room.

'I thought we could do with some brandy,' Sir George said, filling the two glasses. He held one up and I took it gratefully.

He sat down at the bureau. 'What I do not understand, Pepys, is why you came all this way, by yourselves, only to confirm a theory? Is three hundred miles not a long way to come, especially to a land with which we shall soon be at war?'

I took a sip of the brandy, relishing the warm taste. Sir George may have been sceptical, but at least he was not dismissing me out of hand.

'In this, our hands were tied by the need to rescue my man, Will Hewer.'

'The boy downstairs? Was he a prisoner?'

'Not exactly, Sir George.'

'Then what?'

I shifted uncomfortably. 'He... was engaged in an investigation on board when the ship left unexpectedly.'

'A stowaway then.'

'I would not put it quite like that, sir.'

'Then how would you put it?'

I opened my mouth to speak, but could not quite find the words. Admonishing myself for the misstep, I tried to steer the conversation back to the conspiracy. 'We were all witnesses. Both to the smuggling of the explosives and to what we discovered at Brakspur Point. Mr Hewer can also corroborate what I said about Governor Arden.'

'The stowaway.'

'The conspiracy does not end there, Sir George. We know that Arden and Harcourt are working together, but also that they are not the ones ultimately in charge. Instead they take their orders from a man called—'

'These mysterious soldiers of fortune,' Downing cut in. 'They told you everything that they knew – willingly?'

'We interrogated them, Sir George.'

'I see. And where are these men now?'

'They… I cannot say for sure.'

'How inconvenient.'

He held my gaze for a moment, the candle in between us casting long shadows across his jowly face. From down on the street, I could hear men talking in Dutch as they passed by at a brisk pace, perhaps on their way home from some tavern. A pair of gulls screeched overhead. Somewhere, a dog was barking.

But inside the little room, there was only silence.

'Think before you speak. Is that not what I was always saying to you, Pepys?' Downing said, eventually. Without taking his eyes off me, he refilled his glass. But not my own.

I began to feel the urge to quail once again. I told myself this was ridiculous, that I was a man of thirty-six with money and status. So why did I still feel like a junior clerk in the presence of my former master?

'Sir George, I know this is a lot to ask you to believe. But every word I have said is the truth.'

'You know what I could do to you, don't you, Pepys?' he said, darkly. 'Just a few words from me to the right ears and you would find yourself in serious trouble.'

'I came here to warn you. There is a conspiracy and I believe you are in danger. Whether you believe me or not makes no difference – I know it to be true.'

He balanced a pair of eyeglasses on his nose and picked up a piece of paper, examining it close to the candlelight. I saw that it had a royal seal.

'Governor Arden is a trusted servant of the King. Indeed, as His Majesty says in this very letter, it is for this reason that he chose him to escort me from Amsterdam back to England. When we reach Folkestone, I understand that I am to be transferred to a smaller, more comfortable vessel, and taken up the Thames to White Hall, where I am to attend His

Majesty. Now if I could only find the name of the Captain who is to meet me there... Ah, here it is, yes. Harcourt. James Harcourt.'

He sat back in his chair, regarding me with those familiar, cruel eyes. From outside, horses' hooves and heavy wheels echoed around the empty street, then came to a halt nearby.

'I do not know what madness this is, Pepys, but Governor Arden is expected here on a mission from the King. And this man Harcourt is to meet me in Folkestone. There is no conspiracy.'

I pursed my lips in anger. 'God blind you, man. Why won't you listen?'

There was a pounding on the door downstairs. A moment later came shouts and the sound of boots running on floorboards. Suddenly I was afraid for Will and the others. Leaping to my feet, I threw open the door, but it was too late. Two men in English naval uniform were running up the stairs, their swords drawn.

I turned back to Downing. He smiled triumphantly.

'It appears you have overreached yourself this time, Pepys.'

I was dragged downstairs to the parlour, where the others were being held at gunpoint. A hard shove in the back told me that I was expected to join them.

'I demand to see Governor Arden,' I said.

'You will soon,' sneered the man who had pushed me.

I went and stood next to Will.

'How did that go, then?' he said, brightly.

At that moment there was the sound of a struggle from outside, then the door opened and Jack Gale was dragged into the room. The captain was badly hurt, his face livid with bruises, and one of his eyes appeared to be swollen shut. Will and Belle took the old man's weight.

'Gale, you're hurt,' I said.

He spat out a globule of bloody phlegm and smiled. 'They'll have to try a lot harder than that.'

Suddenly he began to sway, and for a moment I thought he would collapse, but he raised an arm to indicate that he did not want any help. It was then that I saw the deep gash on the back of his head. Blood was running down his back, soaking into his clothes.

'What did they do to you?' asked Belle, through gritted teeth.

'Searched the docks, didn't they? Don't worry, lass, I gave them a good fight.' He coughed and a line of blood dribbled from his swollen lips.

Voices approached from the corridor, and a moment later Ben entered, followed by Downing. I stared at my old friend through the near-darkness of the crowded room. He looked back at me, and for a moment I thought I saw pain in his eyes.

'This man needs a physician,' I said.

'He will be seen to,' Ben responded, as curtly as if he were addressing an underling. 'Search them.'

Two of the guards began examining us for weapons. I recognised them as the men who had chased us through the streets earlier in the night. From the roughness with which they treated us, I understood that they knew it too.

Ben turned to Downing. 'You are unharmed, Sir George?'

'Quite, though sorely vexed at this disgraceful intrusion. What took you so long to get here, Governor?'

'We came as soon as we got your message, sir.'

Charlotte let out a cry of protest, and I turned to see one of the men pull the flintlock out from underneath her shawl. He tossed it down on a side table, next to Belle's knife and pistol.

Downing walked over and stood with his face mere inches from hers. 'You brought concealed weapons into my house, Mistress de Vere?'

She said nothing. He slapped her face. Belle jerked forward, but Will immediately held her back.

'No. Not yet.'

'I suggest you control your property, madam, or I shall do it for you,' said Downing, striding out of the room.

Belle's nostrils flared with anger. 'Mistress?'

'I am fine, Belle,' she replied, rubbing her jaw. 'Worse things have been done to me by better people.'

Ben had been watching all of this from the open doorway. I tried to read his expression, but was unable to judge what emotion it was that I saw etched upon his tired face. Was it anger? Or guilt?

'Why, Ben?' I said gently. 'What has happened to you?'

'I could ask you the same question, Samuel.'

'I know about you and Harcourt. About the explosives.'

His eyes shifted uncomfortably to the men standing guard. 'What explosives?'

I turned to the guards. 'Do you know what was in those barrels? Has the Governor told you anything about this mission?'

'My mission is to escort Sir George safely to England,' said Ben. 'Nothing more, nothing less. I know nothing of any explosives.'

'Why are you lying?'

'You are deluded. And I think it best you address me as Governor from now on.'

'Who were those men? The ones who took the cargo?'

'That is no concern of yours.'

'What about Downing? Is he involved in this sordid enterprise too?'

'*Enough.*' He turned back to the guards. 'These people are dangerous criminals. Tie them up; make sure they are secure. Sir George wishes to leave immediately.'

'What will happen to us, *Governor*?' I said, emphasising the last word as if it were a curse.

Ben took a step towards us. Just hours ago, I would have looked upon the familiar, kind face of my old friend and felt nothing but love and warmth. Now, all I could see was betrayal.

'We sail for England at dawn, Samuel. And we are taking you and your friends with us.'

August 15ᵗʰ

It was hard to judge the passage of time in the darkness of the hold.

Our hands and feet were bound tightly with ship's rope, the knots joined in such a way as to leave us all but immobile. There was no way out.

Worse still, it was black as pitch. We had been left with no light, nor had we been afforded provisions of any kind. My lips became so dry and cracked that I began to taste blood.

We had been thrown down here after being transported on the back of an open cart, like the condemned being taken to the gallows. A while later we felt the motion of the *Rupert* putting to sea.

At first, we had talked among ourselves in an attempt to keep our spirits up. But as time passed, and the rough motion of the waves began to make those among us who were not used to life on board ship feel sick, silence took over.

'Is everybody alright?' said Will. It felt like hours since last anybody spoke.

'Yes,' I replied.

'I too,' said Charlotte, her voice as hoarse as mine.

'Could do with scratching my arse, elsewise I'm fine. Jack?' Belle paused. There was no answer from the Captain. 'Jack?' she repeated, louder this time.

'Aye, I'm still here,' he said at last, though his voice was weak and slurred. I feared that the blow to his head might have done more damage than we knew.

Will spoke again. 'How long do you think we have been at sea?'

'Been a while and we got a long time to go yet,' replied Belle.

'If we ever get there,' said Charlotte.

'Aye. True enough, that.'

There was a sense of dejection in Belle's voice that I had never heard in her before. I tried to sound encouraging.

'We will get there. And when we do, I shall demand to see Albemarle. The duke will listen to me – I know he will.'

'Your faith is touching, but I fear that is precisely why we shall never reach London,' said Charlotte.

'What do you mean?'

'Why don't you ask your friend the Governor?'

'He is not my friend.'

'A poor jibe. I apologise.'

'Whatever else Ben is mixed up in, he is no murderer.'

'If he gives us up to the authorities, he knows we will get a chance to put our side of the story. He also knows you saw him unload the gunpowder.'

'The gunpowder,' said Will. 'If only we knew who those men were.'

'Foreigners, stealing English gunpowder with the aid of the Governor of Portsmouth? Whoever they are, I will wager it is not information he will want shared.'

'Another reason for him to do away with us before we get to London.'

I closed my eyes. 'I need you all to know that I am sorry. It was I who brought you here. I should never have involved you.'

'We all knew the risks,' said Charlotte. 'We came because we wanted to.'

I was about to thank her for those words, when Gale began coughing violently.

'You alright, Jack?' The unease in Belle's voice was palpable.

'Aye, I'm alright,' he said, when the coughs finally subsided. 'I tell you all this much, though. She's right, this ain't nobody's fault except them bastards up top. But that don't mean we ain't done for. It's a death sentence, right enough. Just a matter of time.'

The words sent a chill through me. A death sentence. How apt a term.

I listened as the ship heaved and creaked. Above us, the waves broke against the mighty hull of the ship. It struck me how alike a cell this was, although even the wretched prisoners in Portsmouth Gaol had a little window for light.

Yes, we were under a death sentence alright. Just like poor Wolfert Jansen.

Suddenly, something clicked in my mind. 'My God. Wolfert.'

Will sighed. 'Yes. I suppose he is beyond help now, too.'

'No, no, that's not what I… Will, do you remember what Wolfert told us, when we went to see him? About why he had to flee from Holland?'

He thought for a moment. 'The Dutch rebels. Sam, you don't think…'

'Those men on the docks. It fits, does it not?'

'Will one of you explain?' said Charlotte.

'When Will and I interviewed Wolfert Jansen, he confided in us the true reason for his coming to England. He had got himself mixed up in a rebellion against the Dutch Republic. But his group was discovered, so he had to flee or be hanged as a traitor.'

'And what did Lord Maynard tell you before he died?' Will said to Charlotte. 'That he suspected there was treason among the officers?'

'I do not think he meant treason against the *Dutch*, Will. What motive would they have to help Dutch rebels?'

'The same as has spurred on traitors since time immemorial,' I said. 'Avarice.'

She considered the idea. 'So, traitors aiding traitors. It is not a bad theory. But it still does not seem right. Think about it. Harcourt and Arden have coordinated the mass theft of explosives from the navy's arsenal, even hired soldiers of fortune, probably using stolen treasury funds. Do we seriously think a bunch of Dutch rebels have the money to pay them handsomely enough to make such risks worthwhile? You are talking about high treason.'

'Aye, you're right,' said Belle. 'All men got a price. But this ain't the kind of risk men take for small profit.'

'Yes, but there is one other thing to bear in mind,' I interjected. 'Whatever this conspiracy is, Ben is not the man in charge of it, is he?'

'William Jackson,' said Charlotte.

'Precisely. What are his motives, whoever he is? And remember the order Ben spoke of? Could he have meant an order to supply the Dutch rebels?'

'Quiet,' said Will suddenly.

We fell silent. At first, all I could hear was the movement of the ship. Then I heard it too – the creak of floorboards directly above us. A chink of light opened up at the top of the staircase. I held my breath. Then slowly a familiar, stooped figure stepped into view. I watched as he descended into the hold and stood in front of us.

In one hand, he carried a candle. In the other was a knife.

'Samuel.'

'Ben.'

His voice was quiet and filled with anguish. 'Upon my soul, I curse the day you ever came back to Portsmouth. Why could you not have stayed in London?'

'I came to investigate corruption and murder, Ben. And I seem to have found both.'

'Did you kill John?' said Charlotte, her voice clear and unwavering.

Ben turned to face her. He seemed to pick his words very carefully. 'I had no quarrel with Lord Maynard, madam. But he meddled in places he had no business, despite warnings, and in doing so, he sealed his own fate. Just as you have.'

'Is that a confession?'

'I was not the one to wield the knife, thanks be to God. That particular task did not fall to me.'

The anxiety in his voice seemed real. A sudden memory flashed through my mind. The morning of the murder: Ben, arriving at Admiralty House, furious at the mention of Captain Harcourt's name.

'You didn't want it to happen, didn't you?' I said. 'But you were under orders?'

He said nothing. I noticed that the hand carrying the knife had begun to tremble.

'Orders from William Jackson,' I added.

He looked at me, aghast. 'How do you know that name?'

'I know more than you think, Ben.'

'Your mind was always one step ahead of everybody else's, my friend.'

'Friend? You make a mockery of the word, Ben. My apologies – Governor.'

To my surprise, he looked genuinely hurt. 'Oh, Samuel. I hold you in the highest esteem. My love for you is what makes this task unbearable.'

'Then why do it? What is more important to you than friendship?'

'Duty.'

'You cannot truly believe that. How is arming some Dutch rebels a matter of duty?'

'You… you cannot understand.'

'Then tell us. If this man Jackson has some power over you, maybe I can help.'

'No one can help me.'

'Who is he, Ben? If we are to die, at least tell me that.'

He covered his eyes and groaned with anguish. Will and I exchanged a glance. This could be our chance.

'Ben?' Will said. 'Are you alright?'

'I am tired. So tired.'

'Then let us go,' said Charlotte, softly. 'If you free us, our score will be settled.'

'You do not understand. You cannot.'

I leaned forward. 'Who is William Jackson? Please, Ben. Tell me.'

He rubbed his wrist across his sweating forehead, his expression filled with pain, as if he were battling some inner demon. Then, finally, he shook his head in resignation.

'Very well. William Jackson is the head of a secret Order, of which I am a member.'

It took a moment for his choice of words to sink in. 'We are sworn to the order,' Ben had said to Harcourt. Only he hadn't. Not quite.

We are sworn to the Order.

'What does this Order do?' asked Charlotte.

'Certain… tasks, for a great person. Tasks that are not pleasant, nor even sometimes honourable, but which must be done in service of a greater good.'

'Downing?' asked Will.

Ben let out a humourless laugh. 'No, not Downing. He is not fit to kiss William Jackson's boots.'

'I take it Harcourt is a member of this Order too?' I said.

'Yes. But Captain Harcourt is not the man you think he is. I do not care for his methods any more than you do. But what he does, he does out of duty.'

'That word again. Duty! Tell us more about William Jackson.'

'I have already said far more than I should.'

'Is that even his real name?'

'I can say nothing more.'

'Even now, when we are about to die?'

'Even now.'

'You are nothing but criminals,' said Charlotte, contemptuously.

He pointed the knife at her, raising his voice in sudden passion. 'No. That is not true. We do what we do in service of the highest ideals.'

'Though the act condemns the doer, the end may justify him. Is that it?'

'In this case, madam, yes.'

'You are a poor student of Machiavelli, Mr Arden.'

'Ben,' I said, desperately. 'You do not have to do this. Whoever this Jackson is, whatever power the Order has over you, you are still the same man.'

'You do not understand, Samuel.'

'Think, man, think, for God's sake. You are about to commit murder.'

'I… Samuel, I cannot.'

'Ben. Look at me. This is not the man you are.'

I stared into his eyes as he held the blade aloft, his hand shaking wildly. Then he lowered the knife.

'You are right. I cannot do this.'

I breathed a deep sigh of relief. He set about slicing through our bonds, first mine, then Will's.

'You must hurry. Take the launch boat. I will get you on board. Then as soon we are in sight of England, you must leave. I rendezvous with Harcourt in Folkestone and if he discovers that I let you go free—'

Suddenly, Ben was cut off by the noise of an explosion. He started running up the staircase. 'What the devil…?'

'Ben, the knife!' I shouted, and he threw the blade down behind him. Will picked it up and undid Belle's bonds next, before moving swiftly on to Charlotte and Gale.

'What was that?' he said.

'Sounded like cannon fire,' replied Belle.

'Something's wrong.'

Gale attempted to get up, but stumbled, wincing with pain as his knee cracked against wood. Belle went to help him, but he waved her away, rising unsteadily to his feet.

'I'm fine, girl.'

'You don't look fine.'

From somewhere overhead, I began to hear shouting.

'Quickly,' I said, running up the stairs and out into the passageway, the others close behind me.

'Are we under attack?' shouted Will.

'I don't know. But we must hurry.'

We raced along the orlop deck, and up the ladder into the lower gun deck. At that moment, there was another explosion and we were thrown back against the wall. Smoke started drifting down through the hatch.

I felt the cold grip of fear in my chest, but we pressed on up the ladder, then raced through the upper gun deck. There were two levels to go. My legs cramped violently after so many hours bound tightly, but I did not stop. Up ahead, I saw light from above. One more level.

'We're nearly there,' I yelled, racing towards the hatchway.

Gripping the rails for support, we ran up the stairs and emerged into the open air of the main deck. What I saw there stopped me dead in my tracks. Right off the starboard side of the *Rupert* was another, smaller ship, its deck on fire, smoke billowing from its cannon. And it was heading right for us.

'My God, Sam, look!' Will pointed at the ship's prow. There, painted on the side, was its name: *The Nonsuch.*

'The stolen cutter,' I gasped, just as a cannon ball smashed into the deck.

'It's a fire ship,' shouted Belle. 'We got to get to the launch now.'

Nearby, I saw Ben issuing orders to some of his men. He looked up at us, his face ashen with shock and confusion.

'Samuel…'

'Downing,' I said, coughing as the acrid smoke filled my lungs. 'Where—'

'Get down!' Charlotte pulled me backwards as the *Nonsuch* crashed into the ship, cutting a swathe through part of the deck as if it were made of paper.

We dived for cover as best we could, just as a small group of men jumped from the blazing ship onto the deck of the *Rupert*, their muskets drawn. There were maybe half a dozen of them at most, all dressed in plain, unmarked clothes, with swords at their belts – except for one, who wore the uniform of an English officer. A man we recognised instantly.

'*Fire*,' shouted Captain Harcourt.

Several of the *Rupert's* crew went down in the first assault. Harcourt and his men were outnumbered but they had the element of surprise, and they used it to deadly advantage. Bullets flew through the smoke and flames, mowing down the hastily assembled defence.

'William?' yelled Ben desperately, over the deafening noise of the assault. 'In God's name, why?'

'I am sorry, Benjamin,' the Captain shouted back. 'But he will listen now.'

Then he raised his gun and fired. Ben flew backwards in a spray of blood and slammed into the deck.

'No!' I screamed, lunging forward, but Will held me back.

'I have to help him,' I protested.

'He's already dead. We have to go.'

With a last, anguished look at Ben's unmoving body, I allowed myself to be dragged away.

I looked around in confusion. 'Where are the others?'

Will pointed ahead and I saw that Charlotte, Belle and Gale were already making for the stern. 'Launch boat. Come on.'

We ran to catch up, keeping as low as we could to avoid being seen. As we passed the mainmast I nearly fell over a tangle of bodies. Looking down, I saw that the one on top was a man in a long black coat.

'Will, wait.'

I turned the body over and immediately recoiled as the boy's head lolled sideways at a ghastly angle, exposing a wound that was so deep I could see his spine. It was Peck. Beneath him was the lifeless body of the young purser's mate, Dimmock. I wondered fleetingly if he had died trying to protect the young secretary.

'There's nothing we can do for them,' said Will.

By the time we caught up with the others, the fire had already started to take hold on the masts. Soon it would reach the sails and turn into a conflagration. The smoke was so thick that we could barely see the battle that was raging behind us.

Then, without warning, our path was blocked by one of Harcourt's men, who stepped out of the smoke, twin pistols raised. He fired, but Gale had already lunged forward, knocking the man off balance and sending the bullets harmlessly over our heads. With a furious roar, Gale set upon him, pounding him over and over with blood-drenched fists. I heard the sickening crack of bone as he pulverised the man's face.

'Gale, come on,' Charlotte shouted, but her words were cut off by the deafening sound of another gunshot. A moment later, the back of Gale's head exploded.

Belle yelled with rage, looking around for the assailant. Her face was splattered with blood and grey matter.

Charlotte grabbed her arm. 'We must keep moving.'

Through the hideous maelstrom we went, until at last we reached the little boat. Charlotte and Will immediately worked at untying it from its fastenings.

It was then that I saw him.

The smoke to my left cleared just enough to reveal Downing, cowering on the ground behind the mizzen mast. Two English sailors lay beside him, dead.

'Sir George,' I shouted, running towards him.

'God damned fool,' I heard Belle shout through gritted teeth, followed by the sound of running footsteps as she followed.

Bullets whizzed overhead and I nearly stumbled on the violently pitching deck, but at last I reached Downing. He recoiled with a scream as I placed a hand on his shoulder.

'Sir George, we must leave,' I said, pulling at the man's arm, but he would not move. He was in a state of shock.

'Come on, you useless bastard,' said Belle, slapping the back of his head and grabbing his other arm. This seemed to spur him into action, but rather than come with us, he cried out in panic.

'They are here! Help!'

Belle silenced him with a blow to the stomach, winding him, just as a shot narrowly missed our heads.

'Still think they are on your side, Sir George?' I said, as we dragged him in the direction of the launch. But before we could get there, there was a tremendous crash, and our path was blocked by a section of burning mast.

Then another bullet thudded into the deck.

Belle pushed Downing and me to one side and ran back to grab the guns from the belts of the fallen men.

'Go. I'll cover you.'

'Belle, no—'

'Go.'

She fired back into the smoke. I looked around in desperation, water streaming from my stinging eyes, but I could see nothing. I began to choke. We were trapped.

Then the wind changed direction just long enough for me to see the way around the fallen mast. Pulling Sir George behind me, I ran as hard as I could.

'Where's Belle?' Charlotte shouted as we reached the boat.

'Behind us.'

We turned to see Belle facing off against the attackers. There were two of them. Without the smoke to act as a shield, she was exposed. We watched, horrified, as they fired in unison, but Belle had already anticipated their move and thrown herself down onto the deck, rolling over and returning fire with both guns at once. One of the shots went wide, but the other hit its target, and the man fell down.

'Belle, come on,' Charlotte shouted.

Belle looked back at us, momentarily distracted. The surviving attacker charged right at her, drawing his sword. Belle leapt to one side, but the blade caught her arm, slashing through the sleeve of her leather coat. She cried out in pain, diving at a nearby corpse to grab the man's sword before swinging round to parry the next blow.

Metal clashed against metal as they fought, while all around them the flames were getting higher. Charlotte started to run towards her, but I held her back.

'No. It is too dangerous.'

'*Let me go,*' she demanded, but I did not loosen my grip.

I turned again to see Belle parrying blow after blow from the man's blade, then she caught him off guard and rallied with a powerful thrust that went right through his neck. He convulsed, then slid off her bloodied blade.

It was then that I saw the other man. Belle's shot had only wounded him, and now he loomed out of the smoke behind her, his own sword raised, poised to deliver a killing blow.

'*Belle!* ' screamed Charlotte, and her friend wheeled round just in time, plunging her blade into the man's stomach. Then she jumped straight through the wall of flame, reaching us seconds later.

Will and Charlotte both held out their hands to help Belle onto the launch boat first, but she had just taken the first step when a shot sliced through one of the four ropes. She tried to hold on as the little vessel swayed, and fell back onto the deck. I turned, and with horror, saw Captain Harcourt standing a few yards away from us, holding a pair of flintlocks.

'Drop your weapons,' he shouted.

Belle did not move.

'Drop them or she will be the first to die.'

He jabbed one of his guns towards Charlotte. Belle set her jaw and slowly threw down her sword and pistol.

'Can't take us all,' she growled.

'I don't have to, you insolent little bitch. Listen.'

Though my ears were ringing loudly, I strained to hear. He was right. The firing had grown less. The battle was almost over – and they had won.

Any moment now, Harcourt's men would subdue all remaining opposition, then they could pick us off together. All he had to do was hold us back until then. I searched my mind, desperately trying to think of something, anything, that might save us.

Harcourt's mouth twisted into a vengeful smile. 'It is only a matter of time. But I can wait just a minute more.'

'You do not have to do this, Captain. We are not your enemy.'

'You miserable cur, Pepys. I should have taken care of you when I had the chance.'

Sir George began to whimper. 'Please, Ca–Captain, I am not with these people. My name is Sir—'

'I know who you are, Sir George.'

'Then you must know that I am a close friend of His Majesty.'

'Indeed. That is why we are here.'

'Captain.' Charlotte's voice rang out, loud and commanding. 'You will stand down.'

'Is that so, madam? And tell me, why should I do that?'

'Because we are in the Order too.'

'That's right,' I added quickly, understanding what she was trying to do. 'Mistress de Vere, Mr Hewer and I. We are all members of the Order.'

He hesitated slightly. 'I have no idea what either of you are talking about.'

'Yes, you do, Captain. William Jackson will be angry if you kill us.'

His eyes widened at hearing that name, but then he grew angrier, all but spitting out the words. 'Then tell me this, Pepys, you lying dog... Who is he?'

I tried desperately to think of the answer for which we had been searching, these past days. I recalled everything we had learned, every scrap of information I knew about the man at the head of this deadly conspiracy. But I came up with nothing.

At the very last, I had failed.

Harcourt smiled. 'I thought as much. Time to die, Pepys.'

He raised the guns. I clamped my eyes shut. A moment later, a shot echoed around us and I stiffened, bracing for the agony that I knew would follow. But nothing happened. I opened my eyes again.

Harcourt was standing there, guns still raised, an expression of shock upon his gaunt features. Blood was gushing out of a large hole in his neck. His eyes glazed over and a second later his legs gave way. The last thing he did before hitting the deck was to fire one of his guns.

Behind him, lying on the ground with a smoking pistol in his hand, was Ben. A trail of blood stretched out behind him. The old man looked at me for a moment, trying to speak. Then he, too, slumped forward and was still.

I was so transfixed by what had just happened that it took me a moment to register that Belle was screaming.

'*No!*'

It sounded distant at first. Will pushed past me and bent over something on the ground. Then I realised my face was wet. Was it raining?

I raised my fingers to my cheek.

Blood.

Suddenly I was alert. Charlotte was lying on the deck, blood pouring from a wound just above her chest. She was gasping for breath, her body shuddering violently.

Around us, the deck was almost completely ablaze. The firing had stopped. Somewhere, men were screaming.

Belle lifted Charlotte off the ground and handed her to Will, who had already climbed aboard the launch, ready to take her. Belle followed him on board, then Sir George, then I went last. Will laid Charlotte's body down gently and I knelt next to her, lifting her head to rest on my legs.

Behind us I heard a rush of flame, followed by a cacophony of screams, then a great wave of heat billowed over us. My skin felt scorched. Will grabbed hold of the winch, immediately pulling his hands away with a sharp cry. He pulled up his sleeve for protection against the hot metal, then gripped it once again, setting his teeth against the pain, and began turning the handle.

I took off my coat and pressed it as hard as I could against Charlotte's wound, trying to staunch the flow of blood. Belle knelt next to me, gripping her beloved friend's hand, tears streaming down her face.

As we descended to the roiling sea below, I became dimly aware of burning shapes falling into the sea, accompanied by the sound of screaming. Whether they were Harcourt's men or Ben's, I could not say.

I was too busy looking at her.

Then we hit the water. Will and Belle started rowing with all their strength. The battle was over. We had escaped the *Prince Rupert*.

But Charlotte de Vere was dying.

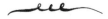

It is so cold as I write this that I can hardly move my fingers. At first, I thought my little notebook was lost forever, until I remembered that I had hidden it inside my coat last night. Now I do my best to record the events that have led us to this point, lost at sea, floating under the moonlit sky.

We have not stopped rowing since we left the burning wreckage of the *Rupert*. Each of us is taking a turn at the oars. At times, my arms ache so badly that it feels as if the muscles will tear.

But still, we keep going.

Charlotte's breathing has become irregular and shallow. We managed to fashion a makeshift bandage out of Will's shirt, which we tied as tightly as we could over her wound, stemming the flow of blood at least. Belle and I gave up our coats to use as blankets to try and keep her warm. But it all seems futile. We know how unlikely it is that we can save her now.

As we rowed away from the ship, we saw that there had been another small vessel, a twin-sailed caravel, waiting nearby. It must have been the boat in which Harcourt planned to make his escape, I thought, as the burning hulks of the *Nonsuch* and the *Prince Rupert* sank beneath the water. As it fell, the hull of the *Rupert* brushed the caravel, setting light to its sails. Within moments the little boat was ablaze, soon after to join the others in the deep.

I am still trying to assemble the last pieces of the plot in my mind. Was their plan to assassinate Sir George Downing on the journey home? Ben was as shocked as we were by Harcourt's assault on the *Rupert*. Was this where the conspiracy had diverged?

In any case, three burning ships are unlikely to have gone unseen. It is imperative that we get word to London before it is too late.

Will I ever fully understand why men would do such a monstrous thing? I suppose we may take comfort from the fact that the conspirators are dead, but it is the emptiest of victories. Ben is gone. Perhaps Charlotte too.

When sorrows come, they come not single spies, but in battalions.

For hours we were unsure if we were heading in the right direction. But then night fell, and between us, Belle and I were able to navigate well enough from the stars to confirm that we were indeed heading towards the coast of England at least. How far we had to go was anybody's guess.

I had just finished my latest shift at the oars when Sir George sat down next to me.

'It would appear I owe you a small debt, Mr Pepys.'

If I had had the strength, I might have laughed. Either that, or killed him myself.

'Your friend…' he continued. 'I doubt she will survive.'

'I know.'

'I would like to make a request of you, Mr Pepys. When we return to London, I would be grateful if you would tell no one about… certain details.'

'You mean, that you were a base coward who cared about nothing but saving his own skin?'

He grunted, but did not argue.

Then an idea started to form in my mind. 'As a matter of fact, Sir George, as much as I despise you, it is possible that we may come to an arrangement.'

'Very well, how much would you—'

'No, Sir George, I do not want a bribe. This is a different kind of bargain.'

I told him my plan. At first, he flatly refused, but then I reminded him of the strong bond of honesty that existed between myself and the Duke of Albemarle, and the obligation I had to leave nothing out of my report. He turned away and has said nothing to me since. But I think he will cooperate. The man will do anything to avoid being painted as a coward in the eyes of the King.

Now I must try to sleep. It has taken the last vestiges of my strength to record the hellish events of yesterday and today in my little notebook, while they are still fresh in my mind. Though I find it impossible to believe I could ever forget a single moment of what has gone before.

All I can do is pray that, when dawn comes tomorrow, it shall bring a shred of hope along with it.

August 16ᵗʰ

'Sam, get up.'

I opened my eyes with a gasp as Will shook me by the arm.

'Is she—'

'She still lives,' he said, then pointed up ahead. 'But look.'

Dawn was breaking and, far ahead, I could just make out the shape of cliffs through the early morning mist.

'Is that…'

'Yes,' he said, excitedly. 'The Seven Sisters, we think. Which would mean we have passed Beachy Head. Portsmouth is about sixty miles from here.'

I felt a surge of hope as I took over his place at the oars.

We were all so thirsty. There was a small water ration stored on the boat, but we had only been able to share it out in tiny sips to avoid running out too fast. My throat was bone dry and my lips cracked, but still I rowed as hard as I possibly could.

Belle sat at Charlotte's side, wetting a scrap of fabric and dripping the water a little at a time into her open mouth. The wound on Belle's arm opened up again every time she took to the oars, and now her shirt was soaked through with her own blood, as well as that of her friend.

All the while, we could hear Charlotte breathe in little gasps. The sound of her clinging desperately to life gave us hope. But we knew that she was fading fast. The end was near.

Salvation came in the form of a fishing sloop, which spotted us three or four miles away from the coast. We managed to hail the vessel and they agreed to take us the rest of the way to shore.

As soon as we made landfall, Will and Belle ran off together to find help. They returned a short while later with a surgeon, a stout man of about forty, who was complaining bitterly about having been roused from his bed so early. But as soon as he saw Charlotte, lying on the jetty, his demeanour changed.

'Dear God,' he said, performing a rapid examination of her wounds.

I drew Will to one side. 'Promise to take care of her. Spare no expense in her care. Tell the man I will cover it.'

'You are leaving now?'

'I must. It is our only chance to save Wolfert.'

He pulled me into a tight embrace. 'Courage, my friend,' he whispered.

The surgeon leapt to his feet. 'Quickly. It may already be too late.'

Will hoisted Charlotte up in his arms, the cold sea breeze whipping at his torn shirt, and followed him in the direction of the town. Belle started to go with them, but I held her back.

'No. I have something else you must do.'

'I ain't leaving her.'

'Please, Belle. Wolfert's life depends on it.'

I thought she would refuse, but with a final look towards Will carrying Charlotte up the road, she relented.

'What do you want me to do?'

Quickly, I outlined a message for Albemarle, telling him what had happened. I implored him not to act on any reports of English ships being sunk near Dutch waters.

'Ride hard to White Hall Palace in London. The guards will not let you in, but you are to ask for a man called Thomas Marshall. He is the duke's secretary. If he does not believe I sent you, tell him… Tell him that I hope his garden has had some rain. Have you got that?'

'Yes.'

'Good. Now go.'

<hr>

It took an agonisingly long time for us to find horses, but after I persuaded Downing to open his purse, a local farmer agreed to hire us his best steeds.

I knew our chances of success grew slimmer with every passing moment. Wolfert might already have been executed. But we had to try.

Sir George and I rode hard all day and managed to reach Portsmouth by evening. As we entered the town via the west gate, I noticed a large crowd gathering around the entrance to some kind of yard. Thinking nothing of it, we spurred our horses and rode on to the gaol.

Pitt answered the door, his expression quickly changing from irritation to delight when he saw it was me.

'Oh, it's you. Sir Thomas, the – what was it, Inspector of Prisons, you said? Come to see the show now, I shouldn't wonder.'

'Pitt, I demand you fetch Wolfert Jansen here now.'

'Demand, do you? Well, well. Who's your friend here?'

'My name is Sir George Downing, churl. You will release your prisoner to me, in the name of the King.'

Pitt scratched his head in mock disappointment. 'See now, that's the problem, sirs. I am afraid you just missed him.'

'What do you mean?' I asked.

'If only you'd come an hour ago I would have been delighted to be of assistance, but alas…'

'God's death, man,' bellowed Downing. 'Speak plainly or I will fetch the constable and have you whipped.'

'Now, now, sirs, calm yourselves, I am just the messenger. If it's the Dutchman you seek, you will find him near the west gate. Up that way.' He jabbed a finger in the direction from which we had just come. 'Bound to be quite a spectacle. If you're lucky you might just catch it.'

Suddenly I remembered the crowd we had seen on our way in. 'Come, Sir George. We must hurry.'

We mounted our horses and rode as fast as we could back up the road, weaving in and out of the crush with shouts of 'king's business,' but I feared we were too late. I felt my guts twist with anxiety. Had we really come this far, only to fail at the last moment?

Approaching the yard from the south side, I could see more clearly what was going on. A crowd was gathered in a patch of open ground, at one end of which had been erected a platform with a crude wooden scaffold on top. Leaning against the scaffold was a row of ladders, on which stood a line of poor, bedraggled men and women with hoods over their heads. Nearby stood a priest, finishing off a prayer.

We pushed our way through the braying crowd, shouting for people to stand aside and let us through. Some moved, but others ignored our pleas, angrily pushing back as if were merely trying to find a better view from which to see the terrible spectacle that was about to unfold.

Then it all happened so quickly. The kicking away of the ladders, followed an instant later by a series of hideous cracks and the condemned prisoners jerked and kicked in the air, as if suspended in some awful dance. The crowd roared its approval.

'No,' I shouted, desperately. 'This must stop. In the name of the King, it must stop.'

A few people pointed and laughed at me, but they were drowned out by yet more whoops from the crowd as one of the dying prisoners pissed themselves.

We were too late. It was done. I prayed that Alice Scovell was not here, among this braying mob, to witness her husband die this way.

Then the executioner stood aside to let a small group of onlookers climb up onto the platform. Many were in tears as they grabbed onto a pair of the wildly kicking legs and pulled down hard.

Families of the condemned, I realised. They must have bribed the executioner into letting them end the suffering of their loved ones more quickly. I craned my neck to look for Alice, but she was not among them.

I felt a nudge and turned to see Cobb, Gaoler Pitt's loathsome young assistant.

'See that, Mr Pepys? No finer way to spend a Saturday evening, I says.'

I rounded on the boy. 'One of those men was innocent. Now his wife is a widow and his son will grow up without a father. Have you no heart?'

He sniffed nonchalantly. 'That right, is it? Well, at least you're in time to see the Dutchie.'

'What do you mean?'

'Up next, in't he?'

I grabbed his bony arm. 'Wolfert Jansen is not one of them?'

'Nah, them's just the petty thieves and pickpockets,' he said, as if it were obvious. 'We're all here to see them hang the dirty Dutchie for what he did to the Governor. Thought that's what you was here for too, what with you being sweet on him and all…'

I did not hear what else he had to say, for Downing and I were already pushing our way to the front of the crowd to speak to the Justice. I could only hope that the word of a senior officer of the Crown would be enough to stay the execution…

August 17ᵗʰ

Sir George and I sat in the parlour of Dione House. It was dull and grey this morning, the sound of distant church bells smothered by the steady pattering of rain on the window.

We had arrived last night, filthy and exhausted. The door had been opened by Kitty, who was shocked to see me in such a piteous state, and gave orders for rooms to be prepared immediately.

Then, while Sir George was shown to his quarters, I took her to one side and told her the news. 'Oh God,' she said, raising her hand to her mouth. 'Oh please, no.'

I tried to stay strong, but in spite of myself, tears welled up in my eyes. 'Will Hewer is with her now. Belle will return to her as soon as she has delivered the message to London. But I... Kitty, I must tell you plainly, I do not expect her to live. I promise you this, though. If she does not, your mistress will have died a hero's death.'

Her green eyes glistened with tears. We embraced and wept quietly together.

Now it was the morning and we were waiting as our coach was prepared for the journey to London. I needed to get back as soon as I could.

But first, we had a visitor.

Alice entered the parlour, carrying her babe in her arms. We exchanged warm greetings and she assured me that Wolfert was well. A little shaken, she said, but he was alive. That was the important thing.

Then the smile disappeared from her face and she looked at me with great sadness. 'I heard what happened to poor Mistress de Vere. 'Tis an awful thing, sir.'

I nodded sadly. She placed her hand upon my arm.

'"How unsearchable are His judgements and His ways past finding out." I shall pray for her.'

'Thank you, Alice. What news of Wolfert?.'

'Well, they say he will need to stand trial again. Not that he had much of a one the first time around, mind.' She smiled once more, and it was like watching the sun come out. 'But they tell me I can see him today. He shall meet our son at last.'

'That is very fine news.'

'While there is life, there is hope. Always remember that. Will you be returning to London today?'

'Yes. I have urgent business. And I must find out...' I stopped, suddenly unable to form the words.

'I know,' she said.

Her baby began to cry. She shifted the boy in her arms, gently bouncing him up and down, then turned to Sir George.

'I hear it is you I must thank for his stay of execution, sir.'

Sir George inclined his head. 'No doubt justice will prevail, madam.' The baby let out a loud wail and Downing recoiled slightly. 'A spirited infant you have there. What is the child's name?'

'The boy has no name yet, Sir George,' I began to explain. 'They are waiting—'

'Samuel, sir,' said Alice. 'We are going to name him Samuel.'

Kitty and some of the other girls gathered in the courtyard to see us away. The mood was sombre, although Kitty did her best to remain cheerful, wishing us well for the journey as she handed over a hamper filled with food.

Jane and Cecily had volunteered to take us back to London. At least this time, I knew we were unlikely to be waylaid by outlaws.

With all that had happened in the past two days, the prospect of finally returning home did not fill me with the joy it should have. Instead, as the coach pulled away from Dione House for the last time, I felt numb. There was too much unfinished business. Too much that had been lost along the way.

But before we left Portsmouth, there was one final stop I had to make. It was time to confront the killer of Elias Thorne.

It was raining even harder as I stepped from the coach and entered the churchyard. A flock of crows wheeled overhead, agitated by the change in the weather. The faint sound of metal against metal echoed from the smithy nearby.

Otherwise, all was quiet in the village of Farlington.

The last time I had been here, two months ago, the little tower of the Norman church had stood out like a beacon against the cloudless blue sky. Now, on this dark and grey morning, it seemed to me like a sentinel of melancholy.

I pushed open the ancient oak door and stepped inside. A figure was kneeling on the floor in front of the altar, their head bowed in prayer.

The sound of my footsteps echoed off the stone floor as I walked slowly up the nave. Around me, the rain cast shadows on the whitewashed walls, like ripples in a stream. I came to a halt and spoke gently.

'Tamsin?'

She did not look around. 'How did you find me?'

'I called at the Four Feathers. Goody Brown told me you were here. Visiting Piety.'

She said nothing in reply. I took a deep breath.

'Tamsin. I know that you killed Elias Thorne.'

Tamsin turned to face me. Her eyes were red from crying, her voice drained of emotion. She looked exhausted. 'I wondered when you would come.'

'I did not realise the truth of it until recently.'

'And now you are here to arrest me, is that it?'

'I am no officer of the law, Tamsin. But it is my duty to take you to the Justice.'

Slowly, she rose to her feet.

'Well, let's be done with it. You can take me away. I am ready.'

'Tell me how it happened.'

'What's the point? I just want to get this done.'

'You truly are prepared to give yourself up?'

'Yes.'

'First, tell me. Please, Tamsin.'

She stared out at the rain for what seemed like an age, then let out a deep sigh. 'Alright. But not here. This ain't no place to talk of murder.'

We stood underneath the branches of a yew tree, looking down at the headstone. It was small and cheap, with a simple epitaph:

Piety Blake
Departed this life May 23rd 1669
In the 20th year of her age

I had not expected to feel such sadness in my heart at the sight of her humble little grave. Until now, the killing of Piety Blake had felt like an incidental thing. Hers was a story we had learned along the way, not the reason we had come.

And yet, just a few feet under this earth, lay the remains of a woman who had meant so much to so many people. To Tom Wilkin, she was an unrequited love. To Charlotte de Vere, a beloved ward. To Belle and the other women of the Hidden League, a comrade in arms. To Tamsin, a friend.

And now, she was nothing.

Tamsin broke the silence. 'God help me, Mr Pepys. When I heard you was dead, a part of me felt relieved. But that was nothing compared to the relief I feel now someone else knows the truth.'

'Tell me this, Tamsin. It is one thing to suspect a man of murder, even truly believe such a thing. But to commit murder against him in turn... You were there, weren't you? The night it happened?'

She closed her eyes. 'It was late. They were fighting like dogs, out in the street, screaming curses at each other. I'd seen them fight before, but this was different. I'd never seen such a rage in either of them. I came out to tell them to stop, but Pie told me to mind my own business. Said she could handle it. Then they went off together, back to Farlington. But I could not stop worrying that he would do her more harm. So... I followed.'

'Alone?'

'It was foolish of me, I know, but I know these roads backwards. I can take care of myself. The moon was full that night, and I'd not long been on the marsh road when I saw them up ahead. At first...' She faltered.

'Go on.'

'They was both on the ground. At first I thought they were kissing, God help me. But he had his head on her chest, like he was crying. Then I got closer and... saw she weren't moving. Then I knew.'

'Did he see you?'

'Yes. He ran off into the woods. I tried to help her, but... she was already dead. Strangled.'

'But Tamsin, if you saw all this, why did you not tell the authorities?'

'What, the word of a common serving girl against a king's man? No. Elias just laughed. Told them I was a whore trying to blackmail him. They'd never have believed me.'

'But could you not have sworn to it? Taken the matter to the governor if needs be?'

She looked at me with something akin to pity. 'You are a clever man, Mr Pepys. But you will never know what little power there is in being a poor woman alone in the world.'

I wanted to protest, to tell her that I did understand, more so than I ever had before. But now was not the time.

'So you murdered Elias for revenge?'

'Not revenge. Justice. Nobody cared who did for Piety. To them she was just another young slut who got what was coming to her. So I did what the law would not.'

'How did it happen?'

'He stopped coming to the Four Feathers, but it was easy enough to find him. I followed him one night. He was almost blind drunk, but I know he recognised me when I came up behind him and said his name. Right up until he turned and looked at me, I didn't know if I had the strength in me to go through with it. But when I looked into his eyes, it were easy. I just drove the knife into his gut and left him to die.'

Until now, she had confessed all this in a tone almost devoid of emotion, but at this point she grew agitated, placing her hand on my arm. 'But Mr Pepys, I swear to God, that is all I did. All the other things, the carving up of his corpse, them disgusting things done to his body…. That was not me, I swear it.'

'I believe you.'

'Thank you. I don't know if the judge will. Don't expect it'll make much difference anyways.'

She knelt in front of the grave, placing a hand on the mound with its covering of young grass. I watched as her lips moved in what could have been a silent prayer, or perhaps just a final farewell to her friend. But by the time she stood to face me again, my mind was already made up as to what I would do.

'Well, sir. Shall we go to the Justice?'

'No.'

'I don't understand.'

'Tamsin, there are things about this world we can never hope to change. But sometimes we may at least choose the right side.'

'You mean...'

'You must make your own peace with what you have done. Perhaps one day, God Himself will be your judge. But I will have no part in it. Your secret is safe with me.'

At first, she seemed almost angry, as if I had cheated her of a reckoning that she had come to believe was inevitable. But at last she smiled, and I saw a touch of hope in those bright blue eyes. She embraced me.

'You are a good man, Mr Pepys. You are a good man.'

I offered to take her back to the Four Feathers. At first she refused, but then we heard a roll of thunder in the distance and she relented.

'I've never been in a coach before,' she said, as we walked through the churchyard.

From inside the coach, Sir George gestured at me furiously.

'Who's that?' she asked.

'That, Tamsin, is Sir George Downing. A very important man who will not be pleased that we are to make yet another detour. But ignore him.'

'Looks like a right charmer.'

'The late Governor Maynard had the perfect description of him, so I recall.'

The flock of crows that had been wheeling overhead had by now settled into the trunk of the dead tree, where they sat cawing angrily, as if to echo Sir George's temper.

Tamsin looked up at them absently. 'That tree used to be the tallest thing for miles around, till the storm of '56. Used to come up here when I were a girl, and play hide-and-seek in the branches like William Jackson.'

I froze. 'What did you say?'

'William Jackson. You know... the story of the Royal Oak?'

For a moment, I did not understand what she meant. Then all of a sudden it came to me. How could I have been so stupid?

I knew the identity of William Jackson. And the truth of it chilled me to the bone.

*August 19*th

It took us two days to reach London. Sir George remained mercifully quiet on the road, other than ordering me to see to his various needs, and find food when he was hungry.

At least he had the good sense to be civil towards Jane and Cecily. He made little attempt to engage them in conversation, which seemed to suit them both well enough. The girls spoke little to us at the inns at which we broke up our journey, choosing instead to take small meals and retire immediately to the bed they shared.

More than once, I wondered if they blamed me for what had happened to Charlotte. I am not sure I could argue if they did.

We spent last night in Guildford, once more at the Red Lyon, where I wrote up my report and dispatched it by fast rider to White Hall. I put in as much of the truth as I could, and tried to make the rest believable. I doubt Albemarle will accept it, but there are secrets I dare not share. I made no mention of the Hidden League, nor of William Jackson.

After all, I knew who else would be reading.

The rest of our journey progressed well enough until we reached Southwark. There, once again, we moved at a crawl, with hundreds of people waiting to cross London Bridge. We sat for a full hour on the approach to the south bank of the Thames, before finally the bridge loomed into view ahead of us.

As we passed the row of traitors' heads by the entrance, I saw that a makeshift set of gallows had been erected nearby. From these hung the bodies of several men. I looked up at them as we passed, curious as to who they were.

Then I noticed that all of the dead men had spiked hair. I peered closer and could just make out rows of teeth that had been filed down into sharp points. Despite myself, I smiled. So Mother Quick had got her justice in the end. Good.

Now that I was so close to home, I longed to tell Sir George that I was not coming with him to see Albemarle. I could just get out here and walk straight up to Seething Lane, I thought, and leave all of this behind. But I knew that would have to wait a little longer.

We arrived at White Hall Palace a little after two. Sir George was admitted straight in to see the duke, while I waited in the clean white anteroom. As I sat there, going over in my mind what I would say to him, I fell so deep into my own thoughts that I did not hear Thomas Marshall approaching.

'Mr Pepys?' he said in his broad Yorkshire accent.

I rose and shook his hand, warmly. 'Mr Marshall. Sir, I sent somebody to see you, a young woman—'

'The Jamaican girl? Aye, now she was a wild sight, I can tell you.'

'She gave you the message?'

He smiled. 'I liked the code you gave her. Well remembered. My garden's bloody parched, thank you for asking.'

'How is…' I raised my chin towards Albemarle's office.

'In an ill humour. Feeling his age more than ever, though he is not saying it. And neither did I, mind. How is that lovely wife of yours?'

'I… have not been home yet.'

He smiled, in a way that once again suggested that he understood more than he was saying. 'Well, I have no doubt she'll be most pleased to see you.'

The door to Albemarle's office opened and Sir George stepped out. He saw me and puffed out his chest.

'He is all yours, Mr Pepys.' Then, as we passed each other, he said in a low voice, 'You will remember our bargain, won't you?'

'I assure you, Sir George, your secret is safe with me.'

I opened the door to see the duke sitting behind his desk. He looked thinner and paler than when I had seen him last, over two months ago.

'Sit,' he said, curtly. 'Well then, Pepys. I suppose you deserve to be congratulated.'

I inclined my head respectfully, although I suspected that it was the last praise I was to hear from him that afternoon.

'I have read your report and I have… questions. The last time you wrote to me, the murders had been solved, the missing money accounted for, and you were fêted as a hero. The next I hear, the whole thing was in fact a plot by a senior officer in His Majesty's Navy. Furthermore, you now say that none of what you previously said was true.' He made a steeple with his hands. 'Tell me Pepys, was it all lies or just a catastrophic failure?'

'It was not lies, Your Grace. The conspiracy we uncovered was a very complex one.'

'Ah yes, this so-called conspiracy. Explain it to me again, from the beginning.'

Taking care to stick closely to the version of events I had already submitted to him, I explained how Harcourt had planned to kidnap Sir George Downing in order to extort money from the Crown. Ben, I claimed, was duped into going along with the plan, only to discover the truth at the last minute, before Harcourt killed him.

The look Albemarle gave me when I had finished told me how little credibility he accorded the tale – and with good reason. I was dissembling and he knew it. But I could not risk telling the whole truth, even to him.

'Is that so? And what of Lord Maynard's murder?'

'He came close to uncovering the plot and had to be silenced.'

'Why do I feel that you are holding something back from me, Pepys?'

I began to reply, but he kept on talking. 'Sir George mentioned a woman called Charlotte de Vere. What was her role in all of this?'

'She provided us with assistance, Your Grace, as a loyal subject of His Majesty and the widow of a noted captain, Edmund de Vere.'

'I see. And where is this woman now?'

'She was mortally wounded in the assault on the *Prince Rupert*. I have had no news of her since leaving Portsmouth, but she was not expected to live.'

He grunted, as if that were the only acknowledgement such news warranted.

'And what of the other matter I sent you down there to investigate, the murder of Elias Thorne? You seem certain that the foreigner, Jansen, did not kill him. And yet you offer no evidence to suggest who did.'

'Portsmouth is a dangerous place, sir. We believe he was set upon by robbers.'

Albemarle stared at me with hard, suspicious eyes.

'Believe, yes. That word again. I am asked to believe rather a lot from you, Pepys. If Downing had not vouched for your story I think by now I would already have thrown you into Bedlam.' Suddenly he erupted. 'God's blood, man, why did you not find out the truth sooner? You play me for a fool. How many men dead? How much treasure lost? As it is, we have nothing to show for it except your word and what little Sir George could corroborate. Unless you count two damned ships at the bottom of the North Sea.'

'Your Grace, we uncovered a major conspiracy…'

'Conspiracy,' he spat, dismissively.

'People died. Good people. Friends.'

He picked up a quill and started to write.

'The king will be told of everything you have said. He will decide what is to be done with you.'

Unable to contain my anger any longer, I stood up and slammed my fist onto the desk. 'May I go, sir?'

He stared up at me furiously, then waved me away and returned to his work. I stopped at the door.

'Tell William Jackson that too many good people have died because of him.'

I left without saying another word. As I passed through the anteroom and out into the corridor, Mr Marshall looked up curiously from his desk.

I arrived at Seething Lane just as the bells of St Olave's struck three. As the coach rounded the corner, and I saw the familiar old street rising in front of me, I found myself choking back tears.

I was here at last. Two months had gone by, but it seemed like a lifetime. Still, there was yet one more stop to make before I could finally go home.

'Sam! God be praised, you are back.' Will greeted me in the little parlour of his house. 'What of Wolfert? Is he safe?'

'He lives. Not yet a free man – still rotting in that hole – but he lives.'

Will exhaled with relief. 'That is good news.'

'And Charlotte?' I asked, though I suspected I already knew the answer.

'I left her with Belle. The surgeon did his best, but he did not think she would live much longer. I am sorry, Sam.'

I closed my eyes. It was the news I had expected.

'Sit down,' said Will, changing the subject. 'Tell me more about your journey.'

'Will, I swear: never again will you hear me complain about you as a travelling companion.'

'I do not envy you three days on the road with Sir George Downing.'

'And you?'

'Well enough. I have been back since yesterday. Have you seen Albemarle yet?'

'I have. He remains as gracious as he ever was.'

'What about the rest of the conspirators? Did he know who William Jackson is?'

Do I tell him, I thought? Do I dare?

'It is out of our hands now.'

I sensed he knew there was more, but he did not press me.

'Have you been home yet?'

'No. I came straight here from the Palace.'

'Go. See Elisabeth.'

'How is she?'

'Missing you.'

'Thank you, Will. You have been a true friend, these last months.'

'It was nothing,' he said, modestly. 'But if you need me tonight, I shall be at the Haunch of Mutton.'

I took my leave. Outside, Jane and Cecily were waiting to start their return journey to Portsmouth. I bade them farewell and sent them on their way.

As I approached my house, I rehearsed in my head what I would say to Elisabeth. I felt like a different man from the one who had left here, almost as if my life were now divided in two. There was the time before and the time after.

I thought back to what had passed between us, months earlier. I recalled with shame how I had reacted with pity for myself when she told me she wanted to live apart, rather than sorrow for the hurt I had caused her. How I blamed her for finding my diaries and reading them, more than I did myself for their contents.

I stood outside my door, practising the words out loud.

'Elisabeth, my dear, it has been quite a time...' I shook my head. 'Elisabeth, there are things that must be said. Perhaps we could sit in the parlour and...'

Suddenly the door opened and Elisabeth was standing before me. For a moment, I could say nothing. Then I threw open my arms and she fell into them. We stood there for a very long time, holding on to each other, not letting go.

'Elisabeth,' I whispered softly. 'I am sorry.'

August 27ᵗʰ

For the past week, life has almost returned to normal.

After taking a day to rest and spend time with Elisabeth, I resumed my work at the Navy Board. The familiar routine of daily life has been as welcome to me as if it were a favourite pair of slippers, even though I have been careful to return home from the office at a reasonable hour each night.

Elisabeth and I have been happier in these last few days than we have been in a long time. Word had indeed reached her that I was safe, just as Charlotte had promised, although this had only served to make her anxious.

As it happened, we need not have troubled her. Harcourt never sent news of our disappearance to Albemarle. What was it that Will said? 'A pair of dead heroes would be most convenient for him.' Evidently, the boy was right. Harcourt must not have wanted to risk anybody else joining in the search until we had been safely eliminated.

Elisabeth and I are learning to enjoy each other's company once again. It has not always been easy, and sometimes we have fallen back into the familiar pattern of argument and reconciliation that has so benighted our relations. But at least I can say our efforts have been sincere.

We have also been able to allay any concerns I might have had that Doctor Grey's ministrations had left me deficient, *hazer con elle*.

I told Elisabeth most, but not all, of what had happened in Portsmouth. Some details I left out so as not to cause her hurt; others, for her own safety. In more ways than one, I had sailed in dangerous waters and she did not need to know it all.

Will has gone back to his carousing ways, albeit without me to join him. I have so far managed to avoid further confrontation with Albemarle;

indeed I have not seen the duke since the day I walked out of his office at White Hall.

The fragile peace with Holland holds steady. England is not yet at war.

Of course, I knew these days of blessed normality could not last for long. I was at the office this morning, going through some papers on my desk, when there was a knock on the door. When a liveried messenger entered, I knew there was to be no more running away from the inevitable.

The time had come for my reckoning with William Jackson.

The king stood in his solar, looking out over the grounds of St James's Palace. He was dressed in a velvet robe over a white silk shirt, with a large black wig that fell down past his shoulders. My heart racing, I stepped forward, bowing deeply.

'Your Majesty.'

'Ah, Mr Pepys.'

He beckoned me over. I stood silently as he continued to stare out of the window. The sun cast harsh shadows across his handsome, aquiline face.

'What am I to do with a man like you?' he said at last.

'Sir?'

'Albemarle tells me you foiled a whole conspiracy, and saved the life of one of my most trusted advisors. And yet he also thinks you are not telling him the whole truth.' He turned to face me. 'Of course, you and I both know that you were lying. Is that not so?'

'Your Majesty, I…'

'You what, Pepys? You would deny it to my face?' He waited for me to respond, but I dared say nothing. 'I would have you tell me what you believe to be the truth of this conspiracy. No lies, no dissembling, or I fear it could go very badly for you.'

I swallowed nervously. 'Ben Arden and James Harcourt were members of a group known as the Order. I believe their mission was to deliver weapons and explosives to the Dutch rebels. In doing this, the hope was that the Republic would be destabilised enough to delay and possibly avert war with England. But Harcourt thought this plan inadequate and wanted to go a step further.'

I faltered. The king betrayed no emotion.

'Go on.'

'He was the more belligerent of the two. Like Lord Maynard before him, Harcourt believed that the defence of the realm was so badly compromised as to be all but ineffective, and that the threat of an invasion was not taken seriously enough – even by you, Your Majesty. So he devised a counter-plot, to steal the *Nonsuch*, kill Sir George Downing, together with Governor Arden and the crew of the *Rupert*, and blame the attack on the Dutch. Thus forcing your hand.'

'Most interesting. And Lord Maynard?'

'He came too close to discovering the plot. So they were told to silence him.'

'Told, Mr Pepys? By whom?'

'A man named William Jackson.'

There, I had said it. There was no going back now. The king stared at me with those dark, piercing eyes I had come to fear. My legs began to shake and I felt beads of sweat rolling down my neck.

'Tell me, Pepys. Have you ever heard of the Order of the Royal Oak?'

'No, sir. I have not.'

'I am glad to hear it. A poor kind of secret society it would be if you had. The Order of the Royal Oak is a network of intelligencers and hidden agents, unconnected with any part of government, that reports only to me. You see, I have enemies, Mr Pepys. At home and abroad. And if there is one thing my years in exile taught me, it is to take nothing for granted where enemies are concerned.'

The Order of the Royal Oak... *O.R.O.* The key had been there all along.

Every schoolboy knows the story of how, after his father's execution, the young king had hidden in the branches of an oak tree to evade capture by Cromwell's army. He had even disguised himself as a servant.

A servant by the name of William Jackson.

The king continued. 'Captain Harcourt was ever the hothead, believing his way to be better than anybody else's. At first, I saw his zeal as an asset to the Order, though in this I was sorely misguided. Never thought he was a traitor, though. But the one thing I do not quite understand is, who else was involved in the plot with him? I take it the Captain did not steal a ship and use it to attack the *Rupert* all on his own?'

'I suspect the other men were mercenaries, Your Majesty. We encountered two of their kind in Portsmouth.'

'Ah, yes. I fear the late wars have left England with far too many masterless men. Old soldiers with no loyalties, nor useful skills other than killing.'

'Why are you telling me all this, Your Majesty?'

He clasped his hands behind his back. 'Because, Pepys, I want you to join. You have a fine analytical mind. I believe you would be a most valuable asset.'

I was aghast. 'This is... most unexpected, sir.'

'The Order operates... not above the law, exactly, but outside it. There is no organisation in the land more secret, or more secretive. You would work under my direct command, and with my protection. But of course, if you were ever to be caught, I would deny all knowledge.'

'But my work, my life...'

'All of that would continue as before. Only from time to time you would be called upon to carry out, shall we say, special missions.'

'Is Albemarle a member of the Order?'

'No. But his secretary is.'

'Sir, I have seen enough killing. I could not take a life, even in your service.'

'Ah yes, you are thinking of Lord Maynard. A great tragedy. You were wrong on that score, Pepys. His death was not of my doing. My agents are free to act independently in the course of their duties – up to a point – but in this case they went too far. Harcourt, I presume?'

'So I am led to believe.'

'I deeply regret Lord Maynard's death. And I give you my word that I had nothing to do with it.' He took a step towards me. 'Pepys, the business of the Order is to protect my person and to keep England safe from its enemies. To prevent wars, not cause them. Yes, our methods may sometimes be underhand, but they are a means to an end. Join and you would become one of my most trusted advisers. And besides, our work continues with or without you. At least as a member, you could help shape what the Order becomes.'

Do not be persuaded, I told myself. This life is not for you. But then a thought came to me, and before I could stop myself, I had spoken it out loud.

'There is a man languishing in Portsmouth gaol. His name is Wolfert Jansen. I know him to be wholly innocent of the charges levelled against him.'

'Ah yes, the man accused of Lord Maynard's murder. You wish him to be freed and given safe haven?'

'I do.'

'Then it is done.' He smiled. 'You see how useful it is to have the favour of a king?'

I probably should have walked out of there, returned to Seething Lane, and turned my back on this life he was offering. But for better or worse, I did not.

'Very well, Your Majesty.'

'You will do it?'

'I will.'

'Excellent.'

He turned away from me and picked up a letter from a small wooden bureau. I noticed a curious design on the broken seal – a closed knot, wrapped in the branches of an oak tree.

I stood in silence as the King read, awaiting his next instruction. It was only when he looked up again that I realised our audience was already at an end.

'Did you want something else, Pepys?' he said, with a frown.

'No, Your Majesty.'

'Good.'

He returned to his correspondence. Taking this as a signal that I should leave, I bowed as low as I could and backed swiftly out of the room.

I stepped through the door of my house to find the place strangely quiet.

'Elisabeth? Mary?'

I went through to the parlour. It, too, was empty.

'Mary? Where are you, girl?'

In urgent need of something to steady my nerves, I poured a glass of brandy and sat down on the settle. My hands were still trembling.

I struggled to bring order to my thoughts. What did this mean? Had I made a terrible mistake?

Rising to fetch myself another brandy, I heard footsteps in the corridor.

'Mary, is that you?'

Elisabeth appeared in the doorway. 'There you are. Where did you go?'

I hesitated. 'The office.'

She frowned. 'I went to find you there. Your man said you'd left.'

'Yes. That is, I mean, and a brief visit to White Hall and back. Nothing important.'

She seemed to accept this and I felt a pang of guilt. That lie came to me too easily.

'Where is Mary?' I asked, changing the subject.

'I sent her to Jorkin's. Are you quite well, Samuel? You look pale.'

She stepped forward and placed her hand on my forehead. I put my arms around her waist, drawing her close. 'I am fine. And you are fussing.'

'You should be at rest, Samuel. Until you are recovered, you would keep to the office and home, unless I go too – that was our agreement.'

She kissed me.

'But I am recovered, my dear,' I protested.

She kissed me again, pressing her body closer against mine.

'Do you know why I had Mary go to the cook shop for supper?' she asked.

'Because the girl is bone idle?'

She gave me a slap on the rump. 'Because I thought I might give her the night off.'

Another kiss.

'Mrs Pepys, you are a shameless wanton.'

'Do you not like me so?'

We kissed once more, deeply this time. Then suddenly she paused, looking out of the window.

'That woman is staring at us.'

I turned to look. On the other side of Seething Lane was a black coach trimmed with gold. Velvet curtains were drawn across the windows. On the perch sat a woman with long red hair, tied back underneath a riding hat. She inclined her head in greeting.

My heart skipped a beat. It was Kitty.

'Wait here, my dear,' I said to Elisabeth, trying not to hurry as I went out into the street.

I hesitated at the door, watching the stationary coach. For a moment nothing happened. Then the curtain drew back to reveal Charlotte de Vere. She smiled. Her face was a little pale, but otherwise she seemed well. Her hair was pinned up in the French style, a string of pearls gleaming against the deep blue silk of her dress. Next to her sat Belle, dressed once again in the simple attire of a servant, smoking a pipe.

Charlotte held up a piece of paper. For a moment, I didn't recognise it. Then I realised that it was the letter I had written as a boy.

The letter that could still condemn me for treason.

Belle took out a thin taper, which she lit from her pipe. Charlotte held the letter out of the window, then passed the taper underneath until it was alight. She held it for a moment until the flames had taken hold, then let it fall into the gutter, where it slowly turned to ash.

I whispered, 'Thank you.' She smiled and inclined her head.

Then she drew back the curtain and the coach drove on.

Historical Notes

Samuel Pepys (1633–1703) kept a diary for almost ten years. Starting on January 1st 1660, he wrote meticulous records of his daily life, both at home and in the course of his work as a civil servant in the court of King Charles II. Pepys did not intend for his diaries to be read in his lifetime. They were written in a complex shorthand, designed to protect his words from prying eyes (a reproduction of which can be seen in the opening pages of this book). And yet, his contribution to the historical record is incalculable. A lot of what we know about daily life in Restoration England is down to him.

Pepys' accounts of, for example, the plague of 1665, or the Great Fire of London of 1666, are considered essential primary sources. They are also gripping pieces of reportage. And yet, for me, some of the most captivating passages of his diaries are more ordinary in nature – among my favourites is a lovely description of a day out Sam and Elisabeth shared in St James's Park, for example. Pepys' writing can be funny – intentionally and otherwise – and it can be tender. It is also racy, at times shocking, and utterly indiscreet. He was a cultured man, who loved the theatre and knew how to have a good time. He was also a snob and a social climber. In short, like all the best literary heroes, he was a deeply flawed individual.

Pepys was a philanderer who did not stint from describing his sexual escapades (albeit lapsing into an oddly coy mixture of Latin, French, Spanish and Italian at key moments – the passages Elisabeth quotes to him during their argument are genuine). He caroused and misbehaved. He sexually exploited women, including his servants. He cheated on his wife. A lot. His diaries are frank and honest, not stinting on painful details, whether or not they paint him in a good light – and, it must be said, they rarely do.

But then, after more than a million words, detailing all manner of misadventures, he just stopped. Why? An oft-repeated answer is that it was because of his failing eyesight, but that only tells part of the story. After all, he could see well enough to correspond, keep accounts and various other records for the next thirty years. More significant, I think, is that he was simply going up in the world. Given the choice between sanitising his memoirs or the risk of having the more salacious parts fall into the wrong hands, it makes sense that he chose to stop when he did. Yet we know that, during the rest of his life, Pepys would rise to dizzying heights, becoming both an MP and Chief Secretary to the Admiralty. He also experienced crushing lows, even spending a brief time imprisoned in the Tower of London. It is tantalising to wonder what secrets his diary might have revealed, had he kept going.

Which is, of course, what gave me the idea for this book.

It is important to stress that my Pepys is not *the* Pepys. And while I have tried to stay as true as I could to his voice and the world he inhabited, I take a firm line that my first duty is as a storyteller – not an historian. To that end, the book you have just read contains a handful of anachronisms that I trust Pepys devotees will forgive in the name of a good story. The greatest of these is his lithotomy. Pepys really did undergo this terrifying operation to remove bladder stones. (I'm afraid the procedure I describe is not at all exaggerated for effect.) But in reality it happened in 1658, when he was 25. In her peerless biography, *Samuel Pepys: The Unequalled Self* (Penguin, 2002), Claire Tomalin describes how he endured the procedure with great fortitude, taking pride in the fact that he was up and out of bed after just a month's recuperation. For many years afterwards, Pepys commemorated his ordeal with lavish and well-lubricated suppers. Never let it be said that he lacked irony. Readers with strong stomachs can read more about the horrors of pre-anaesthetic surgery in Lindsay Fitzharris's compelling *The Butchering Art* (Penguin, 2017), which I found extremely useful in researching that particular scene.

I have also taken a few liberties with the history of Portsmouth in 1669. Admiralty House is my invention, though the rush to rebuild the city's defences is not. The Governor of Portsmouth – a hangover from a medieval office that was to last until 1834 – was in fact the King's brother, the future James II, although holders of the office were usually not quite so grand as that.

It is difficult for us to imagine just how profound an impact the civil war of 1642–51 had on English society, nor how long-lasting its scars. The young Pepys really did watch the execution of Charles I on January 30th 1649. Eleven years later, after a decade of rule under Oliver Cromwell – a dictator in all but name – and briefly by his feeble son, Richard, Parliament invited the exiled Charles II back to reclaim his father's throne. Just as he describes to Charlotte de Vere, Pepys was part of the delegation sent to bring the King back to England. The first few months of his diaries describe the preparations in fascinating detail, culminating with Charles' triumphant return to London on May 29th 1660.

Although the restoration of the monarchy was initially popular, by the end of the decade the King's image was tarnished by the perception (largely deserved) of his indolence and extravagant living in the face a devastated economy. There were plenty who wanted to topple the King and return once more to Parliamentary rule. Lord Maynard would certainly not have been alone in the Republican sentiments that so astonish Sam during their first meeting.

Charlotte de Vere's tale of resistance during the Siege of Chester is inspired by real-life events during this extraordinary chapter of civil war history. The women of the city played the key role in breaking the brutal siege, which ended after eighteen months in February 1646. The Siege of Chester seems to have been somewhat overlooked by historical fiction (and popular non-fiction, for that matter), a situation which I sincerely hope someone will remedy, because it's a gripping tale. The best account I could find was in an episode of Melvyn Bragg's wonderful 2004 series for BBC Radio 4, *Voices of the Powerless*. At the time of writing, it is still available as a paid download from various sites.

A common thread running through this book is the fear that England might be facing war with the Netherlands. It was a very real concern. The nation had gone into the last Anglo-Dutch war, in 1665, eager for a fight ('mad for war' as Pepys himself put it). It was to emerge from the conflict two years later, battle-scarred and humbled, forced to sue for peace after a series of crushing naval defeats. The worst was an attack on the port of Chatham, Kent, during which the Dutch not only torched the English fleet, but towed away the *Royal Charles* – the very vessel in which the King had made his triumphant return to English shores. As if the humiliation was not complete enough, the Dutch king was Charles' own nephew – William of Orange (who would go on to become joint ruler of England, along with Charles' niece, Mary, in 1689). The war proved to the world that the Dutch were an economic and military force to be reckoned with, while England was a power on the wane. In this context, it is easy to see why the atmosphere in the country was so febrile – and why there was a genuine fear that Charles was not taking the defence of the realm seriously enough. Another defeat like that could mean total ruin. Ben Arden, Captain Harcourt and the other conspirators were right enough in that.

The Order of the Royal Oak was, believe it or not, a real thing – although I have no evidence to suggest that it was a secret network of clandestine operatives. Sorry about that. It was, in fact, an honour that Charles II planned to create for those subjects he felt deserving of the highest reward. It never came to fruition. A brief discussion of the Order can be found in Charles Spencer's thrilling *To Catch a King* (William Collins, 2017), which also contained plenty I didn't know about Pepys' own relationship with the King.

Other books that were invaluable to my researches include Stephen Porter's *Pepys's London* (Amberley Publishing, 2012) and Liza Picard's *Restoration London* (Weidenfeld and Nicolson, 1997), both superb studies of this great city in a turbulent age. Likewise, I couldn't have got to grips with Portsmouth of the same period without William Gates' *The Portsmouth That Has Passed* (Milestone, 1987) and Lake Allen's *The History of Portsmouth* (Life is Amazing, 2012, updating the 1817 edition). I owe further debts to Simon Schama's *The Embarrassment of Riches: an Interpretation of Dutch Culture in the Golden Age* (Alfred A. Knopf, 1987); Nadine Akkerman's *Invisible Agents: Women and Espionage in Seventeenth-Century Britain* (Oxford University Press, 2018); and Ian Mortimer's essential *The Time Traveller's Guide to Restoration Britain* (Bodley Head, 2017) for furnishing me with a variety of extremely useful historical details. And it should, of course, go without saying that I made extensive use of the diaries of Samuel Pepys themselves. The two main editions I consulted were the beautiful, four-volume set published by Hurst and Blackett in 1854; and the doorstop-size Penguin Classics edition from 2003. It is the latter that sat on my desk for two years, extremely well-thumbed and dog-eared.

Finally, I should mention that a handful of supporting characters in this book were also real people who appear throughout Pepys' diaries. They include the cantankerous Duke of Albemarle; Will Hewer, who became like a son to the childless Pepys; and of course, his long-suffering wife, Elisabeth. Though he treated her appallingly, he really did love her. I think the best monument to their relationship is, well, literally a monument. Sam and Elisabeth are buried in London, at St Olave's Church on the corner of Hart Street and Seething Lane. There, high up on the walls, sit two memorial busts, both commissioned by Pepys himself. The first is his own. The second, facing him across the nave, is Elisabeth's. She is depicted mid-laugh, with a playful look on her face. It's as if she is frozen in time, telling a bawdy joke.

Jack Jewers
February 2022

Acknowledgements

This book began life at the tail end 2017 when I pitched the idea to my friend (and later agent) Giles Milburn. His response – 'if you don't write that, I will' – was the final push I needed to actually try writing the historical novel he had been pushing me for years to attempt. Thank you, Giles, for your confidence, and I'm sorry it took quite so long.

I owe an enormous debt of thanks to my editor, Flora Rees. I would have been lucky enough to work with an editor of her calibre and reputation had this been my tenth book, let alone my first. Not only did her insight and experience make this book so much better, but she even had the patience to weigh in on some frantic, last-minute revisions by phone from a booth at the Dubai Expo. Now that's the kind of editor authors dream about.

Thank you to my copy editor, Helen Grant, whose eye for historical versimilitude makes me wonder if perhaps she is a time traveller. (Either way, she is also a brilliant author and you should check out her books – particularly her ghost stories, which would make M.R. James sleep with the light on). Thanks also to my proof editor, Sarah Hulbert, for her eagle eye in correcting the final manuscript.

I cannot begin to give enough thanks to the team at Moonflower. This book wouldn't look anything like as good as it does were it not for the work of Jasmine Aurora, a designer whose business cards should really just say 'Genius.' Thanks also to Tory Lyne-Pirkis, who is quite literally the best PR in the business (sorry, everyone else, that's just a fact); to Martin Palmer and Katherine Rhodes for being the finest sales team I could wish for; and to Emma Waring for her outstanding skills in herding cats.

An eminent author who I am pleased to call a great friend, Dr Alexia Casale, was my beta reader. I'm not sure I really believed my work could amount to an actual book until her notes came back, filled with positivity, enthusiasm, and the filigree of excellent suggestion. Thank you, Lexi, for sharing your insight. And all those delicious bowls of pasta.

I am fortunate to count several other authors as dear friends, and I would like to thank them for their words of encouragement when I shyly told them I, too, was trying to write a book – in particular, Emma Trevayne, Tom Pollock and Amy Plum. You are all wonderful, and you probably don't realise how much even just a simple 'you can do it' from writers of your talent mattered.

Thanks also to various work colleagues without whose support I don't think I could ever have finished, especially Hermione Spencer and Roxy Caron, who absolutely get free copies of this book.

Sincere thanks are due to several individuals whose specialist knowledge on certain subjects far exceeded my own and who were kind enough to share it with me. Any errors that remain are most certainly mine. Chiefly, to Mina Witterman, friend and adventurer extraordinaire, I must say *echt heel erg bedankt* for her help with some of the more obscure aspects of maritime history and the Dutch Golden Age.

Merci beaucoup also to Justine Duhart for helping me shape my poor French into something that sounded credibly arcane, for the scene with the French ambassador who refuses to speak English. And thank you to George Pliotis and Fiona Dunbar for helping me craft the correct Latin for Charlotte de Vere's proud axiom, 'women are equal to anything.' (It would feel remiss if I didn't at least tip my hat to the UK Supreme Court Justice, Lady Hale, whose family motto I shamelessly cribbed here. I trust she'll forgive the appropriation.)

There is an audio edition of this book available to download from all the usual outlets, narrated by Gareth Armstrong. Gareth, who has a voice like liquid velvet, brings the story to life in ways I'd never imagined, and I'm very grateful for his time.

For other pieces of help and advice which, though small, proved hugely valuable, I would like to extend thanks to Catherine Sutherland at the Pepys Library, Magdalene College, Cambridge; Dianne Cawood and the staff of the Portsmouth History Centre; Dr Helen Tudor; Hallie Rubenhold; and Ashley Rose Kaplan. Thanks also to my wonderful mother, Philippa Urquhart, who instilled in me both a love of history and a desire to own more books than I could ever possibly read. I hope you enjoy this one, Mum, for the half-day it takes you to get through it.

Finally, I come to the biggest thank you of all – my wife, best friend and partner in all things, Christi Daugherty. It would be easy for an aspiring writer to feel a little intimidated by the fact that they happen to be married to an author of her dazzling talent and ability, but she has never made me feel anything other than inspired. Thank you for your advice, support and encouragement at every step of the way. Thank you, my darling, for everything.

The Coming Darkness by Greg Mosse

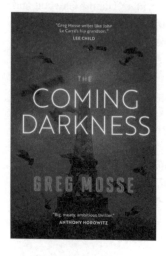

Paris, 2037. With a double threat of rising temperatures and new diseases jeopordising public health, the world has never been more dangerous.

French special agent Alexandre Lamarque notices signs of a new terror group and connects it with an ominous sequence of events: a theft from a Norwegian genetics lab; a string of gory child murders; a chaotic coup in a breakaway North African republic, and the extraction under fire of its charismatic leader. And as the one man able to see through the web of lies, Alex may be the world's only hope.

About the author

Greg's first career was in theatre as actor, director and writer. He has lived and worked in Paris, New York, Los Angeles and Madrid. Having worked as an international interpreter, in 2015 Greg returned to theatre. Since then, he has written and produced 25 plays and musicals. He took advantage of 2020's lockdown to fulfil a long-term ambition to write a powerful thriller.

SCAN ME TO FIND OUT MORE

Praise for The Coming Darkness

"Admirable audacity. One of the best thrillers of 2022."
THE SUNDAY TIMES

"A clever, fast-paced thriller."
THE INDEPENDENT

"Superb. Greg Mosse writes like John Le Carré's hip grandson."
LEE CHILD

Out now from Moonflower Books

MOONFLOWER

www.moonflowerbooks.co.uk

Blue Running by Lori Ann Stephens

'Gripping.'
THE GUARDIAN

'Brilliant.'
HEAT MAGAZINE

BLUE RUNNING

LORI ANN STEPHENS

BOOK OF THE MONTH · THE INDEPENDENT & THE FT

SCAN ME TO FIND OUT MORE

Out now from Moonflower Books

MOONFLOWER

www.moonflowerbooks.co.uk

In the new Republic of Texas, guns are compulsory and nothing is forgiven.

Fourteen-year-old Bluebonnet Andrews is on the run across the Republic of Texas. An accident with a gun killed her best friend but everyone in the town of Blessing thinks it was murder. Even her father – the town's drunken deputy – believes she did it. Now, she has no choice but to run. Because in Texas, murder is punishable by death.

About the author

Lori Ann Stephens is an award-winning author whose novels for children and adults include Novalee and the Spider Secret, Some Act of Vision, and Song of the Orange Moons. She teaches creative writing and critical reasoning at Southern Methodist University in Dallas, Texas.

Praise for Blue Running

Book of the Month
THE INDEPENDENT & THE FT

"If there's one teen novel this year that readers will never forget, it's this one…"
BOOKS FOR KEEPS

"Brilliant."
HEAT MAGAZINE

"Gripping."
THE GUARDIAN

Number 10 by C.J. Daugherty

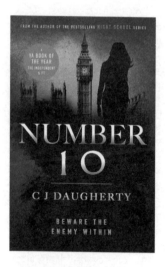

SCAN ME TO FIND OUT MORE

Out now from Moonflower Books

MOONFLOWER

www.moonflowerbooks.co.uk

Eight months ago, Gray Langtry's mother became Prime Minister. Now, someone wants her dead.

Gray's life has been in turmoil ever since her mother was chosen to lead the country. First, they had to leave their home and move into the Prime Minister's official residence at Number 10, Downing Street. Now, everywhere she goes, she must be accompanied by bodyguards. Worst of all, the media won't leave her alone - she's in every tabloid, and her behaviour, appearance, the length of her skirts... everything is judged. And she doesn't like this life.

About the author

A former crime reporter and accidental civil servant, C.J. Daugherty best-selling young adult series, *Night School*, was published by Little Brown and went on to sell over a million and a half copies worldwide. Her books have been translated into 25 languages and have been bestsellers in multiple countries.

Praise for Number 10

"YA Book of the Year... CJ Daugherty is a YA big hitter."
THE INDEPENDENT

"Exciting and unique... action packed and thrilling."
THE GUARDIAN

"The most exciting teen book series to hit our shelves in ages."
NOW MAGAZINE

The Fortunes of Olivia Richmond by Louise Davidson

After a terrible tragedy, governess Julia Pearlie finds herself with no job, home, or references. When she's offered a position as companion to Miss Olivia Richmond, she's relieved. But Mistcoate House is full of secrets.

Olivia has a sinister reputation. The locals call her the Mistcoate Witch, thanks to her tarot readings, and her insistence that she can speak to the dead. Her brother believes this to be girlish fantasy and is looking to Julia to put a stop to it. But it seems there may be more to Olivia's stories than Dr Richmond would have Julia believe – not least because Olivia seems to know something of the darkness that Julia desperately hoped she had left behind.

As the danger grows, and the winter chill wraps around the dark woods surrounding Mistcoate, Julia will have to fight to uncover the truth, escape her past – and save herself.

About the author

Louise Davidson was born in Belfast and has always worked in the creative arts some capacity, from working as an assistant to theatre directors, to holding scriptwriting classes in prisons and teaching English and drama to A-Level students. Louise lives in London with her husband and step-son. The Fortunes of Olivia Richmond is her debut novel.

SCAN ME TO FIND OUT MORE

Out 2023 from Moonflower Books

MOONFLOWER

www.moonflowerbooks.co.uk

About Moonflower Books

Young, UK-based and independent, Moonflower Books is a commercial publisher with an indie heart. Our aim is simple: to find hidden gems by incredibly talented authors and share them with the world. The books we choose to publish are the ones that make us sit up in our seat a little. Books that break the mould. That are a little hard to categorise. The "it's like this, but only sort of" ones. In short, the kind of books that deserve your attention.

Join us in our mission.

www.moonflowerbooks.co.uk

Follow Us

 @moonflowerbooks

 @moonflower_books

 /moonflowerbooks